Twisted Heart

Twisted Heart

Eden Maguire

Hodder
Children's
Books

A division of Hachette Children's Books

First published in Great Britain in 2011
by Hodder Children's Books

1

A Catalogue record for this book is available from the British Library

ISBN 978 1 444 90187 0

Typeset in Berkeley Book by Avon DataSet Ltd,
Bidford on Avon, Warwickshire

Printed and bound by CPI Group
(UK) Ltd, Croydon, CR0 4YY

Hodder Children's Books
a division of Hachette Children's Books
338 Euston Road, London NW1 3BH
An Hachette UK company
www.hachette.co.uk

For Anne McNeil, who was in at the birth

It will have blood; they say, blood will have blood.
Stones have been known to move and trees to speak . . .

William Shakespeare's *Macbeth*

1

I sleep with a dreamcatcher above my bed. I use it to filter out bad dreams – I had enough of those earlier this summer. Flames eating up the forests, leaping across canyons, shooting firebrands through the night sky. Plus the visions and psychic connections and the dark angel voice slithering through my brain with a warning – 'We will all rise. There will be other times, other places – a million other willing souls!'

I travelled halfway across the world to get a break from all that flesh-creeping stuff and if my good angel isn't around any more to protect me, which she doesn't seem to be, I'm not too proud to rely on old superstitions, ancient beliefs, whatever.

My dreamcatcher is a circle of slender willow branches about thirty centimetres wide, wound with a narrow leather strip and with cotton threads woven across the centre in a geometric petal pattern. A pendulum of turquoise beads and white and black feathers hangs from the bottom of the hoop. Good dreams find their way through the net but bad ones can't get past. It works some of the time, I guess.

Since the last big burnout on Black Rock, I also avoid going up on to the flame-seared slopes whenever possible. And it's not just me – my best friend, Grace, and all the traumatized kids in Bitterroot, if I'm honest.

I prefer valleys and water – cool streams, white-water rapids, Prayer River and Turner Lake.

I mean, I love the lake, totally adore the light sparkling on its surface and the way your feet and ankles turn pale and distort when you wade in from the pebble shore, the icy feel of the water between your toes. It's where Orlando and I first fell in love.

It was midnight, and just remembering it makes my soul soar. The night sky was huge, the Milky Way streaming across it – a glittering banner made out of a million stars. We were tiny and unique. We took off our clothes and swam in the lake.

'You're my midnight swimmer,' he tells me even now.

Or he would do if he was here.

It's Saturday and he promised he would be home Friday. What the hell happened to his afternoon flight out of Dallas, I wanted to know. I had to fly across the whole freaking Atlantic and I still made it on time – Friday, 8.00 p.m., my parents' house on Becker Hill. They were in Denver so we would have the place to ourselves. A chance to celebrate after two whole months of love famine.

'They oversold tickets,' he explained. 'The airline gave me a three-hundred-dollar credit for transferring to a later flight.'

I almost tossed my phone out of the window. 'Jeez, Orlando.' Words failed me, as you can see. In my opinion, our romantic reunion was worth more than three hundred lousy dollars any day. Evidently not to him.

'I'm out of here first thing tomorrow,' he promised.

'I won't be here,' I snapped back.

'Why? Where will you be?'

'At the lake.'

'What for?'

'The New Dawn thing – the triathlon.'

Silence while he computed this. 'You're not – I didn't know . . .'

'I'm not *competing*!' Insert the word 'Stupid!', tag it on the end of the sentence, hear it in my tone of voice. With me, disappointment turns to anger in a flash. I drew breath then spoke more calmly. 'Yeah – maybe the swimming. I'm OK with that. And cycling. But can you see me running 10k?'

'Gotcha,' he mumbled. A pre-recorded warning to keep your bags with you at all times sounded in the background, so at least he'd made it to the airport and that bit of his story was true.

Two grey doves flew across my view and landed in the red-gold aspens behind the house.

My old buddy Paranoia (worse since my bruising encounter with the whole dark angel thing) lay in wait on the back porch, ready to pounce – I figured that Orlando had spent two months in Dallas and found someone new to love. A girl on his fashion design course; a catwalk model; a fabric designer. He was finding an excuse not to leave, to stay with her for one more night. I was absolutely certain. Then, get a hold of yourself, I thought.

The doves took off in opposite directions as I tried again to take the edge of fear and anger out of my voice. 'No, I'll be at the lake rooting for Holly.'

'Oh yeah, Wonder Woman,' he joked. And then to break the tension; 'To be honest, she scares the shit out of me.'

'Me too.' When I last spoke to Holly on the phone from Paris, she'd been in the gym for weeks performing single-leg dead lifts to strengthen her glutes.

Plus, her dad had bought her the best Boardman performance bike on the market and she'd borrowed a seven-hundred-dollar Speedo Tri-Elite wetsuit from a girl who competed at trials for the 2008 Beijing Olympics. So I knew she was serious about this New Dawn triathlon.

'So you're OK if I join you lakeside?' Orlando checked. 'I'll drive straight from the airport.'

What could I do? What could I say? 'I missed you so much.' My anger dissolved and my voice broke. A sigh escaped.

'Me too.'

'I love you.'

'See you tomorrow.' Click. End of.

And now tomorrow was today and my night-time dreamcatcher had let me down, had allowed through a glimpse of hell: a water snake emerging from the dark depths of a lake, bearing a snarling, hissing head at each end of its body, surging to the surface, bringing black rain, floods and disaster. These visions of mine shook me to the core. They chewed me up and spat me out. I wonder all this time – is it worth having these psychic powers if they leave you feeling this wasted and weak?

'Hey, Tania.' Holly's boyfriend, Aaron, found me standing by Lake Turner, my back turned to the knot of early arrivals in the car park at the entrance to the New Dawn Community. 'Orlando didn't make it, huh?'

'Later,' I muttered.

'Good to see you after all this time,' he said shyly, as if a two-month trip to Europe had turned me into a total stranger. And he quickly ducked out of any more conversation. 'Come and talk to Holly; wish her luck.'

Aaron led the way across the pebbles, his boots crunching, the back of his black sweatshirt reading 'Never trust anyone below 14,000 feet' in white letters. He was a climber, a mountaineer trained since the age of ten by his dad who worked for the National Park Service. The training had given him broad shoulders and strong thighs, plus nerves of steel, which you had to have to handle a relationship with my next-door neighbour, Holly Randle.

'Tania!' She stood next to Aaron's grey truck, raised her arm and yelled at me above the rumble of other vehicles pulling into the parking lot. Then she ran at me and held me in her Brunhilda hug. Brunny, by the way, is a legendary princess of the Visigoths who offered to marry any man who could defeat her in a trial of strength and courage. It's amazing what random information sticks when you're in Paris, Rome, Berlin.

Holly hugged me in her black and gold Speedo wetsuit, glutes duly strengthened, corn-blonde hair hidden under a small white rubber helmet, a bold, black competitor number 85 stencilled in waterproof ink on to her upper arm.

'You look different,' she accused.

'No — same old.' I blushed as she held me at arms' length.

'Oh yeah, Tania — look at you! Skinnier, for a start — if that's possible. And paler.'

'I travelled between cities; I stayed out of the sun.'

'Wow, I love that little red purse. Where did you buy it — Paris? How much did it cost?' She didn't wait for answers, just zapped through every item of my clothing from head to foot, wanting to know where I bought it, what size it was and not believing me when I told her European sizes were different than ours.

'No way. Size six is a size ten — that's gross!'

I smiled and shrugged. 'I almost got my hair cut by a top London stylist.'

'No way!' she shrieked. 'You've had beautiful long hair ever since I've known you. You can't chop it off.'

'So I didn't,' I pointed out. Me and long hair go together — something to hide behind, or to brush and

7

style and occasionally be vain about, I guess. 'So you're ready?' I asked, gesturing towards the gathering crowd of triathletes, a mix of toned guys and girls, all with stencilled numbers and swim goggles strapped around their white swimming caps.

'This is a regional championship event.' Holly put me in the picture. 'No elite athletes are taking part, but Amos invited coaches from the national camps to take a look at the talent.'

'Amos?' I quizzed, without too much genuine interest. If I'm honest, I had one eye on the cars pulling into the lot, looking out for you know who.

'Yes – Antony Amos, *the* Antony Amos!'

'The movie director – yeah.'

'Come on, Tania, pay attention. Amos is sponsoring this whole deal.'

'I guess he can afford it.' From the profits of his endless gore-fest movies. It was well known, mostly taken for granted in Bitterroot, that the locally born director was a money-making machine, which was how he'd come back home and spent gazillions setting up the New Dawn community – giving something back if you like.

'Half the New Dawn kids here have entered the event,' Holly went on. 'They're going to be tough to beat.'

'Do they divide the guys and girl into two groups?'

Aaron looked concerned that his girlfriend was about to plunge into the lake with a hundred guys bulked up to the size of your average Super League player.

Meanwhile I was finally paying attention – not to Holly but to the dozen or so figures in wetsuits, numbers stencilled on their arms, strolling down from the row of log cabins set against the rocky hillside – a distance of maybe two hundred metres. Again, they were a mixture of boys and girls, and obviously residents of New Dawn.

'Here come the juvies,' Aaron muttered, looking even more worried.

'Explorers,' Holly corrected. 'That's the name they give them here.'

'Yeah, everyone knows they're kids in rehab, whatever fancy label they stick on them.'

Holly didn't agree. She stared Aaron down. If she hadn't been conserving her energy for the competition, she might have given him an even harder time.

The juvies, the explorers, the boot-camp/brat-camp residents of Antony Amos's New Dawn log cabins – whatever you want to call them – approached the lake in their sleek wetsuits, bare armed and bare calved and, I had to admit, looking downright Neanderthal. That's the reason they grabbed my attention.

Especially number 102. He came down the hill,

between some tall junipers, out of the long shadows on to the beach. The top half of his wetsuit lay in folds around his waist, leaving his chest and shoulders exposed to the early morning sun. And, wow, I'm talking serious muscles. They bunched up around his neck and shoulders then smoothed out over his chest and abs in sleek, undulating curves. There was no body hair on view – did he wax? But the hair on his head was long and blond – kind of Viking. Anyway, primitive and strong was the overwhelming impression.

Then there was number 98. He was taller, more basketball than football, rangy and loose-limbed. His dark hair was cut short, his skin was mixed race, maybe more white than black in his family history but anyway beautiful. His wetsuit fitted like a second skin, and actually yeah, I admit I was looking at these guys like objects. Then again, I'd just spent part of my two-month escape to Europe in artists' studios attending life classes, looking at naked bodies and trying and often failing to make the appropriate marks on paper and canvas.

Two girls followed through the trees, carrying their swimming caps and goggles in their hands. One wore her dark hair in two thick braids and looked scarily serious, like she didn't ever smile. She scowled and didn't make eye contact with anyone as she reached the crowded beach and gave off don't-mess-with-me signals, which the other girl had to heed.

Her buddy wasn't like the others, I noticed. She was more delicate and nervy. There was no strutting her stuff, no guard up against the curious stares of the Bitterroot crowd. I mean, we were all staring at the juvies and not necessarily in a friendly way, with a fair amount of suspicion in the ether.

'Whose idea was it to make the event this big?' Aaron sighed. 'Why not limit entries to regular college kids?'

'Because the New Dawn team want to push the envelope,' Holly told him.

'This is part of a new reintegration programme. From what I hear there'll be a lot more so get used to it.'

'I'm not . . . I didn't mean it that way.'

'I know you didn't,' I sympathized, preferring to think that Aaron was worried about sheer volume of entries, envisaging all the athletes sprinting together into the lake, jostling and shoulder-charging for the best starting point to give them the shortest distance to the finish line.

'So where's Orlando?' Holly asked as she spotted Grace and Jude climbing out of his red Cherokee. She waved again and beckoned our buddies over.

'On a plane somewhere . . .'

'I thought you said he'd be here Friday.'

'Yeah,' I spoke over her. 'That was the plan.' And he wasn't here, was he? All for the sake of three hundred dollars.

Just then my phone buzzed with a text message. Orlando. 'He's in the airport as we speak,' I reported through gritted teeth as Jude and Grace joined us.

'Look at you – you look so cool!' were Grace's first words. She looked like the old, pre-dark angel Grace – soft, fair-haired and curly with wide grey eyes, all over golden, as if evil had never touched her on Black Rock and there'd been no Ezra, no seduction, or any attempt to drag her on to the dark side and steal her soul. I can't tell you how happy this made me feel.

Grace's hug was gentle, her open smile told me how glad she was to see me back. Likewise Jude.

'Where's Orl—?'

'Don't ask,' Holly warned.

'So tell!' she invited, her eyes still smiling.

'Tell you what?'

'How come you didn't stay away until the year end? Was it Orlando? Did you miss him too much?' Joined-at-the-hip, loved-up Grace obviously couldn't imagine being apart from Jude for two days let alone two months and again I took this as a good thing, given what they'd been through at Black Eagle Lodge earlier this year.

'Actually it's my mom,' I told her. 'She's in hospital for tests. The neurology department at Denver General – a brain scan, other stuff.'

'Oh, Tania,' Grace sighed, and she slipped her arm through mine.

'No results yet, but I wanted to be home with them.'

'Europe can wait,' Jude agreed.

Gulping back my emotions, I switched topics. 'I did have an awesome time, met some amazing people.'

'Went shopping, bought some fabulous clothes,' Holly added, quieter since I'd dropped in the news about my mom.

'Visited the Louvre, saw the *Mona Lisa*. It's so small – no bigger than this!'

'So you're still planning on being an artist?' Grace asked as I sketched out a small rectangle in the air. We huddled together to let the stencilled competitors pass on their way to the starting point, skull caps on, goggles down, wading into the water.

'Wish me luck.' Holly took a deep breath. Her goggles made her look like a sexy aviator.

'Go, girl! Good luck! Get out there and whup ass!' we said non-ironically. We all really wanted her to win.

'Right now I'm more into film,' I told Grace. 'The early

experimental stuff – Andy Warhol, Gillian Wearing, Stefano Cagol.'

She looked at me like I was an alien. 'Stop, my brain hurts.'

'And this from the psychology major!' We laughed and watched Holly step into the water with one hundred and twenty other competitors.

There was a whole heap of noise, a lot of splashing, high expectations. Beyond the swarm of swimmers at the lake's edge was an expanse of calm, silvery water, broken only by an island in the middle of the lake – a low, misty green mound with pine trees surrounding a rocky peak – and way beyond that the dam that diverted Prayer River to allow this lake to form, so old and familiar it almost seemed part of the landscape. But it wasn't. The twenty-metre barrier was built fifty years ago to a design by an engineer called Luke Turner. He created a lake where before there was only a river running through a valley, drowning ranches, pasture land, streets, hotels, houses – the entire frontier town of West Point – in order to provide water for Bitterroot.

Back when I was eight years old we had a school visit from one of the workers on the construction project – a really old guy who described in detail how they built the dam and flooded the valley, how they watched the water rise above barn rooftops until only a couple of church spires and the island with the pine trees were visible – nothing else. Church spires with crosses that you can still see in a dry summer when the water level drops.

Aged eight I spent a long time wondering what happened to the graves in the West Point churchyards. Did they dig them up and move the bodies before they let the water in?

I didn't remember that until now, staring out at the smooth surface of the lake beyond the triathletes. Somehow it seemed connected with the water snake of my nightmare, the two-headed monster, even though there was no logical link, only the cold sensation on my skin, the fear of the murky depths beneath the silver surface.

But I love water, I reminded myself – the way it buoys you up when you lie on your back with Orlando and stare at the stars. Midnight swimmers.

And because water is the opposite of fire. 'Nowhere to run!' Zoran Brancusi had mocked me as I fled for my life through the smoke. Fire lights up the sky, turns the world to ash. A tree had exploded into flames above my head, the dark land had burned.

The yells and splashes at the water's edge demanded that I shut out the past and concentrate on present time.

Breathe, focus on the race, remember that Orlando was this very minute driving from the airport towards the lake. Be still, my beating heart.

'Do you see Holly?' Grace asked me. 'Did she get a good position?'

Jude, Aaron and I all tried to pick out our girl in the mêlée. Aaron was the first to spot her black and gold suit. 'See, over on the right-hand side.' He explained to us her starting strategy. 'She didn't want to get stuck in the middle. She wanted to avoid the crowd.'

The mid-section contained many of the bulked-up New Dawn competitors, who were using their elbows and shouldering opponents aside to hold their position in the pack, so I thought Holly's plan was a good one. 'This is worse than football,' I sighed, picking out numbers 102 and 98. 'Does anyone ever get hurt?'

'There's an open-water survival technique,' Aaron told us. 'If you get behind a bunch of slow swimmers, you protect your face from getting kicked by swimming catch-up style with one arm braced out in front of you. But the best plan is to start on the outside the way Holly is doing, and work hard at the beginning to stay way out in front of the others. She's been working on her surge power.'

'You bet she has,' Grace murmured. We all knew

Holly and her will to win.

'So when does it all begin?' Jude wondered, looking around for a guy with a starter gun.

It wasn't a gun but a klaxon, as it turned out.

A young guy came down the hill – a little older than the other New Dawners, but not by much – not more than twenty-two, maybe twenty-three. He was dressed in a white T and jeans, dusty hiking boots and a black Stetson. It struck me he was the only guy this side of a movie camera who could make a Stetson look cool, like he wore it to keep sun and rain off his face, not for any other reason.

I'll take a little time here. He loped out from under the trees carrying the klaxon that would start the race, looking around the beach area with startling blue eyes that seemed to take in every detail. He observed, he waited for competitors to notice that he'd arrived. Only when he was happy that he had everyone's attention did he set off across the pebble beach towards the edge of the lake.

'Would you look at that!' Grace said under her breath. We girls had long-term boyfriends – we weren't meant to register our admiration of stranger hunks, not when one of those boyfriends stood next to us and the other was en route all the way from Dallas to join us.

But stare we did – at a guy who, come to think of it, could have stood *in front* of any movie-camera lens and passed the hunk test with his perfectly shaped jaw, full lips and columbine-blue eyes that would stop your heart dead. And the rest – long limbs, triangle torso, slim hips . . .

'OK, so you all see the green chequered flag to the left of the island?' Stetson guy asked the athletes. He didn't have to raise his voice to make himself heard – he'd been spotted and the competitors had immediately fallen silent. They looked at the distant flag and nodded. 'This is a one-and-a-half-kilometre swim,' he reminded them. 'You reach the flag, swim around it in an anticlockwise direction then head back here to the shore. Got it?'

The competitors nodded and fired themselves up for the start.

'See the boats?' our guy asked.

It looked like he was in sole charge. He pointed out two small boats, motors idling in an inlet about two hundred metres along the shore. 'They'll come and help out if they see anyone in trouble.'

The competitors stayed silent, listening to every word. You could feel the tension rising.

'When you reach the shore and finish this section of the race, you need to head straight for the stand containing your bikes. Each bike is numbered. Choose the correct one, the one that corresponds to your entry number. The cycling section runs in a northerly direction along the track by Prayer River. You'll see orange ribbons tied to the trees – follow these markers for 5k until you reach the highway. After that you'll cycle around Bitterroot on a 25k route, clearly marked and with marshals directing traffic.'

'I'd rather die!' Grace whispered with exaggerated weariness, and I agreed. And we hadn't even got to the running part yet. I watched the athletes, especially the New Dawn kids, give Stetson-guy every ounce of their attention. Fists were clenched and adrenalin was definitely starting to pump, even amongst spectators.

At last he was through with the instructions. You could cut the silence with a knife as he raised the klaxon, waiting for the triathletes to turn and face the water.

The sudden blare from the horn made me jump. Grace grabbed Jude's arm. Aaron's gaze was fixed on Holly; he was praying that her surge tactic would pay off.

Waaagh! The klaxon sounded, the swimmers plunged into the water waist deep, then they threw themselves full length. Everything was white foam and kicking, flailing limbs. They were off.

A hundred and twenty swimmers swam for the

chequered flag. Heads bobbed, arms whirled, legs kicked.

'Crazy,' Grace sighed.

Jude stayed quiet. Serious asthma holds him back big time. Otherwise, my guess is he'd have loved to be in there swimming.

I agreed with Grace – all this sweat and competitive effort – crazy! I was still looking over my shoulder, only half paying attention.

'I've lost Holly – I can't pick her out,' Aaron reported anxiously from the water's edge.

A posse, a gaggle, a herd of athletes still thrashed through the water, destroying the peace. A few super-swimmers surged ahead but most were still bunched together about five hundred metres out, creating people soup.

A black truck pulled up in the parking lot – at last! I turned from the shore and ran.

Orlando stepped out of his dad's truck. My boyfriend's dark hair was shorter; he was wearing a new black jacket. Two months and a hundred metres separated us. I was running, he was running, we flew into each others' arms.

He held me tight. I leaned my head on his shoulder, wrapped my arms around his waist, breathed him in. When he kissed me I knew he hadn't found a new girl, that his heart was still mine.

'You look amazing,' he murmured, unclasping my arms and stepping back so he could take a longer look.

'You too.' My heart beat fast, I felt dizzy with joy to be gazing into his grey eyes, to be reaching up to run my fingers over his smooth, cool cheek, his soft lips. All I wanted to do was jump in the truck and get the hell back to my house on Becker Hill. 'Oh God, I missed you!'

'I'm sorry about yesterday.'

'Don't. It's cool.'

'I missed you every single day. But I needed the extra three hundred.'

'It's OK, honestly.'

'I hadn't planned for this trip and Dallas is expensive. I have to move out of my apartment to a cheaper place.'

'Where will you move to? Who with?'

I plan to share a room with a guy called Ryan. He's on my course.'

'Is he OK about it? Will there be space for all your stuff? God, I sound like your mom!'

Orlando smiled and pulled me back in for more kisses. 'How was Europe?' he mumbled.

'Exciting. Confusing. Different. But it's really helped.'

'You feel better?' he checked.

I nodded. 'I so needed to break free from what happened on Black Rock – literally to put a physical distance between me and the whole Zoran trauma.'

'Cool,' he sighed, then kissed me some more.

'When I go back, swear you'll visit,' I urged.

'If I can find the airfare. You're going back for sure?'

I nodded. 'Mom made me promise. Before I stepped on the plane in Paris, she laid down a condition: "Only come home if you buy a return ticket."'

'What date do you fly back?'

'It's an open return.'

'Any news from the hospital?'

'Not yet. Later today maybe.' I was clinging on to his hand, I realized, holding on like I would never let him go. Spectators stood on the shoreline behind us, yelling their support for the swimmers. And two new people were walking down the track from the direction of the New Dawn cabins – a girl with short dark hair wearing sunglasses, white capri pants and a pale pink shirt, and an older, grey-haired guy with glasses. They walked through the parking lot on their way to join the noisy group by the shore.

A nightmare vision slams hard against the backs of my retinas, giving me a flash of pain. I see decomposing bodies escape from underwater coffins and drift up through murky water – whole skulls and ribs lurk out of sight, tiny metatarsals bob on a dark, oily surface.

Hell is always close to where I stand – a blink of the eye and I'm there.

Orlando realized that I'd got the queasy, gut-wrenching feeling that comes with my visions and he grabbed hold of my hand and held it tight.

'That was Antony Amos!' he whispered after they'd passed by, in the breathy tone of an anthropologist who's just spotted a rare Amazonian tribesman. Amos moved back into the neighbourhood seven or eight years ago, but he's hardly ever seen in public.

I was still intent on putting a lid on the nightmare vision so I didn't waste more than a glance on the writer and his chic companion. In the flesh our local celeb didn't look too much out of the ordinary, I thought. Rather tall but slighter than he looked on screen at the Oscar ceremonies, though the swept-back grey hair and tailored shirt did cut him out from the jeans and sweatshirt crowd. 'He's the sponsor,' I told Orlando. 'I guess he wants to see what he's spending his money on. Hey, what do you say we get out of here, back to my place?'

Orlando grinned and started to pull me towards the truck. We'd have been reversing out of our spot and totally out of there in under a minute if it wasn't for what happened next.

2

The crowd on the shore fell suddenly silent, but only for a split second. Then people started to point and yell, a warning klaxon sounded, the boats in the inlet set off full throttle towards the middle of the lake.

'Someone's in trouble,' Orlando realized. He took hold of my hand and we ran back to join Grace, Jude and Aaron.

'Out there, to the left of the flag!' Aaron pointed to a swimmer waving both arms, crying for help. 'I knew this would happen – didn't I say?'

That there were too many competitors all bunched together, that it was dog-eat-dog out there on the lake. I swallowed hard and focused on the girl waving her arms. 'That's Holly!' I gasped.

'But she's not the one in trouble,' Jude was quick to point out. 'See the guy next to her – the one who just dove down beneath the surface? It looks like he's searching for someone.'

'What's Holly doing? Why has she dropped out of the race?' It was Orlando's turn to ask questions as the two boats roared towards the flag. Other competitors stopped or changed course to give them a clear channel. Meanwhile, Holly quit waving and dived down to join the swimmer who had just disappeared.

Ten, twenty, thirty seconds went by and I found I was holding my breath. The boats reached the spot as the first diver broke the surface. A guy in one of the rescue boats leaned over to speak with him.

'Holly, come up, come up!' I muttered.

'How long can she stay under?' Grace asked Aaron, who ran futilely knee-deep into the water then groaned and stopped.

The second boat slowly circled the flag. Back on shore, Antony Amos and the girl in pink hurried to speak to the guy in the Stetson. Amos snatched what looked like a two-way radio receiver from the race starter.

'Holly, please come up!' we all prayed.

At last, after what seemed an impossible length of time, Holly's head broke the surface. She yelled to the nearest boat, pointed frantically into the water.

Meanwhile the first diver had strapped on a yellow life

vest handed to him by a guy in the nearest rescue boat. He let himself be raised out of the water then flopped face down on the deck. On shore, a crowd gathered around Amos and his girl companion.

'We lost a swimmer,' Amos reported to his companion after he'd spoken to a lifeguard on the first boat. 'Number 85 saw him go down. Number 102 went after him then 85 followed.'

'Who's missing? Do we have his number?' the girl asked.

'Tell Holly – number 85 – tell her to get on board a boat!' Aaron broke in between Amos and the starter. 'We don't know what the deepwater currents are like out there. Tell her to quit playing the hero!'

But the organizers had more important things to establish before they started thinking about Holly's heroics. Amos clicked a switch then spoke into the radio. 'Give us the number of the missing swimmer.'

There was another click. '43, repeat 43.'

'Is it one of us?' Amos asked the starter, his hand shaking as he clutched the radio.

'Number 43 – Conner Steber.' The guy with the klaxon sounded certain but he pulled a printed list from his pocket to check anyway.

'Conner,' the girl repeated softly. She let out a soft

sigh, a confirmation that the missing swimmer belonged to New Dawn.

'Holly!' Knee-deep in the lake, Aaron yelled her name as many of the athletes realized what was happening, abandoned the race and began to head back to shore. Holly must have heard the call but chose to ignore it, taking a deep breath and diving down a second time. Almost simultaneously, two members of the rescue team jumped from the second boat to join the search.

Amos clicked the switch to speak again. 'What happened exactly?'

'We're not sure. All we know is number 43 went under and 102 couldn't find him. 85 and two of our guys are down there to try again.'

'Tell her to quit!' Aaron begged.

The starter nodded then took the radio from Amos. 'Ziegler here. Get 85 out of the water and into a boat. When she comes up, don't let her dive again.'

'I hear you,' the rescuer replied. 'Here she comes.'

There was a gasp of relief amongst the crowd as Holly's head reappeared a second time. We saw the rescue boat glide towards her, watched as a woman in the boat flung her a vest and talked hard at her, eventually grabbing her by the arm and hauling her on board.

A groan followed the gasp – the two professional

rescue divers had just returned to the surface and were hauling a dark, motionless shape with them. I shuddered and held fast to Orlando's hand. Down in the depths there was a whole town. I imagined streets with wooden sidewalks worn away by the water, steel and timber skeletons of houses, gas stations and grocery stores, spires with rusting crosses. Now only the bones of the dead jostled at shop counters and sat in weed-veiled Sunday best along the church pews. The divers swam slowly towards the nearest boat, hauling their burden with them. Close to the shore, distressed swimmers turned back to look and cry out. 'Oh my God!' 'Can you believe it?' 'Don't even look!'

'Is it Conner?' Ziegler asked, eyes narrowed, staring out across the water.

'Conner Steben,' the rescuer confirmed.

'Any vital signs?'

There was a long pause while the divers struggled to hand their find over to the team in the boat.

And I'm still down there in the deep, dark water, amongst the skulls. A cold current draws me down, a strong pull of water which I can't fight because my arms hang useless, my legs refuse to kick and my lungs, my heart are choked with weeds. My eyes are blind. I sink, I twist. I roll this way and that.

Click. We hear a muffled reply from the boat. 'We found a pulse,' the tense voice reports. 'Call an ambulance. We're heading for the shore.'

Extreme emotion is hard to read. Jaws clench, lips are stretched in joy and agony, both the same.

So I couldn't make out if Antony Amos and the starter were relieved or disappointed that the kid from their community was still alive as the rescue boat reached the shore and two divers carried him through the shallows on a stretcher, laid him out on the pebbles and stood back to let a paramedic try every technique she knew to resuscitate him.

All I saw of the half-drowned swimmer was a glimpse of grey and black wetsuit, a face turned towards me with eyes staring wide, mouth gaping open and a slick of dark-blond hair plastered to his forehead.

A crowd closed in with mixed motives, I realized. Some hoped the kid would make it, even praying aloud. Others with phone cameras at the ready just wanted an image to post on Facebook. Still in charge, Ziegler piled in and roughly shoved the rubber-neckers aside.

'Cancel the event,' we heard Amos instruct the girl in the pink shirt. Back in control of his facial muscles, he turned to her. 'Aurelie, call your brother. Tell him to contact the traffic marshals, send them home.'

'Papa, are you sure?' She spoke with a foreign accent – maybe French, maybe Italian. 'Shouldn't we wait until—'

'Call Jean-Luc,' Amos insisted. He looked at the swimmers wading out of the water, spotted number 102 in his life jacket, still breathing hard and standing hands on hips slightly apart from the action. 'Tell Jarrold to go to his cabin,' he ordered the girl, who this time didn't resist.

She went and spoke quietly to 102. He turned and walked barefoot up the hill without glancing back, his long fair hair dripping on to his shoulders. No one said thanks for trying to save a kid from drowning.

They ignored Holly too, who by this time was sitting with Aaron, huddled in the shade of the nearest trees. Nobody expressed any gratitude for raising the alarm and diving down to the rescue. Maybe that would come later, we told ourselves.

In any case, no one was doing much talking while the paramedic worked. The CPR kit was out, she was kneeling over the patient, intent on airway management, attaching a resuscitation bag to the mask strapped around his face.

'Is he going to make it?' Grace whispered to Jude, who shook his head in a don't-know way.

We stared in silence and watched the medic finally give up on clearing the airways. She shook her head, removed the mask and stood up. Game over. The kid lay on his back, eyes staring, his lips turning blue.

'How long was he under the water in total?' Orlando asked.

Holly was still in a state of shock. She didn't answer.

'What exactly happened – did anyone see?' Jude added.

We'd driven up to Holly's house next to mine on Becker Hill, persuaded her to change out of her triathlon gear into bright-blue sweats, made her drink a lot of water and sat with her until we were sure she was OK. We all had that shock-induced empty feeling in the pits of our stomachs and numbness in our brains.

'This is bad news for the New Dawn people,' Aaron sighed.

'It's bad news, period,' I said. A sunny day had turned to tragedy and it had happened at Turner Lake – my favourite spot in the whole world. And my nightmare visions had started over.

'I'm starting to wish I'd stayed in Europe,' I whispered to Orlando.

'It's OK,' he reassured me. 'I can see what happening

to you but I promise we'll get through this – you and me together.'

'You don't know how it feels, deep down,' I groaned. 'This time it's like I'm drowning, gasping for air. I come out of it and I can hardly breathe!'

'It's cool, I'm here,' was all he could say as he held me tight.

The paramedic had given up on Conner Steben and covered his face. Antony Amos had watched her pack away her kit then had walked slowly up to the cabins with Ziegler and the girl who'd called him papa.

I thought how lonely Conner's last journey – the drive to the hospital morgue – must have been.

I saw his face under the water, tilted up towards the light. The picture in my head was as real as the room I was sitting in now, shockingly vivid but with a weird underwater silence – a white face tilted upwards, eyes open but unseeing, fair hair billowing forward across his brow. I saw him sink without a fight to the bottom of the lake, just letting himself drift down. I hoped it was peaceful, that there were no monsters, no two-headed serpents writhing in the muddy bed, rising to meet him.

'How are you doing?' Orlando asked me as he squeezed my hand.

'I'm good,' I murmured, though my body language

told him different. I was hunched on Holly's sofa, arms crossed, shivering.

'Holly, did you actually see him go under?' Jude was the curious one who pushed her to speak.

She nodded then frowned and shook her head. She too was shivering.

'Sorry, I didn't mean to pressurize you,' Jude mumbled after an elbow nudge from Grace.

'No, it's cool. I need to vent,' Holly said in a shaky voice. 'The worst thing is, I thought I caught sight of him – the first time I dived down.' She paused for a long time and we waited uneasily. 'Yeah, I did see him. But I couldn't reach him. I had to come up for air.'

'Was he conscious?'

Maybe Jude should take up a career as a forensic scientist.

Again Holly shook her head. 'I guess not. He wasn't trying to save himself. He was just kind of drifting down, going with the underwater currents. Anyway, when I dived down a second time, he'd disappeared.'

'And by that time Jarrold – number 102 – had been hauled into the boat and you were the only one left trying to save him until the rescue people joined in.'

'I kept on searching as long as my lungs would hold out,' Holly said. Her eyelids flickered at the painful

33

memory and she began to cry. 'I said to myself, he must be here somewhere: he can't just vanish.'

'But the currents . . .' Jude pointed out. 'And the lake must be forty metres deep at that point.'

'I saw him and I couldn't save him,' Holly whispered, turning her face towards Aaron and burying it against his chest. This was the one fact she couldn't get her head around.

'You did everything you could,' he told her gently then steered her away from the guilt that was tearing her apart. 'It was crazy out there – too many people. Something bad was bound to happen.'

'That's right. That's exactly what you said before the race started,' Jude remembered. 'It was up to the organizers to stagger the start.'

'I guess there'll be an investigation.' Orlando tried to think ahead. 'An autopsy, a pathologist's report, that kind of stuff.'

Oh, didn't we have enough of this on Black Rock – of kids dying in weird circumstances, of parents having to be informed?

The battle between good and bad angels hadn't only been about Grace. Jude had been dragged in too. Plus me, of course. I relived Zoran's party and the time the love thief had tried to snatch me away from Orlando –

spectacular Daniel in his sun god costume, dancing me to the edge of darkness.

Then a boy called Oliver had walked out of Black Eagle Lodge and fallen into a sink hole – a burning underground chamber, the gateway to hell. The Forest Service rescue team had found him and carried his body off the mountain. That was the reason I'd fled to Europe, to escape the memory of these things.

'I'll take you home,' Orlando offered, seeing how I was reacting. He raised me from the sofa and led me towards the door.

'You all want to know what happened to Conner before he went down?' Holly asked, her voice suddenly loud and clear. She had stood up, as if she had wanted to make an announcement. 'I was there. I can tell you.'

'So were twenty or thirty other guys,' Aaron reminded her, wanting to spare her the responsibility and Conner. 'I could have reached out and touched him.' The glazed look in her eyes told us she was back there in the surge of bodies through cold, clear water, rocking in the wake of other swimmers, cutting through the waves.

'Connor got kicked in the head,' she announced. 'Wham! Right between the eyes. One kick was all it took. He went under, dropped to the bottom like a stone.'

* * *

'Shit happens,' Orlando told me after he got me back home.

The day was still sunny and there was light streaming into the house as we sat on the porch overlooking the mountains. A wind rustled through the trees and shook golden leaves from their branches. The sky was a deep, impossible blue.

'I know it does. I'm good, thanks.'

'There's nothing weird. A pure accident, that's all.' Orlando knew I was still wrestling my demons and he was trying to help.

'Thanks.' I managed to smile at him.

He spoke with total conviction. 'This has no connection with what happened with Zoran on Black Rock.'

'I know.' I sighed, I closed my eyes, fought the vision of Zoran Brancusi strutting his rock-star stuff to a pounding drumbeat, melting, shape shifting into a black-winged demon, rising with me into the night.

'You fought him, you won.' Orlando refused to let me go there. He held my hand and fought to draw me back into the light. 'It's over.'

'It's never over,' I sighed. 'Anyway, another kid has died. Conner Steben. We knew nothing about him, but somewhere there must be parents who would have to be told.

Frustrated, Orlando left me for a while and walked in

amongst the aspens at the bottom of the garden, hands in pockets, staring at the ground. One of the doves from the pair I saw yesterday rose from a branch with a whistling flurry of feathers. Only one? What had happened to its mate, I wondered.

I watched it fly. It struck me as sad and lonely, and I cast my mind back to the family tragedy that had taken place here on this plot on Becker Hill. Before my dad had built our house, there had been a forest fire, a burnout. Three people had died – a husband, wife and baby girl. Deep in my psyche I was connected to those people, especially to Maia, the mourning mother. She'd been my good angel, my support during the worst times on Black Rock.

'What was it like in Europe?' Orlando asked me from the aspen stand.

'What do you mean?'

'How exactly was it better for you?'

'Not so many nightmares,' I told him. 'No psychic episodes, so I didn't live my life in constant fear that my dark angel would come back.'

'It was good for us both to get away from Bitterroot,' he agreed. 'Plus, I was focused on my course. There was nothing in Dallas to remind me either.'

'But did it feel real?' I'd made a trip of a lifetime, been

to all the major galleries, studied film, met cool new people. Lucky, lucky. But there was a barrier there, like I was trapped inside a bubble, not making contact.

Orlando walked back towards me, stopped with one foot on the porch, leaned in and gazed at me intently. 'Yeah, Tania, it did. Real and important. I'm totally into what I'm studying. There's a History of Theatre Costume module – that's my favourite.'

I nodded, glad that he had a key into the future, a door to open which I still didn't know how to find. Maybe with him – with Orlando – I could. 'OK,' I decided. 'You're right. We're through with all that stuff.'

He smiled with relief and took me inside the house. Goodbye, post-traumatic stress and paranoia. Hello, real world.

Did it seem inappropriate to make love with Orlando with all that was going on around us – Mom in hospital and the dead kid in the lake? The thought flitted through my head, stayed about five seconds and left.

Then I was in the moment, in his arms, feeling the smooth warmth of his skin and sighing, kissing, telling him how much I'd missed this. After two whole months so strange, so familiar.

I love the way Orlando scoops me off the floor and

lets me wrap myself around him. I love the effect of being so close to his face that his grey eyes and dark lashes blur. We lie on the bed and I eat up every bit of him. He gives himself totally. It was like our first moonlit time all over again. And afterwards the afternoon sun slanted across the bed and we talked.

'Are you OK now?' he asked, stroking my face with the pad of his thumb, smoothing it across the arch of my eyebrow.

I let my eyes close then half open for the blurred-vision effect I love. 'Yeah, when I'm here with you, I'm good.'

'I'm scared for you,' he admitted. 'All the time. I just want to know you're OK.'

'I'm good,' I insisted. The sunlight was dappled and warm, I was where I most wanted to be. 'And I'll be better still when we get the results from Mom's scan.'

'I love you,' he told me for the tenth, maybe eleventh time. 'And listen, you're not the only one with extra-sensory perception. It's my turn – I have a gut feeling.'

'About what?'

He smiled a brave smile, which I tried to mirror. 'Your mom is going to get through this. Everything will work out fine.'

I lay back and closed my eyes, let Orlando's comforting

words flow through me. At that moment in time I would have believed black was white – anything so long as it was him who told me.

'"Mourning dove – *Zenaida macroura*."' Dad read from his *Native Birds of America* book, which weighed a ton. He had opened it and spread it out on the kitchen table to identify the new visitor to our aspens – the lone, greyish-brown dove with the black wings markings and the soft pink belly. There was still no sign of her mate – missing, presumed dead.

'Mom has to stay for more tests,' Dad had told Orlando and me when he arrived home alone from the hospital.

'More tests?' We were wrong: we hadn't expected this. Mom should have been with us, she should be here, sinking down on the sofa and asking for a glass of red wine, saying 'Thank God that's over!' They should have given her pills to cure her headaches.

'Yeah. Doctor is very thorough. Blood tests, more scans.'

'Do they know what's wrong? Can I call her?'

'Not yet. Call tomorrow. She sleeps now.' Dad had kept it short as always but he'd sounded calm, not as abrupt as the bare, Romanian-accented words look on the page. Calm and strong – as always, come to think of it. 'She's fine, Tania. Doctor is good. Knows what he's doing. Mom says no problem.'

And he'd got beer from the fridge, sat on the porch a while then spotted the lone dove. He'd taken down his most recent doorstop volume, sitting on the shelf alongside the political histories and literary biographies to identify the visitor. '"Also known as the rain dove, up to six broods per year, two squabs per brood."'

'Let me see the picture,' I insisted. Yeah, I recognized the flash of white on the wings, the dark eyes, the reddish legs and feet.

'"A popular game bird,"' Dad read on. '"Up to seventy million are shot annually for sport."'

'Ouch!' I said, then, 'Ugh!' I don't like guns. I especially don't like shooting for fun.

'"It has a plaintive coo-woo-oo-oo-oo call, which changes to roo-oo under threat. The wings may make a strange, low whistle at take-off and landing."'

'Yeah, I heard it.' I put my hand on his shoulder, leaned over and read with him. Stuff about a flight speed of up to fifty-five miles per hour, a preferred habitat of grassland and lightly wooded area, not thick forest. A diet of corn, millet and sunflower seeds. And finally, '"The mourning dove is monogamous and partners for life."'

Dad finished reading a few seconds after me, closed

the book and took out another beer. 'Maybe white-winged dove, *Zenaida asiatica*,' he said, thoughtfully staring out of the window towards the aspens. 'Maybe inca dove – *Columbina inca*. Maybe not mourning dove after all.'

Holly dropped by next morning with questions about my mom and news about poor Conner Steben.

It was when I was getting ready to drive into Denver with Dad and Orlando. I'd already spoken to Mom and she was expecting a visit at ten thirty so I didn't have much time.

'Your mom will be good.' Holly echoed my boyfriend's optimism. 'People like her don't get sick, remember.'

A reminder – Mom is a multi-tasker. She runs a home and family alongside a job that jets her across the world to find and rent commercial properties for an international energy company. She does it without stopping to draw breath so I took Holly's point.

'How are you?' I asked.

'Cool.'

'Sure?'

'Totally.' She was like a sleek yellow Labrador, running out of the river, shaking herself dry. Not a drop of yesterday's trauma seemed to have stayed with her.

'Aaron made some phone calls. He found out Conner Steben has been at New Dawn since May. His time was almost up.'

'God, that makes it worse,' I groaned.

She agreed. 'The courts gave him a six-month sentence for stealing Dexedrine tablets from his local pharmacy – a first offence. Amos's rehab community was his best option. They say he did real well there.'

'Worse and worse.'

'I know.' Holly sat down at the kitchen table as if we had all the time in the world and Dad and Orlando weren't hovering in the driveway ready to leave.

'These halfway-house situations don't usually work that well but you have to hand it to Anthony Amos and the guys who work with him.'

'Tough love,' I reminded her. 'They set the kids big challenges, they don't take no for an answer. All that wilderness therapy.'

Between us we pieced together what little we knew about New Dawn – facts we'd picked up second or third hand from the Internet and by word of mouth.

'The juvies form a team and they hike up the mountain,' Holly said.

'What do they do up there? I mean, exactly.'

'They explore. That's why they call the kids Explorers.

The leaders make them live like native people did before white men came and civilized the hell out of the place.'

'They have to learn how to make a fire, find food, all that stuff?'

'Yeah, and more. There's a spiritual content too.' Holly obviously knew way more about it than I did. 'They have a motto: "From heart at war to heart at peace."'

I said I liked the sound of this idea. 'If only it was that easy,' I sighed. I bet Holly didn't have recurring nightmares and visions the way I did. I made a private bet my non-psychic buddy would outrun, outswim, outcycle any dark angel that came winging her way.

'I hear you. And what do you bet it's not all sweetness and light. Imagine living there month in, month out with only other juvies to talk to. Yeah, these kids are in rehab and they're all supposed to show respect and find inner peace, but don't you just bet some of them hate each others' guts?'

Through the window I noticed Orlando tap his wristwatch and mouth for me to move my ass. 'Hey, I have to go,' I told Holly, scraping back my chair. But she has this way of holding back the most important thing until last – like yesterday's fact about Conner being kicked before he sank. Now she did it again. 'I saw who kicked him,' she said, looking me in the eye.

I sat down again to give her my full attention. 'Are you certain?' There was too much spray, too many arms and legs. 'How can you be sure?'

'I told you – I was right behind Connor. The guy I'm talking about was ahead and to my right. I saw him get Connor in his sights. Then he rolled on to his back, aimed and lashed out with his foot, made contact, wham!'

'You're saying this was deliberate!' I took a deep breath, tried to visualize the choppy waves, the chaos. 'So who?' I said again.

Holly was definite – no hesitation, no doubt in her mind. 'Number 102,' she said. 'Tarzan with the long blond hair. One kick from him and Conner went down.'

3

People say I'm the drama queen, that I go through life pulling in the bad stuff, but I'm nothing compared with Holly, believe me.

'Honestly, that's the way she sees it!' I told Orlando and Dad as we drove into Denver. We were coming down from the mountains, seeing the flat plain of the city spread out below us. High-rise blocks lay half hidden by the morning mist. 'She told me Conner's death was a deliberate, cold-blooded homicide.'

'That girl.' Dad grunted in disbelief as he swung a right off the Interstate.

'Yeah, I'm with you, Andrey,' Orlando agreed. 'Holly watches too many straight-to-video crime movies. There's always a mystery.'

I sat in the car recalling the theories she and I had developed about the aftermath of Zoran's Heavenly

Bodies party. Was it mere alcohol that killed a million brain cells and stopped us from remembering what had happened at Black Eagle Lodge? No, Holly's theory involved Rohypnol and date rape oblivion. For twenty-four hours after the event she would have sworn on her life that serious substance abuse was involved – until she showed up in the ER for a test to prove that it wasn't.

'So Conner's death was an accident,' I said quietly. Safe inside the car, swooping down on the city into Cherry Creek and stopping on Bannock Street to buy flowers for Mom, I was happy to believe it.

Then, after we'd parked the car and were making our way through the main hospital entrance, we had an unexpected brush with the reality of Conner Steben's death.

There was a small crowd gathered outside, jostling to attract the attention of three people leaving the reception area – a grey-haired couple and a girl aged thirteen or fourteen.

'Mr Steben, have you carried out a positive identification of your son's body? Have they given you an exact cause of death? Mrs Steben, can you tell us how you're feeling? Do you attach any blame to the organizers of yesterday's event?'

'Jeez!' Orlando steered me around the knot of reporters.

I took another quick look. The parents seemed totally traumatized – as if the soft tissue on their faces had been dragged down by some terrible g-force – and the expression in their red-rimmed eyes was dazed, exhausted. The girl, though, looked angry. Her teeth were clenched, her jaw set. She caught my eye and I saw straight away there was hurt beneath the anger and she was probably holding her jaw tight to stop herself from falling apart.

'Where will you hold the funeral, Mr Steben? Will you take Conner home to Oregon to bury him?'

What sleazeball editor ordered these guys to doorstep the grieving family? What level of heartlessness does it take to push a camera into their faces? I was glad when two muscle-bound security officers showed up to shove the journalists to one side.

Dad strode on ahead of me and Orlando, leading us into the elevator and showing us the way to Mom's ward on the sixth storey. 'She got good sleep,' he told us. 'But still tired. Doctor goes on looking for reasons.'

He slowed down as he reached the door into a private room – Mom's medical insurance is the best – and he pushed the purple orchids we'd bought into my arms.

'Go ahead,' he told me and Orlando. 'Talk to Mom. I'll find doctor, nurse, someone to ask.'

So we went into a small white room with white slatted blinds to keep out the sun.

My mom smiled at us from her crisp white bed. Her dark hair was loose around her shoulders. Her face looked thinner and more shadowed than before her illness. 'Flowers!' she murmured as if they were the last thing she was expecting.

The clear wrapping crackled as I lay them on a table by the window. 'Hey, how are you doing?' I asked. I hovered. I didn't go right up to her.

'Come here,' she said. And she hugged me. We didn't speak for the longest time. Then she reached out to Orlando and squeezed his hand. 'Sit,' she told us. 'Not on the chairs – on the bed where I can hold your hands.'

I hesitated. 'What about the nurses?'

Mom raised her eyebrows in a so-what way – a look I was totally familiar with, though seeing her confined to bed was the weirdest thing. 'Sit,' she repeated. She waited a while then said, 'So they made a diagnosis.'

I took a deep breath. 'But Dad said . . . he thought . . .'

'The doctors were just in here. They finally know what we're dealing with.'

Major headaches, blurred vision, extreme fatigue.

There'd been a quick consultation with our family doctor then immediate admission into the neurology unit for tests. The news couldn't possibly be good.

'There's no tumour,' she began.

I allowed myself a sigh of relief. 'But?'

'They say I've had a series of small brain haemorrhages,' she told us, perfectly calm. 'Intra cerebral – that means bleeding inside the brain tissue.'

I shook my head, found nothing to say that would help. This shouldn't be happening.

'Don't look so tragic,' Mom said gently. 'They call it ICH for short. The pressure from the bleeding is what gives me the headaches. All they need to do is get in there and relieve the pressure.'

'Surgery?' I whispered.

'Today,' she confirmed. 'Like, right away.'

'But how . . . what causes it?'

'Too many glasses of Merlot,' she joked. 'Well, they say alcohol is a major risk factor.'

'But you don't . . . I mean . . . not that much.'

'Plus menopause, plus high blood pressure,' Mom added. 'A lethal cocktail, apparently.'

'But the surgery will fix it?' I was so scared I couldn't look her in the eye. This was my mom, the strong one, the one who always made the right decision, who was never ever sick.

'You bet.' She held my hand, squeezed it tight.

The room was too white, the orchids too purple, the sun too strong beyond the blinds. I fought back tears, thinking, I'm not the one who matters here. Be strong, be like her.

'So, Orlando, you take care of my baby,' Mom told him. 'Promise?'

He nodded and then he had to leave the room to hide his own tears, making the excuse that he would go find Dad.

'And, Tania, you take care of Daddy,' Mom told me in the silence as the door swung closed. 'I'm talking about these next few days. I'm not talking for ever because I plan to sail through this and get back to doing what I've always done. But help him through this difficult part, OK?'

'I will.'

'I'm glad you came home,' she said with a sigh, after a long silence.

'Me too.'

'And look at you – my grown-up girl.' Mom leaned her head back against the pillow but she didn't let go of my hand. 'How many languages do you speak now – fluent French, Italian . . . ?'

'A little bit of both. Not as much as you.'

'You know what they say about travel? It broadens the mind. I'm a true believer.' She took a rest but she wasn't through talking yet. 'And you and Orlando?' she asked.

I smiled back. 'You know what they say about absence?'

'It's true too. That's how come Daddy and I do so well after all this time – I fly home from a trip and each time I remember the reasons I love him all over again. Likewise, he works out of state, comes home and, magic – his heart has grown fonder!'

'My God, you're a pair of old romantics!' Like the mourning doves who find a mate for life.

'And what's wrong with that?' she asked.

'Nothing. I'm with you.' That's where I get it from – being romantic is in my DNA.

We were chatting in the white room, warding off the big, scary reason she was here. 'And, Tania, you still want to go back to Paris to study film?' she asked, sounding exhausted.

'Maybe.' I wouldn't commit until today was over. Right now it felt as if my future was a blank screen waiting for keys to be pressed.

Mom's eyelids flickered shut and she sighed.

'How bad is the headache?' I asked.

She didn't answer but her eyes opened again. 'I want

you to know how very proud I am,' she murmured. 'From the day you were born, always proud of my girl.'

'Even when I'm trouble?' I kidded. Angsty teen agonizing over which jeans to wear, refusing to clear up my room, fighting her authority. And, as it turned out recently – a psychic medium messing with dark angels. My simple question was loaded with all this significance.

'Especially then. Always.'

So now my tears fell. Mom couldn't be this sick. She couldn't be.

'And your intuition, your psychic power – call it what you like – I want you to know that you should go ahead and trust it one hundred per cent.'

'So I'm not crazy?' All those times she'd heard me wake up from nightmares of the forest blazing, of the house burning, of hearing the child cry. The nights when she'd come into my room and soothed away my fears.

'Be strong,' she insisted, hours away from life-saving surgery, thinking only of me. 'Follow your star. Believe in yourself the way I believe in you.'

That same evening, after Mom's surgery, Dad began to feed the dove. He threw down sunflower seeds, sat under the trees and waited. 'Here, pretty bird. Fly down, eat.'

Coooo-woo-oo-oo-oo! She whistled down to the ground,

scattering the seeds with her fluttering, black-spotted wings. Then pecked with her short dark beak.

We called her Zenaida because it sounds exotic. They shoot gazillions a year like vermin, but, hey, ours was unique.

'Where's your mate?' Dad asked her.

Mom had survived the procedure to drain blood from her brain. It was only afterwards, while she was still sedated, that the surgeon gave us the bald statistic – a mortality rate of over forty per cent.

'Your wife is one tough lady,' she'd told Dad. 'But even she will need to sleep through the next twenty-four hours, so we have sedated her and you have time to go home, relax. We'll call you if we need to.'

So when Dad spoke to Zenaida it came from the heart. 'I'm sorry you lost mate,' he said in his deep, un-American voice. 'But stick around here, mend broken heart.'

'Mourning dove,' I called from the porch swing. I had the bird book on my lap. Orlando was with his laptop inside the house, researching costume design for the first Paris production of *The Firebird* in 1910. He had to submit an assignment before the end of the week. 'Predators include falcons and hawks.'

And black eagles.

I shiver as the dark angel in eagle form sweeps across

the rain clouds gathering over Carlsbad. There will be other times, other places. We're talking about his thirst for revenge, his twisted heart, and I never for a moment doubt that he'll be back.

Zenaida saw the Randles' white cat crouched on the porch roof next door. She took off with a whistle of wings.

The next day, Monday, Dad drove into Denver alone. According to the latest report, Mom was doing well but she was still sedated until the swelling in her brain reduced. 'Visit tomorrow is better,' Dad advised. 'Today, you and Orlando take hike, make bike ride – have fun.'

Easy to say but more difficult to do when all my energy for the past twenty-four hours had gone into living and reliving every agonizing moment of Mom's surgery.

'It's a good idea.' Orlando showed up at the house as Dad left. My heart eased the moment I saw his black truck come up the hill. He was my cavalry, my knight in shining armour. 'Your mom told me to take care of you. What do you want to do – cycle or hike?'

'Neither.'

'How about the hot springs – help you relax?'

Indoor activity was more what I had in mind, I

told him with a sigh. 'Hold me,' I said. 'Don't speak. Just hold me.'

We went to my room. We stepped into the moment, his cool skin against me. I love that he's so strong and lean. I love the prickle of his chin on my cheek, the pressure of his lips on mine, that he can kid around and be funny when we make love, not serious all the time.

It's afterwards that he gets intense. 'Come to Dallas,' he begged, lying back with one arm behind his head, staring up at the ceiling.

I turned on to my side, folded myself into him.

'Come with me, Tania.'

'I don't know. There's a film festival in Prague next month – small indie stuff, then another editing course in London.'

'But I miss you. I miss all of this.' He stroked my arm and shoulder, turning and tilting his head so that his eyes reminded me of a puppy dog, soft and pleading.

'I miss it too. I can't tell you how much. But it won't be for ever.' A few more months. He'd be busy with his own course. We could Skype every day. I was about to go down Mom's absence makes the heart grow fonder route, until his mood suddenly changed and he cut off from me.

He sat up and put on his clothes. 'Come on, let's take the bikes down to Prayer River,' he said.

* * *

That was Monday, when Mom was still sleeping. Dad came home and said everything was good. They were pleased with her progress.

Tuesday morning I visited. I sat by her bed and watched her wake up.

'Oh boy!' Mom sighed when she finally opened her eyes, like she'd slipped back a few decades to the language of her childhood and her own parents. 'I sure am thirsty.'

She was propped up on pillows, connected to monitors and drips. They said I shouldn't tire her and I left after an hour.

Tuesday evening Orlando and I took another cycle ride, this time to Turner Lake.

'But not on New Dawn territory.' I insisted on using the track on the opposite shore, keeping a distance from Saturday's tragedy. I wanted to enjoy the lake, remember all my special times with Orlando. And actually I loved every minute – cycling hard, steering the bike around raised tree roots, seeing the golden aspen leaves flutter and fall.

'Shall we swim?' I asked when we reached one of my favourite spots. I longed to plunge in and let the water refresh me, to recreate our midnight swimmer moment in full daylight.

'Too cold.' Orlando was keeping his distance, still feeling rejected. He would probably still be this way when he took the plane back to Dallas. After that he would miss me and shower me with long-distance love.

'I bought my plane ticket,' he said as we continued on. 'I'm out of here, tomorrow midday.'

I put on my brakes, stopped dead. I felt the blood drain from my cheeks. 'You really have to leave?'

'Really,' he insisted. Stopping a few metres ahead of me, he turned to judge my reaction. 'Thursday I meet with Dr Greenaway to talk through my assignment.'

He said it in a way I couldn't or shouldn't argue with, but I tried anyway.

'Postpone the meeting. Tell them your girlfriend's mom is sick, you need to be with her.'

'Tania, don't make me feel bad. Anyway, I'm packing up and moving to Ryan's place, remember.'

'I'm only saying . . . Is this because I decided I wouldn't come to Dallas?'

'You figure I'm that immature?' he challenged. 'I have to complete my module, end of. Like you said, we can Skype.'

Ouch. He was leaving for sure and I felt like I was falling, sinking, drowning again. To our side the water glittered, the far-off island shimmered. Above our head the aspens quivered.

A body sinks without a struggle. Bubbles rise towards the light, the body twists and turns in the currents. He, or is it she, stares blankly into the darkness. The corpse is down in the lost town, drifting through doorways, looking without seeing. Ghosts watch the spirit depart.

I drove Orlando to the airport and we walked hand in hand to the departures gate. My hand in his, a perfect fit.

'You'll think about it?' he asked after we'd kissed goodbye.

My lips tingled, my heart yearned. 'About Dallas?'

He nodded. 'I know you said no, but we could make it work, believe me. You could still travel to Europe whenever you need.'

'I'll think about it,' I promised. I knew I totally loved him, but did he know it too? Would I have to go to Dallas to prove it? 'I'm not making any decisions until Mom gets out of hospital.'

'Yeah, cool.' He kissed me again, this time wistfully. 'We're good, aren't we? You're still my midnight swimmer?'

I nodded. I watched him go, the back of him – tall, loose-limbed, perfect.

* * *

59

'It's not a funeral, it's a memorial service,' Grace explained as she drove me and Holly to the lake late that afternoon.

'Obviously,' Holly said. 'The family already took Conner home to Oregon.'

'So whose idea is the memorial?' I asked. I'd agreed to go without really wanting to and partly to fill the hole of Orlando's leaving. It was either that or staying home with Zenaida, who was getting fat on sunflower seeds.

Grace drove the familiar route through town towards the lake. 'The New Dawn people think it's appropriate, I guess.'

'It's the least they can do,' Holly muttered from the back seat. 'But if you ask me it's some kind of PR exercise.'

'How do you figure that?' Grace didn't get it.

'The community is under pressure. One of their Explorers dies in weird circumstances.'

'Will you stop this!' I shook my head and stared ahead. 'What?'

'Making stuff up, developing theories.'

'Tania's in denial,' Holly told Grace with a patient sigh. 'So anyway, the New Dawn people set up the memorial service to make it look as though they care.'

'How can you know that?'

'That's what these boot camp places have to do. I read about it. They cover up abuse with slick PR. It's a known fact.' Holly's position didn't soften. She was sticking with her hard-line view.

'You're sure you want to be there?' I asked, turning to look at her. 'What if you see the guy with the blond hair – number 102, Jarrold?'

'Yeah, Holly, don't make a scene,' Grace warned. 'We don't want you sharing your homicide theory with people. This is not the right time or place.'

'So did anyone start investigating?' I'd been out of the loop since Sunday because of Mom's surgery. 'Is there going to be an inquiry?'

'Who knows?' Holly shrugged. 'I already called Antony Amos's office to remind them I was a witness.'

'And?'

'They said thanks but no thanks. The woman – the French one – cut me dead, if you really want to know.'

'So what about the cops?' Grace turned off the highway and followed the rough track to the New Dawn Community. We drove through junipers and redwoods which eventually opened out to give us a clear view of the lake.

'I called them too and they said so far they're not directly involved. They're waiting for the autopsy report.'

'So you think you can handle this?' I checked. Knowing

61

Holly and her reaction to hitting her head against a wall, I doubted it.

'A kid is dead,' Grace added quietly. 'That's all we need to focus on right now.'

'Sure I can handle it,' Holly sulked, opening the car door before Grace had even finished parking. She got out and slammed the door. 'What do you think I am?'

4

It wasn't what I was expecting, not in a million years.

In fact, I had zero expectations because most of my mind was still on Orlando walking through the departure gate and my heart was wrung out with regrets and longing.

But here we were, walking from the car park down to the lakeside to join a group that was about to celebrate a departure of the final kind.

It turned out there were around fifty people at Conner's memorial. Twenty or so were from Bitterroot, responding to the message on the New Dawn website that everyone from the town was welcome. The rest were staff and juvies from the community. I picked out and recognized straight away the girl called Aurelie, who'd been by Antony Amos's side. Today she was dressed in a floaty orange skirt and long-sleeved cream top, standing next to a guy who could only be her brother, maybe even her twin, who had the same shiny, dark hair and dark eyes and that quiet way of holding himself slightly apart from those around him, who were mainly Explorers by the look of them. I mean, they didn't have the classy look. I know I shouldn't say that, but I just did.

For instance, there were the two girl triathletes I'd seen last Saturday – the scowling one with thick black hair who again established personal space with a hostile stare. Today she was dressed in frayed jeans and a tight white T, with plenty of silver jewellery including a couple of face piercings. She stood reluctantly with the nervy, skinny one – pretty but awkward, whose denim jacket was buttoned to her chin and whose long hair blew across her face as she stood with her back to the wind from the lake.

The moment Aurelie saw me arrive with Grace and Holly, she came to greet us. 'Thank you for coming,' she said with a smile. 'I'm Aurelie Laurent, Antony's stepdaughter. Antony will be here any moment.'

Stepdaughter. I registered this and stored it. We all smiled and felt embarrassed, mumbled hi and followed her into the crowd.

Dainty and delicate are the words to describe our guide. And charming. *Charmante*. You felt that right away. Huge, wide eyes gave her an alert, intelligent look, her hair was cut so well you immediately wanted to ask who was her hairdresser at the same time knowing you couldn't afford it. Groomed, delicate, dainty, charming. And French. Some girls have it all.

'Come and meet my twin brother,' she invited.

Twin – first impression confirmed. Another fact for the Aurelie file.

I didn't know about Holly and Grace, but Aurelie Laurent made me feel like a dork. That's the only way I can describe it. Compared with her, we were hicks. We should have been playing our banjos on the back porch, chewing tobacco, spitting and eating grits. I exaggerate to make my point.

'This is Jean-Luc.' Aurelie began the introductions.

'Hi, I'm Grace.'

'Tania.'

'Holly.'

Here we were again – Jean-Luc was another drop-dead gorgeous guy, to which one-word responses were all we could manage. His almost black hair swept across his forehead and was long enough to curl on to the collar of his blue and white striped shirt. He wore the cuffs rolled back to reveal tanned wrists, the collar turned up and the two top buttons undone.

'Thank you for coming,' he said, mirroring his sister's perfect manners. Add 'sophisticated' and 'refined' to charming, groomed and the rest. I tried not to stare open-mouthed at this second picture of perfection.

'Tania was just in Paris.' Grace told him the first thing that entered her head.

She blushed, stepped back and left me and Holly in the firing line.

'Really?' Jean-Luc glanced from me to Holly and back again, unsure which was which.

Pay attention, *monsieur*.

'This is Tania,' Holly said quickly as she gave me a small shove.

Aurelie's brother kept his attention on Holly. 'Number 85,' he recalled, fixing her with an unwavering stare. It was enough to make the stoutest heart go flip-flop, pitter-patter. 'I heard you tried to save Conner.'

'I did,' Holly mumbled, her tanned face flushing. Here was her moment. I saw it all – the kick to the head, the moment of homicide. But no – Jean-Luc's powerful gaze seemed to stun her into silence.

'You did a brave thing,' he told her, his dark eyes seeming to dig deep into her consciousness.

Holly swallowed and took a step backwards. All her usual bravado seemed to have deserted her.

Jean-Luc stared at her for a while longer then finally turned his attention to me. 'Tania, when did you leave Paris?'

'Friday.' I was so nervous I couldn't be sure I had my tongue under control, so I kept it short.

'Where in Paris did you stay?'

'Rue du Temple.'

'And why were you there?'

'I went to study art. Well, film actually.'

'You saw the Picasso museum?'

I nodded.

'A friend of my father's is curator there.'

Wow. How do you top that?

'Our father, Claude Laurent,' Jean-Luc explained. 'He is a banker there, in Paris.'

Again I was tongue-tied and Aurelie had to step in with a change of subject.

'We wanted to hold the ceremony here, in the place where it happened. It makes us feel . . . connected.'

'We're so sad for you.' Grace always speaks from the heart. She's an open book – no games, no barriers. It makes her both vulnerable and strong. 'It's important – we have to show we care,' she'd told Holly and me when she was persuading us to come here.

'Thank you, we appreciate it. Especially your bravery,

Holly.' Aurelie smiled graciously then went to mingle with other guests. At last – a recognition. Her brother, Jean-Luc, stayed to chat with me about Paris, explaining that he liked to spend part of each year there: 'Whenever I get the time. Antony's foundation keeps me pretty busy actually.

'Antony', not 'Papa', I noticed.

'My job is to be the bridge between our Explorers and their families. A lot of parents ask for daily progress reports, though we don't allow direct contact during the time kids are here. The idea of New Dawn is to open up Explorers to a completely new beginning. "To turn hearts, to walk together in the sight of the Great Creator."'

Jean-Luc delivered the quote straight from the New Dawn manifesto, it seemed. I wondered if there could be a touch of irony in his voice but I didn't see any sign of it in the serene expression on his face. Anyway, I was happy just to enjoy the foreign inflexions, to admire the perfect grammar. Gorgeous *and* smart. *Incroyable*.

'So,' Holly blundered in. 'Your mother divorced your father then married Antony Amos?'

Too personal. I thought about giving her a dig in the ribs to make her behave, but Jean-Luc didn't seem to mind.

'It was ten years ago. They met while Antony was filming in Greece – an epic horror, lots of dark mazes, snakes, minotaurs. Our family owns a holiday villa on Crete. Aurelie and I were eight years old.'

'And where—' Holly began.

Jean-Luc read her mind. 'Unfortunately my mother died earlier this year.'

I straight away felt bad for him and Aurelie – for their loss, and I thought of my own mom in her hospital bed.

'Wow, I'm sorry,' Holly said, by now totally under Jean-Luc's charming spell.

'She helped Antony to set up the community. She was a psychotherapist in Paris and it was her idea to give New Dawn an experiential basis. Our programme stresses assertiveness and group work, it consists of a series of tasks to challenge Explorers and bring them into harmony with the wildernesses of the world.'

The text-book speech fell fluently from his tongue – again no hint of cynicism. I bet he gave this same spiel ten times a day. And believed it, it seemed.

'Excuse me – duty calls,' he said next, smoothly sliding away when he saw more people coming down the track from the cabins on the hill.

He left Holly, me and Grace practically open-mouthed on the lake shore.

'Not behaviour modification but experiential,' Grace echoed softly. This was her field and she sounded interested.

'A series of challenges in the wilderness,' Holly murmured. She had that bring-it-on look in her bright-blue eyes and before we could comment she went right over to Aurelie Laurent to ask her whether New Dawn ever took volunteer helpers.

Grace threw me a puzzled glance. 'Wow – she changed her mind!'

'Yeah, what happened to the homicide theory?'

'One talk with a good-looking guy and she drops it, just like that,' Grace frowned. 'Suddenly she loves this place enough to volunteer.'

'Typical, huh?' I followed the back view of Jean-Luc as he walked halfway up the hill to meet his stepfather, Antony Amos, accompanied by three more of the Explorer kids including Holly's ex-chief suspect, Jarrold.

Blond and muscled, smooth-skinned and strong. Did he look like a guy with a guilty secret as he strode down through the trees?

I glanced up amongst the pines and experienced a stomach-wrenching flip into the past, vivid and powerful as a lightning strike.

I see Red Cloud, Red Dog, Little Wound wearing crows'

feathers in their black, braided hair. There will be no surrender. They stand at the edge of a forest with blankets around their shoulders, arms crossed. The Ogala Lakotas send war pipes to their friends, the Arapaho. Together the tribes swoop down to the South Platte in a thunder of hooves, the whole valley lights up with burning cabins and stage stations, pine trees twist and explode into flame.

'Do not trust the enemy. In one hand they hold a peace pipe, in the other is a rifle.'

Red Cloud with his long black hair falling to his shoulders. His eyes are hooded, his mouth is a wide, thin slash across his broad face, his shoulders are strong. He says, 'The white men have pushed the Indians back season by season until we are forced to live in a small country north of the river. And now our last hunting ground, home of the people, is to be taken from us. Our women and children will starve, but we will die fighting.'

White Ghost, Sitting Bull, Crazy Horse. Names like sighs, like wind blowing across the plains. Braids and beads, headdresses made of fluttering eagle feathers, faces built out of rock, out of earth.

'A bird, when it is on its nest, spreads its wings to cover the eggs and protect them. We will protect our wives and children.' Sitting Bull rides bareback by the river, amongst the tipis. 'Make a brave fight!' he cries.

71

Snow comes and falls deep. Soldiers appear on the hill. A black rattle of rifles, a swoop of a thousand horses. They shoot and burn. Nothing remains but smoke and ash, smoke and ash.

Sitting Bull, Rain in the Face, Crazy Horse live on. Thousands are slain in the valley, by the river. Their blood stains the snow.

'When I was a boy we owned the world. The sun rose and set on our land. Where are the warriors today? Where are our lands? Am I wicked because I am Lakota, because I was born where my father lived, because I would die for my people and country?'

A bearded man with a wolf-skin headdress walks with Amos out of the moonlit forest. He is half man, half wolf with a hairy jaw. Is this past, present or future?

Wolf man beckons me and leads me into thorns, I crawl after him, my clothes are ripped to shreds. His amber eyes draw me in, he breathes soft words into my ear. The grey-haired wolf howls his song.

'Tania?' Grace said. She tugged at my sleeve. 'Are you OK?'

I was on the edge of a fantasy forest peopled by ghosts and nightmares, sensing danger. 'I'm cool,' I told her, getting a grip, shrugging the wolf man off.

* * *

Through the whole ceremony Amos kept Jarrold by his side. He stood by the water's edge, his back to the lake, facing us. And his quiet dignity claimed our attention. Like Red Cloud talking to his warriors before battle, he made us listen.

'Our brother, Conner, walked with us in the wilderness,' Amos began. 'We saw greatness in him, we saw peace.'

New Dawn kids and staff raised their arms above their heads. They gazed out over the water.

'He sat by our fires, high on the mountain. His heart was healed.'

The Explorers raised their arms and poured out their emotions on the shore of the lake. Some of the girls wept while their leader spoke.

'He is gone yet he remains. He's in the trees over our heads, the rocks beneath our feet. He is every drop of water in the lake.'

'Hey, Conner, this is Channing speaking. We're here to say we love you.' The mixed-race guy with the tall, rangy physique spoke softly. A low chorus of voices echoed his words.

'We know you're here,' Channing murmured. 'We know you're at peace.'

'Go but stay,' Amos said. 'Walk with us in harmony.'

73

The ceremony was short and simple. It ended with hugs, handshakes and tears, with smiles breaking through and a kind of quiet joy. Then we split into groups and talked amongst ourselves.

'Are you in a hurry to leave?' Aurelie asked Holly, her fall-coloured skirt blowing in the breeze, suggesting great legs beneath the flimsy fabric.

'Are we?' Holly checked.

Grace and I shook our heads.

'So why not walk up to Trail's End with us?' Aurelie invited. 'Papa's cabin,' she explained. 'He'd love to talk with you about volunteering, Holly. And you too, Tania and Grace.'

We nodded. Shake, nod, shake, nod, like banjo-playing puppets on strings.

Anyway, we followed Aurelie, Jean-Luc, Ziegler and Amos up the track, under the trees.

What had happened to Jarrold, I wondered. I turned and saw him sitting alone on a rock, staring out across the lake.

'So did you actually volunteer?' Grace checked with Holly.

'I decided I want to help out,' she explained. 'I can do survival skills, no problem . . . What?' she protested when Grace and I looked sceptical. 'I was a girl scout, I went to summer school – gathering berries, rubbing a couple of sticks together to make fire, boiling water. How hard can it be?'

'But . . .' Grace was tempted to bring up Holly's old homicide theory, which had apparently been blown clean out of the water.

'Don't even bother,' I warned. 'Holly was at the ceremony and now she's a convert.' Amos's words had been impressive – sincere, calm and convincing.

And his face had really and truly looked like one of the old tribal chiefs – lined and beaten by the wind, hair swept back from his noble features. If I switched off the critical part of my brain, I could see the attraction.

So we trailed on up to the New Dawn leader's cabin, where we were caught off guard again.

'No way do I call this a cabin,' Grace whispered from a distance of thirty metres.

Trail's End was way too big for a start, with wraparound porches and main windows looking over the lake towards the distant peaks of the Bitterroot Range. The porch furniture – swings, chairs and tables – were five-star quality with leather cushions and expensive ranch styling. An air-con unit stood next to the log store and the main door was open, showing a glimpse of a living room with a round table bearing the weight of a bronze statue of a bucking horse. So I agreed with Grace – this was no ordinary cabin, more the kind of ranch house you see in realtor ads, with moose heads on the wall and bear rugs on the floor.

'Come in!' Aurelie invited. 'Can I get you iced tea?'

'Yes, come in.' Antony Amos stood in the porch. He must have been fifty-five years old, but he'd walked up the steep hill without stopping to draw breath.

'He's in good shape – it's all that wilderness walking,' I muttered to Grace as Holly stepped forward to accept the offer of tea.

Fifty-five, with thick grey hair swept back from his square-jawed, lined face. His eyes were deep set and dark brown behind small, wire-rimmed glasses, his clothes western style today, but not flashy – jeans, tooled boots, white leather belt but no cowboy buckle, a plain grey shirt with white piping around the collar and across the chest, a gold band on his wedding finger. 'Which of you three girls wants to help out?' he asked as Grace and I stepped up into the porch.

'That would be Holly,' Grace told him. 'But I guess we might be interested too.'

We were? Had she forgotten I was heading back to Europe as soon as the doctors gave Mom the all-clear?

'The point is, you don't need to know in advance the

76

survival techniques we use here,' Ziegler was explaining to Holly as we walked into the house. Ziegler with the black Stetson, columbine eyes and white T-shirt that emphasized his pecs – the man with the klaxon.

Self-conscious and hovering in the doorway, I focused on the bucking-horse statue, burnished and big as a lurcher, resting on a polished, dark-wood table with ornate carved legs. The artist had made the mane and tail fly, had sculpted to perfection the horse's wild eyes and flaring nostrils, plus every muscle in its chest and neck. 'You learn our methods while you're out there in the wilderness with our Explorers,' Ziegler said.

'All you need is to be fit and healthy, period,' Amos added.

'I play tennis, I ski,' Holly said eagerly.

Ziegler nodded and made a note. He asked Holly more questions in a quiet, relaxed voice, exploring her motivation for volunteering, how many hours per week she could give, how she saw herself relating to the Explorers in her team. She answered meekly and obediently, like a child at a magic show.

'And what's your interest?' Jean-Luc asked Grace, leading her to the window and looking out over the lake.

'That would be more the theory, the therapeutic approach.' She plucked up courage and told him she was hoping to enrol in a course as a psychology major, starting next summer. 'If I could get hands-on experience at a place like New Dawn, it would look great on my resume.'

'And you?' Amos turned to me as Jean-Luc concentrated on Grace. 'What's your focus?'

'The kids here,' I said without hesitation. Jarrold, Channing, the girl with the face studs – all of them.

'Good answer. Tell me more.'

'What brings them here to New Dawn? How do they deal with it?'

Amos listed criminal offences on his fingers. 'They come here for larceny, violence, drug and alcohol dependency, the fall-out from family break-up – you name it. The conventional system processes them and spits them out. We pick up the damaged pieces. And each Explorer reacts differently. Most are pretty reluctant when they first get here.'

Like the scared girl in the denim jacket, looking like she wanted to run. I tried to picture where she'd come from and why she'd been sent to the community but found that I couldn't guess.

'But we ask them to turn their hearts, make a new beginning,' Amos said.

I was growing used to the jargon, getting an inkling of what it might actually mean. So I tried not to take a cynical step back when he talked about turning hearts.

'The wilderness helps them to learn respect.' Amos paused, studied me then began again. 'You don't totally believe me, do you, Tania? But take Ziegler.'

The drop-dead-gorgeous coach sat with Holly at the central table. He heard his name mentioned, glanced up and smiled briefly.

'Richard came to us aged seventeen.'

'As an Explorer?' I'd lost count of today's surprises.

'Juliet, my wife, spotted him on the set of one of my movies. He'd lied about his age and found work as a stuntman and body double. Then he got into trouble – street fights, petty larceny, that kind of thing.'

'That's hard to believe.'

'Yes, when you look at him now. Originally we took him in for a ninety-day period.'

'And he's still here.'

'On staff, as a team leader. How about that?'

'Awesome,' I said. From what little I'd seen of Richard Ziegler – at the lakeside on Saturday and again today, he seemed like one of those totally together people who can make decisions and take action in an emergency. It was hard to picture him as a punk kid in trouble with the cops.

'My stepson says you were living in Paris.' Amos

cut across my thoughts. 'Don't look so surprised. We talked on the walk up to the cabin. I hear you want to study film.'

'Yeah, it was fine art originally – painting. But then in Europe I saw a lot of video art, starting with Warhol. I got interested in instant playback and different ways of editing, especially when things went digital.' Wow, I was loosening up at last, talking about film to Antony Amos, who was only one of the most successful directors of all time. 'I like the underground Italian film makers.'

'Stefano Cagol?' he asked. 'How about the home-grown guys – Matthew Barney, Gary Hill? And David Lynch – everyone knows *Twin Peaks*, huh?'

'Yeah, cool.'

'You know that Explorers here take footage of their wilderness experience?' Taking off his glasses, Amos slipped them into his shirt pocket, accepting iced tea from Aurelie, who had reappeared from the kitchen.

'No, I didn't know that.' This sounded really fascinating – I imagined some kind of fly-on-the-wall documentary, except here there were no walls, only forests, lakes and mountains.

Amos was still staring at me intently, weighing up what I'd said, the way I sounded. 'So, Tania, why don't you join us?' he asked. 'We could use some of your recently acquired editing skills.'

I was shocked. Truly. And I was on the spot, squirming. 'I can't,' I told him in a rush. 'I'm only home in Bitterroot for a couple of weeks at the most. Then I get on a plane and fly back to Europe.'

I left the cabin ahead of Grace and Holly, needing to walk and put distance between myself and the decision that had fallen out of my mouth under pressure from Antony Amos.

I was going back to Paris, end of story. Because I loved film as much as Orlando loved fashion, because I felt further from dark angel danger over there. And because I'd promised Mom. Sorry, Orlando. So sorry, my love. I strode away from Trail's End along the track, my heart pumping hard. Tonight, when I got home, I would Skype him, check he was safe then explain my plan. It would be one of the hardest things I'd ever had to do. I would tell him and hurt pride would make him do his cut-off thing again. He would act like it was no big deal, start talking about his new room mate or his Firebird assignment. But we would both know that he'd practically begged me to go to Dallas to be with him and in the end I'd said no.

Why, for Christ's sake, was I going to wound him so badly?

Walk, get a distance. Remember how much you love him and he loves you.

Look up at the branches of the redwoods, breathe in their sharp, resin scent.

Breathe.

The grounds of the New Dawn Community were beautifully laid out, I realized. A row of small log cabins was hidden amongst stands of aspens, connected by a trail just wide enough for two people to walk side by side. Surrounded by silver trunks and rustling branches, each one was secluded and simple, totally the opposite to Amos's showy spread. Behind them, the hill rose steeply to a granite cliff and a jagged horizon which stood in deep evening shade. Below was an almost sheer drop to the lake shore, meaning the trail through the aspens was the only way in and out.

I carried on walking, ready to double back whenever Grace called me to say she and Holly were all set to leave. It didn't happen so I left the cabins behind and followed the trail through thicker aspens until I came to a creek tumbling over rocks on its way down to the lake. Should I cross it? Did the path continue on the far side? I stood a while, the palm of one hand flat against the rough bark of a nearby tree, looking down at the clear, gushing water. Then I glanced up across the creek and came face to face with Jarrold. He must have been there all along, hidden in the trees, only stepping out when I stopped to consider my options and still blending into the background in khaki sweatshirt and black jeans.

'Sorry, I didn't . . .' I began. I turned around, ready to quit bothering him and walk away.

'You were at the ceremony,' he said in a deep, slow drawl.

So I turned back, spoke above the splashing, gurgling stream. 'I saw you there too.'

'We all were. Channing, Regan, Kaylee, Blake, Marta, Ava – everyone.' Jarrold stepped across to my side, totally sure-footed on the sloping, wet rocks.

'You were a triathlete. You dived down to rescue Conner.' And you either did or did not deliberately kick your fellow competitor in the head before he drowned, I thought. Depending on which of Holly's versions I choose to believe.

He met my gaze but his grey eyes were troubled. 'Conner was my buddy.'

'I'm sorry.' Instantly sorry for even thinking that Holly's homicide theory might be true. Honestly, I felt guilty as I looked him in the eye.

'We shared a cabin – him, me and Channing.'

'Really, it sucks.'

'Me, Conner, Kaylee, Ava – we were a team. Just last week we walked the wilderness.'

I ran out of apologies, shook my head and stared at my feet, shaking off the guilt and starting to feel actively angry that Holly had planted the seed of suspicion against Jarrold, who looked and sounded to me like he was genuinely suffering. And I was knocked off balance for a different reason. This guy's presence was strong and physical and I sensed that I could easily find him way too attractive. So I refused to look up again and take that risk.

'You were there on Saturday to watch your buddy?'

'Holly Randle.'

'She has guts,' Jarrold said. 'The currents were strong down there. They dragged us all to hell.'

The double-headed serpent hisses. A corpse drifts and turns amongst the weeds and silt. Coffin lids lift – skulls, ribs, thigh bones float free.

'Yeah, Holly – she always gives one hundred and ten per cent.'

'So she's OK?'

For some reason Jarrold's question bothered me and I made myself look up again. 'Why shouldn't she be?'

'No reason. An experience like that could be traumatic, I guess.'

'For her but not for you?'

'Not when you believe.' He gazed steadily back, half in the setting sun, half in shade.

'Believe in what exactly?'

'That we all belong to the earth, the sky, the water. We belong to fire. Like Amos and Channing said, Conner's spirit surrounds us.'

'Sorry, I honestly don't get that.'

'Neither did I, at first. You have to be in the wilderness a couple of times. Then you know.'

I spread my hands, palms upwards. 'What can I say?'

Jarrold began to smile in sympathy at my confusion but the expression froze before it was fully formed. He'd obviously spotted someone coming along the trail towards us. I glanced over my shoulder to see Aurelie, skirt blowing in the breeze, her pale top standing out amongst the shadows.

And before I knew it, without saying another word, Jarrold had jumped back across the creek and started to scramble quickly down the steep scree slope towards the beach.

'What was that about?' I asked Aurelie, gesturing down the cliff towards Jarrold.

'I'm sorry,' she sighed, waiting until he'd made it safely down. 'Jarrold just broke one of our guiding principles, and he knows it.'

'Why? What was he doing that was so wrong?' I was still watching and secretly admiring him from a safe distance as he strode along the very edge of the lake, heading towards the inlet where the two rescue boats had waited on Saturday.

'He spoke to you,' Aurelie explained, slowly and simply like a kindergarten teacher.

'And?' Did they have a vow of silence here at New Dawn? If they did, it was news to me.

'Right now Jarrold holds the status of Outsider. He's forbidden to speak.'

He was walking away, growing smaller, turning the corner into the inlet and disappearing from view.

'He did something bad?' I asked.

'Not really.' Aurelie slipped her arm through mine and started to lead me towards the cabins. 'Here at New Dawn we don't make judgements about bad and good. No, Jarrold is simply excluded from all group activities. He needs to be alone with his pain.'

5

My laptop screen showed Orlando surrounded by cases and cardboard boxes in the room in Dallas which he was about to vacate.

'I move out tomorrow,' he told me on Skype. 'Ryan already gave me the key to the new place.'

'It's exciting,' I told him.

'How's your mom?'

'She's doing good. Dad just came back from the hospital. They told him that getting through the first forty-eight hours is the tough part. Now they start doing tests to find out if there's any permanent damage.'

'Oh, babe.' He commiserated on screen, so near yet so far away. It made me ache to be there in the room with him, to be able to touch him and kiss him, feel his warm breath on my cheek. 'There's nothing major, is there?'

'Dad says they don't know yet, it's too early to say.'

And besides, I wasn't certain if Dad was telling me everything, or if he was holding some things back. 'I'll visit her tomorrow morning.'

'So don't stress, OK? Not until after the doctors come up with a verdict. Who knows – maybe she escaped any bad effects.'

'Let's hope. How was the flight?' I asked, ready to switch topics. I still had to give him my decision about Paris and it was weighing heavy. There he was, pixillating and breaking up on the small screen, lips out of sync with the sound of his voice, surrounded by boxes, moving on.

'Good flight, no problems. Hey, and I spoke with Aaron.'

'Holly's Aaron?' I asked with an air of distraction.

'Yeah, Holly's Aaron. What other Aaron do we know? So now he tells me his girlfriend has another crazy plan that he's not happy about.'

'You mean the New Dawn volunteer thing?'

'The last I heard she hated the juvies – one of them especially. The one she blamed for the kid's drowning.'

'Oh, Jarrold.' Jarrold the Outsider, forbidden to speak so that he could be alone with his pain. 'But you know Holly – she comes out with this high-octane junk without stopping to think. It was just the first thing that came into her head.'

'So she didn't actually see this Jarrold character kick the guy?'

'Who knows? She hasn't mentioned it lately, not since Conner's leaving ceremony where she became a convert.' I gave a wry smile and moved the conversation forward. 'Anyway, what did Aaron say?'

Orlando tidied his desk as we spoke, stacking books into piles and sliding papers into folders. 'Only that she volunteered to walk the wilderness with a bunch of screwed-up juvies. The New Dawn people have decided they like volunteers – it's part of the rehab, reintegration programme.'

'Yeah, they do. And yeah, she did. And Aaron's not happy?'

'No, and I totally get that. We don't know this organization, or any of the guys who run the place. Holly's getting herself into something she might regret.'

'Why, what could happen?'

Orlando stopped tidying and frowned into the camera. 'What about Amos, the big movie mogul?' he challenged. 'What kind of guy is he?'

'OK, I guess. He made a cool speech at Conner's service.'

'You were there?'

I picked up the surprise and disapproval combined into three small words.

'Yeah, and I was there when Holly volunteered. Grace is thinking of doing the same. Amos was kind of cool. Actually, he reminds me of Sitting Bull or Red Cloud – one of those old chiefs we read about. And he believes in the ethos at New Dawn, no question.'

'Believing in something doesn't make it good,' Orlando pointed out. 'Remember Zoran Brancusi.'

Other times, other places. A million other willing souls. The dark angel name sweeps like a shadow across my life, threatening my whole being.

'This is different,' I protested. 'I'm talking about a talented guy who has everything going for him – brilliant career, high profile, multi-millionaire. And instead of cruising his yacht in the Bahamas, Amos chooses to set up an organization to help kids who are disadvantaged, damaged, whatever. And he's hands-on. He doesn't just pull in a team of people to work it out for him.'

'Run that back,' Orlando suggested. 'Rewind. Substitute the name Brancusi for Amos, Black Eagle Lodge for New Dawn. See what I mean?'

Wings beat. My dark angel and love thief, black eyes glittering, circles silently overhead, ready to drop on to his prey.

His mission? To destroy young lovers and drag their souls on to the dark side. And to revenge himself against me, Tania Ionescu. To punish me for knowing him, for speaking his

90

name. *'Malach!'* I said, and his power crumbled. *Spirit of death, dark angel.*

His method? To lurk, to lie low or circle the earth, never to go away. To shape-shift and rise again.

'No, really.' I spoke louder than I intended. Orlando was wrong about Antony Amos. It didn't feel the same. I had psychic powers and would know in my heart it if it did.

'Tania, listen to me.' Leaning across the desk closer to the camera so that I was staring straight into his eyes, Orlando grew intense. 'Holly can do what she likes and we know no one's going to stop her. But I'm serious, Tania – I've seen what getting involved in bad spiritual stuff does to you.'

'To all of us,' I pointed out. 'Remember Grace.' How the dark angel targeted her because she was innocent and in love with Jude. In his twisted view of the world, she was his ideal victim, and he almost drew her on to the dark side and claimed her.

'OK, I hear you. I'm not saying it wasn't real – the fires, the poor kid who died on Black Rock.'

'Oliver,' I reminded him.

'But you, Tania – you have to be aware.'

That my psychic energy made me borderline crazy? Is that what we were back to? The idea that super-sensitive me could so easily slip from reality into nightmare visions of dark angels out for revenge.

Out of the window I saw Dad throwing down grain for Zenaida and somehow the sight of it kept me grounded. I felt this was a time to back down from argument, to let it go. 'I know. I hear you.'

'Good. So no volunteering?' Orlando was strident, demanding in a way I didn't recognize or like.

'No,' I agreed reluctantly. 'In any case, how can I?'

The puzzled frown came back, the uncertainty behind his beautiful grey eyes.

'What do you mean – how can you?'

It wasn't exactly the way I'd planned the break the news – not after our difference of opinion over New Dawn, but it came out anyway. 'How can I volunteer when I'm not going to be here?'

'Why, where will you be?' His eyes widened, he had a moment, a flash of hope that I would be in Dallas with him.

'Paris,' I murmured. And God, forgive me, I saw the hope die. 'As soon as Mom is well enough, I fly back.'

I lay for a long time without sleeping, remembering how Orlando had walked away. He'd left the room without switching off the camera, without saying anything.

'You OK?' Dad had asked when he came in from feeding the dove. 'You and Orlando, you had fight?'

'Kind of. I told him I was going back to Paris. He walked out on me.'

'He wants you in Dallas?'

I'd nodded, bit my lip to stop it trembling.

'He loves you,' Dad had pointed out. He'd said this to comfort me but it only brought on the tears. 'Big passion, you're his first girl. I remember this.'

And now I couldn't get to sleep for running over the options – Paris and my career, or Dallas and the guy I loved. And was it possible to have both? Was it greedy to *want* both?

I turned over to my right side, stretched out the cramp in my legs, turned over on to my left. A breeze disturbed the dreamcatcher hanging over my bed.

And the wolf man leaps in through the window, teeth bared. Bearded and with amber eyes, he creeps out of the forest, out of the thorns and thickets where he has his lair. He leaps and tears me apart.

I sat up in bed, in the dark, trying not to cry out, remembering all the times I dreamed of fire, smoke and the child in the burning house who called for her mother. And how Mom was always there to comfort me.

Where is Maia, my gentle good angel, to protect me from

danger? I don't know my enemy. I don't know him yet but he is in the room, he has me between his jaws. One more bound takes us out into the night, across the water to the island in the middle of Turner Lake. 'Help!' I cry, knowing that no one hears.

I didn't sleep and my head felt dull and empty when I got up the next morning, I wasn't so much tired as confused and not wanting to talk to anyone as I left the house to drive into Denver.

Luckily Dad had already set out to check out a new construction job, locally in Paloma Springs, but unluckily Holly caught me in the driveway.

'Hey, Tania, you want to drive down to New Dawn with me?' she called over the fence.

I waved my car keys and shook my head. 'Sorry, I'm visiting the hospital.'

'Not now. Maybe later this afternoon. Richard wants to show me some video footage.'

'What video?' I noticed she was already on first-name terms with the fascinating Mr Ziegler.

'A documentary shot by the Explorers last week – Conner and Jarrold went up to Carlsbad, above the snowline. The video shows the type of survival skills I'll need when I accompany the next group. They call them

94

bands, named after natural objects. Mountain Lion, Falling Leaf – that kind of thing.'

'So you're definitely still planning on volunteering?'

'Why wouldn't I be?' Holly paused to consider the implied challenge behind my question then understood. 'You talked to Aaron?'

'No, to Orlando.'

'And he'd already talked to Aaron. Those guys trade gossip faster than we do! What did Orlando say?'

I shrugged, got in my car while we were talking. 'He said, don't do it.' I closed the door. 'We don't know enough about New Dawn: he doesn't like the sound of Antony Amos, yabber-yabber.'

'Just like Aaron, blah-blah.'

I released the handbrake and noticed Holly keep pace with me on her side of the fence. We reached the end of our driveways at the same time and she leaned in through my open window. 'You know what this is?'

'A conspiracy?' I said, making it light. Two guys talking behind our backs, trying to control their girlfriends' actions.

'They're jealous!' Holly declared. 'They've seen the muscles on those mean and moody juvies, and they don't want us to go within half a mile.'

* * *

95

Holly makes me laugh, the way she's so dramatic, so black and white. I don't always agree with her, but the things she says leave a mark.

Jealous or not? I thought of Orlando as I drove down to Denver, and I tried to reverse the situation – would I feel OK about him volunteering in a situation where there were gangs of good-looking, needy girls? If I'm honest, probably not. I'm the girlfriend who stresses about those waif-models and wacky designers on his college course, remember.

So I tried to be open-minded, to tell myself that Orlando's jealousy was kind of flattering, that it was something I could handle and I decided I would be adult enough to run Holly's latest theory by him the next time we spoke. *If* we spoke! I had a sudden picture of Orlando's back turned as he absorbed my Paris news then strode out of the room full of boxes. I saw the door swinging shut.

Sure, we'll speak, I told myself, driving into town past the high chain-link fence of the Three Peaks Correctional Facility and the roadside notice that read 'Do not pick up hitch-hikers along this section of highway', as if some dumb-ass driver would be stupid enough to do it.

I drove on, stopped in Cherry Creek to buy more flowers for my mom – bright-orange gerberas this time,

96

no pastel shades for my mom – and went into the hospital
to see her.

'They say I lost my sense of taste and smell,' Mom told
me. 'That's careless of me, huh?'

I sat on the edge of her bed, holding her hand.

'It's because some part of my sensory cortex is bruised,
but they tell me I'll slowly get it back.'

'That's good, Mom.' Trying not to stare at the curved
scar across her scalp and the row of neat sutures, I smiled.

'Lucky for me the bleeding occurred where it did,' she
went on. 'Any closer to the vagus nerve and it would have
been a different story.'

'You don't have to talk,' I assured her. She seemed so
tired, so pale. 'Just listen. You'll never guess what
happened with Holly last Saturday. You know she entered
the triathlon at New Dawn? Well, a kid from the
community gets into trouble during the swim stage. And
who's there, right on the spot to try and rescue him?
Holly, naturally. Only she can't get to him and the poor
guy drowns. Yesterday we went to a memorial service. It
sounds tragic but actually it was awesome.'

Mom listened and gave tiny nods, as if moving her
head was painful.

'The doctors did find another small problem,' she told

me when I paused for breath. 'There's a disconnect between my brain and my left hand. I tell it to move and it refuses to cooperate.'

I gasped and looked at the hand lying free of the sheets, resting palm down on the bed.

'Watch,' she told me. She stared at the hand and willed herself to raise it from the bed. All she got was a faint tremor of her fingertips. 'Dyspraxia,' she explained. 'Don't worry. They'll put me on a rehab program and before you know it I'll be good as new.'

'So I'll stay longer,' I told Dad on the phone. I'd called him in Paloma Springs to update him on Mom's latest news.

'How long?'

'A week, maybe two. Until I'm sure she's going to be OK.'

Dad didn't argue with my decision. And he didn't say he was glad, but I knew he was. 'What food tonight?' he asked. 'Take-out pizza or fried chicken?'

'Pizza.'

'OK. Don't tell your mom.'

'I won't. See you later.'

We finished speaking and I walked out into the garden. For the first time this fall I felt a wind cold enough to bring snow down from the mountains, though the sky was still blue and the sun dazzling through the branches of the aspens. I walked through the trees, kicking up russet red leaves, hearing above my head the call of our resident dove.

'Sorry, no food,' I told her. 'Maybe later.'

She sat on a branch, staring down at me, head to one side.

'I know, I'm mean. But it's for the good of your waistline. And I'm sorry you lost your mate. What happened to him?'

The noise came from deep in her throat, her pink chest was puffed up.

Suddenly the blue sky is filled with a hundred mourning doves. Their grey wings speckled with black whistle as they land in the trees. The sun shines. My bird gazes down through golden leaves. A predator approaches through the long grass – fox or coyote. Wolf, even. Bearded jaws, amber eyes. Who are you? The dove takes off with a whistle and a whir of wings. She soars into the sky and away.

For a moment I thought I smelled burning wood and I raised my hand to shield my eyes from the sun. I checked out the forested slopes of Black Mountain, afraid to spot the tell-tale spiral of smoke rising – the start of another burnout. But no, there was nothing. I looked at my watch and made a sudden decision, found my keys and set off down the hill.

Holly's car was already parked in the lot at the entrance to the New Dawn Community. It was two thirty and the cold wind was still blowing down from Carlsbad. Clouds were gathering over the lake, I noticed. The first snow of the winter – it'll be here before nightfall, I predicted.

Leaving my car, I set off up the trail in the opposite direction to Amos's luxury pad, towards the row of cabins on the hill, not exactly sure who I was looking for or the real reason I was here.

I was still curious to find out more about the New Dawn kids – I admit that, and I was tempted to take a look at the documentary video footage of their wilderness walks. Plus, the fight with Orlando had brought out my not-so-inner rebel. I was convinced he was wrong about wilderness-walking Amos's parallels with Zoran Brancusi, even though Holly might be right about the jealousy thing.

My feet crunched on the dirt track as I came to the first cabin in the row – a small log building hidden amongst the aspens. It had the formulaic porch with a log pile, a porch swing and a row of coat hooks by the door, which stood propped open by an iron boot jack. As I drew level, one of the girls I'd noticed before – the skinny, nervy one – ran out on to the porch, followed by the girl with the face jewellery. She was yelling and the first girl cowered against the log pile.

'Hey!' I called and began to walk towards them. It didn't make any difference – the second girl carried on yelling.

'I know you took them! Who else goes into my room? That's where I left them – on my bed!'

The first girl looked terrified. She shielded her face with her arm.

'Quit yelling. What are you fighting over?' I demanded as I reached the porch.

Close up, I saw the skinny girl was no match for her attacker. She was shorter and lighter, and looked like she needed to eat better. Her small face, dominated by huge dark eyes, was shadowed: her wrists so thin they looked like they would snap.

The tall girl swung round towards me, ready to hit out. I thought she was going to leap down the step and swing a punch but something stopped her. Instead, she pushed her hands into her jeans pockets, scowled and walked past me down on to the trail. The girl by the log pile slowly lowered her arm.

'I'm Tania,' I told her, letting her draw breath.

'Ava.'

'You OK?'

She nodded.

'You sure?'

Pulling herself upright, Ava, flicked her long hair behind her shoulders and made a weak attempt to push aside what I'd just seen. 'Why shouldn't I be? Kaylee's cool – she doesn't scare me.'

'Really? She scares the hell out of me!' Over my shoulder I saw face-piercing girl disappear down the trail towards the creek where I'd last seen Jarrold. 'You two share a cabin?'

Ava nodded.

'So what did she lose?'

'Her socks.'

'All that yelling over socks?'

Another nod and Ava's long lashes flickered down over her glistening eyes.

She sniffed back the tears. 'I have to go,' she told me, but she didn't move.

'Was that really it?' I couldn't believe a girl could get so angry over a pair of socks.

And suddenly the floodgates opened. 'Kaylee caught me talking with Jarrold,' Ava sobbed. 'Yesterday, in the social area. We were only talking – end of story.'

'Oh!' I paused to let this settle. 'I heard Jarrold is

on a no-talk regime.'

'He is. We broke a guiding principle.'

'So I won't tell anyone,' I promised. 'Kaylee and Jarrold – they're an item?'

'She thinks they are,' Ava said in a rush of bitterness as she pushed past me and ran down the track. 'But it's all in her head. Jarrold isn't really into Kaylee. He's only into himself!'

The social area that Ava talked about was a big old ranch-style building surrounded by pinon pines and standing in a secluded inlet on the shore of the lake. There were rooms with pool tables and table tennis, a cinema room and a cafeteria, but the main room was a sitting area with a big open fire and half a dozen leather couches, where the walls were hung with moose, deer and elk antlers and the floor carpeted with a huge bear skin, head included. Those glass eyes stared at you every time you walked by.

'Tania, welcome!' It was Antony Amos himself who spoke as he spotted me in the doorway. He sat on one of the couches, surrounded by staff and kids, apparently in the middle of a meeting. This is where I finally found Holly after half an hour of searching.

'Come in,' Aurelie insisted, sending Kaylee to fetch me.

I want to make it clear – I didn't walk into this with

my eyes closed. I was definitely on my guard, looking out for the whoosh of wings, the sudden dark angel swoop. And honestly, there were no wings or sharp black beak, no hairy jaws, amber eyes and snapping teeth – no enemy, nothing.

'Follow me, please,' Kaylee said, just like a waitress showing me to my table. She wore her black hair loose, still parted down the middle and kinked by her usual braids. I noticed a white-and-red beaded belt around her jeans.

Jean-Luc was the one who stood up to offer me his seat, in between Jarrold and Channing, with his short, thick hair and basketball physique.

'Hi, I'm Channing,' he told me, as if it was information he'd rather have kept to himself. Since he'd spoken at the ceremony by the lake he'd definitely closed down the shutters and seemed more your stereotypical juvie – silent and sullen, with a huge chip on his shoulder.

'I know. I'm Tania,' I told him.

'She's here to volunteer!' Holly announced brightly from a couch on the far side of the roaring log fire. She looked totally at home with the situation, kind of fired up and wanting to make a good impression. Richard Ziegler sat close by her with photographs and what looked like maps on the coffee table in front of them.

'I'm not sure yet,' I muttered. Like I said, I wasn't certain what had brought me here. Maybe I was a moth drawn to a flame. Or else I was bidding for independence from Orlando, dead set on making my own decision and following my star.

Amos was seated away from the fire, his feet stretched out and almost touching the bear head. 'Richard has spent some time explaining to Holly our philosophy here at New Dawn,' he told me with a smile. 'To sum it up, we could say it is walking in the wilderness to find the greatness of the Creator in each and everyone of us.'

'Our wild walks allow us to move in harmony from broken heart to whole heart, from heart at war to heart at peace,' Ziegler added with all the zeal of a convert, the firelight flickering across his handsome face.

'There is greatness in us all,' Amos repeated. 'We learn from Mother Nature how to survive. She teaches us.'

Ziegler chimed in with more beliefs while, sitting beside him and basking in his warmth, Holly lapped it up. 'At the start of our journey we learn to drop the burdens of our previous lives and allow greatness to take their place. In the wilderness we eat what we find, we walk, we sleep. We give thanks to the Creator.'

'So anyway, I'm sure Tania and Holly have heard enough philosophizing,' Amos said at last. He broke the spell, stood and came over to me with a smile. 'Call in at Trail's End when you're done here,' he invited. 'I have footage from last week's wilderness walk that you might like to see.'

Then he left the room, inviting Jean-Luc to take the seat that he'd vacated, and allowing the meeting to continue.

'Holly, as a volunteer next week, we'd like you to join the Hawk Above Our Heads band,' Ziegler told her. 'Out in the wilderness, a band is like family. You make sure each member of your band stays safe. You trust each other completely.'

'So who else is in my group – the Hawk Above Our Heads band?' she asked eagerly.

Ziegler leaned forward to consult a list on the table. 'That will be Blake and Marta, plus Channing and one other.' Then he glanced up towards a geeky-looking kid on the outside of the group, not sitting but standing in the shadows. 'Regan, you'll take Conner's place in the Hawk Above Our Heads band. You'll be Explorer number 4, out on Carlsbad. That makes Blake, Marta, Channing and Regan, plus Holly as Friend. The other group out there next week is the River Stone band, comprising Kaylee, Ava and Jarrold. You'll be lakeside. You need to take this location into account when you make your preparations.'

Kaylee, Ava and Jarrold would be wild walking together by Lake Turner. I tried to picture it – paranoid Kaylee yelling at Ava to go find sticks for the fire, suspecting her of sneaking illegal time with her beloved Jarrold every step of the way. Neurotic Ava too scared to stand up for herself. Jarrold the Outsider and still a possible killer, not permitted to talk but hey, who cared? He was definitely the type to break every rule in the book.

It would never work, I decided as the group split up and Jean-Luc offered to take me to visit his stepfather at Trail's End.

6

'Tell me something,' I said to Jean-Luc as we walked. 'If Jarrold is an Outsider on a no-talk regime, how does he integrate and become part of the River Stone band?

'Good question,' he replied, striding on.

I ran to keep up. 'So?'

'You're right, it's difficult,' he agreed in that so-charming accent. 'An Outsider is forbidden to speak to the band or share in band activities.'

'To be alone with his pain?' I quoted Aurelie then waited.

'Yes, until he can't stand it any more.'

'And then?' Trail's End was twenty metres away, set back on a bank of golden grasses that waved in the cold breeze, so time for conversation was running out.

Jean-Luc stopped and shrugged. 'Then Jarrold breaks through a spiritual barrier, he finds peace.'

'And it works?' I couldn't hide my surprise at the unconventional methods used here.

'According to my stepfather, yes.'

'And you – what do you think?'

He gave a second shrug and knotted his dark eyebrows, dropping his voice so that he couldn't be overheard from Amos's cabin. 'I wouldn't like it to happen to me – alone in the wilderness. I don't know, maybe I'm not strong enough to come through such an experience.'

'Does it ever go wrong?' I asked, looking down on the lake, on monsters hidden in the depths, on bones floating free of their coffins, on the secret dark side of what might happen here at New Dawn.

'I sank beneath the surface fifty years back,' a corpse confides. It's night-time, he is whispering in my ear. 'The water rose, I drowned. I am bone, I am buried in the depths of the lake. I am dirt, I am weed, I am water.'

Three words rise to the surface – Death. Darkness. Suffering. The corpse floats away on the black water, his voice fades.

'Are you OK?' Jean-Luc checked as I halted my stride and felt the usual chewed-up pain in my gut. He took my arm. 'Listen, don't let Antony scare you. He's just a regular guy.'

I steadied myself. 'Yeah, a regular guy who happens to

have made some of the highest-grossing movies of the past two decades,' I quipped. '*Evil Birth, Main Street Massacre, Dark Secret* . . .'

'Yeah, well now he's returned to his roots and found a new role,' his stepson reminded me.

'Here at New Dawn, as a kind of spiritual leader?'

Jean-Luc nodded and, putting his arm through mine, began to walk on slowly. 'Scratch the regular-guy surface and you'll find he's busy working on his charisma.'

'Wait – you mean, he's faking it?' Honestly, I hadn't expected this level of frankness from my guide, who paused a second time.

'No, he believes it,' he corrected me. 'The Native American stuff about the Great Creator, the existence of ancestral spirits within the rocks and lake – all that.'

'But?'

'But it leads him into extremes. In my opinion, his methods are a little harsh.'

'I hear you,' I murmured, eager to learn more. But then Antony Amos appeared at the door of his cabin.

'Tania, here you are!' he said with outstretched arms. He wore a collarless white shirt over loose black chinos, his silver-rimmed glasses perched on top of his head. 'Again, welcome. Step inside.'

'So this is the video shot by the Black Crow band,'

Amos explained, pressing the remote to start the show. 'Richard just gave it to me so I haven't had a chance to view it yet. Remember, it's totally raw and unedited, shot on a hand-held camera. See what you think.'

We were in his cinema room at the back of the cabin – a small, claustrophobic space without windows and with only a black leather couch facing a large screen on a wood-panelled wall.

'Conner, Jarrold, Ava and Kaylee – they were wild walking up on Carlsbad. You know it?'

'Yeah, it's the highest peak around here.' Carlsbad was where I'd ended up with my dark angel, where black, bat-like monsters emerged from shadowy crevasses. It was white, it was frozen. It was endgame. I concentrated on the screen and tried hard not to remember.

'I won't talk any more,' the great director promised in his flat, rather dry voice, which reminded me of a physics professor or a hospital surgeon. 'I'll let it speak for itself.'

So we watched four Explorers set out from a campsite in the foothills of the Carlsbad range. They were dressed like any other group of hikers in Ts and combat pants, wearing heavy laced boots, with their thick jackets tied around their waists. Their feet crunched on grit, the long morning shadows of the tall lodge pole pines fell across the pinkish granite rocks.

'OK, so we're about to head above the snowline,' Jarrold explained to camera when the band stopped for a break. His broad, regular features filled the screen. At this point it felt like one of those wildlife programmes for TV, where the presenter is sent on an adventure into the Brazilian jungle, along an African river, whatever. They carry sharp knives to hack through undergrowth and spear their supper. They know how to create a spark by rubbing sticks.

Only Jarrold didn't exactly fit the presenter profile – instead of photogenic smiles there seemed to be resentment lurking close to the surface. 'We make a shelter out of what we can find on the mountain and spend the first night.'

Turning the camera on his three companions, Jarrold went close in on their faces. Ava, wide-eyed and on edge, looked scared to death as she put on her jacket and zipped it to the chin. Cut to Kaylee, who stuck out her tongue then put up her hand to knock the camera sideways. Her blurred fingers obscured the lens. Cut. Then Conner appeared. He stared straight into the lens and grinned.

My heart missed a beat. Conner Steben's wide eyes and smile made him look twelve years old. His fair hair was curly, he had a chip on one of his front teeth. That was a week ago. He was relaxed, confident, full of life. 'Enough already,' he eventually told Jarrold, who focused on him for maybe a full minute. 'Dude, point that thing at someone else.'

There was more hiking, fewer trees, a midday sun. Conner walked with Ava, Jarrold with Kaylee. At times Jarrold had his arm around Kaylee's shoulder and she didn't shake it off. Conner patiently waited for Ava, who often lagged behind. All four covered a lot of ground until they reached a place where the trees stopped and the dazzling white snow began.

'So last week Jarrold wasn't an Outsider?' I checked with Amos, sitting beside me on the couch.

'That came later,' he confirmed. 'Right now he's walking in peace.'

Walking on up Carlsbad into the frozen wilderness as daylight dimmed and snowflakes fell.

The next shot was of mountain peaks through flurries of snow. We heard Jarrold's low, back-of-the-throat voice-over.

'So would I rather be locked up in the Denver correctional facility or hiking up Carlsbad in a blizzard?' A long pause. 'The mountain wins,' he decided with a hollow laugh.

I glanced sideways at Amos who seemed happy so far

with what he was seeing and hearing.

'Conner caught two salmon in a creek,' Jarrold went on. 'That's supper. Ava doesn't eat fish, but she will tonight. It's only her second walk so she doesn't get it yet. Kaylee found berries. She got it from the start – we eat what we find, we share everything.'

Cut. Fade in again on a setting sun. The snow had stopped falling.

'Jarrold, quit talking into that machine. Come and eat,' Kaylee's voice said.

The Black Crows had built a shelter in a rocky gully, rising sheer on either side. They'd found a ledge where the snow didn't fall, used rough poles bound with rope, covered by a blue plastic tarp. The space was unisex and basic.

'Something's wrong,' Conner told the camera as the last daylight faded. He was hunched over a steaming cooking pot. In the background you could make out Ava wrapped in a red blanket, sitting cross-legged on the ground. There was no sign of either Kaylee or Jarrold.

'Jarrold's heart isn't at peace,' Conner confided to the camera.

'What did he do?' Ava came to sit beside Conner, her doe eyes unblinking.

Conner shrugged. 'He ignored a guiding principle,

that's all I can say.'

Cut.

Fade in. A cold grey dawn. Jarrold spoke urgently to camera. He was unshaven and looked like he hadn't slept. 'I can't do this any more.'

Amos paused the video, frowned, reran the sequence of Conner confiding that Jarrold had broken a guiding principle, then Jarrold alone and obviously in trouble.

Cut to Kaylee and Conner in the entrance to the gully, arguing with each other but too far away to be heard. Conner tried to grab Kaylee. She pushed him off and strode towards the camera. 'Ava, quit filming!' she demanded.

'Where did Jarrold go?' Ava's scared voice asked.

There was no answer. Cut to a long shot of a lone figure walking in the snow.

The figure was wrapped in a blanket. He was leaning into the wind, walking hard. The wind blew and the blanket flapped like wings. It was Jarrold, striding on and not looking back, like he wanted to walk off the edge of the world.

Red Cloud stands with his blanket around his shoulders, arms folded, watching his people die. He will die fighting. His name is in the wind, his footsteps mark the snow. Rattle of guns, stain of blood. The sun rises and sets on our land.

I stared at Jarrold growing smaller and smaller on the mountain. What made him walk away?

'Excuse me, Tania,' Antony Amos said as he left the video playing but stood up from the couch. 'I need to speak with Aurelie. Please stay here and watch the rest of the footage. When I come back, you can give me your views on how we should edit.'

Alone in the wood-lined, claustrophobic cinema room, I watched the filmed events of last week grow jerkier and even more disjointed. There were endless long-distance shots of Jarrold walking up the mountain, a couple of sequences showing Kaylee and Conner still arguing.

'I don't see why,' Kaylee said angrily, her back to the camera. 'Why does anyone have to know about me and Jarrold?'

It must have been Ava who kept the focus on Kaylee while Conner did his best to calm her. 'I'm not saying I blame either of you, especially Jarrold – he's my buddy. Besides, I know how it feels. All I'm saying is – you two should be more careful.'

'Oh yeah, mister squeaky clean.' Kaylee weighted this one short phrase with scorn – jab, jab leading to knock-out punch.

Conner stood his ground, his face mostly hidden by

the peak of his black cap.

'If you break the first principle, you don't do it while the camera's rolling,' he warned.

'Do me a freaking favour!' More scorn, more poison.

'Kaylee, you know how it works – officially no emotional attachments here at New Dawn, no romance. It's basic. And if I don't spill the beans, which I totally won't, someone else sure as hell will.'

I hit pause. 'No romantic involvement.' Huh. This was new and fascinating.

And in a way it made sense. New Dawn obviously couldn't allow their kids to form relationships here in this closed community where the focus was firmly on spiritual development. In other words, they were celibate – guiding principle number one.

Jeez, how hard was that! Totally unnatural, actually. It demanded more self-control than I would have in this situation, I guarantee that for sure.

I pressed play to see Kaylee laughing and glancing over her shoulder at Ava who was still holding the camera. ' "Attachment"?' she scoffed. 'We all know that's code for fucking.'

'I didn't say that.' Conner felt the killer punch and backed off. The camera wobbled in Ava's hand.

'But that's what you mean – that we're fucking, Jarrold

and me. Anyway, Ava won't say a word, will you, Ava? She has too much to lose.'

'So they'll pick it up on the footage,' Conner pointed out.

'Not if we edit it out before they get their hands on it.' She turned direct to camera and put her hand across the lens. 'Quit that, Ava, for God's sake!' she yelled.

Pause again. So that was it. Kaylee and Jarrold were a couple, even if Ava had doubted it. They hadn't been able to stop Aurelie getting hold of the unedited documentary and that was obviously one of the reasons Jarrold had gotten the label of Outsider.

That was a gigantic grudge for Jarrold to hold, I thought queasily. And chief suspects on his list of sneaks and betrayers would be Conner and Ava from the Black Crow band.

And where did this leave the idealistic stuff about the kids learning trust and to respect each other, about turning hearts and walking in peace in the sight of the Great Creator? Yeah, in theory. But in practice how soon did these all-too-human, hormone-driven cracks begin to show?

I pressed the play button, gearing up for more dirty linen being laundered in public.

Maybe it was the wrong button – I don't know how

it happened but no way was this the Black Crow wilderness walk.

I stared at the screen and saw coyotes stealing between trees, through undergrowth, then a close-up of a bison's huge head and wide nostrils, curved horns like deadly weapons of war. There was mist and hissing rain, a long shot of a lake.

Where am I? What is this?

Rain blurs the creatures who trample the prairie grass and creep through the undergrowth. It hisses through the grey air, turns the land to mud.

One bison locks horns with another – a mighty clash, a writhing and twisting of muscled, sweating heads and shoulders, a roar from deep in the chest. Rain lashes down.

And wolf man, more man than wolf, hides behind a rock. His jaw hangs open, a wolf pelt forms a cloak around his bare shoulders. His amber eyes stare at me. Will he snarl and leap, will he carry me to the island in the lake? No – a dark creature rises from the lake, teeth bared. It has no shape I have ever seen before – snake head, body of a mountain lion, broad black wings. Cold green eyes stare from a flattened, scaly face, a forked tongue flicks. It is huge, it fills the screen. It emerges from deep below the surface, sloughing off water, shaking itself and spreading its leathery wings.

The bison, the coyote and the wolf man flee into the forest, but not fast enough. In the mist, in the pouring rain, the monster's claws sink into a coyote's back, they tear into its flesh. The coyote is dead, its bloody body scattered. The bison too – torn to pieces by cruel claws. Only the wolf man escapes.

Death, darkness, suffering, the bones in the lake remind me.

I am cold, like snow, like ice. I am deaf. I cannot speak. My hair writhes like snakes on my head – Medusa. I sink into the mud, in the shadow of the beast's wings. I grow small, I am a child crying out as the water rises, surrounded by snakes.

I am that corpse, sinking without trace, turning to bone.

When I came round, Jean-Luc was beside me. He held my hand.

'Tania, what happened? Are you OK?'

I nodded. My skin felt cold and clammy, I was sick in my stomach. 'I guess so.'

'Did you pass out? Do you need more air?' Offering me his hand, Jean-Luc led me from the cinema room, out through the living room on to the porch.

'It's cool. This happens to me sometimes.' I told him that I had blackouts.

'That's not good. Have you seen a doctor?'

'Yeah, and I researched it on the Internet. There's a medical name for it.'

'So it's a neurological reaction?'

120

I nodded, went deep into the science to distract him from any idea that I might be certifiably insane. After all, Jean-Luc's good opinion mattered to me. 'It's kind of like epilepsy – a small seizure, where something interferes with the electric signals to my brain.'

'So not good,' he repeated, growing more sympathetic by the second.

'I get temporary memory loss. It can happen when I'm exhausted or stressed, and it's triggered by flickering lights.'

In non-medical terms, this is me connecting with the dark side, tapping into my psychic powers, but that was something I didn't tell Jean-Luc. I stuck with the medical labels and kept the super-sensory stuff to myself.

'Should you see a doctor right now?' he asked as he sat me down on the porch swing.

'No, I'm good, thanks.' I asked for water and he disappeared back inside Trail's End, returning quickly with a glass.

'I walked in and found you lying there, completely out of it,' he explained, crouching beside me. 'One of my stepfather's movies was playing onscreen – a scene from *Evil Birth*, the one based on a native American myth about the end of the world.'

'I guess that was it.' The monster rising from the lake,

121

ripping its victims to shreds. All except the wolf man, who escaped.

'Antony did a lot of research on the figure of the wolf in these legends.' Jean-Luc seemed keen to go into more detail than I needed to hear. 'In Navajo culture, for instance, witches regularly disguised themselves as wolves. If they appeared to you in a vision, they sent you crazy. Some victims even died.'

'It sure scared me,' I agreed.

'For the Avesta tribe, the wolf was the most cruel of all animals. They called him Ahriman. Antony used this figure in *Evil Birth*.'

The information flowed over my head as I realized that I was a victim too. I realized no dreamcatcher, no net of string and feathers could protect me from being sucked into these new nightmares, the reawakened visions.

'Scary, huh?' Jean-Luc put his hand on my knee. 'Did you see it in the cinema?'

I shook my head. 'I don't watch that kind of movie.' There's too much horror lurking in my imagination already.

'They make big box office,' Jean-Luc reminded me. 'In the end it's the cunning coyote who jumps down Ahriman's throat on an island in the middle of the lake. He kills him by sawing up his heart with a flint. He's the hero.'

'Happy ending,' I joked feebly. The water and the fresh air were helping me to get my head back together. 'I'm OK now, honestly.'

'Good. I came to tell you Holly is ready to leave. Can you walk down to the social area, or shall I ask her to drive your car up to Trail's End?'

'I can walk.' Standing up, I let Jean-Luc take my arm and lead me down the wooden step.

'You're a guest – Antony shouldn't have left you alone. He has terrible manners,' he apologized. 'Did he say why he had to leave?'

'No. I think it was something on the Black Crow video – a problem about some guys breaking the rules.'

'Ah!' Jean-Luc nodded. 'He found out about Jarrold and Kaylee. I was hoping to keep that information from him.'

'It's on film,' I pointed out. 'Wasn't he bound to find out?'

'No. Antony doesn't always watch the videos – he's not into details, more the broad sweep of what goes on here. Kaylee told me all about it as soon as the Black Crows got back to base and we formed a plan to edit out the sections on her and Jarrold. But Conner . . . other stuff got in the way and my stepfather jumped the gun by showing you the footage, I guess.'

'So what will he do now?' Walking down the hill with Jean-Luc, I spotted the social centre by the lake and several figures sitting on a bench by the main door, among them Holly, Aurelie and Richard Ziegler.

'He'll be angry, you bet. He'll see it as a huge betrayal on Jarrold's part.'

'So Jarrold could stay isolated for longer?'

'Yeah – all next week for sure. But don't worry, it's not your problem.' Everything about Jean-Luc was reassuring – the polite arm through mine, the considerate, slow pace, the openness of his responses – so by the time we reached the social area I'd pretty much put to one side the blacking-out episode at Trails' End.

'Hey, Tania!' Holly called when she spotted the two of us walking arm in arm. 'I'm so excited. Richard and Aurelie have been telling me more about what to expect when I join the band – what clothes to pack, plus survival items like flashlight et cetera. No cell phones, obviously.'

'Cool,' I murmured. I smiled at Jean-Luc, who unlinked his arm from mine, nodded at Ziegler and took Aurelie inside the ranch house, presumably to talk through developments in the Kaylee–Jarrold situation.

Holly's tone was hyper as always and right now it jarred with me. 'Have you thought what you're going to say to Aaron?' I asked her as we walked on towards the parking lot.

'Hey, is that snow?' Ignoring my question, Holly tilted her head back and felt the first white flakes settle and melt on her cheeks. 'Yeah, it is! Cool, Tania!'

'You *want* it to snow?' I asked, getting into my car.

'Yeah, I want it to snow,' she laughed. 'Walking in peace in the wilderness, being a Friend of the Hawk Above Our Heads band, surviving a winter storm – how cool is that!'

7

Grace's house is in the centre of town, next door to a grand, colonial-style bank building. When I called by to see her early next morning, she was out on the drive, clearing ten centimetres of snow.

'Winter began early,' she sighed, leaning her snow shovel against the wall. 'What's it like up on Becker Hill?'

'We got twelve, maybe thirteen centimetres.' It had been a silent, gentle fall – no wind, just soft, floating flakes all night long. I woke up to a new white world.

Grace invited me into the house for hot chocolate then got straight on to the reason why she'd asked me to drop by. 'You and Orlando,' she began. 'What's going on?'

'Nothing. What do you mean?' I was snappy and mean, immediately regretted it. 'Sorry.'

'Listen, I pick up the vibes. You haven't spoken his name since he left for Dallas. So what's gone wrong?'

'Honestly? I don't know.' We still hadn't spoken. It was thirty-six hours since he'd walked out of his room and we were engaged in a battle of wills. For the first twenty-four I was dead set on him making the first move to call me. I kept calm by telling myself he was busy moving house, that he'd call as soon as he found time. For the last twelve, including a night tossing and turning under my dreamcatcher, I'd felt my stomach tie up in knots. Finally, I knew with a sinking heart that I would be the one to weaken and pick up the phone.

'He flew home to be with you last Saturday,' Grace pointed out, sitting me down at her breakfast bar and giving me my chocolate. 'When your mom went to the hospital, he was there for you.'

'I know it.'

'So he loves you.'

I nodded then sighed. Love – deeper than anything I'd ever felt, out of control. I loved Orlando and longed for him. I never stopped fantasizing about him and his fantastic body, his beautiful mind, or fearing that I would lose him. I freely admit it. But sometimes the love game, the battle was just too confusing.

'So?' Grace broke through my sighs.

'He wants me to go to Dallas.'

'And?' When she wants to make her point, which isn't

127

often, she refuses to back off. Which is why I was taking her seriously this Friday morning.

'Dallas.' I spread my hands, palms upwards. 'What is there for me in Dallas?'

'Orlando.' Unblinking, Grace pointed out the obvious.

'So I give up everything and go there to be with him?' I let go of my own life, my ambitions? 'What are we saying here, that we live back in the nineteenth century?' Wear a corset and a bonnet, look pretty, stand by your man.

'I guess not. And I'm not saying that's what I would do. Not necessarily. But did he ask you to go?'

'Yeah, point blank. I said I'd think about it, then I told him no and he stormed out.' I stared miserably at the creamy froth on top of my chocolate. 'I do love the guy, Grace.'

'I know it. But when did you last tell him?'

'Not since Wednesday.'

'So call him. Talk. Don't let this grow into some huge thing between you.'

'I will,' I promised. 'I'll call him this afternoon, after I've visited Mom.'

Satisfied, Grace sat opposite me, her face still glowing from the snow-clearing exercise on her driveway. 'Poor Tania – your life is going great then suddenly everything gets so tough to deal with all over again.'

So I fell further into confessional mode and told her about Mom's dyspraxia and her programme of physical therapy, and how Dad spent a lot of time in the garden, feeding Zenaida and keeping his thoughts to himself.

'I spoke to Holly.' Grace steered me away from problems I couldn't solve. 'Suddenly she's a Pioneer!'

I smiled. 'They call them Explorers, remember. And Holly's a Friend. Upper-case "F". Her bag is packed. She's ready to leave.'

'Go, girl!' Grace said with a shudder. 'All that frustrated surge power is going to be put into practice.'

'Where are you at with the volunteering?' I asked. 'Will you do it?'

'I don't know any more. At first I liked the idea, to build up my résumé for college.'

'But now?'

'Now I'm not sure. I'd like to know more about their reintegration programme. I mean, how is it a good thing to draw in everyday, regular kids from Bitterroot? Not everyone volunteers with a good motive – right?'

'You mean, we know some people who might do it just to snoop and dig dirt?' I totally got what she was saying.

'Yeah. And some who might get a buzz out of

associating with kids from the wrong side of the tracks – drop outs, drug addicts and the rest.'

'I can think of a few,' I agreed. 'Besides, even I'm shallow enough to think that some of those New Dawn guys are totally hot and that's as good a reason as any to volunteer.'

'Tania, you're not serious!' Grace pretended to be shocked. Then she laughed. 'OK, they're hot,' she agreed. 'So will you?'

'What?'

'Do it – volunteer?'

Getting up from the counter, I wandered to the window to see that the sun had warmed up and the snow was starting to melt. Drops of water dripped from the gutter on to the drive. 'Orlando doesn't want me to.'

'But you haven't decided?' Grace worked on intuition, which hardly ever let her down.

'Now I'm here in Bitterroot for longer than I thought,' I admitted. 'I have a couple of extra weeks just hanging around, visiting the hospital. And I don't know what it is, but there's something that makes me want to find out more about New Dawn – and not just the hot guys!' I added quickly.

'I didn't figure it was,' she said quietly. 'Seriously though, Tania – I have a lot of questions about the place.'

'Me too.' And though I didn't mean to, I shared with Grace some of the doubts floating in my head. 'For a start, even Antony Amos's stepson questions the methods. I found out that the kids who live there are not allowed to form any close relationships. And did you know they isolate you if you break the rules? They stick a label on you, call you an Outsider. You can't talk or interact until they're ready to let you back in.'

'Plus I heard they cut off all contact with your family.'

'This thing about not building relationships – that's so tough.'

'And they send you out without a cell phone or a two-way radio, right?' Grace helped me build up the case against New Dawn. 'So why are we even thinking about getting involved?'

'Because it works?' I suggested. 'It really does help people find out who they are. Or, maybe it does – who knows?'

'And we do want to find out. But I think you – *we* should look at all the angles.'

There it was – the tiny suggestion that I was the one with a particular problem. Grace had quickly corrected herself, glossed over my psychic weirdness, tried to move on. 'Hey,' I protested wryly. 'I thought you were my friend.'

'I am. And I'm worried.'

'Me too,' I admitted, turning towards her, spilling out the details about yesterday's blackout experience in Amos's cinema room, sparing her the vision of the wolf man and the snake-headed, winged monster rising from the lake. Instead, I kept it general. 'Since Conner Steben drowned, I've developed this water fixation – nightmares about drowning, about bodies trapped in West Point, the town they flooded to make the lake.'

Grace gathered her long fair hair and pinned it to the nape of her neck in a rough twist. 'You and your nightmares,' she breathed. 'Last time it was fire.'

'You know how powerful water is? Tsunamis, tidal waves that wreck bridges and roads, smash houses to a pulp. A wall of water is unstoppable. You can't fight water, you can't run – it just gets you.' Ask the spirits drifting in the currents of Turner Lake. Ask Conner Steben.

Now that we were being totally honest, Grace didn't duck the issue. 'And is it the same for you as before. Is there a dark angel?'

In our minds we went back together to the Heavenly Bodies fancy dress party – Grace in her Botticelli angel dress, me as a bird of paradise. We saw ourselves at the glitzy gathering, mesmerized by the strutting figure onstage – rock star Zoran Brancusi with his glittering black wings.

'Yeah, he's back,' I shuddered.

'And how about the good angel? Is she around to help?'

'Not so far.'

'Is it Antony Amos? Is he the one?' Grace asked.

A skull speaks from the depths. 'Death, darkness, suffering.'

'Who is my enemy?' I ask. 'Where is he?'

There is no answer.

'Help me.'

There is silence.

'No, it's not Amos,' I said quietly. Still it didn't feel right, so I said it louder. 'No.'

'Then who?'

'Grace, I have no idea. And that's what terrifies me this time around. The first time I knew Zoran was my guy, right from the start. When I understood what was happening with the warring spirits, good versus evil and all that, it was mind-blowingly obvious that he was my dark angel. Now, all I'm really sure of is that he will be back. In fact, he never really left.'

'What is he doing? What does he want?' She was so scared that she was gripping my arm harder than she realized. She relived her time on Black Rock – the mind-control games, her falling under Ezra's spell, being led to the yawning gates of Hell.

'He's twisted and bitter and he wants revenge,' I explained. I didn't need any good angel to explain his desire to get back at me, the one person who had defied and defeated him. 'He won't rest until he gets it.'

'So you're running away?' Grace asked. 'When you're in Europe, you're escaping?'

My lips trembled. Running, always running. Even in London, in Rome, in Paris, I never stopped.

A dark monster rises from the lake, mixture of serpent and lion with snake fangs and glittering claws. The wolf man lurks on the shore. The sky is black. The water rises.

Angel of death, who are you? Are you travelling through time, from star to glittering star? What nightmare do you have in store?

'There's nowhere to hide,' I whispered. 'When he wants me, he'll come for me.'

'Tania, don't say that!'

'It's true.' I was never more certain. 'He'll be there and I won't even recognize him. He'll be a new shape – nothing like he was before. That's how he is – he'll catch me off guard.'

'Tell someone, Tania. Find help.'

I stared at Grace. 'I'm telling you,' I whispered.

Because I knew she'd been there herself with Ezra, and because sharing might help me bear the burden. Only, it sounded so crazy that even Grace might not understand.

'What can I do?' she asked, taking both my hands.

'Believe what I say,' I told her. 'My dark angel is close, getting closer. He'll shape-shift and deceive me, he'll travel through time, make fire and flood, create monsters to drive me crazy, there's no limit to what he can do.'

'Then keep safe,' Grace begged. 'Go to Dallas. Be with Orlando.'

I let out a long, despairing breath. 'Then what?'

She knew what I meant. There was no point running – the dark angel would follow me wherever I went. 'So?' she whispered.

'So I have to be ready,' I told her, grasping at the only answer there was. 'I have to be strong. In the end, there's no escape. I have to stand and fight.'

Grab my devil by the throat.

I went from Grace's house to the hospital and was back home again when Orlando called on my cell phone.

He called *me*!

'Hey.'

'Hey.' I was trembling so hard I had to sit on the bench under the aspens and take deep breaths before I could

135

say any more. The sun was shining, melting the snow.

'How are you doing?'

'Good. I went to see Mom.'

'How is she?'

'Good. The therapist started her on a programme to get back the use of her left hand. They scanned her brain again to make sure all the blood clots dispersed.'

She'd been quieter than normal, said she was determined to follow the recovery programme and be the ideal patient.

'It's tough for her, lying in bed all day,' I told Orlando.

She'd quizzed me – was I taking care of Dad, was I eating right, when was I going back to Europe? Was I following my star?

Yes, I'd said to the first question. Yes/ don't know/ hope so to questions two, three and four. I told her Dad was now the world expert on rock pigeons and Eurasian collared doves. He could even tell the difference between the common ground dove and the band-tailed pigeon.

This had made her laugh and say, 'I love that man!' But why only 'hope so' on following my star?

I'd told her about the Dallas versus Europe dilemma. We'd talked it through.

'Dad says Orlando wants me there for the right reason, because he loves me.'

'So love is a prison?' Mom had turned down the corners of her mouth. ' "Love me. Stay in your cage." '

'It sounds bad when you say it like that, doesn't it? I'm sure that's not the way Orlando sees it. More like, "I miss you, I need you, I want you." '

Mom had sat up in her hospital bed, had stroked my cheek with her good right hand. 'You can love someone without being tied,' she'd insisted. 'Love doesn't depend on being there twenty-four/seven.'

'Don't worry, she'll be back to normal before you know it,' Orlando told me now, caring and sympathetic as if we'd never had a fight and he hadn't stormed out. 'And listen, Tania – what you decided about not coming to Dallas—'

'I don't want talk about it.' I cut him off. Please don't give me a hard time, not right now.

'I'm sorry I walked out on you the other day. I was out of line.'

I pictured him in his new room, still surrounded by boxes, not bothering to unpack. 'No, I didn't tell you in a good way. It was my fault.'

'I understand why it was hard for you, especially with your mom being ill. I shouldn't have pressured you. I know you have to get Europe out of your system.'

'I love you,' I said over him. My cage door was open,

I was taking flight. 'Orlando, I love you so much it hurts.'

Which is when Holly walked in on me. She came through the gate that divides her back garden from mine.

'I need batteries,' she said, wielding her flashlight, trying to ignore the ring tone on her cell phone. 'No time to go down to the store. Do you have any the right size?'

'Answer your phone,' I told her. It gave me time to finish my conversation with Orlando.

'You know Ryan, my new roommate?' he asked.

'I know who he is, but I don't *know* him,' I pointed out.

'His family lives in Boulder.'

'And?' Boulder was a hundred miles north of Bitterroot. Holly was talking in the background. Her conversation seemed important.

Orlando took a while to get to the point. 'He plans to visit there soon for his sister's twenty-first birthday. He'll drive from Texas. So I was thinking maybe I'll take a ride, drive up with him.'

'When? I gasped.

'Actually, a week from now,' he told me. 'Does that sound good?'

I closed my eyes, felt my whole body relax into a smile. 'That sounds perfect!'

'Friday,' he confirmed. 'I can't wait to see you, Tania,

but I'll call you every day as well. I'll Skype you at midday tomorrow, OK?'

'Perfect,' I said again. The call ended on a total high.

'That was Aurelie Laurent,' Holly told me as she too came off the phone. Something had put her off her energetic stride, she was looking puzzled.

'Weird.'

'What's weird?'

'This Conner Steben thing,' Holly explained. 'Aurelie says they have to write a detailed report.'

'For the cops?' This didn't surprise me. You expect an autopsy, an investigation when a seventeen-year-old kid drowns during a triathlon.

'Yeah, and for the Steben family.'

For the parents with their faces blasted by grief, for the angry, devastated sister. 'So what does Aurelie's report have to do with you?' I wanted to know.

'She saw I was close to where it happened so she wants me to write a witness statement.'

Again, no surprises, though I agreed it was a little weird that Aurelie had got to Holly before the cops. 'OK,' I said steadily, suspecting that there was more.

'Aurelie is asking me to make it clear that Conner's death was a pure accident,' Holly told me with a frown.

'Why? What exactly did she say?'

'Word for word? "Write down what you saw, Holly. Say no one was anywhere near Conner when he drowned. He just went under for no reason that you could see."'

'But—'

'I know, so don't say it,' she snapped back before I could form a sentence about Jarrold and the killer kick. She rushed on regardless. 'Look, it's cool. I'll do it. I'll make a statement.'

'So Jarrold wasn't involved?'

Holly shook her head. 'No, I must have totally made that up. I guess I was too shocked to think straight.'

'You're sure about this?'

'You know me – always shooting off my big mouth!' She brushed off my question then she held up the yellow flashlight. 'Batteries, Tania! Do you have any or not?'

Mom's right. When love works, it's not a trap – it's freedom. I went to bed happy under my dreamcatcher, thinking about Orlando, feeling myself float into a vision of our future together.

He'll be a costume designer for major Broadway productions, the best in the business. I'll be involved in low-budget indie cinema, travelling the world to search for locations. In my head, there was a movie I already wanted to make about a girl who has visions and has to convince the world that she's not crazy, just connected to a spiritual dimension that others can't tune into. She has something important to communicate – a message from the world of spirits, a piece of information that will help save the world, if only the world will listen.

You can't fail to spot the autobiographical element in the initial phase.

It'll be a big technical challenge – her 3D visions will be of falling, flying, spinning through time. There will be monsters, perhaps a dark angel – but remember, I can't identify him yet, I don't know who he is. There's a mystery at the heart of my storyboard.

I was up at dawn, before Dad was awake, ready to drive Holly down to New Dawn.

'Don't be late,' she'd warned. 'The Hawk Above Our Heads band leaves the community parking lot at seven thirty.'

'You're telling me don't be late!' I'd mocked. 'Why didn't you ask Aaron to drive you there?'

Holly had made a scornful popping sound with her lips.

'You two had another fight?' I'd guessed.

'Aaron's dad says no way should we be walking in the mountains. There's a severe weather warning and the

141

National Park are telling people to stay off Melrose and Carlsbad – all the high peaks.'

'Aaron tried to stop you volunteering?' After what Orlando had told me, I can't say I was surprised, though I hadn't spoken to Aaron myself.

Holly had nodded. 'Sometimes he doesn't know when to back off.'

Here we were again – the old question. How much do you compromise your freedom to please the guy you love? Because Holly did love Aaron, I was sure. She'd fight like a tigress for him if he was in danger, but she still held on to her right to do her own thing.

They say opposites attract. Well, Holly and Aaron fit that model like no other couple I know. Her – black and white, no compromise. Him – take a back seat, don't speak two words where one will do. But always there for each other, no question.

Anyway, that was how come it was me waiting for Holly in the garden early next morning, and not Aaron. She was the one who was late, of course.

I looked around for Zenaida, hoping for a quiet chat. 'The snow's melted,' I murmured as I strolled down to the aspens. 'But you'd better stock up on seeds while you can. There's more bad weather coming.'

Our mourning dove coo-wooed me from a high

branch. She sat there with her chest feathers puffed out to keep her warm. There was blue sky above her, cold wet earth below.

'Stick around,' I told her. 'Dad will see you through the winter.'

She spread her whistling wings and flew to a branch nearer to where I stood. Now I could make out the circle of blue around her eyes, the white wing patches, the pinkish chest.

'What are you trying to tell me?' I asked.

A flock of doves rises from the trees. They are white, pink, grey. Sunlight shines through their strong, beating wings as they soar into the blue sky.

'You are trying to tell me something, aren't you?'

The birds fly high. They are airborne, beautiful in the sunlight. My lone grey dove soars over my head.

'Speak to me,' I murmured.

'I am here,' a tender voice whispers.

A breeze rustles through the fallen leaves. The voice of the grey dove is familiar.

'Don't be afraid,' she tells me. She is bathed in silver light.

The waiting is over and I'm not afraid. The angel of light who was Maia has risen and shape-shifted into a dove. She's the one who will protect me and tell me all I need to know. I reach out my hand and rise from the dark ground. 'I was

143

waiting for you,' I tell my mourning dove.

'I have always been here,' she replies.

'I know. It took me a while.'

Here she is, my good angel, my spirit of light. Lone angel without her mate, who died in the fire on Becker Hill on the very day I was born. Welcome back! My body tingles. It's as if my flesh melts to leave me weightless, as free to fly as my dove, my Zenaida.

'You know you are in great danger,' she tells me softly. 'The fallen angels, the evil spirits are gathering.'

I nod, I am airborne beside her, wrapped in her glowing light.

'Your dark angel leads them out of the realms of darkness. They have once more pierced the barrier we set up to keep them out. They are everywhere.'

I see devils rising from grey water, constantly changing shape and leaping skywards. They are two-headed snakes and writhing, slimy monsters with deformed limbs, mouth agape. Angels of light arm themselves with flashing swords. They stand fast, but more devils rise – a terrible army that soon outnumbers the shining archangels.

They fight. Sparks fly and fade in dark outer space – falling stars, exploding meteors. The water below the clashing armies turns crimson, the colour of blood.

Still the wolf man stands to one side, watching everything.

'So you must listen to me, Tania,' Zenaida continues. 'It is important. Arm yourself against the dark angel's revenge, against his twisted, wicked heart. Remember he is cunning. He will gather recruits, he will trick and deceive you, use your innocence against you.'

'It's OK. I know not to trust anyone,' I tell her.

'Anyone!' she repeats.

The doves above our heads wheel and fly off in every direction. Only Zenaida remains.

'Gather your strength,' she tells me. 'Suspect everyone.'

She flaps her wings, rises higher, trailing her light. I feel myself sink to the ground.

'Remember, you are not alone.'

These are her last words. She rises into the pure blue sky. She flies away. It's OK, I feel happy. I know that I am blessed.

'Thank you,' I whispered.

I felt happy that my good angel had been transformed and reincarnated. She flew off with a light whistle of wings as the garden gate opened and Holly walked through.

She was wearing grey combat pants and a black T-shirt, boots and a bright-orange jacket. 'Here,' she told me. 'I wrote my statement on Conner Steben. Would you give it to Aurelie when you next see her?'

'Sure,' I told her, shoving the white envelope in my pocket.

* * *

The Hawk Above Our Heads band were ready and waiting for Holly when we reached the parking lot. Richard Ziegler was with them, giving last-minute instructions.

'There's a frozen lake on the north side of Carlsbad, way above the tree line.' Ziegler, still uber-cool in his trademark cowboy hat, had a map spread out on the hood of his Jeep. He pointed to the band's destination. 'You should reach this lake on day three.'

In the background Turner Lake was the colour of lead, its surface dead still.

'Death, darkness, suffering,' my good angel reminds me. For whom? Does she mean Conner? Does she mean Holly? Or me?

I turned my back on the lake, tried to pay attention to the nervous band of Explorers.

The four kids in Holly's team tried hard to cover their anxiety about setting off up Carlsbad. The two guys, Channing and Regan, acted tough without convincing anyone. Regan, remember, was short, skinny and fair-haired – a nerdy type who looked like he'd arrived at New Dawn by mistake. Channing you already know about.

'Holly, Tania – meet Blake,' Ziegler said.

Now, Blake – she was the real deal. Take Kaylee

and multiply her by a factor of five. Tougher than either of the guys, she oozed aggression from the top of her no-frills, magenta-dyed haircut to the toes of her heavy laced boots. When Ziegler said her name, she shot me a hostile look that said, 'Don't even think about saying hi.'

'And finally, Marta.' The New Dawn coach folded up his map as he introduced me to the last member of the Hawk Above Our Heads band.

Marta was the tallest in the group by far – six three maybe – with a long neck and high cheekbones, emphasized by the way she pulled back her long dark hair into a high, tight ponytail.

OK, if you asked me what each of the four had done to be sent to the community, this is what I would guess: geeky Regan – computer hacking, Channing – maybe auto theft, Blake – major graffiti damage to public property, Marta – stealing prescription drugs from a pharmacy. Who knows, I might even be right. And I'll never find out – there's an unspoken code here that you don't get to ask.

So these were the kids who Holly was wilderness-walking with. I shot her a questioning glance – you're sure about this?

She blanked me and went into hyper-Holly, super-surge overdrive. 'So what are we waiting for?' she asked, shouldering her rucksack ready for action. 'Come on, let's do this.'

'Before you leave, you need a blessing,' Ziegler told her. 'Antony's on his way.'

Sure enough, Amos soon joined us in the parking lot, striding down from Trail's End along with Aurelie and Jean-Luc. All three were wearing padded jackets and jeans, and Amos was wearing the serious shaman expression that linked him in my mind to Red Cloud and the rest.

I had to admit I was disappointed that it was Aurelie, not Jean-Luc, who singled me out and paid me some attention. 'Hey, Tania. It's good of you to drive Holly. Now you have a chance to see the leaving ceremony. We do it each time a band sets out on a wild walk.'

'Give me my statement!' Holly hissed as Amos gathered the Explorers in a circle around him. 'Aurelie's here, so I can hand it to her myself.'

Relieved of the task, I handed over the envelope and let Holly explain what it was she was delivering to Aurelie in person. Aurelie thanked her. 'This will help Conner's family. In this type of tragedy they need to hear what happened from someone who was actually there.'

Then there was no time for any more Conner talk

because Antony Amos launched into his leaving ceremony.

'I'll tell you a story,' he said to Blake, Marta, Channing, Regan and Holly, as if they were small kids gathered at his knee. 'It's called "The Swan". The boy, E-tsa-wis-no was growing into manhood. One day his father walked him to the edge of the tipi settlement and told him, "Soon you will be a man. You must walk into the mountains. The Great Spirit will take the shape of a bird or beast. He will speak to you of the moon and sun and stars."'

Outside the circle with Jean-Luc and Aurelie, I watched and listened. Amos's voice seemed more mellow than before, his manner warmer as he got deeper into the ancient story.

'"Listen to the Great Spirit, follow your spirit ally, your Weyekin," the boy's father said. So E-tsa-wis-no walked into the mountains and sat beside a frozen lake. He waited for two days and then the Great Spirit appeared in the moonlight as a white swan. The swan said to him, "I am your Weyekin. I will lead you. Watch and listen, learn all there is to know about the swan and you too shall fly.

'So E-tsa-wis-no studied the beautiful bird. He stayed by the lake for five times the cycle of a man's life and his tribe did not see him. And after that time he was seen

149

again, flying in a formation of swans. He had feathered wings but the body of a man. And every year after this he was seen flying south for the winter and north in the spring.'

Amos finished the story then laid a hand on the shoulder of each of the five kids. 'Trust one another, use what Mother Nature offers you,' he reminded them. 'Turn your hearts to one another, begin anew.'

I was still puzzling over the message of the Native American tale, liking the idea of walking into the mountains to find a spirit ally, a Weyekin – someone similar to my own good angel – when Blake broke away from the group and started walking. She left the parking lot without looking back, just expecting the others to follow.

Marta and Holly were the next to leave.

'Go carefully,' I called after my buddy. 'Come back safe.'

She walked away without acknowledging me, fixing her gaze on distant Carlsbad, taking big strides to catch up with Blake.

The boys left last and at a slower, almost lazy pace. They let the girls forge ahead along the lakeside track.

'Shouldn't they stay together as a band?' I asked, already worried.

'Don't worry,' Aurelie told me with a smile. 'Channing

150

and Regan will soon catch up. By the end of today they'll have bonded.'

You hope, I thought. In spite of Aurelie's confidence, in spite of Amos's deeply held spiritual beliefs and the sincere blessing he'd given them, I had my doubts. After all, look at the no-relationship crap that happened last week with the Black Crow band. Examine what went on beneath the preachy surface.

'Come back safe,' I said again.

I meant all of them, not just Holly. And all five looked so small, the lake and mountains so huge as they walked into the wilderness.

8

'My favourite place in all of Paris is the Rodin Museum on the rue de Varenne.' Jean-Luc didn't let me slip away once the Hawk Above Our Heads band had finally disappeared. Obviously wanting to chat about the city he loved, he took me to the cabin he shared with his sister and offered me a cold drink. Their home was in a great position – next to the social centre overlooking the lake. 'You've been there?' he asked.

I nodded. 'Yes, it was awesome.'

'My father's apartment is close by, on the same street. You can look down from his balcony and see the statues in the garden.' He told me that his favourite piece wasn't the mega-famous 'Kiss' or 'The Thinker' but 'The Gates of Hell'. 'Inspired by Dante's *Divine Comedy*,' Jean-Luc explained. 'In bronze bas relief. Magnificent.'

Then we went on to discuss the collection of

contemporary art in the Pompidou Centre, and the groundbreaking seventies architecture, and the way tourists swarmed everywhere and there were queues for everything and how the small street cafes were vanishing under an onslaught by McDonald's and Starbucks.

Jean-Luc laughed at himself. 'I'm an elitist, I admit. Antony always tells me I'm not a team player.' He smiled in a cool, unconcerned way. 'So when do you return to Paris?'

'I don't know when I leave – I haven't decided yet,' I told him, swirling the ice cubes in the bottom of my glass of orange juice. 'My mom is still in hospital. I guess I'll wait until she gets out.'

'Then we can hope to see you again here at New Dawn,' he said happily. 'Good. I like talking about my favourite city with you.'

'Me too.' I smiled at Aurelie, who had just walked in, and I was struck by how weird it must be to have a twin – not exactly identical, but close enough for it to draw comment from strangers, and both so good-looking and stylish, with their dark eyes and full mouths, so cool.

She kissed me on both cheeks, French style, then sat down beside me. 'So did you persuade Tania to volunteer?' she asked Jean-Luc, laughing as she spoke.

He blushed. 'Aurelie, please. We were talking about Paris.'

'OK, so forget Paris and let me cut to the chase.' Aurelie wasn't the least bit embarrassed. 'Tell us you'll give the community a couple of days of your time,' she implored, still with the smile playing around her mouth. 'It doesn't have to be a full week. You can join the River Stone band as a Friend for a short time, help shoot the documentary, give advice. You can come out of the wilderness whenever you choose.'

'How does that work?'

'Easy. You give us a time and location. Either Richard or Jean-Luc will drive out to pick you up. The Explorers can continue without you.'

'So I'll think about it,' I said.

'It'll change your life.' Aurelie grew suddenly serious and gave me full eye contact. 'It's a truly awesome spiritual experience – something you can't explain. You just have to do it.'

'But no pressure,' Jean-Luc broke in. 'Seriously, Aurelie – Tania has to think of her family first. Her mom is ill in hospital: her dad needs her.'

Plus, my boyfriend and I will have a fight if I volunteer here, I thought. Just like Holly and Aaron. It was time I left. I needed to be back home by midday to talk with Orlando on Skype.

'It's OK, you don't have to come with me,' I told Jean-Luc who had got up to hold open the door. 'I can find my own way.'

So I shrugged off the invitation to join the River Stone band and walked alone along the lake shore towards the parking lot, recalling how much I loved the water since I first learned to swim, lost in a world of my own as I enjoyed the sound of small waves lapping over smooth stones, picking out the pinkest of the pink granite pebbles, marvelling at the richness of the colour amongst the pale brown and grey.

I was on the part of the beach where the triathlon had started – a wide stretch backed by junipers and lodge pole pines that partly hid the trail leading up to the row of cabins where the Explorer kids lived. I was in the moment, back to the old feeling I had about the place when Orlando and I swam together, simply loving it.

Then Jarrold walked out from under the trees and suddenly everything got complicated.

He came towards me, hands in pockets, not looking at me but walking across my path so that I had to stop. He was fifteen centimetres taller than me and impossible to step around.

'Hey,' I said.

155

He stared at me. A breeze from the lake blew a lock of fair hair across his forehead. 'What was in the envelope?' he asked.

I opened my eyes wide. 'What envelope?'

'The one Holly snatched from you and handed over to Aurelie.' Jarrold didn't blink. And he wasn't about to move out of my way.

'Oh that. How did—'

'I was back there, watching.' Jerking his head towards the trees, he made it clear he'd been spying on Holly and me and had most likely been hanging around during the leaving ceremony until he could finally get me on my own.

'It was Holly's witness statement about Conner Steben,' I told him straight, trying to carry on meeting his gaze. I didn't exactly stick out my chin in defiance, but that was pretty much how it felt. 'Are you even supposed to be talking to me?' I challenged. 'Isn't it against the rules?'

'Fuck the rules,' he said then fell silent, which was worse. I mean, some silences are way more intimidating than any words you care to come up with.

I tried to sidestep and walk on towards my car. He let me but then walked with me, stepping in front of me again when we reached the gate. Honestly, it was like a flyweight coming up against a champion heavyweight in a pre-fight press conference, him freaking me out with his muscles and the intensity behind the grey eyes.

'What was in the statement?'

'Nothing, I don't know.'

'Yeah, you do.'

'Ask Aurelie.'

'They won't let me speak.'

'Oh yeah, I forgot.' And so did he, it seemed. Staring up at him, crumbling under his gaze, I felt my knees go weak. 'I have to leave,' I said.

'What did your buddy say?' he muttered. 'Did she mention me?'

I shook my head and let slip a piece of information that I should probably have kept to myself. 'Aurelie told her not to.'

Jarrold nodded then grunted. 'Anyway, it wasn't me. I didn't touch the guy.'

Whoa! Did I ask to have this conversation? Did I look like I wanted it? 'I have to go!' I repeated breathlessly.

'Some people think I did.'

So does Holly, deep down, if you want the truth, until something happened or she was collared by Ziegler and became a convert.

'You want to know why?'

I shook my head.

157

'Conner and I had a fight. It was stupid. But it was on the video so they got to know about it.'

'When you were out on the mountain?' Suddenly I was one step ahead. Jarrold couldn't know that I'd seen the footage of the Black Crow walk, of him wrapped in a blanket – a small, dark figure striding through the blizzard. And I'd also seen the confrontation between Kaylee and Conner over the no-relationships deal. I played dumb, so I could hear it from Jarrold himself. 'So what did you two fight over?'

His mouth twitched and he pushed back the stray strand of hair. 'What do guys normally fight about?'

'Girls?'

He nodded. 'I know it's different here, or they say it is. There's a no-relationship rule, a guiding principle.'

'But?'

'What do you think? It happens anyway.'

'So which girl?' I prompted.

'No comment,' he muttered.

I liked that – the fact that though Jarrold came across as Tarzan swinging through the jungle, he had enough sense of honour to protect Kaylee. 'Conner found out?' I asked. 'Your secret wasn't safe?'

'We fought over it. I won. Game over.'

I pictured the caveman contest on the snowy mountain

slopes and repressed a shudder. 'You won and made Conner promise not to tell? But you both forgot it would come out on the video footage.'

Jarrold shrugged. 'So anyway, out on the lake – I didn't touch the guy.'

I frowned, backtracked to where I wanted to be. 'And maybe Conner did tell someone after all. That's why Ziegler and the others made you an Outsider.'

'I didn't touch him!' he repeated angrily, moving in to threaten me. 'I dove down, tried to save him, remember.'

Did I believe him? I don't know, but I was definitely thrown off balance. For one, I was shocked by the change in Jarrold's attitude towards New Dawn. When I first stumbled across him at the end of the cabin trail, he'd spouted all the right phrases at me. Now he was the arch rebel, saying fuck the rules. I winced and grew more cautious. 'It's OK, Holly actually said in her statement that she saw you try to rescue Conner.'

'That I didn't lay a finger on him?'

I nodded. 'You're off the hook, Jarrold, if that's what you want to hear.' He was officially cleared by Holly's witness statement, no longer a suspect. 'Now, can you please stand aside? I have to leave.'

Slowly he gave way and I stepped through the gate. I picked up speed, headed for my car, relieved that he was

159

letting me go, even though he was following close in my footsteps.

Before I turned my key in the ignition, he leaned into the car and said one more thing. 'So if you join the River Stone walk next week, I'll tell you the whole me and Kaylee back-story.'

I stared back at him, started the engine, headed for the exit. Did I hear that right? Had Jarrold actually invited me to join his band?

Why would he do that? What kind of sense did it make? I panicked and didn't look over my shoulder. With a squeal of tyres over rough grit, I drove away.

My friends tell me that I'm like Holly in that I swing like crazy from one point of view to its polar opposite, and I guess it's true – that I have no fixed purpose, no star to follow. Sorry, Mom.

'First we agree between us – we won't volunteer. Now you say yes you will.' This was Grace speaking to me on the hands-free phone as I drove home to Becker Hill.

'Hey no – that's not what I said.'

'I'm reading between the lines and that's how it sounded.'

'No, I only said Jean-Luc and Aurelie tried to *persuade* me to volunteer.' I was stuck in traffic in the centre of town, anxious to be home and sitting at my computer, ready for Orlando to Skype. 'And I happened to think the leaving ceremony they gave for Holly's band was impressive. It was a native American story about searching for your spirit ally, your Weyekin.'

Grace ignored the spirit ally reference. 'So I'm right – you're getting sucked in.'

I turned left off Main Street on to Queen Street East. 'Hand on heart, tell me you don't find the New Dawn stuff interesting,' I challenged her.

'Do I find it interesting? Yeah. Will I volunteer? No.'

'Why not? And before you say anything, you can forget about lining up Antony Amos alongside Zoran Brancusi. I already went through that with Orlando, plus a hundred times in my own mind and there's no comparison, believe me.'

'More specifically?'

I reminded her that Amos didn't have Zoran's strutting, glittering eagle-eyed arrogance and charisma. 'We're agreed – you don't look at this serious, new-age type of guy and feel mesmerized or brainwashed. No way does he threaten you.'

'Trust no one,' a soft voice in my head warns me.

'Except that he's made some of the goriest horror movies in the history of cinema,' Grace reminded me. 'So you have to agree there's something dark going on.'

'Maybe not. Maybe it just means he's a super-talented director with a direct line into the teen zeitgeist. You know how most kids love a gore-fest. Anyway, New Dawn isn't Black Eagle Lodge and we're definitely into a different ball game,' I insisted as I came off Queen Street on to Becker Hill.

'*Trust no one.*'

I had five minutes to make it to my computer before midday. 'Got to go, Grace. Speak later.'

'Where have you been? Who have you seen? Did you miss me?'

Orlando was thirty minutes late. I'd died a thousand deaths in my imagination. He didn't want to speak after all. Something more important had come up – a new assignment, a new girl. But here he was onscreen, smiling at me, piling up the questions.

'I took Holly down to New Dawn.'

'Uh-oh, crazy girl!'

'Who, me?'

'No, Holly. Where is she now?'

'As we speak she's halfway up Black Rock, heading towards Carlsbad.' It wasn't Holly I wanted to talk about. It was us. 'So how's your new room?' I asked.

'Take a look.' Unhooking the camera, Orlando carried it across to the window then back towards the desk. 'You want to see the kitchen?'

'No. Let me see your bed.'

'It's a mess,' he laughed.

'So what's new?' I watched the tilting, jerky images and made out a single bed piled high with sports bags, unmatching socks, underwear, books and unpacked boxes. I had a sharp pang of wanting to be there with him, clearing a space, sliding between the sheets, getting naked. 'When can I visit?'

'Tonight?' he invited, reattaching the camera to the computer. He came in close. 'I'll fix up the bed specially,' he grinned. Then he turned to someone who had just come into the room. 'Hey, Ryan, say hi to Tania.'

A guy with short dark hair and cute, sticky-out ears came into view. He had one of those permanently smiley faces with white, even teeth that showed his parents had chosen orthodontic work over plastic surgery to pin back the ears when he was a kid. 'Hey, Tania,' he said to the camera. 'I want to know – can your boyfriend cook?'

Unexpected question but I didn't hesitate over my answer. 'No way.'

'Not even bacon?'

'Unless you like it burned.'

'Oh Jeez.' Ryan faked massive disappointment. 'You hear that, Natalie? Orlando can't cook us breakfast.'

Another figure appeared on the screen – a girl with piled-high, tousled fair hair wearing tiny pale-blue pyjamas. She didn't have much flesh on her slender frame but what she had was pretty much on show. Ouch!

'Say hi to Natalie,' Orlando invited.

'Hey.' I made the expected noise but my heart was flip-flopping all over the place. A hot girl in the apartment! How come no one mentioned a girl?

'OK, you two, give a guy some privacy,' Orlando told Ryan and cute, pretty, size four Natalie. He wrestled them out of view and came back centre screen.

'Skyping's cool,' he sighed, 'but it makes me wish you could time-travel and be right here with me.'

I studied his face – that killer combination of wide grey eyes and the sweep of dark hair. 'Are you still planning to drive home with Ryan?'

'For sure,' he murmured. 'We moved it forward to Thursday. Hey, why aren't you smiling?'

'How about Natalie?'

'How about her?'

'Will she come too?'

'Sure. It means we'll split the cost of the gas three ways instead of two. And listen, Tania, it's twenty-four hours sooner than we thought. How cool is that?'

'Cool,' I said with an attempt at a smile. Oh Jeez, a good-looking girl in the apartment, in the car for the journey north. Sure, she was Ryan's long-term girlfriend and Orlando loved me, obviously. But put temptation in a guy's way, throw in a big dose of flirtiness, metres of bare flesh, a beehive of blonde, tousled hair . . .

Relax, breathe, take your time.

It was straight after the Skype conversation and I was in the garden with Dad, who was feeding Zenaida.

'Snow again on Carlsbad,' he pointed out. 'Dark clouds over Black Rock, already minus three degrees in town. Blizzard coming.' He'd learned all this from the guy who ran the gas station outside Bitterroot, on his way back from the hospital.

To prove his point there was a strong, icy wind blowing in from the north-west.

'Holly didn't pay any attention to Aaron's dad,' I said. 'As we speak her band is wild-walking into a storm.'

'She's tough cookie,' Dad assured me. 'So no problem.' Did I say, my father likes extreme weather – ice six centimetres thick on Turner Lake, frozen creeks, cross-country skiing? After a childhood cooped up in grey,

165

concrete, Communist Bucharest, he loves the great American outdoors.

Breathe deep, focus on the dove, I told myself. Banish Natalie and jealousy, 'the green-eyed monster which doth mock. The meat it feeds on.' (William Shakespeare – *Othello*). We studied it in literature class, but I forget the act and scene.

With a whistle of wings Zenaida flew down from the bare trees and pecked at the grain on the ground.

'How was Mom?' I asked.

Dad threw down his last handful of corn. 'Moving hand better,' he reported. 'But slow. Doctors say OK, maybe home in one, two weeks.'

The tennis club has indoor courts and I arranged to play later that afternoon with Aaron, Grace and Jude. Outside, the promised snow had arrived and Holly was halfway up a mountain.

'Wow, Tania, where did that mean little shot come from?' Jude asked as I whacked a forehand down the line.

And, 'Ouch!' Grace winced on the next point. She'd been crouching at the net and I'd missed her head by a centimetre. 'What's up with that?'

'Thirty–love,' Aaron called from the baseline, ready to toss up the ball and serve. He was my partner and keen to ride my wave of unexpected aggression.

I ran, I smashed, I grunted and squealed like a Williams sister. Getting physical is the best way to relieve stress, I find.

Anyway, Aaron and I won the set six games to three. We came off court exhilarated and while Grace and Jude headed off to the locker rooms, we two winners went to the clubhouse, bought Cokes and took them to a window seat where we could watch the snow settling fast.

'Pretty,' I murmured. Fresh and white, smooth and pure.

'Any other time I'd say yeah, but not today.' Aaron frowned into the distance. He was slumped in his chair, brooding over his impetuous girlfriend.

'You're thinking about Holly up there on the mountain?'

He nodded. 'I tried to stop her but you know what she's like.'

'Stubborn.'

'Hot-headed.'

'Never listens.'

'Non-compromising.' Aaron and I ran out of adjectives and sat staring gloomily into his glass. 'I don't get it,' he sighed. 'How come she changed her mind about the New Dawn people?'

I waited a while before I answered. 'I kind of get it,' I admitted. 'All this turning hearts, Native American stuff – if it works the way Amos says it does, it really is cool.'

'Tell me,' Aaron invited unenthusiastically.

'It gives hope to kids who fell down to the bottom of the barrel and most likely through no fault of their own.'

He was in no mood for feeling charitable. 'Whose fault is it then if you turn out to be a junkie stealing cars to feed your habit?'

'That's harsh. Maybe they're from dysfunctional families. I don't know any details. But they're the same age as us, Aaron. I think they should be given a second chance and I guess Holly does too.'

'It's not what she said on Saturday,' he muttered. His dark, straight brows knitted together until they almost met in the middle. 'Back then she was singing a different tune.'

'You mean about the accident on Turner Lake?'

'Accident?' Now his eyebrows shot upwards in scorn. 'On Saturday Holly was talking homicide. Now she's making witness statements saying the exact opposite, like she's been brainwashed.'

The word 'brainwashed' got through to me and made me sit up straight. Since crossing swords with Zoran Brancusi this is not something I take lightly. 'Who would do that to her?' I challenged.

Aaron shrugged. 'I don't know – maybe that Ziegler guy, the one in the black hat who started the race. Maybe Amos. And how about number 102, the swimmer closest to Conner when he went down?'

Brainwashed. When you think it through, it literally means wiping the mind clean of all previous thoughts, being manipulated, getting confused over what is real and what is fantasy.

It's when the Aztec masks leap from the wall in Brancusi's underground house, when carved, painted wood spring to monstrous life. It's murals on chapel walls turning into 3D wolves, coyotes and bears, and men shape-shifting into demons, rising into the air and bending you to their will. And more lately it's monsters rising from Turner Lake, double-headed serpents, the beast with a snake's head and giant leathery wings and the wolf man standing at the edge of the cliff.

'I don't think so,' I told Aaron shakily, taking the route I'd already been down with Grace. 'I'm not feeling it the way I felt it on Black Rock.'

'So you're not getting the bad dreams, the phobia about forest fires?' Because he was worried about Holly, Aaron threw off his casual, neutral stance and pressurized me more than usual.

'Yeah, I'm getting bad dreams,' I admitted. 'But they're about water this time. And yeah, I've already told Grace that I know for sure we're not through with the dark angel. I just don't think it's Amos, that's all.'

Where are you? Who are you? If I'm to stand and fight I need to know my enemy.

Aaron nodded and grunted. 'Tania, I hope you're right,' he muttered as Grace and Jude, freshly showered, joined us in the clubhouse.

That night Dad told me that Mom's mom was taking a flight up from Miami. 'Angelica wants to visit hospital, see Karen,' he explained. 'Stay two days then fly back home.'

He didn't say much but he didn't have to. My high-maintenance, botoxed grandmamma was nobody's favourite person. We knew she would arrive at the airport loaded down with too many Louis Vuitton bags, would use my dad as a cab driver, stress the small stuff and suck all the attention away from the person we really cared about – my mom lying on her hospital bed. I personally didn't want to stick around to see it happen.

'So I guess I'll join the New Dawn guys,' I said suddenly. It's weird what makes you finally quit prevaricating and reach a life-changing decision. 'Sunday,

Monday – I'll be back Tuesday at the latest.'

Dad knew the recent history of open hostility between me and my grandmother too well to try and stop me. Instead, he went into be-prepared, boy-scout mode and pulled out good maps of the Turner Lake area that showed every detail of the topography – the small natural lakes upstream of the reservoir, the major landmarks such as Shaman Overlook and Spider Rock, together with the Jeep trails that threaded through the forest. And he loaned me Mom's expensive, lightweight hiking jacket. 'Tonight snow stops falling,' he advised me. 'Tomorrow maybe blue sky.'

Dad's my all-time hero. By now that must be totally obvious.

Later, I had a conversation with Orlando. It was one of those sad, pathetic ones where not much gets said and a whole lot is held back.

'I'll be home Tuesday,' I promised after I'd told him my new volunteer plan.

He was offhand, dismissive. 'Cool. So I'll be busy too. Tomorrow Ryan, Natalie and I plan to fix up the apartment then take in a movie. Monday we have lectures.'

'Aurelie made a big deal over inviting me,' I explained. 'They'll let me shoot documentary footage. I'm excited.'

'Cool. Listen, Tania, I have to go. The guys are downstairs in the lobby waiting for me.'

'Guys?'

'Natalie and Ryan. There's a college football game.'

'OK, have fun.'

'You too.'

'I will.'

'Bye.'

'Bye.'

Click. Call ended. One minute thirteen seconds.

Then came the avalanche of emotion. Orlando hadn't reacted the way I'd expected. He'd said 'cool' when I told him I'd volunteered, stayed out of any argument, hadn't asked me questions, hadn't even told me to take care. Natalie's name had come up at least six times in seventy-three seconds. So I was swept away by jealousy and while I was floundering there I emailed Aurelie to confirm that I would be joining the River Stone band the next day.

'Good news!' She emailed right back. 'My stepfather will be so pleased. We'll see you tomorrow at dawn.'

9

'So you couldn't stay away!' It was Viking Jarrold, brash and bold, there in the parking lot as the sun rose. I was going to say alone in the parking lot, except that I caught sight of Jean-Luc talking with him as I drove in then slipping away in the grey light without waiting to greet me.

Jarrold was dressed for the cold weather in a black ski jacket and a close-fitting, black knitted hat – a kind of skull cap that hid his long fair hair. There was a video camera slung over one shoulder.

'Yeah, I'm here for your whole story,' I countered as I looked around for the others – for Kaylee, Ava and Regan.

'They got held up.' Jarrold interpreted right without me having to open my mouth. 'Regan has a mega brain but his cabin is a mess. He lost his hiking boots. The girls are helping him out.'

'So are you still an Outsider?' I was confused. 'How come Jean-Luc was here?'

'He had to deliver a message. The Hawk Above Our Heads band didn't make it to the lake on Carlsbad because of the snow.'

'But they're OK?' I asked quickly.

Jarrold nodded. 'They came back down the mountain and camped overnight on Shaman Overlook. Jean-Luc thought maybe we'd run into them some time today.'

'Still, he shouldn't be talking to you. He should give the message to Kaylee or one of the others.'

'Technically correct,' he admitted, looking straight at me and curling his top lip. 'But who here is planning to report back to the boss?'

'OK, no problem. It's not my business.'

'Anyway, Jean-Luc has booked a one-way ticket out of here.' Casually Jarrold dropped the information into our illegal conversation. 'He doesn't give a crap about guiding principles. Are you shocked? Yeah, you are – you're stunned.'

'Not really.' I guessed straight away that Amos's stepson had decided to go home to Paris. 'I would've been more shocked if you'd said Aurelie.'

'Oh no, not Aurelie.'

Still glancing round for the others and feeling uncomfortable under the steel-grey gaze, I blundered on. 'What made Jean-Luc finally decide?'

'He wanted to go, even before his mom died. She drowned in a ferry accident off the coast of Goa early this summer. They were out there searching for a location for Antony's next movie.'

'I knew she was dead but I didn't know the details. I'm sorry.'

'It hit them hard – Antony, Jean-Luc and Aurelie. They were all on the boat with Juliet, but she was below deck and she was the only one who drowned.'

I see an azure sea, a palm-fringed coastline, a badly painted, rusting bucket of a boat overloaded with passengers, cars and trucks. It sits low in the water, rocks from side to side as the waves meet it sideways on. Spray cools the faces of the passengers wedged shoulder to shoulder on deck, a midday sun burns.

And nothing terrifying happens. The boat doesn't hit a reef with a sickening thud and scrape of metal. There's no Titanic moment, just a gradual listing and sinking under its own weight, water washing in through open portholes, people slowly realizing that they're in danger. The ferry wallows in the bright-blue water. Below are dark, volcanic rocks with

175

shoals of blue, yellow and red fish swimming in and out.

Someone cries out. A wave breaks over the prow of the boat, a dark-haired child clings to the skirt of her mother's shocking-pink sari. Some cattle penned in the trucks below deck begin to bellow.

The ferry rolls and wallows, it sinks. Three hundred people jump into the sea. A hundred and twenty souls are lost.

'So after Juliet died, Jean-Luc flew back to New Dawn with the rest of the family, but it was harder to believe in the ethos here without Juliet. Eventually he's had enough.'

'I see that.' Jarrold had just helped me make sense of Jean-Luc's attitude. From the first time I met him, I felt that he didn't belong at New Dawn. 'Does he somehow blame Antony for his mom's death?'

'I guess.'

'The whole thing's so sad.'

'Yeah, but don't feel sorry for Jean-Luc. His own dad's loaded. Jean-baby doesn't have to stay here – he can do whatever he likes.'

'Unlike you?' In a prison without walls, waiting to be released.

'Yeah, unlike me.'

'So I'm waiting.' It was my turn to look Jarrold in the eye and hold my nerve. 'For your story.'

'Later,' he promised, picking up the approach of the

other Explorers long before I did – as if he had sensitive, wild-animal hearing. And he walked quickly to the far side of the parking lot, isolating himself and waiting for Antony Amos to arrive.

Our New Dawn guru followed Regan, Kaylee and Ava down the track. Aurelie and Ziegler came a couple of paces behind, each carrying a long, red-and-white-striped pole decorated at the top with clusters of white feathers hanging from leather strips. Aurelie wore a small cap embroidered with turquoise beadwork and her soft suede boots were styled like moccasins with fringes and beads. Ziegler was all in black, his Stetson pulled low over his forehead.

Eventually we all came together in the centre of the parking lot. It was cold enough to see our breath in the pale morning light. Our faces looked pinched and we hunched our shoulders against the icy wind.

Amos gathered his Explorers close to him, beckoning for me to join them. Then he launched into his leaving ceremony. 'You know that today you lose yourselves to find yourselves,' he began. 'Let the wilderness guide you and let yourselves be open to change.'

Hearing the slow, weighty words, I glanced up at the cliffs rising behind the New Dawn cabins – rugged rocks where snow clung to shadowy ledges. For a second I imagined the lone figure of the wolf man standing on the cliff top watching us.

'I give you the advice given to Running Chief, a young Pawnee warrior, by his mother who raised him. "Now you are grown, be brave and face whatever danger may await you. If I should live to see you become a man, I want you to become a great man. If I live to see you go off on the warpath, I would not weep if I were to hear that you had been killed in battle. That is what makes a man: to fight and to be brave."'

I looked to the horizon again. There was no wolf man – only the big, grey, snow-laden sky.

'And here's another voice belonging to these lands,' Amos went on, drawing us in with his powerful shaman stare. He was the oldest of us by far and the only one besides Ziegler who didn't hunch his shoulders, who seemed not to notice the arctic temperature. 'This is the voice of Satanta, a great Kiowa chief. "I love the land and the buffalo and I will not part with it. I will not settle. I love to roam over the prairies. There I feel free and happy, but when we settle, we grow pale and die. When I go to the river I see camps of soldiers on its banks. These soldiers cut down the timber, they kill my buffalo. I see this and my heart feels like bursting."'

I sneak another look at the jagged ridge. There is a

different figure. His hair is long and black, the bottom half of his face is painted vermilion, his upper body is bare to the elements and he wears a feathered headdress.

'"This is our country,"' Amos tells the band, speaking in the voice of Satanta. '"We have always lived in it and there was plenty. We were happy."'

Hooves thunder across the open plain. A herd of black beasts with huge necks and curved horns raise dust as they gallop heads down, pursued by men on horseback. The men hold painted sticks adorned with feathers. They herd the fleeing buffalo towards the edge of a cliff. They funnel them, urge them on, kettle them and force them over the edge.

The beasts fall. The noise of thundering hooves stops. The hunters on horseback look down calmly on the broken bodies of fifty dead buffalo. Winter approaches. The tribe will eat.

Here again, at the rim of the cliff stands the tall, lean wolf man, his head turned towards me, his amber eyes gleaming.

'You will walk in the wilderness and these are the voices you will hear,' Amos promised us. 'Respect them and pray that their hearts are at peace in this beautiful land.'

I listened to his voice in the cold grey morning and I was lifted out of time, out of place into another existence. Call it spiritual because I can think of no other word. It was a world where men and women were at one with the land they lived in, where ancestors lived on in the rocks, the trees and the water, and when the invaders came and took the land by force, it was a world of pain, of death, darkness and suffering.

Amos told us the simple truth of this. He lifted me above the small stuff, the details, and spoke to my heart.

I only came back down to earth when Ziegler approached. 'Hey, Tania. We need to fix a rendezvous point for Tuesday.'

'You'll come and pick me up?' I checked.

He nodded. 'Name the time, the place.'

So I pulled out the map that Dad had given me and together we fixed on Spider Rock – a lookout point directly above the dam. From here you could see for miles – way down the valley as far as the point where Prayer River joined the Platte.

'A good choice,' Amos confirmed, looking over my shoulder at the map. 'Spider Rock is a sacred place. It's where a young boy of the White Water Sioux tribe would go to seek wisdom. He would fast there for many days and wait for a vision in the shape of a deer, a horse, an elk or an eagle – any animal spirit to guide him through life.'

Like my Zenaida, my spirit ally, my Weyekin, my good angel. She told me I would never be alone.

'So what time will you meet me?' I asked Ziegler. And we fixed on six in the evening – early enough for us to trek back down from Spider Rock to Ziegler's Jeep and drive to New Dawn before the sun went down.

'Are you comfortable with that?' he asked, fixing me with his startling blue eyes. 'It gives you three days and two nights in the wilderness.'

'I'm cool,' I replied. Actually, no. Scared to death of what lay ahead would be more accurate. But determined to do this, to hold a camera and shoot long shots of the spectacular scenery, plus close-ups of the inter-reactions between Jarrold, Kaylee and Ava. Maybe to discover more about my dark angel's presence and eager at last to stop running and to stand up and fight. This is how it felt. It was a big moment for me.

'So go,' Aurelie told us, planting her striped and feathered staff firmly across the exit to the parking lot and raising it as each Explorer approached. 'Open your heart to the Great Creator,' she chanted as they passed through.

I was last to leave. 'You are a Friend. You must open your heart,' Aurelie murmured. The feathers hanging from her staff brushed my cheek.

A bitter wind blows. Ice freezes the tumbling, splashing creeks. Snow blinds me. Stink of wolf's breath. Sweating,

stinking wolf man in his winter lair, a dark place of thorns.
His claws are bloodstained, his slack jaw hangs open.
He pants.

In that visionary second, it was as if my brain had split in two with the sound of an axe cleaving a log – the swish of the blade, the clunk as it met solid wood – then a blur as the two halves of my brain shunted back together and I was whole again. Reeling a little, I followed the three members of the River Stone band along the lakeside track.

This was it, the reality of wild walking.

Ahead lay snow-covered mountains and ice-covered Turner Lake, voices from the past, visions of a terrible future. I am not running, I am moving forward. And somewhere my dark angel hides.

From the beginning Jarrold led the way. He set a fast pace but Kaylee easily kept up, her red jacket vivid against the grey of the tree trunks. Twenty paces behind, Ava stumbled over tree roots and struggled with the weight of her backpack.

'It's OK, take your time,' I told her as I caught up.

She turned her head away from me, tried to make out that she wasn't having a hard time but soon gave up the pretence. 'This sucks,' she said as snow started to fall.

'You have to be crazy to volunteer.'

'Right,' I agreed. I helped her shorten the straps of her pack and got it sitting more comfortably between her shoulder blades. 'It doesn't help that we're being frogmarched out of here by Tarzan.'

Large snowflakes drifted down between the juniper branches and settled on the track so that already we could see the footprints of the two Explorers forging ahead.

'Tarzan and Tarzan's mate,' Ava muttered sarcastically. 'It was the same when we were the Black Crow band, actually. Only then I had Conner.'

The name brought on a cold tingle down my spine but I tried to keep things light. 'Well, this time you're stuck with me,' I told her.

Ahead of us, Jarrold and Kaylee had reached a creek that ran down into the lake and they were figuring out the best way to cross it. It involved stepping on to a flat rock and leaping, praying that you made a safe landing on the far side. And I'm talking smooth granite covered in ice and snow.

'I see a better way,' I told Ava, heading off the trail to a spot where the creek narrowed and allowed us to step safely across.

'You and Conner,' I began as I waited for Ava to cross. 'Were you like Kaylee and Jarrold – a couple?'

There was a long pause, a flicker of pain in her huge eyes. I held out my hand and she took it.

'You loved him but you couldn't go public with it?'

Ava sighed then nodded. 'Not until after we left this place. You know – Conner was the first guy I've ever met who didn't treat me like a kid. He made me feel grown up and good – he didn't care what I'd done.'

'So what did you do?' I asked her as we hiked on through the trees. 'How come you're here?'

'Talk to my parents,' she replied bitterly. 'This was so not my choice.'

I totally got that. It was obvious that skinny, fragile Ava wasn't cut out for wild-walking.

'How come I end up freezing to death by a lake?' She hesitated then decided that she'd shared plenty already and she might as well continue. 'The cops caught me walking out of a store with a jacket I didn't pay for.'

I didn't register any reaction though secretly I was surprised. It wasn't the kind of offence that I expected intense, vulnerable Ava to commit. 'Was it a cool jacket?'

She shrugged. 'Plus a pair of shoes and a purse. All on-trend, designer goods but no way worth all this.'

'So your parents decided on tough love – they sent you here?'

A nod this time instead of a shrug. 'They took me out of dance school.'

'Which you loved?'

'Right. I had a major role in a new ballet. I was principal dancer in my year.'

So why risk all that for a designer jacket, I wondered. 'So yeah, this sucks,' I agreed out loud. We'd got into our stride and were walking more quickly, starting to catch up with Jarrold and Kaylee.

'I told them I wouldn't come. I swore I'd stop eating again, starve myself if they sent me to New Dawn.'

'You've done that before?' No surprise here. Ava was like a tiny bird with big dark eyes, thin wrists and slender, tapering fingers. A gust of wind could blow her over.

'Yeah, and the stealing. It's a compulsion. I guess I have a problem, huh?'

'I'm not a psychologist so I have no clue. You'd have to ask my friend Grace. But you don't want to stop eating. What good would it do? You're here now and you have to get through it, go back to school.'

'Easy to say,' she sighed. 'But my dad won't pay any more fees, so that door is slammed right in my face.'

'Maybe he'll change his mind.'

'You don't know him,' she said, lowering her head and walking on in silence.

I had Ava's story – maybe not the whole of it but at least enough for me to begin slotting together the pieces of the jigsaw.

We were still walking by the shore of the lake where the ground was five centimetres deep in snow. We'd stopped for Jarrold to take a pee behind a rock and Kaylee was pointing the camera at me.

'So, Tania, what do you want out of this?' she challenged. 'Are you seriously looking for the Great Creator?'

'The way you say it, it sounds like you don't believe.'

'Oh, I believe,' she assured me. 'From heart at war to heart at peace. I love it out here, every freaking, freezing second.'

'She sounds like she's kidding but she's serious,' Ava confirmed miserably.

Kaylee lowered the camera and grinned. 'I'd live like this twenty-four/seven if they let me. But we want to hear from you, Tania. What's that gold heart and the cross you wear around your neck?'

I touched them with my cold fingers. 'The cross is Romanian,' I told her. 'It belonged to my grandmother.'

'You have a boyfriend? He gave you the heart?' Kaylee quizzed, raising the camera again.

I nodded. 'Orlando. He's in Dallas.'

'So why aren't you there with him?'

I didn't like this. I was supposed to be the one asking the questions. 'Here comes Jarrold,' I told her and Ava. 'Come on, let's go.'

By mid-afternoon it got to be my turn with the camera. I shot footage of the island in the middle of the lake, lost behind flurries of snow. Then I caught up with Jarrold and turned the lens on him.

'It's OK, I won't hassle you right now – I know you can't talk,' I said. 'Not officially.'

He stuck up a finger to the lens then strode away, cutting off the track and up the hillside.

'Thanks for reminding him, Tania.' This was Kaylee, walking into shot, the hood of her red jacket pulled tight around her face. She stuck out her tongue to show a silver stud right through the tip.

In the background, out of sight, I heard Ava asking when we could stop and build a shelter.

'Wait here. I'll go ask Jarrold.' Kaylee took a couple of steps then came back close to the camera. 'Obviously I'll ask him in sign language,' she grinned sarcastically. 'No actual words will be spoken!'

And off she went. She mimed out the whole situation

for Jarrold – made gestures to show that the snow wasn't letting up and we had to build a shelter.

'So funny!' Ava said in a hollow voice. 'Like, she's following the rules – *not*!'

Sighing, I switched off the camera. At least this way Kaylee could cut out the play-acting. 'How serious is Kaylee about Jarrold?' I asked Ava, meaning, was it more than the obvious lust factor?

'Like I said before, she's one hundred per cent committed to the heartless shit.'

'You can tell?'

'Look at the body language.'

Following Ava's advice, I saw Kaylee talking and laughing with Jarrold now that the camera wasn't running. She was sharing a joke, glancing our way, actually full-on flirting as much as was possible for a girl dressed for a snowstorm in padded jacket, scarf and hood. I watched Jarrold shake his head then turn away and start searching under the nearby trees for shelter materials.

'I'm a newbie but it took me less than twenty-four hours to figure out that everyone here – all the girls – think Jarrold's hot,' Ava explained. 'Channing comes a close second but Jarrold is definitely number one.'

'And Power Ranger Jarrold knows it,' I guessed.

'He leads them on then pushes them away, just like

he's doing now. No one knows much about him, not really. He keeps up a wall.'

'That's what he did with me – he promised to tell me his whole story, acted like he wanted me to join the River Stone band.' I was getting to like Ava, to feel that I could trust her.

Trust no one. My good angel's voice echoes inside my head.

Ava laughed. 'You believed him?'

'Not really. I'm here for other reasons.' On the verge of sharing my precarious spiritual situation with Ava, with the words 'dark angel' on the tip of my tongue, I suddenly switched topics. 'So what *do* we know about Jarrold?'

'He lived in Denver. His parents were super-rich, but both big-time alcoholics. He's lived with his grandfather since he was a little kid.'

'Wow, that's not how I figured it.'

'Six months ago he was busted for stealing the old man's credit card and running up thirty thousand dollars' worth of debt.'

'Ouch.'

'He told the judge he did it because he was bored. It was all over the Denver newspapers – you can google it and read the whole thing.'

'Again, ouch.'

By this time, Kaylee was yelling at us to quit talking

and help with the shelter.

'Unless you want to die in the snow like the Hawk Above Our Heads band!'

Straight away I ran up the hill to join her. 'Why, what did you hear?'

'Jean-Luc told Jarrold the Hawk band had to come down from Carlsbad, the snow was so bad.'

'Yeah, I know – they built a shelter on Shaman Overlook.'

'Which is still there,' Kaylee told me, pointing across the lake and handing me the field glasses that hung around her neck. 'Find the peak of Black Rock and focus directly under there, just above the tree line. See the shelter they built on the ledge?'

Following her directions, I managed to zoom in on a rough shelter built from brushwood and plastic sheeting.

'Do you see anyone?' Kaylee prompted.

The plastic roof of the shelter flapped, wind had blown the snow into deep drifts against the wooden sides. 'No,' I confirmed.

'So either they went back down the mountain and headed for home, which is against guiding principle number three, or else they froze during the night and the corpses are still in there.'

Gasping, I appealed to Jarrold, who was gathering

pine branches left on the ground by forestry workers. 'She's kidding!'

'You hope,' he mumbled. 'With Kaylee you never can tell.'

'We ought to go over and take a look, make sure they're safe.'

'What's with the "we"?' Kaylee scoffed. 'You go if you want to, Tania, but I'm staying right here to build a shelter.'

Jarrold agreed. 'We'd never make it to the overlook before nightfall.'

'Anyway, I was joking.' Kaylee gathered more branches and followed Jarrold as he carried his load to a thicket of aspens, where they set them down. 'The Hawk band probably spent the night on the overlook, left the shelter in place and moved on. The snow got worse today so I guess they came lower, towards the lake.'

Using the binoculars, I scanned the far shore for signs of life.

'See anything?' Ava asked.

I shook my head and handed her the field glasses, tried to tell myself that Kaylee's theory was correct. If they had any sense, the four Explorers and Holly had given up the attempt to climb Carlsbad and were roughly at the same altitude as us, at this very moment building a new shelter for their second night in the wilderness.

Meanwhile, we had work to do, constructing our own shelter by bending and binding together the tips of young aspen saplings to form a rough tipi then weaving horizontal branches stripped from nearby pines between the uprights. Then Jarrold showed us how to cover the wooden framework with plastic tarp, strapping it in place and leaving only a small flap for the entrance.

'Good enough?' Kaylee checked after an hour's teamwork.

Jarrold nodded and glanced up at the sky, which was growing dark. 'We're good unless the wind gets up. In case it does, we ought to weight down the tarp with extra stones.'

'But first we eat,' Kaylee suggested, digging into her backpack to produce bars of high-energy cereal and dried fruit plus packs of juice. 'It's not much but it's all we have – unless you want to go out and trap rabbits, break the ice and catch a fish, shoot a deer . . .'

Gratefully Ava and I took the bars, sat cross-legged on some spare tarp and chewed in silence.

By now the light had almost faded and the snow clouds had cleared. A pale moon rose above the ridge.

'Do you hear the wind?' Jarrold said.

I hadn't until that moment, but now I listened and

sure enough the branches of the nearby trees were rustling, the aspens were beginning to bend.

'We need more stones.' Ava sprang to her feet and began the task of weighting down the bottom rim of our shelter. Kaylee too found heavy rocks and lowered them into position but now Jarrold didn't seem interested. Instead, he stared at the moon and slowly wandered off through the aspens. Something made me follow him. I kept him in sight until the trees opened out on to a clear view of Carlsbad in the distance. Moonlight made the snow shimmer with a silver glow. Over our heads there were a zillion stars.

In the valley there is a large band of men marching in single file under the moon. They chant, they cry, they howl as they leave their land for the last time and walk into the mountains. It is a trail of tears.

'I wouldn't have left,' Jarrold said quietly, as if he shared my vision of the defeated tribe. 'I would have stayed to fight.'

'What with? Bows and arrows against guns?'

'I would still fight.'

I believed him. Nothing on this earth would have made Jarrold walk away from a battle. 'How can it be so peaceful up here?' I wondered.

'With all the blood that was spilled?' He shrugged.

'You think you'd feel the anger, the loss.'

'But you don't.' Maybe it was the eternal moon, the mountains rolling on for ever. I relaxed, breathed deeply and felt my worst fears slip away as I stood at ten thousand feet with snow on the ground and with Jarrold beside me.

10

For me, having a night without dreams is heaven.

I had no dreams, either bad or good, and without even my dreamcatcher to filter them. I slept like a baby inside our tarp shelter, glad of the body warmth generated by Ava, Kaylee and Jarrold as we lay nose to toe in our silver sleeping bags like a can of cosy sardines.

I woke at dawn and slid out through the canvas flap to greet the rising sun. And wow, what beauty, what a spectacular, pink-tinged, cloud-banked sky, and pure white snow everywhere – on the mountains, in the valleys and across the frozen surface of Turner Lake.

I breathed in the cold purity and vastness, felt my anxious heart lift. Jarrold followed me out of the shelter, camera in hand. He filmed the sparkling scene then closed in on my smiling, serene face.

'Give me the camera,' I said.

He handed it over without a word then zipped up his jacket and pulled his hat low over his forehead. I kept the camera on him as he walked away.

'Where did Jarrold go?' Kaylee asked, emerging sleepily but glancing at me and injecting a tinge of jealousy into her voice.

I pointed to the figure heading up the mountain, leaving a trail of fresh prints in the snow.

'It's his day to be alone, I guess.' She looked anxious. 'Let's hope he doesn't do anything stupid.'

'Like what?'

'Like decide this is all too hard – again.'

'And then what – get the hell out of here?'

Kaylee nodded. 'Jarrold wouldn't be the first. He won't be the last.'

'Really? You guys go on the run? Tell me more.'

Maybe she would have talked if she wasn't suspicious about me and Jarrold and if I hadn't had the camera, but as it was she grunted, turned and crawled back into the shelter. Half an hour later, my new buddy Ava surfaced.

'Did you sleep well?' I asked.

There were dark shadows under her eyes as she pulled up the fur-edged hood of her jacket. 'I had bad dreams.'

So it was her turn, not mine. 'What about?' Her confession drew a sympathetic smile.

'About Conner,' she replied, going tight-lipped and retreating into the shelter when I waited for more.

So I quit filming and sat listening to the wind in the trees.

My mind cleared as I absorbed the silence, the space. I internalized what I saw – the neat pawprints of a coyote between the aspen trunks, a blue jay huddled on a snow-laden branch (but no mourning dove, no Zenaida), the diamond glitter of snowflakes.

After an hour I felt totally calm until Jarrold came back down the mountain. I watched him closely, admiring his combination of strength and long-legged litheness as he skirted around icy boulders and waded through soft drifts. In the clear, early morning light he raised clouds of snow that seemed to form a sparkling halo around him. I held the camera steady, captured every move.

'Is that what you do, Tania – sit here and chill while your buddy is in deep trouble?' he demanded.

His voice was a gunshot shattering my peace. I let the camera drop to my side.

'Come and look,' Jarrold invited, grabbing my elbow and leading me out of the stand of aspens, giving me a clear view of the lake.

I saw another lone figure toiling up towards us –

unrecognizable from this distance but it could only be an Explorer from the Hawk Above Our Heads band.

'What makes you think . . . ?'

'It's Regan.' Jarrold handed me his field glasses. 'The only reason he's on his way up here is because his band needs our help.'

'So let's go!' I set off out of control down the mountain, half running, tripping, skidding and clutching at snow-covered bushes.

Behind me, Jarrold had raised the alarm with Kaylee, and Ava and all three were now following.

'Tania, take it easy!' Kaylee bawled. 'You want to break a leg?'

I didn't care. I only wanted to reach Regan and get the facts.

The thin, geeky Explorer saw us coming and slumped forward, hands on his knees, arms braced while he caught his breath.

'What is it? What happened?' I yelled as soon as I thought he could hear me.

'Holly fell through the ice!' His hoarse voice barely made it up the slope but it stunned me to the core.

My friend is down with the corpses – the skulls and coffins. She doesn't resist as she drifts through the church door. The minister is the dark monster with snake head and lion body,

his wings outstretched. Double-headed water snakes make up
the hissing congregation.

'Thank God, she made it to the island in the middle of the lake,' Regan said.

'But now she's stranded. She can't get back?' I stumbled and slid the final few metres, grateful when Regan put out an arm to halt me. We were both caked in snow, our faces blue with cold. Regan was like Ava – not cut out for these conditions.

'Exactly,' he confirmed, repeating the situation for the benefit of the rest of my band.

'Crap!' Kaylee muttered. 'How come she was on the ice to start with?'

Regan shook his head. 'Channing's our leader – you'll have to check with him.'

'What does Channing want us to do?' Jarrold asked.

'He says two of you should inform Ziegler, and two of you should head back with me.'

'I'm coming with you!' I cut in before anyone could speak.

'Me too,' Jarrold decided. 'Kaylee, you and Ava report back.'

There was a short argument – Kaylee said she was stronger than me and would be more use, and anyway she was keen to film the rescue. But no way was I going to leave Holly stranded on the island. Before anyone could stop me, I set off in the direction of the lake.

'How long has she been there?' I asked Regan when he and Jarrold caught up with me.

'A couple of hours. There's a zip-line between the lake shore and the island. Marta thinks Holly tried to use it to get across but the wire snapped and she went straight through the ice.

'Awesome!' Jarrold gave a heartless smile. 'Your buddy acts like we're in a theme park and almost gets herself killed.'

'Channing blames himself,' Regan told us. 'This is his third wilderness walk. He should've warned Holly to stay away from the ice.'

'God, she must be so cold!' The more I tried to run, the worse I stumbled in the snow drifts, so I was the last to arrive at the Hawks' temporary lakeside shelter and it was Blake who had to come and dig me out of the last hole I fell into.

'Give me your hand,' she grunted, her red hair flaming in the early sunlight.

She held on to a tree trunk and leaned out towards me.

'How's Holly?' I gasped.

Blake shrugged. 'We tried to fix the zip-wire, but no luck. Right now she's lying under the trees – see?'

As we reached the pebble beach and I squinted across the ice at the small island, I saw Holly in her orange jacket slumped against a trunk. 'Is she conscious?' I gasped.

'She was, but now we're not sure.' The answer came from tall Marta, helping to brush caked snow from my jacket.

'If anyone can survive this, it's Holly,' I tried to assure them as Jarrold discussed with Channing our next move. Who was I kidding? It didn't matter how tough you were – anyone who fell through the ice in these sub-zero temperatures was in serious trouble from hypothermia.

'What we can't do is walk on the stuff,' Channing explained, testing the surface with one foot. The second he put any weight on the newly formed ice, it splintered and his foot went through.

'We need a boat,' Jarrold said.

'What we need is a miracle,' Blake countered. 'The girl is dying out there!'

'Yeah, so no boat,' Channing disregarded his band member's gloomy prognosis. 'What we do have is the top of a picnic table we scavenged from the Grey Goose camp ground a couple of hundred metres south of here, plus some planks from a bench.'

'To make a raft and paddles?' Jarrold quickly got the

picture. 'You think we can break through the ice as we go?'

'Let's find out.'

The two guys were already heaving the makeshift raft into the lake when I stepped up to join them. 'I'm coming,' I insisted above the sound of cracking ice. 'Holly doesn't know you – she knows me and the sound of my voice.'

'That could work if she's already losing consciousness,' Jarrold agreed as he made room for me between him and Channing.

I squatted down, eyes fixed on the island. We had to cross a gap of about a hundred metres. 'Holly, hang on. We're coming to get you!' I yelled at the dark shape huddled under the tree. No response. I felt my guts tighten and my heart thump against my ribs. So typical! I thought. Trust Holly to try something like this.

The two guys made slow progress through ice that was around a centimetre thick. Their planks cracked and crunched into the surface to open up an area that was big enough for them to paddle through. Then they had to stop and begin the procedure all over again, a couple of metres at a time.

I stared down into the water, watched the loose shards of white ice swirl around the raft. I held at bay all images of slimy monsters deep under the black surface, of skulls trapped inside houses, stripped of flesh, grinning up at us as we rowed.

It took maybe thirty minutes for us to reach the island. When we did, I was the first to leap from the raft with stiff, shaking legs and run towards Holly.

She was propped against the tree without her hat, her head slumped forward, eyes closed. Her lips were blue, I noticed, and the weirdest thing was that the zipper of the new orange jacket was broken and her T-shirt was ripped from the neck band almost to the waist.

'Holly, wake up!' I cried. I'd seen a TV programme about an expedition to Antartica where victims of hypothermia were tempted to drift slowly into what seemed like comfortable, warm sleep, but what was in fact their final moments of consciousness. 'Holly, wake up. It's me – Tania!'

I was shaking her, pulling her jacket closed and pushing frozen locks of fair hair from her face, still trying to rouse her when Channing crouched down beside me.

'Holly, we're here,' he said in a low, intimate voice, stooping so that his lips were against her cheek. Then he slid his arms under her and effortlessly lifted her.

'Wake up!' I pleaded. Her head fell back, her arms hung limp but her eyelids began to flicker.

Thank God – she's alive!

'We're here for you,' Channing murmured. His broad shoulders protected her from the cold wind; his body heat seemed to revive her.

Holly's eyes slowly opened. She was dazed, weak as a kitten in Channing's arms. And as she opened her eyes and tried to raise her arms to put them around his neck, her whole body convulsed and she shook from head to toe. Channing carried her down to the shore and on to the raft. He held her close as Jarrold and I rowed her to safety.

Back on shore we swaddled Holly in sleeping bags and lay her in the overnight shelter. We took our orders from Channing. 'Marta and Blake, make a fire. Regan, go back on to Shaman Overlook, watch out for Ziegler's Jeep and direct them here. Jarrold and Tania, build a windbreak.'

Everyone got busy while Channing stayed in the shelter next to Holly.

'Where am I?' she whispered in a weak, slurred voice that didn't sound like her.

'With me – Channing. You're safe.'

'What happened?' She spoke like a heavy pebble weighted her tongue, slurring and stumbling over consonants.

'You fell through the ice. You don't remember?'

'No. Not a thing.'

'Cool,' he murmured. 'Everything's good. No problem.'

I could see him cradling her, still holding her close. She was shivering and gazing up at him with a vacant look.

Why was it cool that she couldn't remember? What did this remind me of?

'All I know is, I woke before dawn,' Holly whispered. 'It was dark. I crawled out of the shelter. You were there.'

'Hey,' Channing said, rocking her gently. 'Don't try to talk. Ziegler will be here. He'll bring a medic.'

I got busy gathering brushwood while Jarrold found a heavy stone and hammered stakes into the frozen ground. But when I glanced into the shelter, I swear I saw Channing kiss Holly's shivering lips.

Grace and Ezra! I got it in a flash. Ezra, the dark angel's henchman, had brainwashed Grace into falling in love with him on Black Rock. He'd created the same confused, empty stare I now saw in Holly. He'd smothered her in promises and kisses.

Dark angel – stealer of innocent souls, twisted tormentor. The love thief is back to claim another victim. He has risen again. Holly isn't saved by Channing. It's the total opposite – she's in terrible danger.

I broke into the shelter, spotted an angry look flash across Channing's face when he saw me. 'Try to remember!' I urged. 'Holly, it's important. What happened when you crawled out of the shelter?'

'Back off, Tania!' In the small, dark space Channing put himself between me and Holly. 'Can't you see she's confused?'

I argued back. 'What do you have to hide? Was it you? Did you do this to her?' I pointed to the broken zip, the ripped T-shirt. 'Is this all down to you?'

'I said, back off!' he snarled. His temper snapped as he shoved me backwards out into the snow. I lost my balance and sprawled between the two girls, who were fanning the first flames of the fire.

Marta pulled me to my feet while Blake tutted then sucked air through her teeth. 'You don't want to argue with Channing,' she advised. 'The last kid who did that was Regan and he ended up in the ER.'

'Holly is my friend!' I protested. 'Her clothes are ripped. There's a big hole in her memory. I need her to tell me what happened.'

'No, you don't,' Marta advised, standing back from the flames.

'You definitely don't,' Blake agreed. 'What you need to do is listen to Channing and act exactly the way he tells you to. If he says jump, you jump. If he says make a fire, you make – no question.'

206

I shook my head in disbelief. 'What happened to trust? What happened to walking together?' And to the peace and harmony I'd personally felt as I'd watched the sun rise.

The huge black monster slithers across the ice towards the fire. His eyes bulge and reflect the flickering flames, his body shines like burnished bronze – lithe and muscled like a giant cat – with claws and fangs and a foul breath. His wings cast a deep shadow over us.

High in the morning sky, my glorious grey dove sails on an air current, keeping watch. Trust no one.

Don't believe Channing, I told myself. Or any of this New Dawn philosophy. Scratch the surface and what do you get? Secrets and lies.

Above the crackle of the fire Jarrold swore at me for not helping with the brushwood windbreak.

Richard Ziegler arrived with Regan and a woman I recognized as the paramedic who'd tried but failed to resuscitate Conner at the lakeside. It took me a while, but finally I placed the wide face and neat cap of mid-brown hair, the strong, capable hands as she entered the shelter and strapped a blood pressure cuff around Holly's arm, listened to her heart and diagnosed atrial fibrillation. 'It's an indication of stage three hypothermia,' she decided. 'The patient needs an immediate shot of intravenous fluid – dextrose and saline.'

'Did you bring some?' Ziegler checked, standing by the entrance to the shelter.

'It's in the bag I left in your car,' she told him.

I shoved my way past Ziegler on sentry duty, ready to stand up to Channing in spite of the warnings from Marta and Blake. 'Did you talk to her?' I asked the paramedic. 'Can you get her to answer questions about what happened?'

'Not right now. She's too severely hypothermic, which means she's likely to be incoherent and irrational.'

'What about this?' I demanded, pointing to Holly's wrecked jacket and T-shirt.

'Also typical,' the woman explained. 'The hypothalamus malfunctions and they start to take off their clothes.'

I glanced up at Channing, who returned my stare with a blank expression.

'OK, let's go.' Ziegler moved in, as calm and decisive as he'd been at the triathlon tragedy. He instructed Channing to wrap extra sleeping bags round Holly then help him carry her to the Jeep. The paramedic followed close behind.

'She'll be OK?' I asked her, hesitating as they loaded Holly into the back of the car.

'She's young, she's healthy,' was the non-committal answer.

'She'll be fine,' Ziegler assured me. 'You could drive with us if it'd make you feel better.'

Inside the car, Holly shook her head. 'I want Channing to come with me,' she murmured.

My heart jolted. In that shuddering, fearful heartbeat, Channing had pushed me aside and climbed into the Jeep beside her.

'Stay with the band,' he told me with a smile he definitely didn't mean. 'Your buddy will be cool with me.'

And that's how I had to leave it – doors slamming, an engine starting up, Holly being driven away and me left there by the lake with Marta, Blake, Regan and Jarrold.

'Form a new group,' Ziegler told us as he leaned out of the driver's window. 'Call yourselves the Wolf in the Snow band. Jarrold, you'll be leader. Tania, you'll be their Friend. I'll see you in thirty-six hours at Spider Rock.'

'See you,' I agreed, trying to ignore my hammering heart as Holly was driven away.

'What did you expect?' Blake asked as we shouldered our backpacks and walked on. 'Life's not a beach – not around here anyway.'

I looked straight ahead towards the stand of dark

redwoods laden with snow.

'So accidents happen all the time?' I muttered.

'Hypothermia, busted legs and arms, cracked ribs, emotional meltdown – yeah.'

'Perfect.'

Blake laughed. 'It's not meant to be easy. Amos's system follows a military model. Quote: "It's tried, tested and proved to maximize deterrence."'

'You follow orders, ask no questions?'

'Right.'

'And you can do this?' For myself, I had a thousand questions buzzing around my brain.

'Some of us can. Me and Kaylee, but not Regan or Ava, for example.'

'How about Jarrold?' I spotted him ahead of us, already deep in the shadow cast by the trees.

'Jarrold still has some aggression issues to work on,' Blake told me in that deadpan, between-quotes way that allows cynicism to filter through. She still reminded me of Kaylee minus the piercings – tough and in-your-face, totally at ease with physical challenge. Taking the camera from its case, she began to shoot our new surroundings – the ten-metre-high, dome-shaped rock to our right, covered in unmarked snow, Carlsbad in the distance, Regan and Marta bringing up the rear, Jarrold up ahead and disappearing into the shadows.

As Blake filmed, Marta picked up speed to walk beside me. 'Cowboy up, Tania,' she teased as we ploughed through a deep drift. 'Only four hours to go until we stop and make camp!'

Our Wolf band walked all day under a clear sky.

It's indescribable. You put one foot in front of another, hour after hour. You don't talk. In spite of all the high drama that happens, you become at one with the space around you.

We were at ten thousand feet with the sun in our eyes, crunching through a frozen crust of sparkling snow, sinking into the soft stuff, climbing higher, away from Lake Turner towards a peak, a fourteener, which according to my map, was named Melrose Mount after a Presbyterian preacher who scaled it solo in 1856.

No one spoke and the silence was a big part of growing closer to the people I walked with. I learned that words can distract and disguise, that not speaking and walking together was what bonded me with Regan, Marta and Blake. As for Jarrold – he was out of sight, following his own star.

'Tired?' Regan asked me with massive understatement when at last we put down our bags.

I eased my back, hands on hips. A groan was all I could manage by way of reply. And my exhaustion meant I wasn't good with the shelter-building and fire-making on this second night so I was given the task of getting it all on camera.

'Has anyone seen Jarrold lately?' Blake asked once camp was made and we all sat around the fire in the fading daylight.

We worked out that we'd lost track of our Outsider around three p.m. 'No problem,' Marta insisted. 'Jarrold can take care of himself.'

'He's tough but not that tough.' Regan argued that Jarrold had better show up before nightfall if we wanted to avoid a second hypothermia crisis. 'So, Tania, how was your day?' he asked, making space for me so that I could get closer to the fire. 'Come on – stay warm.'

'Actually, awesome,' I confessed.

'You let go of your burden.' Marta put her arm around my shoulder and grinned at me. 'You forgot about your problems, lived in the moment – am I right?'

'Totally. Only . . .'

'Now that we made it through the day and you can relax, you have some questions?' Blake interpreted. 'I'm not mind-reading. It's just that we all go through the same process the first time we wild-walk. So go ahead, ask.'

'OK.' Checking that the camera was off, I rushed to share. 'First thing on my mind is Holly. I know the paramedic explained about the memory loss and stuff, but I want to know how come she did the stupid thing on the zip-wire in the first place. Did any of you see?'

Marta shook her head. 'We were asleep.'

'And what about Holly and Channing – how did that happen? I mean, she only knew him a couple of days.'

Blake grinned at me from the far side of our tight circle. Firelight flickered and played across her face. 'Yeah, but this is Channing we're talking about – right?'

'Babe magnet,' Regan sighed.

'But what about the guiding principle – the no-romance one?'

'Only between Explorers,' he said. 'It doesn't apply to Friends.'

'So, Tania, you could fall in love with Regan, no problem,' Blake joked, and she shoved him sideways against me.

He sprawled across my lap and drew down one corner of his mouth. 'Except I don't work out and have a six-pack like these other guys, huh?'

I started to lie to him to make him feel better, said stuff like that wasn't important to me when Marta interrupted.

'But Regan's brain is amazing,' she insisted as he pulled himself upright. 'As soon as he gets out of here, he's going to start inventing and selling apps for smart phones. He'll be a zillionaire by the time he's twenty.'

'But no more hacking into government computers and leaking national defence secrets, you hear me, Regan?' An unrepentant Blake wagged her finger then turned to me. 'More questions!' she demanded. 'We'll give you the truth – trust us!'

'Conner,' I said, taking advantage of Jarrold's absence and screwing up my courage to ask the big one. 'Was that really an accident?'

The fire crackled, sparks flew up and logs shifted. There was a sudden tension in the air.

It was Regan who finally broke the silence. 'You're talking about a cover-up?'

'Don't listen – Regan sees a conspiracy around every corner,' Marta interrupted. 'That's how he arrived here in the first place.'

I leaned forward to share my suspicions. 'We – that is, Holly – thought Jarrold might have got too close. There were arms and legs thrashing about in the water – maybe Jarrold kicked Conner in the head, but Ziegler, Aurelie, Amos – they don't want to focus on that?'

'Wow – that's why they changed Jarrold's status to

Outsider?' It was obviously the first time Marta had heard the theory. She sat back and thought it through. 'And we all figured it was because of his thing with Kaylee.'

'Jarrold had been fighting with Conner,' I explained. 'Conner had challenged Jarrold over his relationship with Kaylee – that's what I heard.'

'This stupid, stupid no-sex rule!' Regan muttered. 'It's unnatural. Who does Antony Amos think he is – God?'

'Hush!' Blake warned him again, narrowing her eyes. 'The point is – Conner should never have been in the water in the first place. It's not Amos I blame – it's Ziegler!'

'Why? What do you know that we don't?' Regan demanded.

'Ziegler is the one who's covering stuff up,' Blake insisted. 'He holds all our personal details, including our medical records.'

'And?'

'And he knew Conner had major heart surgery when he was fourteen years old.'

'Whoa!' Marta sprang up and backed out of the firelight, almost bumping her head on a low branch. 'He had a weak heart?'

Blake nodded. 'I talked with Ava. She says his doctors gave him a programme of exercise, diet, et cetera. They put Conner on a list for further surgery, maybe even a transplant. They made it clear he shouldn't put too much strain on his heart.'

'But Ziegler ignored their advice?' I asked.

Blake spread her hands, palms upwards. 'Well, he makes Conner enter the triathlon and the poor kid's heart can't take it. Conner drowns and Ziegler's in big trouble. It's just a typical example of the way they run this place.'

'It must be part of the reason why Jean-Luc is quitting.' I broke the conversation-stopping news without warning. 'Even I can see he doesn't fit in around here – there are too many big egos; he can't make himself heard.'

'Jean-Luc is leaving?' Regan said at last, his voice filled with disbelief. 'You know for sure?'

'He's going to live in Paris with his dad,' I insisted as I saw a tall, dark figure step into our small circle of firelight. 'He told Jarrold early yesterday. Ask him. He'll tell you it's true.'

11

For a second I saw a lean, mean wolf-glint in Jarrold's eyes. His face was honed and harsh, his jaw clenched.

'Where did you go?' Marta demanded. 'We were worried about you.'

'Not true,' Blake argued. 'We knew you'd be cool. It's OK, Jarrold – the camera's switched off. You can talk.'

'Yeah, tell us about Jean-Luc,' Regan said.

Slinging his backpack on to the ground, Jarrold was slow to respond. 'What do you want me to say?'

'Tania says he's quitting New Dawn. We want to know why.'

'Go figure.' Sullenly Jarrold took out his sleeping bag and threw it inside the shelter, crawling in after it.

'You mean, who except a crazy person would stay here if they had a choice?' Regan didn't need to have it spelled out.

'Me,' Marta contradicted. 'And Blake, Kaylee, Channing . . . I could give you a long list.'

'Count me out,' Jarrold grunted, already zipped up inside his bag and ready to sleep. 'The sooner I'm out of here the better – zap. I'm history!'

The others muttered and grumbled, but Jarrold's reappearance had put the brakes on our confessional. Soon we were following him into the shelter, where it turned out the only space left for me when I crawled in was next to Jarrold – exactly the place I least/most wanted to be. So we lay waiting for sleep in a tightly packed row – Marta, Blake, Regan, Jarrold then me.

'I can't even breathe. All move a couple of inches to your right,' Marta complained.

I felt Jarrold's shift of weight, grew hyper-aware of his presence. Though it was pitch-dark in the shelter, I pictured him with eyes closed, his skin smooth and clean, his fair hair falling clear of his face.

I lay too close, felt the attraction at the same time as the fear. I remembered Blake's mocking voice telling me that a Friend was free to fall in love with an Explorer and saw again Holly's doting gaze when Channing kissed her lips.

'Thanks and goodnight,' Marta said from the far end of the row. 'Sleep well, everyone.'

I crawl through thorn bushes after the wolf man. I enter his lair.

It is humid, dank with sweat and spilled blood. A gleam of amber light in the darkness – his eyes.

He drags me out into the open. A whole pack of wolves hunt in the forest. They rear on to their hind legs, snap their jaws and morph into creatures you only hear about in folk tales where man becomes beast, ogre or frog. Which one do you run from before he eats you up? Which one do you kiss?

I run. The beasts shape-shift again and carry axes. They paint their naked bodies crimson and black, they wear feathers in their black hair and ride horses across the plains.

Only one has hair that is fair, the colour of ripe corn. His face is streaked with red clay, he wears a dagger in his belt. The wind whips his hair from his face as his horse gallops. He comes straight at me with a thunder of hooves, he leans out and sweeps me from my feet, carries me away. I am saved.

I am in his arms when I look again and see that the golden hair is dull and matted, there are yellow fangs in his mouth, blood on his breath.

'Tania, are you OK?'

I crawled out of the shelter, gasping for breath. It was still dark – the middle of the night.

'Are you OK?' Jarrold asked again.

'I had a nightmare. I was scared,' I admitted.

To my surprise, he wrapped his arms around me and held me close. I felt the strong beating of his heart.

Again, I crept back into the shelter and tried to sleep.

Antony Amos appears dressed in a long buckskin shirt with blue beads around his neck. Ziegler stands beside him, carrying a feathered staff.

They stand on a flat rock in a forest clearing. The rock is the shape of an altar. Storm clouds sweep across the sky, fast-forwarded so that day becomes night – clouds, clear sky, stars and moonlight.

Amos and Ziegler do not move, even when stealthy coyotes, bears and wolves creep out of the shadows and surround them. Ziegler raises his staff then thuds it down on the rock. The creatures howl at the moon then they stop and listen as Amos starts to speak.

'I bring storm and tempest,' he proclaims in the voice of a prophet, a shaman. 'I bring winds of destruction. Watch!'

He takes the staff from Ziegler and thrusts it towards the starlit sky. Lightning strikes, thunder cracks, a savage rain tears the leaves from the trees.

'I turn man into beast and beast into man.'

At his word, the coyotes fall on their backs and writhe in the dust. They snarl and spring to their feet as lithe young guys – each one handsome. The bears roar and strike at each other with curved claws. They wrestle their opponents to the ground, roll and recover. When they leap up, they are as sleek and strong as action heroes. Even the wolves – those sly, stinking, creeping creatures – tear at each other with their fangs then shed their hairy coats and morph into the hot guy you would fall in love with at college and worship from a distance. Exultant, Amos and Ziegler gather their army of dark angels. 'You will go from here and seek out your victims,' Amos exhorts, raising both arms above his head and grasping the staff in two hands. 'They will be young. Each one will know in their heart what love is.'

His followers listen intently, like extras being given direction for the next take. They are eager to enact every move Amos gives them.

'Carry their souls back to me!' he cries, his voice rising. 'Like thieves in the night, you will steal their beautiful, unspotted, loving spirits. You will drag them to the dark side. So our army of dark angels will grow until we outnumber the angels of light!'

I woke again, stunned and cold as death. The questions that had drilled into my brain for days were answered by hammer blows of certainty. Right from the start, when I first saw Amos by the side of the lake, I had

221

been deceived. He had been too clever for me.

I'd been deep in denial, I realized. I'd refused to listen to Grace and Orlando's warnings and, worse still, had ignored both my good angel and my nightmare visions. I'd been so busy preparing to stand and face my enemy that I'd missed the thing right in front of me – Amos was my dark angel after all.

This time I didn't crawl out of the shelter and look to Jarrold for comfort, but drifted like a corpse sinking into murky depths of panic, waiting until the dawn light sluggishly appeared.

My first thought when I finally emerged from the overnight shelter was to flee from my Wolf in the Snow band and head back to New Dawn to find Holly.

Jarrold found me kneeling in the crisp snow, studying my map and working out my route. He quickly snatched the map and ripped it to pieces.

'Hey!' I cried out, scurrying after the paper fragments, which the wind had lifted into the air. 'What are you trying to do?'

'Save your life?' he suggested.

'By destroying my map!' I was furious and helpless, turning on him with fists clenched. 'I'm going to see Holly!' I yelled. 'I want to find out exactly what happened to her!'

Jarrold gave me his speciality blank stare. 'Boring, Tania,' he muttered as he began to build a fresh fire. 'Change the freaking track.'

Grabbing my bag from just inside the entrance to the shelter, I was about to swing it on to my shoulder and head out of the camp when Blake sprang into action. She grabbed my wrist and dragged me inside. 'You heard Jarrold – don't even think about it!'

'Let me go! I'm leaving. You can't stop me.'

Blake pushed me against Marta and Regan. 'Funny – I had you down as smart,' she mocked.

Knowing I didn't have the brute strength to resist, I appealed to Regan and Marta. 'My friend's in big trouble. Would you stick around if you were me?'

'Actually, yes,' Marta said.

'Yeah,' Regan echoed. 'I'd stick with what Ziegler told you.'

'You're all brainwashed!' I cried, struggling to get past Blake, who blocked my exit. 'I thought you got it after the talk we had yesterday. All this crap about trust and teamwork – it's just mind control.'

'And you're hysterical,' Regan said quietly, as if any girl who splurged her emotions was an alien creature. He'd already turned his back on me and got busy rolling up his sleeping bag.

'OK, look at this rationally,' Marta cajoled, squatting beside me. She seemed to be the only one willing to spend more than five seconds on my fragile state of mind. 'We know the incident with your friend has spooked you big time, and we understand that. But Ziegler is a good guy in an emergency. He'll get Holly the best possible treatment and by the time he picks you up in the Jeep later today, she'll be fully recovered and back to normal, believe me.'

'I don't trust him, or Channing,' I confessed. 'I think there are things going on here that you wouldn't even believe.'

Evil things, fuelled by my dark angel's desire for revenge. A great cosmic battle between good and evil. And Holly is under the spell of a love-thief, losing touch with reality. She's being drawn into a tormented shadow world which you're part of, even if you don't know it.

I thought these things, hunched in the dark corner and staring pleadingly at Marta, but I didn't dare to say them out loud.

'Smart but paranoid,' Blake scoffed as she left the shelter.

'So, like I said – cowboy up,' Marta whispered. She was concerned about me, enough to show sympathy while the others mocked and turned their backs.

'Don't risk your life by trying to make it out of the wilderness alone. That really would be dumb, Tania.'

'OK, I'll stay with the group,' I promised.

Scraps of my map flew in every direction. Members of the Wolf band were my jailers for the day. What choice did I have?

At eight a.m. we deadened the fire, shouldered our bags and left camp, hiking in single file towards a small frozen lake called Mule Pond, an old watering station for the wagon trains heading west through the mountains. Jarrold led the way.

Ten hours to go, I told myself, focusing on my meeting with Ziegler and praying that he'd show up as promised but fearing that it was already too late to rescue Holly from Channing's clutches. Remember the dazed look she gave him, the slurred words, the hole in her memory, I thought.

We walked through the morning under a cloudy sky. At noon, a hot sun broke through.

'So now we get the snow melt,' Blake predicted.

We were walking along a narrow ledge with the force of the sun directly overhead. Already the frozen surface had developed the slippery wet quality of water on top of ice. I watched Regan lose his footing and grab on to

Marta, who stood firm until he got his balance. My heart skipped a beat as I looked down at a sheer drop of thirty or forty feet.

The melt happened incredibly quickly, almost before we were off the ledge and entering a narrow valley between ridges. Already there were new streams forming, clear water cascading down the rocks, snow disappearing to reveal flattened vegetation below. Above us, the noon sun blazed.

And we'd fallen into the deep silence that develops on a wild walk. Our feet slithered through mushy snow, water splashed down rocks, steam rose from the dark ground.

At two p.m. we came to a lake surrounded by pines. On the near side there were the crumbling remains of wooden shacks, old fence posts and rails where horses had been tethered while the pack animals drank.

'Mule Pond,' Jarrold announced.

'Kodak moment!' Blake got ready with the camera, lining us up with the dripping cabins in the background. 'To prove that we made it,' she explained. She gave a voice-over as we posed. 'This is the newly formed Wolf in the Snow band by Mule Pond. The noise you hear is the sound of snow melt. See the creek has burst its bank.'

Panning round to her left, she captured a stream gushing over a succession of pink granite ledges. 'The ice on the pond has totally melted,' she commented, turning the lens on the flat, blue surface. 'Pretty, huh?'

'OK, cut,' Marta told her. 'I'm heading for that rock and I don't want the camera on me when I'm squatting.'

'So what's for lunch?' Regan asked.

'Whatever we can catch in the lake.' Jarrold's answer came as he strode along the shore to a crumbling wooden jetty where he lay on his belly and stared into the water. 'Salmon,' he told us. 'Plenty of them.'

Smiling, Blake joined him on the jetty. 'Here, little fishes!'

'Like they're going to jump out of the water right into our hands,' I muttered. I was counting the hours, worried that we wouldn't get from here to Spider Rock in time for six o'clock.

Regan laughed and told me to start collecting firewood. 'Only the driest stuff,' he recommended. 'Take a look inside the old cabins, see what you can find.'

Thirty minutes later, we had a fire blazing on the shore and three salmon from the lake, gutted and beheaded, magically sizzling in a pan.

* * *

In the afternoon I took a turn with the camera.

'Isn't that why you came?' Jarrold reminded me in that mocking way.

Had I imagined it? Was it part of my dream last night that Jarrold had crawled out of the shelter and held me in his arms? 'Why are you mad at me?' I asked, remembering the strong beat of his heart as I trained the camera on his face.

He stared back. 'Do you even have to ask?'

'Yeah, I'm asking.'

'Because you wanted to break up the band.'

'Oh, the band! Well, I'm sorry I was more concerned about Holly's safety than about guiding principles. How stupid am I?'

'Sarcasm doesn't suit you,' he snorted.

'And you think it suits you? God, Jarrold, you're so arrogant!' The camera wobbled in my hand as emotion took over.

He looked as if he was about to walk away as usual but them changed his mind, raising a hand to cover the lens until I eventually turned off the camera. 'You don't fool me,' he whispered. 'I can see right through you, Tania. You only came on this trip so you could find something to pin on me – something about Conner.'

'No,' I began, my heart in my mouth. 'That's not true.'

'Sure it is. But now you know about Conner's heart problem – yeah, Blake told you. And you also realize your friend Holly lives in la-la land. So why can't you put two and two together and come up with the right answer?'

'I do,' I protested. 'I know you and Conner had a fight but it was over. I believe you – really!'

We were standing closer than I'd realized, glaring at each other – near enough for me to see a small, tense muscle jumping in Jarrold's jaw and the fleshy, pink softness of his lips. He had two days' blond stubble which brushed my cheek as he leaned in to kiss me. 'I'm not mad at you,' he murmured. He drew back, stroked my hair, turned and walked.

Now it was me who was mad at Jarrold. How dare he? What made him think that he could do that? We'd been arguing, not flirting. He was way out of line.

Maybe I'm the character in Hamlet who protests too much – 'Methinks the lady . . . whatever.' William Shakespeare again. That guy knew everything and it was four hundred years ago, back in the dark ages.

So anyway, I was confused.

And I was convinced that Marta, Blake and Regan had seen and heard it all – the sarcasm, the fighting, the kiss.

'Is this genuinely the way to Spider Rock?' I asked Marta, who was as close as it got to being on my side. I'd begun to doubt every little thing, including the direction we were headed.

'Sure,' she shrugged. End of conversation.

'Don't tell me – Marta has a thing for Jarrold,' I sighed as she walked off and Regan approached me. 'She saw what he just did.'

He laughed in my face. '*Everyone* has a thing for Jarrold, remember.'

'Or Channing.'

'Which is why guys like me don't stand a chance in this environment. But wait until I'm king of the apps universe . . . !' He gave a lopsided grin, dropped back and brought up the rear.

Regan was the one who saw me slip down the sink hole. These are the craters created by forest fires, when tree roots burn underground for weeks and carve out great hidden chasms that you never see until it's too late.

I screamed as I dropped out of sight, felt wet earth and soot fall on my head, reached out with both hands and tried to claw my way back to the surface.

'Hey, you guys!' Regan called to Marta, Blake and Jarrold. 'We have a problem.'

His voice was muffled. I was deep underground, cut off from the light. I felt suffocated, as if the breath was being squeezed out of my lungs.

Soon I heard other voices.

'Tania, can you hear me? Hold on, we'll get you out . . .'

And other long-lost voices whispering down the years.

Men with crows' feathers in their black, braided hair, they speak to me. 'We are with you. We are part of this land.'

I am in their underground world. Above our heads horses thunder by, gunfire rattles and echoes down the valley.

'They drive us from our hunting grounds, from our homes. But we will never leave.'

I hear the dead men's sighs, the ghostly laments in my crumbling chasm. Earth falls on my face. Down below my wolf man silently waits.

'Tania, listen. Regan and the others will lower me on a rope.' This was Jarrold's voice, issuing orders, taking the lead. 'Don't try to move. Just call out and let us know where you are.'

My mouth was filled with soot and ash, there was still a sharp smell of smoke.

'Be quick,' I pleaded. 'The ground is giving way under me.' The soft mud crumbled each time I shifted my weight. How much further could I fall before Jarrold got to me?

It seemed like an age. More earth fell from above.

Jarrold descended. I made out his shape, abseiling down, legs braced against the soft sides of the chasm, dislodging dirt and ash. Too soon I reached towards his outstretched hand and fell another two metres, groaning and slipping out of his grasp.

'Don't move!' he insisted. 'Wait for me.'

Another age passed. They lowered him further into the darkness until his body swung into mine and he put one arm around my waist and took my weight.

'Pull!' he yelled to Regan, Marta and Blake.

They inched us up. Still I didn't think we would make it. I thought the walls of the sink hole would collapse in on us and we'd be buried together, like Red Cloud and Little Wound, like a thousand slaughtered warriors.

At last I saw daylight and the faces of my rescuers peering down. I clung to Jarrold as they raised us, buried my head against his chest when the sun dazzled me.

'Lift her,' I heard him say. 'Lay her on her side, make sure she doesn't choke.'

Hands raised me to safety and lay me down, covered me in a blanket. Jarrold untied the rope from around his waist. He was covered in soot and ash, gasping for breath, his hands burned by the rope as he'd descended too quickly in his rush to save me.

'Don't do that again,' he gasped, sinking on to his

knees next to where I lay. 'You hear me, Tania? Don't disappear on me.'

After that, Jarrold never let me out of his sight. Instead of striding ahead, he slowed his pace to walk by my side, helping me over creeks and around rocks, taking me by the hand and leading me.

He made me feel safe.

But my thoughts were chaotic. Don't fall for this, I told myself. This is exactly what happened with Holly – she joined the Hawk Above Our Heads band and immediately fell under Channing's spell. And look what happened – within forty-eight hours he made his dark-angel move on her.

Another part of my brain was saying, it's more complicated. Jarrold is a rebel, an Outsider – he doesn't belong with Antony Amos at New Dawn. And lowering himself down the sink hole to rescue me proves that he really cares.

So maybe Jarrold is on the side of light. The thought pierced the dark chaos of my mind like a burning arrow. He's Zenaida's secret spy, he's my hero!

He walked beside me towards the meeting place with Ziegler. 'You OK?' he asked.

I nodded, smiled back and tried not to betray my new

feeling for him. 'What are your plans when you get out of here?'

'No plans.'

'Will you go back to Denver?'

'No. Maybe California – San Diego. I don't know. How about you?'

'Back to Paris,' I said with a frown. 'When Mom gets out of hospital.'

He asked me for details, told me about his dad, who died of liver failure. 'I was eleven. They didn't let me visit.'

'That sucks. I'm sorry.'

After that, we were silent for a while, until we reached an overlook that gave us a view of Turner Lake. This was where Jarrold lined up behind me and pointed over my shoulder to a landmark finger of rock on the horizon. 'Spider Rock,' he told me.

Again I felt the beat of his heart, the strength and heat of his body, the warmth of his breath.

'Jarrold!' Marta called from the edge of the overlook.

We looked round to see that Regan had got himself wedged in a narrow gap between a tree trunk and a rock, with a drop of five metres below.

'What the . . . ?' Jarrold ran to grab him. 'Throw me the camera. Use both hands. Don't talk, just do.'

I joined Blake in the shadow of the rock. 'Don't even ask,' she muttered before I could open my mouth.

'Regan was climbing the tree for the best shot of the lake,' Marta explained. 'He fell from the second branch – see?'

Slowly Jarrold encouraged Regan to place his feet on the safe ledges and to catch hold of his hand. 'To your right. Don't let go with your left hand. Take it easy.'

Regan's arms were grazed and cut. A trickle of blood ran from his forehead. 'This is taking up too much time' was my selfish thought, and I decided to start making my own way towards my destination.

I'd made it from the overlook down into a gully, where I lost sight of Spider Rock, though I still knew which direction to follow. It meant a tough, almost vertical climb of about twenty metres, out of the gully on to a stretch of flat rock that sloped down again at an angle of about thirty degrees. I made it to the top of the cliff then took the slope slowly, making sure with each step that my boots had a good grip on the wet granite before I shifted my weight. Every so often I glanced up to check that Spider Rock was still in sight.

'The four winds are blowing,' a spirit voice tells me. A soft, reassuring presence guides me towards the tall red rock. 'Call for the spirit of the hawk to guide you, for he is the surest bird

of prey. Call for the deer, who can endure thirst in the desert, or for the crow, who is swift in flight.'

I look up and see a flock of doves, speckled grey and white in the sunlight. They are high overhead, borne by the wind, brilliant and free.

'I choose Zenaida,' I say. My mourning dove – without a shadow of a doubt.

I was across the smooth slope, crunching through a snowdrift that still lingered in the shadow of an overhang. Spider Rock was to my left, Turner Lake straight ahead.

The lake was still, smooth as a mirror reflecting wispy white clouds. I could make out the straight wall of the dam, even the row of New Dawn cabins and the social centre by the shore.

A cold wind blows. It carries ice and snow. 'Bring me the gift of courage,' I say to my spirit ally, my Zenaida. 'The courage to stand in the blizzard and not to turn back and run from the wolf, or the monster rising from the lake amid the lost and drifting skulls.'

All of a sudden the surface of the frozen lake erupts. The creature's snake-head appears through the splintering ice, then his massive shoulders. Filthy, weed-strewn water spills from him. In his strong arms he carries a corpse.

He rises from the deep, this unnatural creature. He spreads

236

*his dripping wings, offering up the body, raising it over his
black, scaly head.*

It is Conner.

*'He is gone, yet he remains.' Amos's voice rises above the
wind, reminding me.*

*Conner is an offering. A sacrifice. He lies limp in the
monster's outstretched arms.*

*Ice cracks again and a hundred double-headed serpents
appear. They slither towards me.*

'Give me the courage to stand fast!'

*But no – the serpents swarm out of the lake, they grow
huge and tower over me. I am not strong enough.*

Crushed, breathless I turned and ran towards Spider
Rock. I heard members of the Wolf in the Snow band call
after me – first Marta, then Jarrold.

Painfully I dragged air into my lungs, forced my tired
legs onwards over the rough ground scattered with thorn
bushes and yucca.

'Tania, wait!' Jarrold yelled.

I ran. I stumbled towards the tower of pink rock. The
distance was too great, the fear too strong. I stumbled
again, sank to my knees, forced myself up on to my feet
and carried on.

'Stop, Tania. Wait for me.'

I looked over my shoulder and saw that Jarrold was

gaining on me. He was crashing through willow bushes, leaping across the creek. Soon now he would catch me.

I sobbed; I sucked in air. I was on my hands and knees, crawling towards Spider Rock, out of the sun into dark shadow. Jarrold's footsteps were near but I was still ahead when strong hands lifted me.

I looked up and groaned.

The dark brim of a black hat cast a shadow across a stern face, and eyes the colour of columbines – a beautiful cobalt blue – stared down at me.

12

'Drink. Eat,' my dad ordered as soon as Ziegler had driven me home. It's his way of taking care of me.

He fed me and put me to bed under my dreamcatcher, took my ash-covered clothes and threw them into the washing machine. He asked me hardly any questions.

'Angelica is on plane home,' he told me in his gruff, deep voice.

'Good?' I asked from between the sheets.

He nodded. 'That woman.'

'I know. So how's Mom?'

'You know. Hating the hospital, giving nurses hard time.'

'And you?'

'Good,' he insisted. 'Everyone, everything good now you come back safe.'

* * *

I tried to sleep but Ziegler's intense blue stare kept getting in the way.

He'd stooped and picked me up from the ground in the shadow of Spider Rock. He'd led me to his Jeep, instructing Jarrold and Marta to regroup with Blake and Regan and to carry on with their wilderness walk.

'You get no further contact with anyone until midday on Friday,' he'd warned. 'Follow the guiding principles. If you hit any problems, solve them together. You know how it works.'

Maybe I'd expected an argument from Jarrold along the lines of wanting to come back to New Dawn with me the way Channing had done with Holly. But no, he hadn't said a word, just turned and strode away.

Marta had been the one who'd helped me into the Jeep. 'Jeez, Tania,' she'd sighed. 'Are you always this much trouble?' And she'd promised to look me up after her time with the community was over. 'That is, if you want me to.'

'Sure,' I'd said. And I'd given her my phone number.

Ziegler had driven away from the rock and Marta had waved.

'She's a cool kid, considering what she's been through,' Ziegler had commented, glancing in his mirror to check that Jarrold was following orders. But he'd blocked my questions, hadn't given any more Marta facts because of course it was one of the guiding principles not to divulge this stuff.

He did let me see Holly though.

'Your friend is totally fine, recuperating faster than you'd believe,' he'd reassured me as we drove into the parking lot and he opened the passenger door to let me out. 'Come and see for yourself.'

Holly was in the social centre with Channing, Kaylee and Ava. They were playing pool. I'll say that again – Holly, who had been in stage three hypothermia last time I saw her, was smacking the red ball into the corner pocket. There was a log fire blazing in the hearth. Flames reflected in the glass eyes of the bear-rug made him seem alive.

'Hey, Tania!' she greeted me with her old energy, invited me to grab a cue and join in.

'How come you're here? Why aren't you at home?' I asked, under a hostile stare from Kaylee – a look that warned 'Keep your dirty hands off Jarrold – he's mine!'

'Holly didn't want to leave right away,' Channing explained, sticking close to her side. 'She knew we'd take good care of her.'

'And you did.' Holly smiled and planted a kiss on his cheek. She stood with an arm around his waist as Ava played the next shot.

The same old warning siren blared inside my brain: Grace-and-Ezra, Grace-and-Ezra! Holly's jacket and T-shirt had been torn and there was a wall of silence. 'Did you speak with Aaron?'

'Not yet.' She brushed the question aside, smiled up at Channing, who looped his arm around her shoulder.

Click. Ava's cue ball hit another red, which missed the pocket by a mile.

'Maybe you should,' I suggested.

Holly shrugged. 'Why? No one's expecting to hear from me for a couple of days. Meanwhile, chill.'

'Holly!' I couldn't stop myself. I grabbed her by the hand and tugged her to the far side of the hearth. 'What are you doing?'

'What's it look like? I'm playing pool.' Irritated, she shook herself free.

'No!' I grabbed her a second time. 'This isn't what's meant to happen. They were supposed to drive you home, inform your parents, get you checked out at the hospital or something!'

'They didn't. They took care of me here and I'm fine,' she retorted.

'And what's this thing with Channing?' I hissed. He was watching us from a distance, probably trying to lip-read our conversation. Dressed in jeans and a white T, with his close-cropped black hair and amazingly fine North African features, I had to admit that he did fit the babe-magnet picture that Blake and the others had painted.

'Isn't he totally cool?' Holly breathed. A coy smile played on her lips. 'Tania, did you ever see anyone so beautiful?'

'La-la, not interested,' I snapped. 'Listen. Tell me how come Channing let you try out the zip-wire? I thought he was there to take care of everyone in the Hawk band.'

A frown flitted across Holly's face and for the first time I saw her falter.

Click, click. Channing leaned over the table and pocketed a yellow, hardly taking his eyes off us.

'I don't remember exactly,' she murmured. 'I guess I thought it would be fun.'

'Yeah, fun to almost get yourself killed. Think harder. Concentrate. Was Channing involved?'

The frown turned into a bright, superficial smile. 'Let's ask him. Hey, Channing, Tania wants to know what happened with the zip-wire!'

He leaned his cue against the green baize table and came across, stepping right over the bear's stuffed head.

It morphs. It rises to its feet with a terrific snarl, lips drawn

243

back and fangs exposed. It swipes out with curved claws. I
duck sideways. It falls on to all fours, fixes me with its fire-
glint eyes.

'Sure, I'm happy to share with you,' Channing explained, calm as anything. 'Tania, you know better than anyone that no one tells Holly what to do. And she has more energy than anyone I know. So she was up yesterday morning before any of the band, taking pictures on her cell phone camera, getting the idea into her head that if she used the zip-wire to reach the island, she could get some super-cool shots.'

'Not knowing that no one used the wire for years.' Kaylee had come across and joined in the conversation uninvited. 'It was rusted to hell, totally unsafe.'

'Trust me to jump in with my two big feet!' Holly laughed and gave a goofy shrug.

I was short of breath, feeling the pressure and not able to ask her in front of the others if she knew how come her clothes were torn.

'Anyhow, Tania, look at you,' Kaylee mocked. 'You look like you got run over by a truck.'

It was true – I was covered from head to toe in soot, my clothes were wrecked, my arms and hands scratched.

'She fell down a sink hole,' Channing told her.

I shot him a glance. How did he know? Had Ziegler told him? 'Come home with me,' I appealed to Holly.

She sidled closer to Channing, who locked his arm around her waist. 'Not yet,' she murmured. 'You go if you want to, Tania, but I'm staying right here!'

What happened to surge power girl? Where was the strong, independent Holly I knew and loved?

'She's changed,' I told Aaron when we met on Main Street for coffee. Surrounded by everyday sounds – the clatter of coffee cups, the hiss of the espresso machine, I'd had time to fill him in on the latest developments and asked Jude and Grace to join us. 'The same way you did, Grace, when . . . you know.'

'When Zoran's guys did their brainwashing thing on you.' Jude stepped in, knowing how painful it was for her to talk about it. 'They dragged your head into a different space. Nobody could reach you.'

'I guess,' she murmured. She still carried a heavy load of guilt towards Jude because of what she'd put him through.

He held her hand across the table.

'It was so not your fault,' I insisted. 'You have to believe it's all-out war – good versus bad. Evil for its own sake. You and Holly are just collateral damage.'

Grace smiled bravely. 'So what do we do about Holly? We're not the cavalry. We can't just ride in there and rescue her.'

'And in my opinion she's not totally fallen for it – not yet.' Trying to put an optimistic gloss on things, I told them that Holly had pulled through the dazed and confused stage and was halfway back to normal. It was just that I didn't trust Channing, and I especially didn't trust Antony Amos and the whole ethos at New Dawn. 'I had a dream,' I explained. 'You know – a vision. My dark angel appeared.'

'As Amos?' Grace asked. 'But I thought you'd decided against that idea.'

'I was wrong,' I said, pushing away my half-full coffee cup. 'I was so dumb I can't tell you. And he's clever, twisted, really hard to read. I was thinking maybe Ziegler, maybe Jarrold, but definitely not Amos.'

'Let me get this straight.' Aaron hadn't spoken for a while, but he'd been thinking plenty. 'We're into Black Rock territory. Tania, you're psychic so you see this stuff before any of the rest of us?'

'And the dark angels know this,' I agreed. 'It means I'm especially dangerous to them.'

'So why don't they target you instead of Grace or Holly?'

'Good question.' I leaned across the table and spoke to Aaron in a low, urgent voice. 'What you need to understand is something I learned a long time ago from my good angel – that these love-thieves plan to steal as many souls as possible before I can identify them. They trap someone who's deep in love – like Grace with Jude, or Holly with you – and they spin a kind of web around them, mess with their minds, make them fall in love with exactly the wrong person – who of course turns out to be a dark angel in disguise.'

'Then what?' Involuntarily Aaron shuddered and his voice grew quiet.

'So they totally brainwash their victims. It's like an hallucination – you get to believe you can fly, change shape, kick planets around the heavens. You name it, they trick you into thinking you can do it.'

I gasped as suddenly I thought of Holly and the wire. 'That's it! That's what Channing did to Holly. He made her think she could do anything, even fly! She lost her mind, tried it but fell through the ice. Luckily she made it to the island. Afterwards Channing faked the whole thing with the zip-wire.'

'But then what?' Aaron said again.

'They make them fall in love with the dark side; they steal their identity.'

'It's like living a nightmare but ten times worse,' Grace confirmed as her eyelids flickered shut. She took a deep breath, remembering her own experience. 'For a start, you can't wake up to reality. And you'll do anything they ask you to. You go through a ceremony, like a kind of marriage. What's happening is that you're saying you belong to them and there's no going back. They've stolen your soul.'

'And?' Aaron's voice was full of fear for Holly.

'Then they're through with you,' I explained. 'Once your soul is on the dark side, they don't need your body any more.'

'In other words, you die,' Grace added quietly. 'You wander off into the mountains, you freeze to death. Or you jump off a cliff, fall hundreds of metres. You disappear.'

This is where Aaron comes into sharp focus.

Normally he's the quiet guy in the background, the perfect foil to Holly's big personality, but not any more. Now he's Action Man.

He swung out through the doors of the diner dead set on driving straight out to New Dawn, raiding the place and coming back with Holly.

I ran after him, telling him to wait. 'It's not that simple.

You can talk to her all you want but she won't listen to a word you say.'

'I don't care, I'm getting her out of there.' Aaron sprinted to the parking lot, jumped in his car and started the engine.

'They won't let you in,' I warned.

'Show me the prison walls,' Aaron muttered, his jaw set in determined lines. 'Anyone can get in or out if they really want.'

'And if they do let you see her, what are you going to do? Are you going to kidnap her? Believe me – now that they've got Holly and they're inside her head, they won't just let her go.'

Revving the engine, he got ready to back out. 'I'll figure that out when I get there.'

'But this is too dangerous.' Opening the passenger door, I slid in beside him. 'Aaron, you've no idea what these guys are capable of!'

'Yeah, I do, and I'm still going to do it. Are you with me or against me?'

'With you.' His choice was no choice. 'Go ahead, drive.'

Tyres squealed at we left the parking space and headed for the exit. We shot down Main Street, past Grace's house next to the bank, then the hairdresser's and the pharmacy, heading on to the highway that took us to

New Dawn. The windows were open, a wind blasted through the car as we reached fifty then sixty in a forty mph zone.

'I still think we shouldn't be doing this,' I told him. 'We should be taking our time, working out a plan.

Aaron was manic. He didn't take his eyes off the road ahead and his foot stayed hard down on the accelerator. 'There's one thing you don't seem to realize,' he muttered, his arms braced, hands gripping the steering wheel.

'Slow down, please wait.' I heard the faint sound of a siren coming up from behind, growing louder.

'I'd do anything for Holly,' he muttered. 'I love her.'

It broke my heart to hear him. 'Enough to die for her?' He'd be no match for Amos's army of dark angels. Aaron going into New Dawn would be like a Christian being thrown to the lions.

'If I have to,' he said grimly.

We were doing eighty when the speed cops stopped us. They overtook us, lights flashing. They made Aaron pull over on to the hard shoulder.

'Get out of the car.' Cop number one leaned in through the window. The smell of burned rubber drifted in.

Cop number two ordered both of us into the back of their car. It didn't look like it at the time but they'd just done Aaron the biggest favour of his whole life.

'So they busted him for exceeding the limit. They took him to the sheriff's office and called his parents,' I told Orlando on Skype. It was past noon and I was due to drive into Denver to see Mom.

'We're talking about Aaron, right?' he said doubtfully. 'Laid-back, fade-into-the-background Aaron?'

'Yeah. He was scared for Holly,' I explained. But this didn't feel like the time to go into too many details with Orlando, who I was missing like crazy. Now that things were getting tough with Holly and the dark angels, I wanted him with me, holding me without speaking, just touching and kissing and making me feel safe. 'How many hours before I finally get to see you?'

'In the flesh instead of digital? Twenty-four. Twenty-six max. We plan to set off early tomorrow, but it depends on the traffic.'

'I'm counting the minutes.'

'Wait, Tania. Show me your arms.' Orlando was peering into the camera with a puzzled frown as reluctantly I rolled back my sleeves to reveal the cuts and bruises from my fall down the sink hole. 'What happened to you?'

Shoot! I closed my eyes and grimaced. 'I didn't want to talk about it until tomorrow.'

251

'Talk about what.' His hair flopped forward, his eyes narrowed.

'I went on a wilderness walk.' I confessed my guilty secret.

'You volunteered at New Dawn?' He looked totally shocked then fierce. I saw the stubborn shutter come down.

'Yeah. But only for a couple of days.' Make it light, make it seem like nothing.

He stayed angry. 'But we agreed you wouldn't.'

'No, it was you who didn't want me to. I actually said I hadn't made up my mind.'

'Tania, are you crazy?' Orlando leaned back in his chair. 'How could you do that?'

'Don't be mad. Try to see it my way. I have a choice – confront this dark angel thing head-on or keep on running. Well, it turns out I'm tired of running.'

'And you couldn't wait for me?' he demanded, coming close to the camera again. I caught a glimpse of a willowy blonde figure in the doorway behind him, heard some giggling then a deeper voice that must have been Ryan's. Orlando got up, strode across the room and slammed the door. He came back to the desk. 'All along I said you should stay away from Antony Amos,' he reminded me. 'But no – you said he was an OK guy.

There was nothing weird. So you go out there and get involved with a bunch of juvies doing some stupid wilderness therapy and guess what – you come back covered in bruises.'

'Stop,' I told him. 'It was worth it. I found out what I needed to know.'

'Which is?' Behind him, the door opened and Natalie reappeared, hands on skinny hips. She demanded to know why the hell Orlando had slammed the door in her face.

'I'll explain later,' I promised. 'Wait until tomorrow.'

'I can't believe you did this!' he sighed. I knew from his expression how hurt he was.

'Hi, Tania!' Natalie said, putting her chin on Orlando's shoulder. She waved at the camera and gave a lip-gloss smile.

I left a message with Grace that no way should she and Jude let Aaron out of their sight while I drove into Denver to visit Mom. 'Keep him away from New Dawn,' I texted. 'Meet me at six thirty. We'll make a plan.'

When I arrived at the hospital, Mom wasn't in her room. 'She's with her physical therapist,' a nurse explained. 'She'll be through in five minutes.'

'How's she doing?' I asked.

'You must be the daughter?' he checked.

I nodded.

'You look just like her. She's doing great.' He smiled as he replaced a chart on a hook at the foot of her bed. 'Your mom is one interesting lady.'

I picked up on his choice of words. 'Interesting?'

'I can't believe the places she's been – Italy, England, Romania, Russia, China . . .'

'But "interesting"?'

'Let's say, I never met a patient quite like her,' he grinned.

'You mean difficult? Like, she won't do a thing you tell her?'

'I never said that. No, I mean I never saw anyone more determined to make a full recovery than Karen.'

'And will she?' I asked. There were voices in the corridor, the sound of laughter.

'Why not judge for yourself?' the nurse told me.

Mom came into the room in her sky-blue Japanese robe and satin slippers. The wraparound robe was embroidered with silver swallows. She was walking unaided, joking with the therapist. When she saw me she stretched out her right arm. The left hand twitched but stayed by her side.

I winced.

'It'll take time,' Mom said gently when she saw my downcast face. 'But I'll get there in the end, you bet your life.'

I knew Dad was back in Paloma Springs for work so I didn't hurry home. I took my time, made a detour into town and bought myself a new top that I hoped Orlando would like. It was very fitted and turquoise with lace insets around the neckline.

Back at the car, I picked up a text from Grace. 'Come to my house. Jude will bring Aaron.'

'See you there,' I texted back, working out that I had time to go home, take a shower and still be back in town for six thirty. I was deep in thought as I parked in the drive and went into the house.

Thought process number one – how do we persuade Aaron to hold back and not put his own life at risk?

Thought number two – how long can we risk waiting before Holly goes beyond our reach into Amos's dark realm?

Undressing in my room, I turned on the shower and stepped in.

Three – how much was I prepared to tell Orlando about what had happened to me by Turner Lake? OK, I'll give him my surface reasons for joining the River Stone band in the first place – to keep out of my grandmother's way, to shoot footage of the whole wilderness experience. And the big breakthrough – I'll tell him that while I was out there by the frozen lake I had a vision proving that Amos was my dark angel after all.

Jarrold's name won't come into it though. Best leave him out.

The water was hot. I tilted my head and felt it spray over my face. Music was playing on my sound system, sun shining in through the bedroom window. I shampooed my hair; let the conditioner work its silky magic. Then I reached for a towel and stepped outside the cubicle.

Oh God, I jumped out of my skin! Someone was in the house and I suddenly remembered that I'd left the back door unlocked. Heavy footsteps were coming up the stairs towards my room. Clutching the towel round me, I ran to lock my door.

I pushed and met resistance, got thrown back by the force of the door opening, only just managed to keep my balance.

Jarrold walked in wearing his Explorer's padded jacket and hiking boots. His presence seemed to fill the room.

I didn't scream – I hardly ever do that. But my heart was in my mouth. 'Jeez,' I breathed.

'I didn't mean to scare you,' he said, not making any more moves towards me. An intense flame burned in his eyes.

'Well, you did exactly that. What are you doing here?'

'I quit,' he told me, his jaw so tense that he hardly parted his lips to talk. 'I'm out of there, end of story.'

'You left the Wolf in the Snow band?' Water trickled from my wet hair down my face on to my shoulders. 'You're on the run?'

Jarrold nodded. 'I'm sorry, Tania. I shouldn't have come.' He turned to leave.

'No, wait! Are you OK? What happened?'

'I didn't want to be there any more. I hate the place.'

'But what will they do when they find out? Ziegler will go crazy. You can't just walk away – they'll send people to fetch you.'

Now Jarrold took a couple of paces towards me – close enough for me to take in every detail of his broad, handsome face. And his grey eyes still had the desperate look that made me aware that he was on an emotional brink of some kind, that he might suddenly lose control. 'I don't give a crap,' he told me. 'All I know is that I had to come and find you.'

'Jarrold, don't,' I begged. I tried desperately to focus on the fact that I'd gone shopping and bought a special top to please Orlando.

'Ziegler took you and drove you away. I couldn't bear that.'

Breathe, I told myself. Don't get drawn into this. 'It's OK. He brought me home. Everything's cool.'

Jarrold inched forward. 'I had to see for myself.'

My hands were trembling, my flesh tingling. 'You shouldn't be here,' I whispered. He was close enough to kiss me again, unless I found the willpower to step away. I could almost feel the brush of his lips against mine.

My phone lay on the bed. Its ring tone broke what seemed like a never-ending moment.

With a gasp I reached for the phone and answered the call on speakerphone.

'Tania, it's Jean-Luc here.'

Jarrold took a sharp breath, swore and turned away.

'Jean-Luc . . .' I was breathless, totally confused.

'We just got news from Blake to say that they lost Jarrold out by Turner Lake. We pulled in the whole Wolf band.'

'And?' As I spoke I watched Jarrold back away towards the window.

'We think Jarrold might be on his way to your place.'

'Why? Who said?'

'Just a theory. Blake says he's developed a thing

for you. She figures that's where he's headed. Have you seen him?'

Jarrold's eyes were narrowed and fixed on me. He didn't seem to breathe as he waited for my answer.

'No,' I told Jean-Luc. 'He's not here.'

'Ah.' The voice on the phone was disappointed.

Jarrold's eyes gleamed. Was it victory? Was it relief? Or something else I couldn't identify? 'Thank you!' he mouthed.

'We need to find him,' Jean-Luc told me. 'He's broken the basic condition of his stay here at New Dawn. Before he arrived he signs a contract with us to stay for a set period, during which time he's not permitted to leave. If he goes on the run we have to involve the police.'

'I hear you,' I said softly. My throat was dry, my heart hammering against my ribs.

'So if you see him within the next few hours, before we call the cops . . .'

'I'll tell you right away,' I promised.

'Good, Tania. Thank you. Let's speak soon.'

Click. The phone call ended. At the same moment, a car engine cut out at the bottom of the drive and a door slammed shut.

'Aurelie,' Jarrold reported from his position by the window. 'It looks like they sent reinforcements. So where's the walk-in wardrobe for me to hide?'

'This is not funny!' A fresh panic set in now that I'd lied to Jean-Luc. 'Stay here. Let me go down and talk to her.'

Running downstairs, I opened the front door before Aurelie had chance to ring the bell. 'Hey. You're looking for Jarrold?' I gabbled.

She nodded then kissed me on both cheeks – mwah-mwah – and smiled as if this was an ordinary social visit. 'Can I come in?'

Stepping aside to let her pass, I smelled her gorgeous perfume and noted the gold D&G brand on her shades. 'I just spoke to Jean-Luc,' I explained. 'I already told him Jarrold hadn't been here.'

Aurelie paused at the bottom of the stairs and glanced up. 'You're sure?' she quizzed. Then, without waiting for an answer, she walked on into the kitchen and looked around at the coffee cups Mom had brought back from France, the Murano glass fruit bowls, the painted Russian dolls. 'Pretty house.'

'Thanks. Yes, honestly, I haven't seen him.'

'How's your mom?'

'Making progress.'

'Good.' Aurelie didn't miss a thing. She glanced at the Italian coffee machine, picked up a blue and white antique plate and studied the maker's name – Wedgwood. 'How was Jarrold on the wilderness walk?' she asked casually.

'Normal, I guess. You know how he is.'

'Tell me.'

'He doesn't say a whole lot. Well, he couldn't, could he? He was an Outsider.' The more at home Aurelie made herself, the more awkward I grew.

'I didn't pick him out as a guy who would run,' Aurelie mused.

'So what did he do? I mean, when did Blake and the others realize he'd gone?'

'That would be early this morning.' Having finished her survey of the kitchen, she strolled back out into the hall. 'They woke at dawn and he was missing. They had to walk twenty miles back to New Dawn to hand over the information.' She paused at the foot of the stairs and glanced at me shivering in my towel. 'You must want to put on some clothes, Tania.'

'No, it's cool.' I tried but couldn't stop rushing this answer or blushing bright red. So I lurched sideways into a different topic, trying to snatch back the initiative. 'How's Holly doing?'

'Excellently.' Aurelie dazzled me with her white, even smile. 'Well, you saw for yourself.'

'Aaron – her boyfriend – he heard about her and Channing and he's devastated.'

261

'These things happen. He's young. He'll get over it.' She placed her hand on the banister, lightly drumming her slender fingers. 'How would you and Aaron feel about coming to a party on Friday evening?'

Whoosh – she took me by surprise, grabbed back the upper hand. 'At New Dawn?'

'Where else? Jean-Luc is going back to Paris – he said he told you. So this will be his leaving party. We're combining it with Papa's fiftieth birthday.'

'Cool,' I murmured. I was on tenterhooks, listening out for and dreading the slightest sound from Jarrold. 'Can I bring Grace and Jude?'

'It's open house so please bring as many friends as you like,' she said with a smile. She gave the banister a final tap. 'I'm going to miss my twin brother so I want all his friends to be there – to make this party very special for him. You'll come, I hope?'

'For sure.' Leave, please leave! I prayed that she'd believed what I'd said, that Jarrold would stay hidden until she and her car were well out of sight.

'So if Jarrold does try to contact you . . .'

'I'll let you know!'

'Good.' She gave me the mwah-mwah double kiss and another burst of perfume. 'Au revoir, Tania – until tomorrow night.'

I closed the door behind her and raced upstairs. I flung open my bedroom door. There was a note on the bed but no Jarrold – only an open window with the drapes blowing in the breeze.

T, you know how I feel about you, the note said. *I love you and I can't be without you – J x*

13

'What did I do?' I begged Grace to tell me. 'I get this note and I don't know what I did to make it happen.'

'Show me,' she said quietly.

I handed her Jarrold's message written on a yellow Post-it in a surprisingly even, flowing hand.

'"I love you and I can't be without you",' she read. She turned the paper over, examined the sticky strip on the back, turned it over again.

'How did that happen?' I sighed.

We were in Grace's big, open-plan kitchen with maybe ten minutes to spare before Jude and Aaron showed up.

Grace got me a glass of iced water and sat me down at the breakfast bar. 'I have to tell you something, Tania. Knowing you, it's probably not anything *you* did – OK?'

'I gave out the wrong signals,' I argued. 'Guys don't write love letters unless they get the idea you want them to.'

'Sometimes they do. They're blind, or else they misread the signals. Sometimes they're just psychos.'

Ignoring this last remark, I blundered on. 'I did tell Jarrold about Orlando, or I tried to. We were together at the triathlon. Jarrold knows I'm not—'

'Available?' Grace interrupted. 'But that won't always stop psycho-boy. What seeing Orlando on Saturday did in Jarrold's mind was turn the whole of life into a competition where you're the prize. He's the type who has to be a winner.'

'I let him kiss me,' I confessed, my lip trembling.

'Yeah?' She gave me a long look. 'The same way you invited him into your house, into your bedroom while you took a shower?'

'No way! You know I wouldn't do that.'

'Exactly. So cut yourself a little slack, Tania. And remember, this is what they do.'

'"They" meaning the dark angels?'

She nodded. 'You've been here before. Last time it was super-cool Daniel with his party-organizing and his horse-whispering. OK, so Jarrold is a more macho version, but he's basically out there to seduce you and pull you over to their side.'

'I don't know. I can't figure it out.'

'Believe me!' Grace urged. 'Throw the note in with

the trash and forget about Jarrold – the kiss, the whole I-can't-live-without-you histrionics, everything.' The doorbell rang and she set off to answer it, but she stopped in the hallway. 'You do want to forget about him, don't you?'

I took a gulp of water then nodded. 'Totally,' I muttered. Even if she was wrong about Jarrold, I loved Orlando. To show her I meant what I said, I grabbed the note and screwed it into a ball.

I was checking my text messages while Grace brought Jude and Aaron into the kitchen. There was one from Mom, updating me on progress in her latest physical therapy session, another from Orlando saying he was worried about me after our latest Skype session and how we totally had to talk. He signed it with three kisses.

Come home! I thought. Be here now, by my side!

The third message was from Aurelie. 'Sorry, I meant to tell you – theme for tomorrow's party is Native American,' it read. 'No costume – no admittance. See you at seven thirty p.m.'

'Note?' Grace quickly checked with me as the boys took Cokes from the fridge.

'In with the trash,' I confirmed. If only I could screw my doubts and confusions into a ball and throw them away like the note. Or erase the words written on the small yellow page and now firmly lodged in my head. 'T, you know how I feel about you . . .'

'So I say we tell the Randles the whole story,' Jude said as he sat beside me in his grey hooded jacket and black jeans. 'As Holly's parents they're entitled to know what's happening to their daughter out at New Dawn.'

'Then what?' Grace argued. She reminded us she of all people was in the best position to judge how Holly's mind would be working right now. 'Holly is convinced heart and soul that she wants to stay with the community and nobody, especially not her parents, can argue her out of it. Anyway, look what happened when mine tried.'

I remembered the Montroses' doomed visit to Black Rock. They hadn't even got beyond the security gate before Brancusi's security team had used shotguns to blast the air out of their tyres. 'I agree with Grace – I don't think Mr and Mrs Randle can hack it.'

'So let me try,' Aaron said. 'This time I promise I won't break any laws, OK?'

I shook my head and turned to Jude for help. 'He's one guy,' I pointed out. 'And he doesn't know what he's up against.'

'OK, dude, we have to sit down and figure this out.' Jude's analytical brain was what we needed right now. 'Tania's right – you'd have zero chance of getting Holly out of there by just knocking on their door: "Hey, we're here to collect our buddy." So how else can we make it happen?'

'We could wait until tomorrow night.' With a bad feeling screwing up the pit of my stomach, I threw in the new factor that changed the whole equation.

'Why? What's happening tomorrow night?' Grace spoke and all three looked to me to clear up the mystery.

'A party. To celebrate Amos's fiftieth birthday and Jean-Luc's leaving.'

'You have an invite?' Jude asked.

'Me and you, Aaron,' I confirmed. 'In fact, Aurelie said to bring as many friends as I liked.'

I hear the drumming of a hundred hooves over dry earth, a cloud of dust, buffalos with heads down and galloping, driven to the cliff top, kettled and forced over the edge. Running in blind panic, falling to their deaths.

'No, forget that,' I said to Grace, Jude and Aaron as my skin suddenly began to crawl. 'It's a really bad idea. I don't think we should go.'

It's like forest fire – set a spark to dry grass and let the wind get at it, drop one single cigarette butt in a fire hazard area and the whole mountainside goes

268

up in flames – shrubs, thorn bushes, junipers, pinon pines.

'We're going to the party,' Aaron had decided. Like a force of nature, he'd dragged the time and place out of me, made the others promise to be there too.

'Then what?' Jude had asked, always the cautious one, the planner.

'Then we hijack Holly out of there. No talkie-talkie-nicey-nicey, no trying to persuade her – we just grab her and get her out.'

'Yeah, right,' Grace had sighed. How many X-Men movies had Aaron watched lately, she'd wanted to know.

'So what's your idea?' he'd countered.

We didn't have one, we'd admitted. It had to be the party – in the end we'd all agreed.

I drove home from Grace's house with the buffalos still on my mind, competing for my attention with Jarrold on the run. I was in the usual inside-your-car bubble, cut off from what was going on in the streets, barely noticing a change of lights from green to red when I glanced in my mirror to see a guy on a Harley pull up behind me, way too close. His visor covered his face, but there was something familiar . . .

The lights changed, the Harley guy swerved wide and overtook me on the junction, glancing over his shoulder as he picked up speed.

'Costume!' Grace's text reminded me after I'd driven up Becker Hill and pulled up in my drive. 'You need to go Native American and if Orlando plans to come along, so does he!'

'Will get on to it,' I texted back with a pressure around my heart. It was only when I got inside the house and turned on the TV for background noise that I recognized the oppressive sensation. Call it reluctance about the party. Heighten that and it grows into dread. Yeah, big-time dread was what I felt.

The sun went down that night in a spectacular blaze of red. You could almost see it melt on to the black horizon.

I sat in the garden, comforted by the call of Zenaida in the tree above my head. She perched high up, raised her tail and ducked her head forward, shuffled her pink feet along the silver branch.

'Jarrold – good or bad? Dark or light?' I mused without expecting an answer. I tried Jude's method of applying logic. I was thinking hard, building up the negative column. He's New Dawn, so he has to be in with the dark angels. He's arrogant, he keeps secrets. Grace called him a psycho and compared him with Brancusi's henchman, Daniel, which makes him covert, manipulative, dangerous. Maybe he even killed a guy in the lake. Dark side – no contest. Zenaida sat on her branch puffing out her grey chest feathers to keep out the cold. She prepared for the night.

On the positive side, Jarrold had saved my life. This was a biggie. I recalled how he'd lowered himself down the sink hole, risked death to save me. He'd written me a note to say he loved me. Besides, it was clear from the start that Jarrold didn't follow the New Dawn rules. He was an Outsider. And now he'd gone on the run.

Zenaida called softly through the falling darkness. The very last leaves fell from the aspen trees and settled around my feet.

'That must mean he's on our side,' I murmured, looking up. Jarrold was a foot soldier for the angels of light.

There was silence from above.

'Eat,' Dad said. He'd made breakfast of blueberry pancakes before he set out for work. 'Tania, you hear?'

'Yeah, thanks but no thanks.' My stomach was churning so badly that I would definitely throw up if I tried a single bite.

'Too strung out?' He took away the plate, tried me with a glass of milk instead.

'All good when Orlando gets here,' he promised. 'How long now?'

'A few hours.'

Dad picked up his car keys. 'You'll call me?'

I nodded.

'I worry until I hear.'

'I'll text.'

'All good,' he said again as he left the house for Paloma Springs.

I filled in the gap before lunchtime by buying stuff from the art shop to create costumes for Friday's party – beads, feathers, some soft suede material, fabric dyes, et cetera. Then I worked in the garage which Dad had converted into my studio, complete with easels and a large table where I stretched canvases and made silk-screen frames for printing. I played music as I worked – which is why I didn't hear the sound of the motorbike coming up the hill and I only noticed my visitor when he was actually standing in the studio doorway, shiny black helmet under his arm.

'Jarrold, don't do that!' I almost staggered under the weight of the shock when I finally saw him, recognized the broad face and square jaw, the Viking locks.

'Did you get my note?' he asked.

'Yes. Stay where you are. Don't come any closer.'

'What I said is true,' he insisted. 'I can't get you out of my mind, Tania. I had to come.'

'Are you even listening to me?' I'd been working with a craft knife and I kept it in my hand as I advanced towards him. 'You can't keep on showing up like this. Just turn round and leave.'

His gaze didn't falter. 'Give me a reason.'

'One – I didn't invite you. Two – I promised Aurelie I'd tell her where you were if I found out. Three – my boyfriend will be here any minute. How many reasons do you need?'

'You didn't give me the one that matters,' he said, looking steadily at me and reaching out for the knife.

I glanced down at my hand, surprised it was there, not resisting when Jarrold took it from me and put it down beside his helmet on the table.

'Tania, the only way I'd walk away and never come back is if you told me you didn't love me.'

It happened again – he walked all over my reasons, trampled them into the dirt. He was standing close enough for me to read the passion in his eyes.

'Tell me you don't love me,' he whispered.

I shaped the words, had them on the tip of my tongue, in spite of the way he drew me in and made my heart hammer, my palms sweat.

He didn't wait for me to speak. He reached for me and put his arms around me. His lips were on mine. I felt his warm breath, his tongue, his fingertips on my cheek, his eyes searching my soul.

'Say it!' he whispered through smiling lips.

He was tall, strong. His physicality overpowered me.

He felt me submit. 'You do love me, don't you?'

A breeze blew in through the studio door. Over Jarrold's shoulder I caught sight of two thin white trails from jet planes criss-crossing an immense blue sky, and in the garden a grey dove rose from a tree.

'You have to go,' I told Jarrold, somehow finding the strength to push him away though my skin, my lips, maybe my heart wanted him to stay.

His eyelids drooped, his thick lashes brushed my cheek as he pulled back.

'This doesn't alter anything,' he said softly. 'My feelings for you don't change.'

'Go,' I sighed.

I couldn't watch him leave, just turned away and heard his footsteps retreat. When I risked a glance over my shoulder, I saw that he'd left his helmet on the table. Instinctively I ran after him.

He stopped, waited.

'You forgot this,' I told him, handing over his helmet

and watching the sudden glint of victory in his eyes fade.

He left, this time for real. He climbed on to his bike, started the engine, lurched from the sidewalk into the street, sped away.

Ten minutes later, Orlando's truck pulled up in the space Jarrold had vacated.

We were in my room. I was lying on my bed, watching Orlando in the shower. His head was tilted back, he was turned away. His beautiful body glistened as white foam washed away. When he reached out of the cubicle for a towel, I was there to hand it to him.

He grinned then shook his head, spraying me with droplets from his wet hair.

'Hey!' I twisted the control to turn on fresh jets, pushed him back under the shower and let him drag me with him. Together we felt sharp needles prickle our skin. We kissed with wet lips, together again.

I was with Orlando, filled with warm joy, relief, thankfulness. The dread of my dark angel had eased.

'I don't know what happens inside my head,' he confessed when we were dressed and sitting in the kitchen. 'I just have to look at you and my brain turns to mush. All I want is you – I can never get enough.'

'Mush – is that good or bad?' The pizza in the oven

smelled great. We were both hungry and totally happy. 'It doesn't *sound* good!'

'It's you're fault – you're so beautiful.'

'So good.' I decided with a smile. I took out the pizza, sliced it and put it on the table.

'Especially naked,' he added with an exaggerated sigh.

'I hear you.' Leaning over his shoulder as I put down the plate, I kissed him.

'So if we want to have a serious conversation we have to stay fully clothed.'

'Seriously – do we have to?'

'Eventually, I guess.' We were both smiling and laughing, I was giving him small kisses on his cheek and neck.

'So you think we should talk?'

'You're the one who texted to say that, remember.'

'I was worried about you – about *us*,' he said hesitantly. Then he stopped kissing me back and narrowed his eyes. 'Should I be?'

'I don't know.' I sighed as straight away I thought of Blondie always in the background when we Skyped and of Jarrold's lips so recently on mine. Deflecting this last image, I turned it back on Orlando. 'Should you?'

Orlando gave an irritated shake of his head. 'We don't need to do this.'

'What don't we need to do?'

'Play these games. Don't you see the pattern – we get close then we start to pick-pick-pick at each other. Why do we do that?'

'I'm not picking.' My stubborn shield was up. I wasn't behaving well.

'OK then. We put up barriers.' He stood and walked out through French windows into the garden where the bare trees stood stark against a heavy grey sky. 'We have to get through this, Tania. We have to say what we really mean.'

Following him out, I stood beside him. I didn't feel edgy or scared but for some reason incredibly sad. When he next looked at me I was crying.

'I love you.' He whispered our mantra as he pushed stray locks from my face. 'And I'm sorry.'

'What for?'

'For whatever it is I do.'

'You don't do anything. I do it to myself.'

'When we're not together I get incredibly insecure,' he confessed. 'That's why I put too much pressure on you to come with me to Dallas.'

I was shocked. Why would this gorgeous guy feel this way? No way would you look at him and think Orlando was anything except gifted, confident, relaxed in his own skin. But love does this to a person – it makes you fly and fall, soar and plummet. 'It's OK, I understand.'

'You do?' He pushed on, determined to get through a list of things he'd prepared in his head. 'I adore you, Tania, and I put you up there on a pedestal. But sometimes I don't listen when things get tough for you. Like now.'

I nodded. 'Tell me about Natalie,' I said suddenly.

He blinked and jerked his head back. 'Natalie?'

'Yeah – gorgeous, funny, flirty Natalie.'

Orlando began to laugh then stopped himself. 'Whoa!'

Screwing my eyes tight shut, I groaned. 'I know. I shouldn't have said that.' What an idiot.

'Natalie's not my type. You are.' Lots more kisses, lots of tender smiles.

Slowly we were hugging and talking ourselves into a good, safe space. I felt braver. 'There's this guy called Jarrold,' I told him.

My God, it was like I'd flicked a switch. The smiles vanished.

I grabbed Orlando's hand to stop him pulling away. 'We're being honest – yeah? He was one of the triathletes – the one who tried to save Conner Steben, remember?'

'I know who he is. Don't tell me – he was in your

278

group when you did the stupid hike and almost got yourself killed.'

'That "stupid hike" told me everything I needed to know about Antony Amos,' I reminded him. 'Now I know who my enemy is, and it's not Jarrold, believe me.'

'Yeah, just like it wasn't Amos until a couple of days back.'

Our straight talking had run out of control. We were smack back into the paranoid blame-game. 'Listen to me,' I begged. 'We've got to work together on this. It's Holly we have to think about.'

'So tell me about Jarrold,' Orlando said, ignoring me and speaking through gritted teeth.

'What do you want to know? His lousy parents dumped him with his grandparents when he was a little kid. His dad died. He got into bad shit, ended up at New Dawn.'

'Not that,' he said angrily. 'What do I care about this guy's life story? Come on, Tania – tell me what I need to know.'

I looked up at the sky and felt cold drops of rain on my face. 'He's on the run,' I whispered. 'He says he's in love with me.'

My friend Grace found me in tiny, tear-stained pieces

and scooped me up. She came when I called her, after Orlando had stormed out of the house. She drove me straight into town, to his parents' place.

'Man!' she sighed. 'As if we don't have enough problems to solve!'

'I know – I was stupid. I was trying to be honest.'

'There's honest and then there's honest.' She pulled into a McDonald's drive-by to straighten me out. 'Tania, you're not stupid. Will you stop beating yourself up?'

I looked at her through teary eyes. 'Orlando – what if I've lost him?'

'Then you've lost him,' she confirmed quietly. 'And there'll be a good reason for it to end. But until we know for sure, no post-mortems, huh?'

She drove on through town, through the cold rain.

There was no truck in the Nolans' driveway, no sign of life in the small town house next to the wooden Baptist church on the corner of West Amherst Street and Independence Avenue.

I imagined Orlando storming away from Becker Hill, driving into the mountains, staying away all day.

'You guys,' Grace sighed, parking and tapping the wheel with her pearly-pink nails. 'Did you get around to telling him about the party tomorrow night?'

I shook my head then tried my best to focus on something else. 'Did Aaron hear from Holly?'

'Negative.'

'So how's he doing?'

'Jude is with him. That's all I know.'

As we sat and talked, a couple of cars turned slowly into Orlando's road then a cab dropped off a woman in the church parking lot. Three Harleys coasted along Independence Avenue. Their long-haired riders wore bandannas, fringed leather vests and T-shirts, even in the rain.

'What?' Grace asked when she saw me start at the sound of the engines then turn to look.

'Jarrold got hold of a Harley,' I muttered.

'And now he's stalking you?'

'No. I don't know.' This was total misery – sitting in the rain waiting for Orlando to show up and tell me we were through.

At last his truck turned into West Amherst Street. It splashed through puddles, up on to his drive. As he opened his door, he spotted me sitting in the passenger seat of Grace's car.

'Go!' She ordered me out. 'I'm here if you need me.'

Orlando was on the sidewalk, heading our way. He was without a jacket and already soaking wet, looking wildly angry. Hardly knowing where I was, I stepped out to meet him.

'What does this freaking guy mean, he loves you?' he demanded. 'How did he get to that?'

'Don't be mad.'

'Give me a reason why not,' he stormed. The drive hadn't cooled his temper, but at least he wasn't walking away. We both stood on the sidewalk, being rained on. 'How long has he known you, Tania? Did you tell him about you and me? Really – how well does he know you?'

'I did tell him about us, I said for him to leave. Listen, I only felt sorry for him – losing his parents, living how he did with his grandparents. And I knew it was tough for him at New Dawn.'

Orlando put up both hands as a shield. 'I already told you I don't want to hear that. I don't care about any of that crap.'

'Sorry.' I nodded and fell silent. 'Tell me what I can do to make this better?'

He closed his eyes, walked halfway up the drive and spoke from there. 'I wasn't the one who wanted us to be apart, remember.'

My heart sank as we went round in circles. 'I didn't *want* it,' I told him. 'You're in Dallas, I'm in Europe. It's the deal. It's the way it is right now.'

'I was here for you when your mom was ill.'

'Don't, Orlando. I can't feel any more guilty than I already do.'

'What exactly do you have to feel guilty about?' He was striding down the slope towards me for what felt like a final showdown. 'Jarrold says he loves you – big deal. You told him to back off. I hear you. But I still want to know – do you feel anything for him?'

The rain beat down and my whole world was shaking. A tidal wave of fear washed over me as my heart was squeezed and I grew short of breath. 'I love you,' I told Orlando. 'No one else matters to me the way you do.'

I'm sinking down into the depths again, cold and alone amongst those church steeples with only ghosts from the past to keep me company.

Orlando stared at me through the rain. He blinked once then spoke in a flat, empty voice. 'You're soaking wet. Come inside the house.'

I don't know how long we sat in his room and talked. Talking and talking – no touching, no hugging or kissing, but we got through the jealousy and blame and at last made everything OK. He loved me, I loved him. Nothing else mattered. Finally Grace knocked at the door to remind us she was still there. She told me later that she could tell in a nanosecond that the stress was over and that everything was good between Orlando and me.

She wanted to leave us together but we pulled her in, dried her off, sat her down and gave her coffee.

'Thank you for being my friend,' I told her.

'Thank God I was in when you called me,' she replied. 'I should've already left for Melrose but I forgot the time.'

'What's in Melrose?' Orlando asked. He sat next to me on the couch, leaning back exhausted as if he'd run a marathon.

'My mom. She's visiting my aunt. I planned to join them for supper.'

'You're hungry!' I realized, looking at my watch and seeing that it was already five thirty.

'No. I called a rain check. I want to hook up with Jude and Aaron instead. But before I leave, we need to talk about the party.'

'Costumes?' I asked.

'And transport. Who'll drive, how many cars and all that stuff.'

'What party?' Orlando interrupted before we could get any further.

Quickly we filled Orlando in on Holly's situation and made him see how serious it was.

'But the party – do we have to go?' Orlando protested.

'If this guy Jarrold is going to be there, I don't want to know.'

'He won't be,' I promised. Even if they called the cops and found him, no way would he be allowed to join the celebration.

'Anyway, how else do we get to Holly?' Grace pointed out. 'Believe me, we've been through the options and this is the only choice we have.'

'Plus, time is running out.' I laid it on the line. 'She met a guy called Channing and she thinks she's in love. You know how the dark angels do it. They start by flattering their victims, making them feel special. Pretty soon it moves into brainwashing. Then they control every thought. That's how it is with Holly. Now she won't make a move without him. Her head's totally gone. It's tragic.'

'Seriously,' Grace agreed with a sigh. 'Which is why Tania has to be right about Antony Amos. He's definitely the force behind this.'

'My dark angel,' I whispered.

They both looked at me and waited for more. But the words settled into a silent room. Dark angel, stealer of souls, tormentor. Hideous creature who shape-shifts and dazzles, who leads his army through the dark heavens and plots his revenge. We didn't need to say any of this out loud – Grace, Orlando or I. We all remembered it too well.

'I'll be there,' Orlando promised in the end. We'd agreed details about the next night – Jude would drive Aaron and Grace to New Dawn, while I took my own car with Orlando to keep me company. He made his promise to stay by my side as he drove me home.

'So how far would you go to rescue me?' Keeping it light, I started to kid around. 'Would you break a speed limit? Would you drive through a red light?'

'All of that,' he promised.

I upped the stakes. 'Would you swim a white-water river?'

'For sure.' Turning up on to Becker Hill, Orlando got serious again. 'But don't rely on me to stay cool if this Jarrold guy does show up at the party.'

'He won't. I mean, there's no way. Even if they catch him, Ziegler will slap another Outsider status on him.'

'OK, so get some sleep.' Orlando pulled up in my driveway behind Dad's car. He kissed me briefly.

'We're cool?' I checked.

He nodded and kissed me again. 'Let's get through tomorrow night. Once we grab Holly and get her out of there, we can relax.'

'Totally,' I murmured.

'Promise?'

'Back to normal.' Mom getting better, me and Orlando loved up . . . I put all my energy into believing that everything would work out. 'Sleep well.' I sighed as I got out of the truck, stood in the headlight beam and blew him a kiss.

I went into the house, chatted with my dad, went into the studio and put some finishing touches to the party costumes.

At nine thirty Dad put his head around the door. 'I'm pooped,' he yawned.

'So go to bed,' I told him.

'OK. Don't stay up late.'

'I won't. Go!'

He yawned again then said goodnight.

For his sake I turned down the volume on my sound system, snipped and clipped some more, finally held my costume up and checked it out in a full-length mirror.

The suede skirt was long and fringed, the black tunic was knotted at one shoulder, leaving the other bare. I'd decorated it with white and red beads.

Gazing into the mirror, I heard a thousand voices on the wind.

'My fathers are warriors,' the woman with black, braided hair says. 'My son is a warrior. And the Great Spirit rules us.'

I hear loss, I hear the cries of battle.

'The land is ours, the air we breathe belongs to our people, the clouds above, the mountains below and the great lake at my feet.'

She stands alone in the mist.

I see men on horseback, soldiers with blue jackets. The riders wield tomahawks against rifles. The guns spark and fire. Her people lie dying.

She is alone, wrapped in a red shawl. She weeps.

I looked into the mirror and saw not mine but the woman's reflection. I gasped and flung the costume to one side.

Music still played. Above the drumbeat I heard the sound of a motor bike. Or did I? Holding my breath, I went to the door, opened it and looked down the hill. The street was quiet.

It was time to turn off the studio lights and go to bed. There was a moment of total darkness and again I imagined the roar of Jarrold's bike. But it wasn't real, I insisted, convincing myself that after recent events I was even more easily spooked than normal. I headed upstairs to my room, where the bedside light was switched on.

I undressed, washed my face and rubbed in

moisturizer, brushed my teeth. When I came out of the bathroom, the bulb was flickering – on-off, on-off. I sat on the bed to test the switch.

Click. Total darkness. Wolf man roars in through the window. He shatters glass, bursts out of the night, fills my room with his stench. His eyes glitter, he curls back his lips and shows his fangs.

He pounces and I fall back, feel the sting of his claws slashing and ripping into my flesh. I am in his arms, he bounds away. He carries me across mountains, leaps onto the island in the middle of the lake. I am lost.

14

Next morning, the day of the New Dawn party, I hurried to get dressed and leave the already empty house. Taking Orlando's costume with me, I drove into town.

I'd reached the lights on the junction beside the McDonald's drive-in where Grace had stopped the day before. It stood next to a Mexican restaurant whose shutters were down and a faded realtor's For Sale notice hung off a post by the entrance. A rusted steel barrier kept cars out of the disused parking lot.

The whole place was deserted. You could picture tumbleweed blowing across the pitted tarmac, blues guitar, a long road through the desert.

The lights changed and I was about to drive on by when I saw the Harley in the disused parking lot, standing amongst the discarded plastic bags, empty Coke cans and weeds. I heard a vehicle come up fast from behind then I spotted Jarrold using his cell phone in the entrance to the disused restaurant. He glanced up, saw me and then, before I knew it, a Jeep had overtaken me. Quick as a flash, Jarrold saw the Jeep and ran from the doorway. He sprinted for his bike.

The Jeep swerved across the oncoming traffic. It crashed through the steel barrier, drove right at the Harley. Jarrold threw himself clear as the bike bounced off the car's fender, skidded across the tarmac, into the building. Metal scraped, glass shattered but Jarrold was still on his feet, sprinting towards the traffic jam where I sat.

I saw now that it was Ziegler in his trademark hat at the wheel of the Jeep. Channing sat beside him, arms braced against the control panel.

'Watch out!' I yelled at Jarrold as they skidded and turned on two wheels.

Jarrold jumped the wrecked barrier, got to within ten strides of my car before Ziegler burst out of the parking lot and across the stream of traffic. Again he screeched to a halt and Channing jumped out. Car horns blared, a silver Ford inched forward and cut Jarrold off. Jarrold didn't have chance to stop. Instead, he flung himself across the Ford's hood, scrambled down and had almost made it to my car when Channing threw himself forward and pinned him to the ground.

People jumped out of their cars. Someone yelled to check the kid didn't have a gun or a knife. A cab driver dialled nine-one-one.

Jarrold fought back. He kicked and rolled away from a punch that Channing was about to land, was almost up off the ground when Ziegler arrived and kicked him in the stomach. Jarrold groaned and fell back to the ground. Ziegler stamped on his arm, pinned him down and waited for Jarrold to stop resisting, for his body to go limp.

A crowd of fifteen to twenty people watched Ziegler and Channing jerk Jarrold to his feet. The victim's lip was swollen, there was a cut oozing blood under his left eye. He raised his head as his captors led him away. He looked right at me.

What did I see in his eyes? What was he trying to tell me as they dragged him into the New Dawn Jeep?

I didn't have time to decide. They were in the car, reversing into the empty lot, out again on to the highway and speeding away even before the cops arrived.

'You just missed him,' Orlando's mom, Carly, told me when I finally arrived at West Amherst Street. 'Are you OK, Tania? Would you like a drink of water?'

'No, I'm cool, thanks.'

'You look a little pale. Are you sure you don't need a drink?'

'Where did Orlando go?'

'To the mall – the book shop, I think. Tania, you're shivering.'

'I'm good.' Hurrying back to my car, I set off after Orlando. Stay calm, I told myself. Don't overreact – Ziegler was only doing his job.

I remembered how he'd crunched Jarrold's Harley against the wall, the cold, cruel look in his blue eyes when he'd stamped on Jarrold's arm as he lay on the tarmac. Ziegler wasn't a guy to show mercy, I realized.

And now Jarrold was back at New Dawn, a prisoner again.

'It's a good thing,' Grace insisted when I called her en route to the mall. 'Your psycho stalker/potential dark angel is safely off the scene.'

'Yes, but—'

'No buts, Tania. Forget Jarrold, focus on Holly – OK?'

It was good advice and I tried as usual to follow it, tracking down Orlando's truck parked outside the book shop and going into the store to find him in the theatre history section. He was standing by the early twentieth-century shelves, thumbing through a book on Diaghilev. I kissed him and tried to act as if nothing had happened.

'What's wrong?' he said straight away. I swear, when it comes to picking up signals about my mindset, he has my kind of super-sensitivity. I guess that's what having a soul mate is all about.

'Nothing. I brought your party costume.'

'Show me.' Putting down the book, he followed me out of the store.

'I decided to go down the Navajo route,' I explained, pulling a striped blue tunic and matching bandanna out of my trunk. 'We still need a belt, beads, maybe suede boots.'

'Your hands are shaking,' Orlando noticed.

'I figured we'd get beads from the art shop.' I took a deep breath and walked on down the mall. 'Fake coral and silver. That would look good with the blue.'

Catching up with me, he took my hand. 'Chill,' he told me. 'I know you're stressed about tonight, but I'm here. I'll take care of you.'

'Thanks.' I stopped by the door of Artworks, breathed again then smiled. God, how good did that last sentence sound! 'Tell me again.'

'I'll take care of you,' he promised, whispering in my ear.

So good! 'What do you say we buy the beads and head back to my place – yeah?' I asked.

Orlando grinned and nodded.

I was almost over the shock of Jarrold's recapture, browsing with Orlando through the bead section when we bumped into Aurelie.

'Hey!' she said across the stacked units of multi-coloured boxes. 'Tania, what a pleasant surprise.'

'Sur-preeze' was how she said it, to rhyme with 'breeze'. And she smiled at me with real pleasure, came round to our side of the units and began to chat.

'I am so bad,' she sighed, fluttering her dark eyelashes, using lots of delicate hand gestures. 'My own costume for the party – I left it so late!'

'Wow!' In my head I heard Orlando saying this. Any red-blooded guy would, the first time they met Aurelie – so dainty and feminine, so stylish. Today she was dressed in black loafers, narrow black pants and a short red woollen jacket so beautifully cut and tailored that I knew it must have come from Paris and cost a fortune. She wore coordinating silver and red earrings and a cream scarf intricately twisted and wound around her neck.

'I always do this,' she confessed. 'I arrange everything for Papa and Jean-Luc, and never have time for myself.'

'Costumes – that's why we're here too,' I mumbled. 'Aurelie, you remember Orlando? Orlando – Aurelie.'

They shook hands but there was no European kissing. The eye contact was direct, the lips were smiling.

'Orlando came back for the weekend,' I explained. Is it OK if I bring him along to the party?'

'Please – you don't even have to ask!' she protested with wrist-flicking gestures. 'Orlando, Tania is a tough cookie – is that how you say it? She volunteered and went wild walking this week with the River Stone band. I expect you already know this. But did she tell you how she helped to rescue her friend Holly.' Still the eye contact, the lip-gloss smile.

'Yeah, we're kind of worried about Holly,' Orlando replied. I was glad that he hadn't totally fallen under Aurelie's spell – he seemed cagey, as if he was testing her out. 'Hypothermia is bad. People can die.'

'But of course at New Dawn we have a professional back-up team,' she assured him. 'Mountain rescue, paramedics – everything is in place. Holly is fine, believe me. In fact, she had such a good time with her band that she stayed on in one of the cabins. She'll be at the party tonight.'

'Cool. So will Aaron – he'll be there,' Orlando said extra slowly, waiting for a reaction from Aurelie but giving none himself.

'Aaron?' She repeated the name with a puzzled pout.

Orlando helped her out. 'Holly's boyfriend.'

'Ah!' Aurelie turned to me. 'The ex. So he will need a costume.'

I nodded. 'No problem – we already fixed that.' At least, I hoped Grace had thought of it.

Aurelie's brow creased into a small frown as she took me by the arm and led me a little way down the aisle. 'Tania, do Holly a favour. Tell this boy – Aaron – that she met somebody on her wilderness walk, that maybe things are not the same between her and him.'

I stared back at her. 'You want me to warn Aaron about Channing?'

She nodded then sighed. 'It's so important to avoid a scene at the party, don't you think? For Papa's sake. For Jean-Luc.'

'Aaron will want to be there,' I insisted quietly.

'Jean-Luc,' she repeated, switching back to a smile, but this time a sad one. 'I will miss my brother so much, *n'est ce pas?*'

End of conversation. We said our goodbyes, made our air kisses, went our separate ways.

'What did you think?' I asked Orlando when I was sure Aurelie was out of range. 'Did you see how she smoothed over the whole Holly accident thing like it was nothing? And now she wants Aaron out of the picture to make it easier for Channing.'

'Yeah,' he said thoughtfully.

'Don't tell me – you fell for it,' I groaned. The accent, the haircut, the gorgeous perfume.

'I don't know. I haven't figured her out.'

'But she makes a big impression, huh?'

'Sssh!' He nudged me and pointed to Aurelie catwalk-gliding back down the aisle, this time with Antony Amos in tow.

'Tania, Papa wished to meet Orlando before the party tonight,' she called, loud enough for heads to turn, for people to recognize the local celeb and be drawn towards us.

I felt myself shiver, waited for the vision of dark wings spreading over me, of the creature emerging from the lake.

Amos smiled at everyone in the store, shook hands, kept on coming. 'Hey, Tania,' he said, greeting me with a warm smile. 'Why don't you introduce me to your boyfriend and let me tell him more about our volunteer programme?'

Come on, wings! I thought. I never thought I would say this, but I actually wanted the monster to appear, to prove my dark angel theory. And if not the creature from the lake, at least wolf man lurking in the forest, bursting out from behind a tree, jaws snapping. *Where are you, demons?*

Nothing as Orlando shook hands with Antony Amos, even though my psychic sensors were on red alert.

I've said before, Amos has a way about him that you didn't say no to – a lifetime as a movie director created that, I guess. And a natural confidence in the way he walks up to you and shakes you by the hand, an acceptance that people will stare and admire, be drawn in to his point of view.

For the first time I pictured him as a young guy without the wrinkles and the white hair, when he could have had any beautiful girl he wanted, with his intelligent brown eyes staring at you, somehow asking you to share a joke that you didn't quite understand, but soon would if you got to know him.

Here in Artworks, amongst the tubes of paint, brushes and canvases I was still waiting for my dark angel to descend and for a warning from Zenaida. What happened? Really – where were they?

Orlando shook Amos by the hand, called him 'sir' and said how much he admired his movies.

The great man accepted the praise then turned to me, stooping slightly to confide something. 'We have news. Aurelie received the autopsy report and it finally confirmed that Conner died of natural causes. He had an undeclared cardiac condition. No further investigation is necessary.'

I frowned at the word 'undeclared'. If the kids in the camp had known about Conner's heart problem, how could Ziegler, Amos and the rest claim that it was not on his medical record?

'That's good, Tania,' Aurelie pointed out sweetly. 'Jarrold was not to blame.'

Noticing Orlando's knee-jerk react to the mention of Jarrold's name, I cleared my throat and tried to think of a neutral comment.

'Oh, speaking of Jarrold,' Amos jumped in before me, twisting the knife in Orlando's gut. 'One hundred per cent good news as far as he goes.'

'Why? What happened?' Again Orlando was over-quick to react, shooting a glance at me as he stepped in between us.

'We got him back!' Amos exclaimed. 'Richard found him hiding out and sleeping rough in a disused building. He and Channing took him home to New Dawn. Jarrold will re-sign his contract and stay with us a little longer than we originally planned.'

'You already knew that!' Orlando and I sat in his truck

after Amos and Aurelie had left. He was back to being my judge and jury. 'I can tell by the way you reacted – you knew they'd got the guy!'

'So what if I did? I guessed how you'd be if you found out I was there.' Exactly like this – suspicious and jealous again, ready to blame me for something I hadn't done, as if we'd never had the talk at his house.

My last comment slowed Orlando down. 'You were there?' he echoed.

'Freak coincidence,' I shrugged. 'On my way to your house. Ziegler and Channing – they were pretty rough with Jarrold.'

'He's a dangerous guy. They wouldn't want to take any chances.'

'No, for sure.'

'And Amos and Aurelie – they said it all worked out.'

'Meaning, they're happy he's signed up with them for more wild-walking.'

Amos had said there would be an extension to Jarrold's stay at New Dawn, but he didn't say by how much. 'Jarrold will be ecstatic,' I added with a frown.

'Yeah well, don't sound so sarcastic,' Orlando told me. 'Actually I was surprised back there. He wasn't how I expected.'

'Who – Amos?' No way as surprised as I was, I thought.

I still couldn't figure out why I wasn't getting my visions when my vengeful dark angel was around. No shape-shifting, no levitating, no animation of objects – none of the things I'd grown to expect. 'He's clever,' I conceded. Probably skilful enough to block the visions once he realized that I'd pinned him down as my dark angel.

'Yeah. He was impressive, actually.'

'On the surface,' I muttered.

'I'm still not saying I approve the methods they use at New Dawn. You hear too many bad things about boot camps.'

'This isn't a boot camp.'

'Did you hear about the place in Florida – Bay County? They were doing some kind of military drill and a fourteen-year-old kid died.'

'New Dawn is not a boot camp,' I repeated.

'No, but look what happened to Connor Steben. I don't care about exact types of camp – a kid dying is a kid dying.'

'Even so, you were impressed by Amos?'

'Hmm.' Orlando shrugged. 'Interesting, huh?'

We sat without talking, each thinking our own thoughts. Personally, I was still troubled by the lack of monsters, trying to work out exactly how Amos had thrown me off track, getting more and more scared by the power of his mind-control games.

'They predicted more snow,' Orlando said at last, 'coming in from the north west. Winds of 70mph.'

'Well, thanks, Mister Weatherman.'

'I'm only saying. Let's use my truck later.'

'Not my car?'

'In case we get stuck in snow. And I'll tell Jude to drive his Jeep.'

'Cool.' I nodded, kissed his cheek and climbed out of the truck. '6.30, my place,' I said.

It turned out the costumes were fun.

'Check this out!' Grace cried in the living room at her place. She twirled around in a long red skirt gathered in tiny pleats at the waist and a red flower-patterned shirt. Her long strings of beads and her sash belt were cream, her blonde hair braided down her back with red ribbon running through. 'Apache – based on a picture taken of one of Geronimo's wives.'

She'd stuck with the Apache theme for Jude and Aaron. Aaron wore a loose white shirt open almost to the waist and a black vest. Silver beads hung down his chest, his unruly brown hair was covered with a zig-zag-patterned bandanna in red and black. Jude meanwhile was looking mean and moody in a tan leather vest over his bare torso, worn with tight-fitting fringed pants and nothing on his head.

'Jude, are you sure you won't catch a cold?' Grace's mom looked concerned as we all paraded in their living room.

This mom-speak broke the tension and cracked us up. We laughed and fooled around, tossed Jude a throw from the back of the couch to wear as a poncho and fell out through the Montroses' front door, still laughing even though the predicted snow had already begun to fall.

We drove out to New Dawn with our windows open, yelling from car to car.

'Jeez, Mom was right — it's c-c-cold!' Grace called when we stopped side by side at the lights on Main Street. Dusk had fallen and the street lights were on, neon signs shone over entrances to restaurants and bars.

'I sure hope this party is indoors,' Orlando called back.

'Maybe they'll build a bonfire by the lake. That would be cool,' Jude said as we set off on green.

'Maybe we'll even get fireworks?' I suggested, winding up my window.

'Not in this weather,' Orlando decided.

It was as if we'd all made a pact not to show how nervous and how scared for Holly we were as we made it out of town on to the highway, where we pretty soon took an exit on to the narrow road leading to New Dawn, following the snaking track between trees and boulders with the headlights raking across the wild landscape. All the time the snow kept falling.

'Slow down,' I told Orlando, glancing behind to see Jude's Jeep skid sideways into a ditch. His rear tyres spun and turned the freshly fallen snow to slush while his engine whined as he switched into four-wheel drive to get them out of the gully. 'OK, go ahead,' I said.

We plunged further out of civilization into wild country, catching glimpses of Turner Lake ahead.

'Weird – I didn't think New Dawn was so far out,' Orlando grumbled. 'I guess it's the snow – it slows us down.'

'We're definitely on the right road,' I told him, checking out tyre marks from the cars that had gone before. 'There's only one way into the camp and this is it. Yeah, look.'

Two hundred metres ahead of us, the track was lit at either side by a series of braziers with logs burning bright, showing the entrance to the parking lot. A speaker system blasted dance music through the forest and out across the lake. Orlando squeezed into a space looking out across the water. We stepped out of the truck.

'It's f-f-freez . . . !' Grace shivered and groaned as Jude pulled up beside us.

'Quit whining,' I told her. 'The social centre's this way – let's go!'

We ran, slipping, stumbling through the snow, catching up with other guests from town – a girl in tight jeans and a white tunic, with feathers dangling from two braids, three guys with their faces streaked with red and white paint – a pretty loose interpretation of the Native American theme.

'Cool costumes!' the girl told us as we hurried on by.

Soon we came out of the forest and hit the main party venue – the big log building by the water's edge. External lighting played over the entrance – purple turning to green then red, flickering over the walls and catching snowflakes in their beams while the techno beat grew louder, drawing us in.

For a few seconds we hesitated.

'You're OK with these disco lights?' Orlando checked with me.

'Yeah, they're way down on the list of things I'm worried about.' We all stood and looked at each other, starting to get serious and silently remind ourselves why we were there.

'Is everyone still cool with this?' Grace asked.

We nodded. We were here for Holly. How would she be after all these days in Amos's clutches? Would Channing still be in total control? Aaron took the lead, the rest of us followed.

Inside the social centre the music faded and the lights were dim. A giant screen, which filled one whole wall, played scenes from Amos's blockbuster movie, *Dark Secret*.

There was an extreme close-up of a girl's face, her dark pupils reflecting flames, her expression one of sheer terror. Cut to a forest fire eating up pine trees, leaping gullies, shooting firebrands into the night sky. The girl turned and ran. Burning branches crashed around her – she was lost in thick black smoke. I blinked and looked again. The girl was me.

No, of course not – this was an Antony Amos movie. The girl on screen was a twelve-year-old actress named Carey Hart who starred in this one movie but had never made it as an adult actress. They said she later did drugs and went in and out of rehab. I remember she died a couple of years back at the age of twenty-three.

Taking a deep breath, I turned from the screen to check out other guests.

'Hey, Tania!' A voice greeted me and it took me a while to recognize tall Marta beneath a soft cap decorated with feathers and beadwork. She'd chosen a unisex costume of dark-red trousers and sleeveless tunic and seemed genuinely glad to see me. 'You made it safe to Spider Rock!'

'I did,' I said. 'And Ziegler drove me home. How about you – you got Regan back to New Dawn without breaking any more arms or legs?'

'Yeah, Regan!' she laughed. 'He's so not cut out for the wilderness.'

'Did I hear my name? Who's saying negative stuff about me?' Regan showed up at Marta's shoulder and joined in the conversation.

'Hey, how long did your costume take?' I asked with a grin. Regan had streaked his cheeks with red paint and stuck a single crow's feather in a headband – that was it. Otherwise he wore normal jeans and T, his usual glasses and short, unstyled hair.

'Thirty seconds. You like?'

On screen the mountain fire still raged. It had reached the bank of a wide, fast-flowing river. The girl plunged into the water and swam desperately towards the far side.

Soon Blake and Kaylee joined us, then Ava looking fabulous in beads and braids and bold zig-zag-patterned tunic.

On screen we saw another close-up of the girl, head above water, being swept downstream. More fear in her eyes.

'So where's Holly?' Grace asked.

'She's around here somewhere.' Blake glanced vaguely around the dimly lit room. 'Why not ask Channing?'

A figure threaded his way through the crowd towards us, head and shoulders above most of the others. He looked even taller than usual in a soft, hooded mask topped with a fan-shaped, painted crown.

'He's a Mountain Spirit.' Blake explained the mask which covered his face completely. 'He decided to go with a mystical theme, connected with the Great Creator.'

Channing stepped clear of the crowd into a pool of light. My mind did that hideous slamming-and-splitting-in-two thing and for a second I saw what no one else could see.

Moonlight glows on ice-capped peaks. Men in masks perform a frenzied dance. They raise their arms above their heads, they stamp and howl to the moon.

Finally making it to our group, Channing kept the mask over his face as first Grace confronted him.

'Channing – we came to see Holly. Do you know where she is?'

'Still getting ready, I guess.' Channing's voice was muffled. You could see only his dark eyes through the slits in the mask – cold and cruel enough for me to be

309

reminded of the last time I'd seen him, leaping out of Ziegler's car to grab Jarrold. And I remembered him before that, leaning over a semi-conscious, half-naked Holly in the blizzard shelter by the lake, kissing her on the lips.

As my head stopped spinning and I recovered from my vision, I took another look around and ended up with my attention drawn back to the screen. I saw the dark head of the girl desperately swimming through white-water rapids. The head bobbed up and down then suddenly disappeared beneath the rushing water, as if a strong hand had gripped her from below. A submerged camera filmed her sinking, twisted and towed by currents, her hands stretched out, face turned towards the light.

'If Holly is the reason you're all here, let me go check where she is,' Channing offered, pushing his way towards the exit without waiting for a response.

'She'll show up soon, no problem,' I reassured Aaron, who looked as if he wanted to follow Channing out of the building and punch him senseless. Still I kept sneaking glances at the giant screen to see if the drowning girl was saved.

'Come and get a drink?' Kaylee offered, taking Jude and Grace towards a bar set up in the area with the couches, the bear rug and open log fire.

This left Aaron, Orlando and me with Marta and Ava. Blake and Regan had already drifted off to talk to other people.

'I guess Aurelie and Jean-Luc will show up soon?' I asked.

'With Antony,' Marta confirmed. 'I love your costumes. Aurelie chose the party theme. She's good at this stuff, huh?'

Chit-chat, chit-chat. I realize I'm in danger of making this party sound everyday and unexciting. It was, until you recalled what went before, where we were and the fact that my dark angel was lurking. Plus, I reminded myself, we were still at the very start – guests arriving, Explorers showing up in fancy dress, music playing, a movie showing.

And I want to go back to the cross between a mask and a hood that Channing had been wearing. It looked antique – the genuine thing, and was made of some type of soft fabric – maybe even a dark-stained buckskin – that completely covered his head like a Ku Klux Klan hood without the point. Or like an executioner's hood. And the crown on top was shaped like a fan with spokes around ten centimetres tall. It was painted with a pattern of diamonds, triangles and circles in blue, red and white. Marta said he was a Mountain Spirit – obviously

311

something to be afraid of and bow down to, not a Weyekin or anything you would want as a spirit ally.

It turned out Channing wasn't the only one who had gone down the spiritual route. I soon spotted half a dozen figures dressed in long fringed shirts embroidered with stars and black eagles. They were gathered in a small circle in the centre of the room.

'Ghost Dancers,' my interpreter, Marta, explained. 'It was after the white men took over. They danced all night and day to bring back their lost world, to see the buffalo again, to meet their ancestors. They thought that dancing until they fell exhausted on to the earth was what it took.'

'Did it work out?' Orlando asked.

Marta shrugged. 'What do you think? Eventually they got wiped out by soldiers at Wounded Knee.'

'How come Antony Amos is into all this old stuff?' Aaron kept talking to disguise the fact that he was growing more on edge by the minute. His nerves were strung out, waiting for his first chance to see Holly and talk to her, while my own stomach was in knots wondering if, after all, Jarrold would appear. I stared hard at the Ghost Dancers, thinking that he might be amongst them, then at the group gathered with Kaylee, Jude and Grace by the bar.

I had no luck spotting him so I turned back to the

onscreen action. By this time the drowning girl had sunk into an underwater cave. Her eyes were open but she looked dead. Eerie music – mainly drums and steel guitar – played on the soundtrack.

Then suddenly the images faded as the lights in the room brightened and the guests of honour walked in through the main door.

Aurelie led the way looking spectacular in a long white skirt and fringed tunic embroidered in blue. Her short black hair was tucked behind her ears and she wore hooped silver earrings. Jean-Luc was next, also dressed in white, with a sky-blue neckerchief and a broad blue belt – following the party theme but looking ill at ease. I decided straight away that he was only here because his sister had put pressure on him. Third came Richard Ziegler, looking as if he'd reverted to his young days as a stuntman and body double, stripped to the waist, with his torso and face streaked with red and black paint, looking stunning and sinister.

He came ahead of the guest of honour, Antony himself, who wore a simple, black collarless shirt and black trousers. He smiled and walked, attracting every gaze in the room, basking in the attention.

I glanced at the screen and took in some last, fading images of the drowned girl.

She glides between black rocks, her pale face glows amongst skulls and bones. She is me again. She has my face, my long dark hair.

Water fills her lungs, air bubbles from the corner of her mouth. She prays in the church with ghosts, with Conner. The waterlogged walls shake, the praying skeletons disintegrate and float away. The walls cave inwards, the steeple comes crashing down.

My visions were back with a vengeance and I realized how hard I had grasped Orlando's hand as Antony Amos came into the room.

Aurelie's party plan was in full swing. On screen the movie was over and there was now a video compilation of various musicians and singers – all favourites of her stepfather's from the seventies and eighties. They turned up the volume, cleared a central space and we watched people start to dance, only a few at first, until Aurelie came round and drew people on to the floor. She had Jean-Luc in tow, and when she came to where I was standing with Aaron and Orlando, she smiled her charming smile and said she was sure Orlando wouldn't mind if I danced with her brother, because after all he was leaving for Paris in two days' time. Before I knew it I was in a clinch, slow-dancing with Jean-Luc and she was in a dark corner with Orlando, hand-gesturing, explaining something, always smiling.

'So, Tania,' Jean-Luc began as we turned on the spot in the middle of the crowded floor. His white shirt stood out in the dim, multi-coloured light, his cheeks were smoothly shaved and he smelled good. 'How did the wild walking turn out for you?'

'Interesting,' I replied cagily. 'After a day or two I kind of got it.'

He smiled. 'You connected with the spirit of the place?'

'Maybe.'

'You bonded with your band?'

'Again, maybe.'

'Some members more than others?' Jean-Luc asked with his knowing smile. 'So tell me – how was Jarrold?'

If I was cagey before, this question made me totally clam up. 'Jarrold was Jarrold,' I muttered. No way would I tell Jean-Luc that The Outsider had got too close and declared his feelings for me.

'He's unique, for sure.' Steering me to the edge of the dance floor, Jean-Luc took my hand and led me outside. 'Walking in the sight of the Great Creator with Jarrold is quite an experience. Did you know that practically every girl who walks in the wilderness with him comes back head over heels in love, despite the fact that our guiding principles forbid it?'

'No!' I gave a self-conscious laugh. 'Does he come with a health warning?'

'But apparently not you, Tania. You escaped with your heart in one piece?' Jean-Luc's tone was light but his gaze was pretty intense out there under a moonlit sky.

'The snow clouds cleared,' I murmured, looking up at the stars. There was a pause and then I said, 'I'm sorry you're leaving.'

'You know how it is. I don't do well here. I prefer the city.'

'Aurelie says she will miss you like crazy.'

'She's my twin. We've always been close,' he admitted. 'But I live my own life. I knew I wouldn't stay here at New Dawn, even before my mother died.'

'So what will you do in Paris?'

'Play piano, go to college and study music, lots of things. You can visit me if you like.'

'Cool.' We'd wandered from the social centre along a track between more braziers, right to the water's edge, where we watched the reflection of the moon and stars in the lake. The conversation drifted as always through topics we both enjoyed – art galleries, video installations, European culture in general – until Ziegler strode down to the lake shore and interrupted us.

'Jean-Luc, your stepfather wants you to dance with one of the guests from Bitterroot,' he snapped, plainly ignoring me.

'Tell him later.' Jean-Luc turned his back on the messenger to lead me further along the frozen shore.

'Now,' Ziegler insisted. Light and shadow from a nearby brazier played over his face and toned torso. His eyes were narrowed; he stood hands on hips.

My companion sighed. 'You want to know why I'm leaving, Tania? This is why,' he confided with a sullen jerk of his head towards Ziegler. He spoke so that only I could hear. 'This is the way it is at New Dawn.'

And the two guys left me, their feet crunching through the snow. I breathed in the night air and followed more slowly, deciding as I went that I quickly needed to rejoin Orlando and together we would team up with Grace, Jude and Aaron. It was time we tracked Holly down, no question.

Then, as if all this was scripted and he was right on cue, Jarrold made one of his entrances out of nowhere. He stepped out from behind a basket of burning logs – out of the darkness into the flickering red light, his face cut and bruised.

I stopped, turned around, looked for help. Fifty metres from where we stood, the social centre with its flickering, multi-coloured lights was noisy and buzzing. Out here in the dark, no one could see or hear us.

Small waves rippled and washed against the pebbles. Tall, dark juniper trees stood sentry on the hillside.

'Come with me,' Jarrold said.

15

He took me up through the deep shadows cast by the trees towards the cabin he shared with Channing at the end of the trail. 'Don't try running back to the party,' he warned. 'And don't be scared, I'm not going to hurt you.'

'OK, but I still don't trust you.' I made this clear as I tried to figure out what Jarrold wanted. The fact that he wasn't in costume confirmed my guess that he'd been excluded from the party.

'What did I do? Why are you pushing me away?'

I thought of Orlando dancing with Aurelie back in the social centre and I managed to stand firm. 'You know what you did – breaking into my house, the stupid note. I never invited you into my life, you just stormed in. So let's go ahead and get this over with. Tell me what you want.' I shivered in the cold wind that blew down the valley.

With a quick toss of his head and a clicking sound with his tongue, Jarrold strode on. 'I have something to tell you – something you need to know.'

'Stop right there!' If this was more about the way he felt towards me, another chance to get me alone, he'd better know I wasn't about to play his game. 'Orlando's here. He's in there with Aurelie.'

'Scary!' He turned and laughed in my face. 'I've seen your guy, Tania. What does he weigh – 160, 170 pounds? Do you seriously believe he would want to fight with me?'

Angrily I turned to head back down the hillside but he grabbed my arm and pulled me back so that I had a close-up view of the swelling on his bottom lip and the cut under his right eye. 'OK, so I have feelings for you and I always will – you already know that. But don't think of me as some loser who goes down on his knees and comes crying after you more than once.'

'So what is this about?' I said, not knowing whether to believe him but wrenching my wrist free and rubbing my skin where his fingers had gripped me.

'Things have moved on. I know now I can't get out of here just by walking away. They'll come after me wherever I run. Have you any idea how that feels?'

'Actually, I do,' I answered quietly. Running was one of my specialities.

Jarrold acknowledged my confession by a slight, conspiratorial raising of his eyebrows. 'So now I've changed tactics – I want to dish the dirt, dig deep and really expose what goes on here.'

'And I'm going to help you go public?' I shook my head in disbelief.

'Yeah, you are! If it's not you, Tania, who else? It's not going to be Kaylee or Regan or any of those guys. They're victims of the system too, just as much as me, but they know they have to keep their heads down and serve their time without complaining. If not, they end up the way I am now.'

'Try Jean-Luc,' I suggested. 'He hates the place as much as you do.'

Jarrold nodded. 'You're right, but Amos is his stepfather so there's family loyalty in the mix. Plus, he doesn't have the guts. No – you're the only one, Tania.'

'So what is it you want people to know?' Gradually my shock and anger died away and Jarrold and I were sharing confidences. He was starting to get through again.

'This!' he cried, facing me and pointing to his damaged face. 'Plus, the whole deal – the brainwashing, the psychological BS, the dropping your burden at the gate, heart at peace shit.'

'The Great Creator?'

'All of that. Amos built this whole community on a lie.' Jarrold had raised his voice and tilted his head back in exasperation. It exposed his Adam's apple and the muscles in his neck. 'You have to tell it like it really is – that they call it therapy but it's not. It's Ziegler controlling every move we make, Amos spouting spiritual stuff that no one believes.'

'What else? Tell me – I'm listening.'

Jarrold's voice softened to not much more than a whisper. 'It's sticking the Outsider label on to you, taking away your clothes at night, keeping you here until they break you. And listen to me, Tania – did they tell you about New Dawn PCS?'

'No. What's that?' The urgency in Jarrold's eyes was making the hairs on my neck stand up.

'PCS – Positive Control System. Quote from the Guiding Principles; "If talking doesn't lead to compliance, it is legitimate to employ appropriate physical force." Unquote.'

'"Appropriate physical force" – what does that mean exactly?'

'This!' Springing forward, Jarrold seized my wrist a second time and bent it back with a sharp, strong movement.

'Ouch!' I caved in and let him force my captured arm

behind my back, bending my elbow so that my fingertips touched my shoulder. 'Let go of me, Jarrold.'

'Or this!' Moving smoothly behind me, he put an arm lock around my neck. 'Or this!' Releasing me a second time, he stepped back across my path and aimed a karate kick at my stomach, missing by not much more than a centimetre. 'It's any type of physical force – including what you saw early this morning.'

'Stop!' I raised my hands to my ears. 'I've heard enough.'

Jarrold stepped back and let out a long sigh. Then he stood arms by his side, staring at me as if he was a prisoner in the dock waiting for a verdict.

'OK, I believe you,' I whispered.

His eyes lit up and he sprang forward. 'You'll do it? You'll bring the walls crashing down around Amos?'

'No, wait. Listen. I can't. Not until we achieve what we came here to do.'

A wind moaned through the trees, branches creaked. 'What is that exactly?' Jarrold asked, eyes still gleaming earnestly, a frown knotting his forehead.

'To rescue Holly,' I whispered, turning away from him and walking quickly down the hill.

I got away from Jarrold and back to the party in time to

see the Ghost Dancers lead the guests out from the social centre on to the lake shore. In the light of the braziers they formed a circle with a drummer in the middle and began to move in slow, rhythmic steps, red flames reflected in the shining silver stars which decorated their tunics.

'How cool is that!' a voice said from the shadows.

I turned and at last I saw the girl we'd come looking for.

'Holly!' It took me a while to recognize her because her long fair hair was scraped back and her face half hidden by a white mask that covered her eyes. But when I saw Channing in his executioner's mask lurking behind, I knew it was her.

'The dancers,' she said, as if we were bumping into each other at the tennis club or at the end of our driveways. 'They're stepping into the past, searching for their ancestors who lived here by Prayer River, before the lake was made.'

'Holly!' I cried. 'At last! We've been looking everywhere. Where have you been?'

'Here,' she told me. 'Where else?'

'Whoa, it's good to see you!' As the dancers circled and began to whirl on the spot, raising a chant and watched by around fifty guests, I felt a rush of relief. 'You look fantastic. I love your costume!'

'Mexican Indian,' she explained. 'They wore this type of cotton toga tied at one shoulder, with masks or veils, fans made of feathers. Actually, they put silver rings through their noses but I didn't go that far.'

'No really, it's good to see you,' I repeated. 'You wouldn't believe how we stressed over you – the hypothermia and all.'

'But you already knew I was fine.' I began to pick up that the casual tone was fake, that Holly's voice was higher than usual, and I noticed a nervous monotone. I looked more closely at her face, but her turquoise-studded mask hid whatever expression she had in her eyes. 'You saw me playing snooker with the guys here. I told you I wanted to stay, so what's the problem?'

You're deep in denial, I thought. You're not the Holly I know. You're blanking me the way Grace did. This is too scary! 'Grace and Jude are here. Aaron too,' I told her, trying to keep my voice steady. 'They all want to talk with you.'

'Maybe later – after the dance,' she said, turning to check with Channing.

Rewind to Grace and Ezra – the hunky guy with hypnotic powers. Remember this was exactly how Grace turned her back on Jude and swooned, fell, collapsed zombie-like into Ezra's arms. Well, here we had an action replay with Holly and Channing.

'We're busy, we have things to do,' she explained as they began to move away.

'What things?' Now that I'd finally found her and seen the way she was acting, I was desperate to keep hold of her. 'Chill. Stay here with me.'

'Sorry, Tania, we're on duty. It's time to fetch more logs for the braziers then we have to check on the drinks situation.'

'You heard what I said – Aaron's here.'

For the first time she hesitated but Channing stepped right in with, 'Holly, Aaron can wait. I need you to come with me.'

She winced and seemed about to resist, or did I imagine that part?

'For Antony's celebration,' he reminded her as he took her firmly by the arm.

'Oh cool, the celebration!' She was back to the manic monotone. 'We can't miss that part. Come on, Tania, come with us!'

I had no choice so I followed them across the snowy ground until we reached the area where the Ghost Dancers whirled and wailed. They danced to the beating drum with heads bowed and shoulders hunched, stamping their feet and setting up their high-pitched, desperate cries.

Amongst the guests standing at the far side I made out Orlando with Jude, Aaron and Grace and I was about to slip away and join them, tell them that I'd finally located Holly when the dancers broke their circle and gave way for Ziegler and Amos. Immediately everyone fell silent and the leader of the New Dawn community got ready to make his birthday speech.

'This is the day of my birth,' he began in his solemn, preachy voice. He held his arms wide and looked up at the moon and stars. 'We are gathered here at New Dawn. We walk together. Our hearts are turned to each other in the sight of the Great Creator.'

He stood like a man crucified on a cross, arms spread eagled.

'We are changed from our old ways, and the change comes willingly from within,' he continued. 'We begin anew.'

He speaks and only I hear the wind whistle through the trees, across the lake.

'Behold!' *the white-haired warrior addresses his people. Embers from the dying fire cast flickering light over his sorrowing features.* 'I am old. My sun is set.'

Logs shift, red sparks rise and fade.

At our backs the winter wind blows. Ripples disturb the dark water.

'Once I was a warrior,' the old man sighs. 'My people were around me like the grass on the prairie, like the leaves on the trees. Now men come on horseback and seize our land that the Great Creator gave us. Our people die in the snow. They pass over but their spirits live on in the mountains and beneath the rivers and lakes.'

Suddenly, as he speaks, the rough water parts and the creature rises. A great cry of fear goes up. Snake-headed, with a forked tongue, he towers over us and spreads his wings – black wings without feathers. His cold green eyes shine bright as the stars in the heavens.

The old man on the shore keeps his arms outstretched. He doesn't cower as the creature rises from the lake, doesn't resist as it sinks its fangs into his flesh.

Black water rises, the lake bursts its banks. A thousand double-headed, emerald serpents swarm from its icy depths. The black creature turns and plunges back into the lake with the old man hanging limp in his jaws.

I was in the grip of cold, cold fear, knowing I was at a party in the presence of my bitter and twisted dark angel, seeing visions, feeling time melt, stepping into an evil world without boundaries.

There was a time on Black Rock earlier this summer . . . a different party. I took a sharp intake of breath and glanced at Holly, who had taken off her mask and was staring enraptured at Amos, drinking in every word. Her eyes were wide and unblinking.

We were nearer to the end than I'd expected. Holly was ready to enter into her own ceremony and be led on to the dark side. Her soul would part from her body and we'd lose her for ever. We had to act.

'We are changed, we are departed from the old ways,' Amos intoned. 'And we give thanks that our hearts are at peace.'

A murmur rose from the Ghost Dancers, who had formed a semicircle behind him and Ziegler. 'Our hearts are at peace,' they chanted.

I turned to Holly to make another appeal. It was only seconds since I last looked, but now a figure wrapped in a red blanket stood beside me. One side of her skull-like face was painted black, the other was white. Her dark, hollowed-out eyes glittered.

'Holly?' I gasped.

Beside the red-cloaked, skeletal woman there was a tall figure with a winged mask covering his face. He was naked except for a short wrap around his hips and turquoise beads around his neck.

These ghosts had appeared out of nowhere and Holly and Channing had vanished.

'They were there and then they weren't!' I told Orlando as soon as Amos's ritual was over and I could make my way across to my group. It felt as if every second was vital.

'Come inside, tell us what happened,' Jude said, leading the way back into the social centre with the other guests.

My heart raced. 'Honest to God, you have to believe me. I was talking with Holly and she suddenly vanished!'

'You don't know where she went?' Grace asked. We'd stopped just inside the entrance, under the row of stuffed animal heads on the wall.

'Are you listening to me? She vanished! Channing was with her. When she was here, it wasn't really her any more – she couldn't even breathe without asking permission!'

Slam! My brain disconnected.

Next to a roaring fire, the bear-head opens its mouth and roars. I see the ribbed, vault-like roof of its mouth, the white glisten of its teeth. Bears are amongst us, lumbering on their hind legs, lurching, swiping their claws.

'I'm here with you,' Orlando reminded me quietly.

He said exactly the words I needed to hear. He was

cool and calm. I thanked my lucky stars. Then slam and split again.

Outside in the trampled snow there are animal tracks and blood. The wolf man with matted hair and slavering jaws is sated. He drops on to all fours and slinks away.

'OK, so we break up the group and look for her,' Jude decided. 'Grace and I will stay here and check the restrooms, kitchen, pool room – everywhere. Aaron, you check the lake shore where the guys were dancing. Orlando, Tania, you take the trail up to the cabins.'

'So let's go.' Aaron was already halfway out of the crowded room, heading back to the lake. 'We meet back here in fifteen minutes.'

'And what do we do when we find her again?' Orlando checked with Jude. 'Do we force her – knock her out, drag her to the parking lot and drive away with her?'

'Dude, be serious,' Jude sighed. 'As a first move, we talk to her and persuade her to listen to what Aaron has to say.'

'Will that work?' Orlando asked me.

'Maybe. I agree with Jude – right now it's still our best option.' Anxious to get away from the taxidermy on the floor, I led Orlando out into the snow.

'Check back in fifteen minutes,' Grace reminded us as we headed towards the forest trail.

Orlando and I ran up the slope towards the cabins where I'd last seen Jarrold, leaving behind the sounds of partying – the music, the laughter. The rough trail was dimly lit by more braziers, which shed pools of light on gnarled tree roots and loose rocks. More than once we stumbled and fell.

'Take it easy.' Orlando reached for me as I tripped. A thorn bush broke my fall but I got back on my feet and ran on without bothering to pick painful thorns out of my palm. 'Where are we headed?' he asked.

'Channing shares a cabin with Jarrold,' I explained. 'They live at the end of this trail. Maybe Channing brought Holly here.'

We ran on without speaking but thinking plenty – me frantic to find my friend before she got swallowed up for good by Amos's army of dark angels, Orlando probably reacting badly to the 'J' word. In any case, he slowed down and was a couple of paces behind me when I saw two figures standing on the trail ahead. Instinctively I ducked off the track and hid behind a tree.

'What happened?' Orlando joined me in my hiding place.

'Sssh!' Cautiously I took another look. 'It's Ziegler.'

'And?'

'Jarrold!' My heart lurched and my mouth went dry.

The two guys were about fifty metres away and talking urgently. Jarrold was speaking, gesturing back towards the lake. Ziegler listened, interrupted with quick questions and finally put up a hand to stop Jarrold's flow of words. Then, as Jarrold disappeared on to his cabin porch, Ziegler turned and walked towards us.

Swift and easy he strode bare-chested down the track as Orlando and I cowered behind the tree. We were edging deeper into the shadows, trying not to make a sound, as wrong-footed and stupid as kids caught stealing candy.

'Tania.' Ziegler stopped a couple of paces from our tree. Without question he'd spotted us before we dived sideways into the bushes. 'We'd prefer party guests stayed close to the social centre. There's no access to the cabins – I'm sure you appreciate our reasons.'

With our tails between our legs, Orlando and I followed Ziegler down the track. Without mentioning his conversation with Jarrold, Ziegler made small talk with Orlando, talking him through some of the lesser-known guiding principles at New Dawn, such as no guests allowed inside the cabins after dark. As soon as we reached the social centre, he delivered us like naughty children to Aurelie.

'I caught them on the cabin trail,' he told her with a raised eyebrow before he strode off again.

'Oh dear!' Aurelie was amused. Her laugh was musical and beautiful, like everything else about her. 'Ignore Richard. His interpretation of the rules can be a little . . .' Shrugging and leaving her sentence unfinished, she took us inside, under the moose head with its great antlers and glassy stare.

How do they do that? I wondered. How do they predict your every move and take away your power to act? Before either of us had time to think it through, Aurelie had drawn Orlando on to the dance floor again.

I was by myself with no time to lose, had maybe five minutes before the pre-arranged meeting with the others. Whereas before my heartbeat had been spiky and rapid, I felt that now it had flat lined into heavy dread.

Jarrold betrayed me. This was the phrase that played in my head and made me nauseous. He tricked me with the poor-me, get-me-out-of-here-and-bring-the-walls-tumbling-down tactic, when all along he'd only wanted to discover the reason I was here.

To rescue Holly, I'd told him. And now he'd relayed this information straight back to Ziegler, who would tell Amos, and our plan would collapse. Yeah – Jarrold betrayed me.

'Tania!' Aaron dragged me out of my freefall. He appeared in the doorway in his white shirt and vest, breathless and excited, gesturing for me to follow him. 'Holly – I've found her!'

'Where?'

'By the lake.'

'Alone?' I asked as we ran towards the shore.

'No. Still with Channing. I don't know what they were doing – maybe collecting driftwood for the fires. Come on, Tania – that's why I came looking for you. You have to make some kind of scene, divert the guy's attention while I talk to Holly.'

'We need more people,' I protested. 'Let's go back – get the others.'

'No time. You have to do this for me.'

'OK. Go ahead.' The dread was still dragging me down. I had no clue how I would get Channing away from Holly, or what Aaron could say to change Holly's zombified mind.

Aaron stopped in the shadows, a few metres short of the pebble beach. He gave me a few seconds to make out the two figures by the edge of the lake – one in a white robe tied at one shoulder and the other with a high, fan-shaped headdress. They stood together, hand in hand in the moonlight with their backs turned, gazing out over the calm water.

'Go!' Aaron urged.

No way! I told myself even as I took my first step on to the pebbles. This is not going to work.

'The moon is waning,' I heard Channing tell Holly. 'And see the shooting star directly overhead? And another?'

'It's like they fall into the lake and fizzle and die,' she sighed, resting her head on his shoulder in cosmic harmony.

Then Channing heard the crunch of my footsteps, alerted Holly and together they turned and waited.

'Hey, Channing. Ziegler sent me to find you,' I faltered over my words. Who was I kidding? Was this really the best I could do?

Channing didn't reply. He just went on waiting.

'He needs you.'

Holly glanced up at his hooded face without releasing his hand.

'It's Jarrold,' I stumbled on. 'He went missing again. Ziegler needs you to find him.'

Channing nodded and eased his hand out of Holly's. He moved slowly towards me, his face hidden by the hooded mask. 'Did they search all the cabins?'

'Ziegler did. He doesn't want to raise a general alarm

336

because it would wreck the party. He said could you check the boats moored in the inlet?'

'The boats?' Channing echoed, staring into my eyes, reading my twitchy body language. He noticed Holly try to follow him up the beach. 'Hold it right there,' he told her without turning. 'Tania will stay here with you. I'll be back in ten minutes.'

The plan worked! It might have been a feeble strategy, but Channing was falling for it and leaving, cutting over the top of the small headland into the next bay, using moonlight to find his way.

The second he was out of sight, Aaron emerged from the shadows. Holly saw him and at first she didn't react. She looked uncertain, almost as if she didn't recognise the guy who until earlier that week, had been the love of her life and actually she was trying to recall where she'd seen him before.

Reacting to her confusion, Aaron's instinct was to try to take hold of her and embrace her, like a parent trying to protect a child. 'Jeez, what did they do to you?' he murmured, cradling her head against his chest.

She gave a small cry and pushed him away. 'No!'

'Holly, it's me and Tania! It's OK, we know what's happening here – the mind tricks they play. But it's not too late. We'll get you out.'

'What in the world are you talking about?' She frowned and turned down the corners of her mouth. 'This is New Dawn. There are no mind tricks. No one's making me stay.'

'No, Holly – listen!' Aaron knew he had only minutes to get through to her. 'You know how I feel about you – how much I love you. I don't always say it out loud, but you know, we both know that's the way it is – me and you, period.'

'Once upon a time, maybe,' she said quietly. She was refusing to give him eye contact, sighing, turning away. 'Not any more.'

The night sky is full of dark angels. Their tormented souls are the distant stars that twinkle dimly then fall and fade. They are the shooting stars, glorious for a short time, but then spectacularly exploding, falling, falling. I reach out to catch one. My hand is empty.

Aaron wouldn't give in easily. He loved her, poor guy.

'You and me!' he repeated. 'Not you and Channing or you and anyone else. I'll get you out of this place and you'll soon see what's been going on. You'll be yourself again.'

'Myself?' Now she was angry, turning on him and lashing out with her tongue. 'You say you love me, Aaron, but that's so pathetic. You don't even know the meaning of the word. All your emotions are shallow. I know, because mine were too before I met Channing. He taught me that yours is an everyday, conventional kind of love – let's go to college then get married, have babies, be happy ever after. But I'm not an everyday girl and that's not what I want any more. I want something deeper, richer, finer than you can ever give me!'

Wow, she scythed Aaron down, flattened him, turned and left him for dead. She began to follow Channing over the headland.

I left him on the beach and ran after her. 'Stop. You're not going anywhere!'

'Tania, let go of me. You're like the others. You had your chance and you blew it.'

'What chance? What are you saying?'

'With Jarrold.' She was still in a rage. The wind had blown her hair loose and it was flying across her face. 'He saw something special in you, the same way Channing chose me. You could have been standing beside me now – me and Channing, you and Jarrold – not fighting me and making stupid attempts to so-called rescue me!'

We stood there on the dark headland, surrounded by ice and snow. The lake stretched out towards the horizontal line of the distant dam. Stars twinkled and were spent.

Footsteps came running from both sides.

'Holly, if you stay here you're going to die!'

'No. I'm going to live a life so special you wouldn't believe. It's going to be out of this world!'

Channing came scrambling over rocks, up the slope from the inlet where the boats were moored. Aaron had recovered from Holly's onslaught and was running up the hill after us.

'These are dark angels!' I yelled at Holly. 'Ziegler, Channing, Amos! They're dragging you on to the dark side. Can't you see what this is all about?'

The wind blasted us. It howled through the trees, cold as death.

Aaron reached us first, but not in time to take a hold of Holly and drag her back to safety. Channing bounded the last few metres up the rocks, almost as if he was flying, or as if the wind had lifted him off his feet and propelled him on to the ridge. He landed between us and Holly, threw his arms wide. A strong gust tore the hood from his face and we stared into his amber eyes.

'Back off, don't touch her!' Aaron launched himself at Channing, shoulder-charged him and aimed to knock him off the ridge. He hit solid muscle; Channing didn't move. So Aaron locked arms with his enemy, wrestled him and tried to unbalance him. Channing resisted easily.

He flung Aaron to one side, fixed me with wolf-like eyes.

His eyes blazed, the pupils were narrow. Shadows fell across his lean face.

Aaron came back at him from behind. He charged a second time. Channing felt his full weight but was able to flip him aside with one arm. And this is Aaron we're talking about – a mountain climber who tackled fourteeners, who was tall and strong as anyone in our high-school year, totally fired up, ready to kill to save the girl he loved.

Aaron and Channing were locked together on the dark ridge, wrestling, punching, dragging each other to the ground, rolling against a boulder. We heard the thud of fist against flesh, the stamp and scuffle of boots, the exhalation of breath. Channing was up on his feet, unharmed. Aaron lay groaning on the ground. I ran to try and help him, felt myself cast aside, slammed against a boulder close to where Aaron lay.

Holly stood fixed to the spot, her wild hair flying in the wind.

Aaron groaned and Channing wrenched him upright, stood back and thudded his fist into Aaron's jaw. Aaron staggered then toppled backwards. He slid down the rocks. Stones broke loose and rattled downwards into the darkness; Aaron fell for what seemed like eternity.

I heard the splash as the body hit the water. I ran after him – not fast enough. By the time I reached the inlet, Aaron's body had disappeared below the surface. Moonlit ripples closed over him. I threw back my head and screamed.

16

Black water rises.

It laps against the walls of the houses on Main Street, reaches the doors, the windows. It reaches the roofs. Everything is swept away. There is water everywhere.

Pale flotsam bobs on the dark surface – chairs, tables, trees with their roots ripped out of the ground. A mighty current carries them.

Down in the depths, two-headed serpents writhe at the mouths of black caves.

I drift amongst them with sightless eyes.

I screamed for help and no one came. Holly stood like a block of white stone on the rock overlooking the water. Channing turned his back.

'Do something!' I yelled. 'Don't let him die!'

The ripples spread in ever widening circles. I searched for Aaron, prayed that he would return to the surface and strike out towards the shore.

Nothing. No sign of life. I kicked off my shoes, prepared to dive in. I threw myself from the rock, hit the water, felt its icy grip. I plunged down, groped blindly, swam underwater until I thought my lungs would burst. Then I kicked for the surface.

Nothing.

Holly and Channing had climbed down to the water's edge. There was no expression on their faces as I gasped for air.

'Get some help!' I yelled before I kicked and dived down again.

The lake embraces me. I am in its arms, caressed, rocked this way and that. A hundred other lovers stretch out cold arms to greet me. They emerge from silent, windowless houses of West Point as if they've been waiting for years to welcome me home. They drift towards me with dead eyes, hair like weeds billowing in the cold current. They reach out. One is a boy my own age, more eager than the others. He takes me by the hand.

I recognize him, recoil and kick away. I am not Conner's friend. I am here to find Aaron.

'Come back!' Conner pleads. His face is white, his eyes dark as death. He catches me, clutches me to him.

Around us, the water writhes with green and black snakes.

'I will tell you all you need to know,' the dead boy says.

The promise is false. I resist, pull away and swim with all my might.

I swam in total darkness, searching for Aaron. The ache in my lungs grew unbearable; there was pressure behind my eyeballs, I longed to gulp in air. Pain forced me back to the surface.

I saw fire move across the rock, flames dipping and bobbing towards me – Orlando, Grace and Jude carrying firebrands.

Frozen to my core, I raised both arms and yelled for them to join in the search. 'It's Aaron. He went under. Help!'

Orlando was the first to throw down his torch and dive fully clothed from the rock. The splash rose high into the night air. Within seconds Grace and Jude had joined us. So now we were four, diving down with fear in our hearts, plunging and kicking, reaching out with our fingertips to touch only rock and weeds, rising to the surface to suck in air and dive again.

After my fourth dive, Orlando caught hold of me and dragged me towards the shore. 'Enough,' he gasped. Other figures were running to the scene carrying flash lights, blankets and ropes. I staggered out of the water with Orlando, who handed me over to Aurelie. 'Don't let her come back into the water,' he told her as she wrapped blankets around my shoulders and he waded in.

I struggled to rejoin him but others came and held me – Jean-Luc and Marta. Out in the lake, Jude and Grace broke surface. Grace swam exhausted for the shore. There were more blankets, and from the next cove the sound of a rescue boat starting up.

Too late. Way too late. I knew in my quivering, faltering heart.

The boat appeared round the headland as first Grace then Jude and finally Orlando crawled out of the water. They'd found no sign of Aaron; had been forced to give up as the icy cold invaded their bones.

'It's no good – he's dead,' Grace whispered through chattering teeth.

The rescue boat cast a searchlight into the dark water. The beam raked the rocks where we stood huddled and hopeless.

For a second Holly was caught in a blaze of light. She was standing with Channing, staring at the water, unmoved and still as a marble statue in her white costume – no flicker of emotion, no grief-stricken gesture for her dead boyfriend as the searchlight moved on.

Ziegler and his boat crew promised to carry on searching

the lake until dawn. Aurelie put Marta and Blake on all-night standby on the shore. Meanwhile, Jean-Luc led us back to the social centre to organize dry clothes for Orlando, Grace, Jude and me.

We sat stunned and swathed in blankets by the log fire with the party lights still flickering and the big screen playing music videos to an empty room. In the last two weeks the water had claimed Conner and now Aaron. Two kids – one a total stranger, the other our good friend.

'I can't believe he's gone.' Grace was the first to speak in a slow, halting voice. Someone killed the lights and video. 'I can picture him right here and now, walking into this room the same as always.' Silence.

It broke our hearts to lose Aaron – I had memories of him wearing his Never-trust-anyone T-shirt, striding along the lakeside trail in his hiking boots, of him refusing to have his hair cut when Holly asked him to, saying he preferred the wild, heavy metal look. And I remembered him laughing and wrestling with Holly as she came up from behind with a pair of scissors. Samson and Delilah. Mainly laughing – that's how I pictured Aaron.

'There was a fight – Aaron and Channing.' My chest hurt, I shivered all over as I tried to explain to the others how it had happened.

Jean-Luc interrupted to tell us Aaron's parents had

been informed and were on their way. Then he sat on the arm of the couch and invited us to confide in him. 'How much alcohol had Aaron drunk?' he asked.

The question sent a shock wave around our grieving group. 'What kind of question is that?' Orlando wanted to know.

'Blake says she saw him earlier this evening with a six-pack of Budweiser,' Jean-Luc explained.

I shook my head. 'She's wrong. Aaron doesn't drink.' Plus, he was fixated on getting Holly out of here – no time for even a sip of alcohol.

'I'm sorry, Tania, but I felt I had to check it out.' Jean-Luc sounded sincerely apologetic. 'So why did Aaron and Channing fight?'

'Over Holly.' It was so obvious I wondered why he needed to ask. Then I realized that he was leaving tomorrow and had already mentally logged off, so maybe didn't know the full story. 'Holly's decided she wants to stay at New Dawn.'

'Yes, my stepfather has offered her a job.' He put me straight on the being out of the loop theory. 'Aurelie will train Holly to take over from me, liaising with Explorers' families, doing administrative work.'

Yet again it seemed we were caught on the wrong foot. 'Aaron doesn't – *didn't* know that. He thought Holly's decision was down to Channing, period.'

Jean-Luc sighed. 'None of that matters now, I guess.' Seeing Aurelie beckon him from the doorway, he walked swiftly across the room, spoke with his sister then turned and called to us. 'Still no news,' he reported, before going off with her.

Jude turned straight to me. 'So?' he urged.

'You want the whole story?'

Grace and Jude nodded, while Orlando took Jean-Luc's place on the arm of the couch.

'No way was Aaron going to win that fight. Sure, it was one on one, but Channing had phenomenal strength. It wasn't natural.'

'And what about Holly?' Orlando asked.

'Nothing. No reaction. Zilch.' I turned to Grace. 'You remember what happens when the dark angels take over your mind?'

She nodded. 'It felt like I had no free will. I believed everything Ezra told me about the whole universe – the way the planets orbit their suns and how the dark angels have the power to change their course, make meteors crash into them, send stars shooting through outer space, lots of cosmic crap. I was under his spell and I couldn't put one step in front of another without his permission, couldn't think, couldn't react, would have walked through fire if Ezra told me to.'

'That's the way it is now with Holly,' I confirmed. 'And the way I see it, Channing used a lot of force to seduce her out there in the wilderness. She's smart and she's strong – she would have been on her guard. Remember, no one saw what happened and when we finally got to her on the island, her jacket and T-shirt were torn. That wasn't no hypothermic reaction, the way the paramedic described it. That was Channing!'

'OK, wait!' Jude put up his hand to slow me down. 'Let me get this right. Tania, when you say "seduce", do you mean what I think you mean?'

'We're talking rape,' I confirmed. 'These dark angels – they have to go the whole way, make actual love to you. Some of them don't care about consent. They just need to do it and that's the point of no return.'

Still remembering Ezra, Grace retreated inside herself. She hung her head while Jude stood up and paced between the bear rug and the fire. Orlando didn't shift from his place by my side.

'So that was it, out on the wilderness walk Channing did what he had to do. He brings Holly back to New Dawn and prepares for the final ritual – the ceremony where she officially steps over on to the dark side, which is going to happen any time soon. Then tonight, when we show up with Aaron, Channing recognizes him as the only possible threat still standing in his way because not many days ago Holly's heart belonged to Aaron. They were in love and it was the real deal. Maybe she'll set eyes on him and remember her old life. In Channing's place, what would you do?'

'I'd get rid of Aaron,' Orlando said. 'Obviously the guy has no conscience. Stealing souls and killing people is what he does.'

I nodded. 'What happened tonight – Channing was in charge of the whole thing. First, he let Aaron see him and Holly by the lake. He waits for Aaron to run and fetch me, he listens to my pathetic decoy excuse.'

'Which was?'

'I said Ziegler needed him,' I sighed. 'I told him Jarrold had escaped again.'

Jarrold! I glanced up to see him right there, glaring in at us through the floor-to-ceiling window, his palms pressed against the glass, his eyes gleaming.

Unnerved, I went back to my story. 'Channing went along with it – he faked going off to search for the runaway but only so that he could lure Aaron further away from the party towards the lake. Once he isolated him, he picked him off the way a farmer shoots vermin – pow, into the lake!'

Jarrold didn't move from the window. His eyes gleamed and there was a weird smile on his face. Maybe he was lip-reading every word I said.

Grace looked up with tears in her eyes. Jude sat quietly. I leaned my head against Orlando.

Jarrold stared in at us. Behind him, out of the night sky, snowflakes started to fall.

'Stay home, stay warm.'

Dad's advice was easy to follow. Next morning I drew back my curtains on fifteen centimetres of fresh snow and a leaden grey sky. Bad weather was forecast to last at least forty-eight hours, through to Monday.

'And you, Orlando, please stay with Tania.'

So Orlando called home while Dad slogged into Denver to the hospital.

'Stuck in traffic,' he texted two hours later. And again, after another two hours: 'Will visit Mom then find motel in city. Interstate closed – no way back home.'

I went out on to the porch and gazed across the valley towards Carlsbad. Snow lay round about, deep and crisp and even, like in the Wenceslas song.

'I feel so helpless,' I told Orlando when I went back inside. My totally undomesticated guy was trying to keep it together by doing normal stuff like cooking breakfast

352

even though he knew neither of us could eat a thing.

'Can you even imagine how Aaron's parents are taking this?' he reminded me.

We knew Mr and Mrs Baker had reached New Dawn at midnight to hear the latest update from Antony Amos himself. We'd seen them talking in the entrance to the social centre, had heard phrases like 'The search party is still out there . . . We haven't given up.'

The look on Aaron's mom's face showed that she was hanging on to every thread of hope, but Michael Baker was hollow-eyed and haggard. His strong, handsome features had disintegrated the way Conner's parents' did when I came across them at the hospital. After all, he was part of the national park rescue team – he knew exactly what happens to the human body submerged under water in sub-zero temperatures, and how quickly.

So I partly stayed home on Saturday morning out of exhaustion and cowardice, knowing that I couldn't face their grief.

'Try to eat,' Orlando told me as I let the white world close me in.

I pushed away the plate. For the hundredth time I wished I'd done something different. 'I should have come to find you. I shouldn't have let Aaron face Channing alone.'

Orlando pulled me out of the guilt trap as only he knew how. 'Tania, let it go. What happened happened.'

'We were crazy even to think we could get Holly out of there just by talking. I should have known.'

'Let it go,' he repeated. 'You know what this guilt trip of yours is? It's a way of pulling attention in, grabbing sympathy. Well, I do – I sympathize, honestly and with all my heart. Now move on.'

See what I mean – Orlando doesn't bend my way and let us both sink under a mountain of helpless, hopeless emotion. Like me, he was sick with grief over Aaron but he didn't go under. In that way he's stronger than me.

In any case the grief came knocking.

At eleven a.m. the door bell rang and Orlando opened it to Michael Baker. He came alone, desperate to squeeze every drop of information out of the witnesses who had been there when his son died.

When? How? Why? He looked like a dead man walking.

With Orlando holding my hand, I held myself together and gave him the bare facts as I'd witnessed them. He told us he and his wife, Tracey, knew Aaron was in bad shape after the break-up with Holly but they'd thought he'd get over it. They hadn't realized how deep it went.

'He genuinely loved her.' Orlando kept it simple. Both

he and I steered away from good versus evil, from fallen angels and twisted hearts.

'They suspect he'd been drinking,' Michael said with an angry shake of his head. 'I told Amos that was so untypical. I taught my son to steer clear of alcohol.'

'We didn't see him with a drink in his hands,' Orlando insisted. 'We told the New Dawn guys the same thing – in our view, Aaron was sober.'

Aaron's dad seemed to be on automatic pilot, reciting over and over again the few facts he already knew. So he didn't react to Orlando's news. 'They said the alcohol tipped him over the edge, that he lost control and challenged the guy he suspected of stealing Holly from him. Then there was a scuffle and he lost his balance. Afterwards all hell broke loose – people shouting and screaming diving in to save him, a rescue boat, teams of people out there searching.'

I was still hung up on the question of alcohol. 'It's not true,' I insisted, waiting until Michael came out of his manic-recollection phase. I grabbed his hand and made him look at me. 'Believe me, Aaron was stone cold sober. He knew Holly was in terrible danger so he tried to save her.'

Aaron's father met my gaze with haunted eyes from his prison of loss. 'It would have been quick,' he said quietly. 'In those temperatures, with those underwater currents and with alcohol involved, it would have been over in less than five minutes.'

After he left the house and stood talking with Orlando on the drive, I put on my jacket and walked out into the garden. I had to breathe cold, clean air, stand and gaze at the mountains and the lake.

'I will tell you all you need to know,' the body of Conner Steben whispers from the bottom of Turner Lake. 'They say it was my weak heart but I can tell you different.'

I listened intently, feeling something shift in my brain – a door opening to allow in a new idea. Conner is an angel of light. My mourning dove is absent from the aspens, but she can speak through a drowned corpse.

Conner rises from the lake in the distance. He is in my garden, young and full of life again with a chipped-tooth smile.

'How did you die?' I ask.

'They killed me. You know it's true.'

He is risen from the grey water, free of the decaying death-pews and the shards of coloured glass, surrounded by light.

'Not your heart?' I repeat.

'The New Dawn people – they saw I was like you, Tania – psychic and on the side of the angels of light. They discovered

356

that I'd been sent to spy on them. They were many. I was one.'

I shudder and shake with fear, scared of my dark angel's thirst for revenge, certain he will soon do to me what he did to Conner. 'Who did it?' I whisper. I fear hearing his answer as he opens his mouth to speak. 'No, don't say the name – not until I'm ready!'

'Not who you think.' Conner waits for me to grow calm again. 'I was in the lake, swimming strongly with other triathletes all around. One dived below the surface, caught me by the leg, dragged me down.'

'Not Jarrold?' I whisper.

'Listen. This dark soul drags me down. He strikes me with a sharp stone, a flint from the pebble beach.'

'Who? Who struck the blow?'

Conner's voice is soft. He sounds like Maia, like Zenaida. They are all one angel of light.

'The guy who stands at the right hand of your dark angel,' he murmurs. 'His name is Channing, dealer in death.'

To my certain knowledge Channing had now killed two people – Aaron and Conner.

I am not alone. I am not alone. Pacing to and fro in my snowy, fenced garden I repeated the simple phrase like a mantra, and when Orlando finally said goodbye to Mr Baker and came to find me, I was sloughing off my fear and moving on.

'Look at this.' I showed Orlando a recent text message from Aurelie.

'Please come,' it read. 'Papa and Jean-Luc are arguing. JL needs your help.'

'Isn't this the day he leaves?' Orlando asked with a deep frown creasing his forehead. 'Text her back. Tell her no.'

The force of his reaction rocked me back on my heels. 'I don't get it,' I complained. 'Don't you see – this could be a way in for us to contact Holly again!'

'We tried once and look what happened.' He told it like it was – no frills. His stubborn expression told me he was not going back to New Dawn.

'So we give up on her?'

Orlando glared back at me. 'How many people besides Aaron have to die rescuing her?'

'No one. Not if we get this right.' I gathered every ounce of energy to convince him that we shouldn't and wouldn't run away. 'We almost got Holly out of there last night. Until the tragedy with Aaron happened, we had a good chance. And this message has come out of the blue – Aurelie contacting me and asking for my help. It's like another door has suddenly opened. So I vote we say yes, we don't give any sign that we know who Antony Amos is or what he's trying to do to Holly.'

'And to you,' Orlando reminded me. 'You're his main target, Tania. You're convinced he wants to punish you. So what am I supposed to say – yeah, go right in there, girl, and put your own head on the block?'

'I won't. I'll take care. Honestly, I've come this far and I can't turn back.'

I waited for an age for Orlando to back down. He was studying me, thinking it through from every angle, realizing that he couldn't argue me out of this. 'OK, text Aurelie. Ask her how she thinks you can help.'

'Cool.' Fumbling with my phone, I typed in the message.

Straight away I received a reply. 'The fight is about Aaron. JL needs you as a witness.'

Again, Orlando took a long time to work it through. 'So you go and you give Amos the facts – Aaron wasn't drunk, Channing set up the whole thing.'

'And I do it in front of Jean-Luc and Aurelie. They're people who can spread the truth and speak up for Aaron. At least, Jean-Luc will be able to.'

I was already grabbing my car keys and Orlando saw that there was nothing else left to say or do. 'I'll come with you,' he decided suddenly, reaching the door before I did. We'll go in my truck.'

Tilting back my head, I gave a big sigh of relief. 'Thank you!' I mouthed and I kissed him.

I am not alone! The mantra whizzed round and round inside my head.

'So you'll go searching for Holly, find out what kind of shape she's in while I look as if I'm sorting out the fight between Amos and Jean-Luc?'

'Deal,' he said reluctantly through gritted teeth, climbing into the knight-in-shining-armour truck and switching on the engine.

Our plan was agreed. We drove down Becker Hill and through town, out towards the lake. Fresh snow and a blue sky made the whole place look like a scene from a Christmas card, easing our tension and making us exclaim over the beauty of the pine tree branches weighted down by snow, pointing out the drifts piled up two or three metres at each side of the road. Eventually, nerves tightening again, we drove off the highway and along the track to New Dawn until we came to a snow drift that totally blocked the route.

'So now we walk,' I decided before Orlando could change his mind.

We got out of the truck, skirted the snow drift and headed on until the first buildings of the New Dawn

Community came into view between the trees.

'And now we split up,' I insisted. If Orlando wanted to find Holly, he had to do it in secret and it had to look like I'd come alone.

'If you need me, use your phone,' he muttered, kissing me quickly and warning me to take care of myself before striking out up the hill to our left, heading for a stand of pines overlooking the lake.

As I watched him go, I longed to change my mind. 'Come back!' I almost called.

Give me the courage to stand fast in a blizzard, not to turn from my dark angel. Seize him, grab him, fight him down.

And I knew with total, unbending certainty in the core of me that I couldn't run away from this – I just couldn't.

So I waited until Orlando disappeared under the trees then I set off, keeping to low ground by the lake and texting Aurelie as I went.

'Am arriving on foot. Where are you?'

'Come to Trail's End.'

I walked up the hill as fast as I could, though the deep snow slowed me down. Approaching Amos's cabin, I saw other footsteps trampled into the drifts and heard voices through the open door.

'Why did you tell Richard to call in the search parties?'

Jean-Luc demanded. 'They should be out there, looking until we find him!'

'There's no point.' Amos reacted to his stepson's raised voice by sounding steady and calm. It was obvious that this was the way the power balance had always been – Jean-Luc's passion and rebellion versus Amos's stone-walling rationality.

'Don't you care how this will look to the outside world?' Jean-Luc demanded. 'We throw a party and someone dies. We spend less than twenty-four hours looking for the body.'

'It's over,' Amos insisted. 'We'll let the cops do their thing as soon as they can reach us.'

'Yeah, you'll get them crawling all over this one, I warn you.'

'I know it. Plus rescue helicopters, divers – the works.' As he spoke, Amos came out on to the porch and spotted me. He wore a thick blue woollen jacket over the white costume from the previous night – a sign that he hadn't slept. Likewise Aurelie, who came out after her stepfather.

'Tania, thank you for coming,' she said, her tired face brightening. 'Papa, Tania has all the answers to last night. She can settle this fight between you and Jean-Luc.'

Stepping down from the porch, she kissed me on both cheeks then smiled. 'It would break my heart for Jean-

362

Luc to leave New Dawn in anger and never come back.'

'I'll do what I can,' I told her, feeling the tension between the two guys and stepping into the cabin to find Jean-Luc standing beside the bronze horse statue, hands in pockets, his lip curled into a surly expression that didn't alter as I walked in.

As peacemaker, Aurelie drew her stepfather in from the porch. 'The question is – what shape was Aaron in?' she stated. 'Richard has evidence from Blake and a few other Explorers that he was drinking heavily.'

'No.' I cut in straight away; spoke louder than I'd intended.

Amos looked at me sharply. 'Stop and think, Tania,' he warned. 'This is important. It's likely to be a major factor in any investigation.'

I nodded. 'That's why I'm here. I already told Jean-Luc that Aaron never drank alcohol.'

'And I gave you the facts exactly as Tania told them,' Jean-Luc said angrily to his stepfather. 'But who do you believe – Ziegler or me?'

'Channing swears he grabbed the remains of a six-pack from the guy seconds before he fell into the water,' Amos insisted. 'The kid was so drunk he could hardly stand.'

'Not true,' I said, feeling my pulse race and the anger

steadily rising at the way Channing had altered the facts.

'Which is why we have to carry on searching,' Jean-Luc pointed out. 'If we find the body they can test for alcohol in the blood.'

Again Aurelie tried to calm the situation. 'So, Tania, tell Papa again – you're one hundred per cent certain Aaron wasn't drinking?'

'Stone-cold sober,' I muttered. Jean-Luc's talk about blood tests had made me shudder but I measured my words carefully and watched for Amos's reaction. 'Aaron's only motive in being at the party last night was to talk to Holly, which he finally managed to do down by the lake.'

As Amos pursed his lips and frowned, Jean-Luc raised his hand then slapped it down on the table, making the statue shake. 'What did I tell you!' he exclaimed. 'Who do you believe now – me and Tania or your precious Ziegler; he who can do no wrong?'

Amos's temper snapped and he stepped angrily towards Jean-Luc then changed his mind. Without saying a word he turned on his heel and disappeared into his cinema room, slamming the door after him. This was the first time I'd seen the great man thrown off balance and it left me with a queasy feeling in my stomach.

'Jean-Luc . . .' Aurelie began.

He pushed her to one side, went out on to the porch.

'Don't ask me to apologize,' he said over his shoulder.

'Before you go – please!'

But he didn't listen. Instead, he strode off through the snow.

There were tears in Aurelie's eyes. 'I'm sorry,' she told me. 'None of us is handling this well. The boy drowned – it's painful. It reminds us of my mother.'

Right there and then, in a sudden flash, a picture slammed into my brain and shunted me to a different world.

I see the over-laden ferry wallowing in a blue ocean, the sun burning down. Water seeps in through leaking portholes, someone raises the alarm. The engine churns heavily and the boat turns slowly, clumsily for the shore. There is a gut-wrenching smell of diesel. Passengers rush to the deck from the hold below. A dark-skinned woman in a yellow sari is crushed with a dozen others on a metal stairway. She hands her small child to a middle-aged woman in a white linen shirt who is two steps above her. The woman struggles to carry the child towards the square of light above their heads. Water is rushing in, filling the dark hold. It rises up the metal stairway. The boat tilts to an angle of forty-five degrees.

People reach down from the deck, they stretch out their hands. As the water rises to her waist, the woman in white passes the child to safety. Then a man behind her drags her back in his own effort to climb the stairs. She falls under the oily surface without a sound.

The boat tilts, the sea rises.

'I'm sorry I couldn't do anything to help,' I told a weeping Aurelie. I was sure my vision was true and was shocked that Juliet Amos had died trying to save a child from drowning.

'This time Jean-Luc won't forgive Papa,' she cried. 'There have been too many arguments, too much bad blood between them.'

'Richard Ziegler holds a lot of power here,' I suggested. 'That's a big problem for your brother.'

'Yes, ever since Richard was sent here by the court, Papa has seen something in him that he liked – a quality of leadership that my brother doesn't possess. Jean-Luc was always jealous.'

'So shall I go after him?' I asked. Jean-Luc was making for his own cabin on the lake shore, getting ready no doubt to pick up his bags and drive to the airport as soon as the grader went out to clear snow from the track.

Aurelie wiped her tears then nodded and headed for the cinema room. 'I'll talk to Papa. Good luck, Tania!'

As I set off on my mission to reconcile the warring siblings, I took out my phone to check in with Orlando as I went. 'Jeez!' I sighed when I saw that I'd lost signal. 'I only hope you're doing better than me!'

I was rushing along a trail beside the frozen lake, hoping that he'd found Holly and not paying attention to my surroundings when Jarrold did his speciality thing of appearing out of nowhere.

He stepped out from behind a three-metre finger of rock, right across my path. 'It's always great to see you, Tania, but you really shouldn't have come,' he warned mockingly.

'What are you doing? Step out of my way!' Feebly I tried to push past him but quickly gave up.

'It's not safe for you here,' he muttered.

'How, not safe? What do you mean?'

I'm in the dark forest with wolves all around. I smell them – their wet fur, their stink. I expect the wolf man to appear on the ridge above our heads, and there he is – wearing a wolf skin around his shoulders, the mummified head draped back, a glittering knife at his waist. His long yellow hair blows across his narrow face, his eyes are lit with a strange amber glow.

'You're telling tales against Ziegler,' Jarrold reminded me. 'He's Amos's head honcho, remember.'

'Him and Channing,' I added. Yet again I felt overpowered by Jarrold's physical presence, scared to death by the wolf-man vision.

A smile played over his lips. 'Exactly. Your version of the way Aaron died is about to meet with major opposition.'

'This is so not funny. Why do you always make a joke?'

'Why do you always get into places where you're not wanted?' he countered. 'Why can't you see who is your friend?'

'OK, friend, do something for me!' If I couldn't challenge him physically, I could try to stand up to him mentally. 'Tell me where to find Holly.'

'Still on that old game?' he sighed. 'You don't give up, do you?'

'And last night you betrayed me.' I stayed calm on the outside, gave him one more chance to prove whose side he was on – light or dark, good or evil. 'I saw you talking to Ziegler right after I'd told you we'd come to take Holly back home from the party. You let him know our motive and that's why Channing stuck to her like glue.'

Jarrold blinked. 'You disappoint me.'

'Are you denying it?'

'Totally. What I told Ziegler was the exact opposite. I tried to convince him not to worry – you and your little gang were here for the party, end of story.'

I gave a small gasp of surprise and relief that Jarrold hadn't played the traitor. 'And now – what are you doing right now, jumping out from behind a rock when I'm trying fix up the situation between Amos and Jean-Luc?'

'Same as you, Tania. I was on my way to Jean-Luc's cabin. Ziegler gave me the job of driving him to the airport. I thought maybe I could be peacemaker en route, just like you.'

'So let's go,' I said, pushing against him again and this time finding that he let me pass. He kept pace with me as I walked to Jean-Luc's cabin.

'So, Friend,' he said, as if he was using an ironic title that I didn't deserve. 'Let me pass on one more small piece of information.'

'Which is?' There was so much in my brain that I was trying to compute, so much pressure to get to Holly before they finally dragged her to the dark side, that I didn't feel especially interested in anything Jarrold had to say.

'About Aaron,' he said.

I stopped in my tracks under the final stand of pinon pines before we reached the shore. Jean-Luc's cabin was thirty metres away, the ice on the lake sparkled in bright sunlight.

'You want to know why Amos and Ziegler called off the search?'

My heart thudded, almost stopped then kick-started back into life. Finally I gave Jarrold my full attention.

'Because there really wasn't any point,' he said.

I didn't speak. I didn't understand. I waited for more.

'They didn't find a body, and you want to know why?'

Scarcely able to nod, I held my breath.

'Because there isn't one,' Jarrold explained with that strange half-smile.

'Why not? What are you saying?'

'Imagine a different scenario,' he said, still toying with me. 'Say things didn't happen the way you saw them, Tania. Say Holly's ex-boyfriend didn't really drown in Turner Lake.'

The ice glistened, the sun made the frozen surface sparkle like a billion tiny diamonds.

'Aaron's alive?' I gasped. I felt an unreasonable surge of hope mixed with a sense that everything was slip-sliding out of control.

'Maybe.' Jarrold leaned close and put his lips to my ear. 'Don't tell anyone I told you,' he whispered then walked on towards the glittering lake.

17

It felt like freefalling from a plane and plummeting down. You pull the cord and expect the chute to open. If the chute fails, you have no chance. This is how it hit me when Jarrold twisted the facts about Aaron's death – falling without a parachute, dropping through chaos into the dark jaws of the unknown.

He'd walked away and left me falling, gasping, grabbing onto thin air.

He suggested things didn't happen the way I saw them, said to use my imagination.

'*Someone* drowned in that lake!' I yelled after him as he disappeared inside Jean-Luc's cabin. I started to struggle through the snow after him then stopped.

Or maybe they only wanted me to *believe* that someone had died – after all, the dark angels were masters of shape-shifting and twisting the truth.

'Imagine a different scenario,' Jarrold had said.

Last night as I stood in the doorway of the social centre, Aaron had run up to me in the black native American vest and white shirt that Grace had stitched for him. He'd said he needed my help to split Channing away from Holly. I'd said no, we needed the others – Orlando, Jude and Grace. He'd insisted it had to be me, and quick.

So wait. What if that hadn't been Aaron after all? What if it had been one of the shape-shifting angels taking on Aaron's identity? Suddenly it hit me as a new possibility.

And remember how easy it had been for me to persuade Channing to go off into the night on a fool's errand, how Aaron had failed to get through to Holly on the rock overlooking the lake. What if that had been set up to fool me? The whole fight was fake, and Aaron's fall from the rock – all one big illusion.

I was tumbling into confusion, into a nightmare of doubt and not knowing – and this was exactly what my dark angel had planned!

These new realizations shot through my body like jolts of electricity. I'd been tricked. If there was a chance that Aaron was alive, I knew I had to tell Orlando! But before I could set off to find him, Jean-Luc came out of his cabin with Jarrold, both lugging Jean-Luc's heavy bags in the direction of the parking lot. Jarrold called to ask for my help.

'Take the small bag,' he instructed, throwing me a blue carry-on, which I caught.

'You realize the road out of here is impassable?' I said, then told them about the drift blocking the track out on to the highway.

Jean-Luc groaned and muttered something about the whole world conspiring against his leaving New Dawn – including the Colorado weather. 'All I want to do is sit on that plane to Paris and get the hell out of here.'

'So you two wait in the social centre while I fix the snow plough on to the grader,' Jarrold offered. 'It'll take me an hour maximum to get out there and clear the route.' He abandoned us with the bags and forged ahead towards the service area where they parked tractors and other big machinery.

'That Jarrold is quite a guy,' Jean-Luc grimaced as we lugged the bags through the snow. He sneaked a glance my way to judge my reaction.

'Action man,' I agreed. 'Quite scary, actually.'

'Really?' We'd reached the entrance to the social centre and Jean-Luc arranged his bags under the porch. 'I already told you – he's irresistible to women – those muscles, that Viking look.'

'Believe me, here's one girl who can resist,' I muttered, maybe too forcefully.

Jean-Luc grinned and said nothing, and before long, Regan and Blake and a bunch of other Explorers came out on to the porch to say their goodbyes and I saw the opportunity to slip away.

'Hey, Tania!' It was Marta who stopped me. 'Are you doing OK – after, you know, last night at the party, the accident to your buddy . . . ?'

Her voice fell away and I didn't have time to answer before a sudden loud siren tore apart the silence. It started faintly from a distance but soon rose to an ear-splitting wail, bringing everyone, including Kaylee and Ava, running out of the centre on to the porch.

The siren came from the direction of the dam so we all ran to the lake shore and strained to see what was happening. Half a mile away we made out major activity – giant yellow trucks and diggers were chugging along a forest track towards the dam, and still the screech of the siren split the air.

Then Ziegler came running down from Trail's End, a two-way radio in his hand. He slid and skidded through the snow, kept his balance, kept on coming. 'They found a crack in the dam!' he reported. 'Ice damage – a twenty-metre split.'

My heart thudded to a halt then flickered back to life. A breach in the dam. A wall of water waiting to burst through.

'Can they fix it?' Kaylee asked above the general hubbub.

'They're doing all they can.' As usual Ziegler was in control. 'The engineers out there can't pour fresh concrete in sub-zero temperatures so they have trucks carrying sand bags to shore up the crack. But there's massive pressure from the water behind the dam. It depends if they can plug the gap fast enough.'

Desperately I looked along the shore and up the slope into the forest to see where Orlando had got to.

'The concrete in that dam is decades old. Something like this was bound to happen.' Jean-Luc sounded resigned. To him this latest emergency looked like part of the conspiracy to stop him breaking free from his stepfather and everything that the New Dawn Community represented. He stood back and watched Ziegler organize a team of Explorers who would drive out the New Dawn tractors to help with the sand-bagging operation.

Quickly Amos's deputy got his guys together and they headed off to the service area, leaving the rest of us to fend for ourselves.

'What happens if they can't fix it?' It was Ava who nervously asked the question that weighed heaviest on all our minds.

'Yeah, there's two million cubic metres of water behind that dam,' Regan informed us. 'If it breaks, that whole amount of water floods into this valley where we're standing right now.'

My own heart was already flittering and fluttering, but this new information pressed a panic button in everyone else's minds.

'I'm out of here!' Blake was the first to make the decision. She told Marta and Regan that they could ride with her into town and the three of them quickly headed off.

'Not yet.' I yelled after them, raising my voice above the wailing emergency siren to explain that the road was blocked by snow.

'So what now? Do we try to get out of here on foot?' Marta turned to Regan, who agreed that the best tactic was to climb to higher ground.

'If we make it to the ridge above the cabins we should be OK, at least for a while,' he said. 'If the dam does give way and the water looks like it's going to flood the valley, we climb higher until we're sure we're safe.'

So that's where they headed – everyone except Jean-

Luc, who decided to set out along the trail to find out how Jarrold was getting along.

The siren scrambled my brain as I watched a dozen figures struggle up the snowy hillside and disappear into the trees.

I hear spirit voices lamenting in the icy wind, see ghost dancers fall exhausted to the ground.

'Our dream is dead,' Red Cloud sighs from a high ridge. He is silhouetted against a grey sky. 'We give up our land to the rising waters, we leave our own country for ever.'

Satanta, Lone Wolf, Swift Bear and Big Tree stand beside him as flood water surrounds them. They lift their gaze to the snow-capped mountains, they dream of the past, of sweeping across the plains on horseback, of living off the land, gathering food, making medicines from the plants that grow. It is over. The mountains they roamed, the freedom they enjoyed, the rivers they fished in and the buffalo they fed from are lost.

A swirling torrent sweeps it all away.

I stood alone by the shore, overcoming the impulse to run with the rest of the Explorers. Then the siren suddenly stopped and deep silence engulfed me. I looked around – which way should I go, what should I do?

Someone came running down the hill towards me, shouting my name. 'Tania!' I was in my cocoon of bewildered silence, at first not recognizing Orlando's voice, not knowing which way to turn, certain because of my latest vision that the crack in the dam would get bigger, that the water eventually would break through. The corpses in Turner Lake would rise to greet us.

'Tania, come with me!' Orlando grabbed my hand and staggered on. 'I found Holly. She's in Ziegler's cabin. Come this way!'

I ran with him towards a cabin I hadn't visited before, only convinced that it belonged to Ziegler when I spotted his black Stetson hanging from a hook in the porch.

'Holly's in here?' I gasped, staggering the last few steps up the hill.

Ziegler's cabin was isolated beneath a shadowy overhang, overlooking a small frozen pond and hidden from onlookers by a cluster of tall redwoods.

'Alone!' he promised. 'I was sneaking a peek through the side window – when the siren started, Ziegler took a call on his radio, locked the door and left.'

Orlando and I approached without making any noise, stepped into the porch and pushed at the door. It was locked on the inside. 'Where's Channing?' I asked, every nerve stretched to breaking point.

'I have no idea. Come and look through here.' Orlando led me to a small window at the side of the cabin.

The blind was pulled low, but by crouching and

peering through the gap I could make out a couch and a low coffee table with three glasses, a framed picture of mountains and a door into an inner room. 'There's no one here,' I whispered. 'Maybe Channing came for her, probably when he learned about the problem with the dam. There's a big crack in the concrete: they're scared it'll split open.'

'How much time do we have?' Crouching beside me, Orlando took in the bad news and kept a cool head.

'Nobody knows. Ziegler took a team to help fix it.'

'Shh!' He held his finger to his lips and pointed into the cabin.

I took another look and saw Holly emerge from the inner room. She looked totally out of it – her party clothes were crumpled, her eyes wide and staring. In fact, she hardly seemed to know where she was as she stumbled towards the coffee table. She took up one of the glasses and drank.

'Let's go!' Orlando told me, running round to the front of the low, log building and this time knocking loudly on the door. Through the glass panel we saw Holly recoil at the sound then vanish again into the back room.

'We have to break in,' I decided, seizing a log from the wood pile on the porch and using it to smash the glass panel, then easing my hand through the jagged hole to slip the latch and turn the handle. The door swung open and Orlando and I rushed inside.

Holly reappeared carrying a knife – an antique thing with a carved horn handle and a long straight blade. There was a crazy look in her eyes as she pulled the door shut and advanced towards us.

'What got into you? Stop right there!' I cried.

She ignored my plea and kept on coming until there was only the coffee table between us. Suddenly Orlando lashed out with his foot and kicked the underside of the table, up-ending it and sending it crashing against her. She staggered back and dropped the knife. I dashed to pick it up.

'Tania, give it back to me!' Holly's hair had fallen loose out of its ponytail, her face was pale, her voice childlike and desperate as she ran to stand between me and the inner door.

'Who's in there?' I asked, feeling the hairs at the back of my neck start to prickle.

'Nothing. No one. Ziegler and Channing said not to let anyone see!'

'I don't care about that, Holly. Just let me through.' Pushing her forcefully to one side, Orlando opened the door and disappeared into the inner room. I got a glimpse of a bed and a shower cubicle before Holly regained her balance and threw herself towards me.

'Give it back to me, Tania!' she screeched, wrestling the knife from me and shoving me out on to the porch. 'You shouldn't be here. Channing will be angry with me.'

'Who's in that room?' I demanded, wrenching myself free of her grasp. She was still strong and athletic, despite Channing's mind-control. And again she wielded the knife.

'Who do you think is in there?' she screeched. 'Aaron, of course!' Quickly swinging from desperation to manic aggression, her eyes bulged as she jabbed the knife at me. 'We let everyone think that he's dead because he's one of us now,' she yelled. 'He's going to live here at New Dawn, leave his old life behind.'

'Stop!' I cried. Ignoring the knife, I pushed her off the porch then ran inside to find Orlando leading Aaron out of the bedroom where he'd been held captive.

'I don't know what the hell's happening,' Orlando mumbled.

'They tricked us big-time,' I gabbled. 'Aaron didn't drown.'

Orlando supported a figure that was Aaron but not Aaron. The broken figure stumbling towards me, hands bound and with duct tape over his mouth, had the crazy, wavy hair, the broad shoulders and sturdy figure of the guy I knew, but his face was unrecognizable – almost bloodless and vacant, like a zombie. His eyes were swollen, his head hung forward.

'Tania, grab him!' Orlando gasped as Aaron's knees buckled and he slumped to the ground.

Together we lifted him, peeled off the tape and untied the rope then helped him stumble across the room. Holly was out on the porch, blocking our exit.

'You can't take him!' she whined, confused and desperate. Without being aware, she loosened her grasp on the knife and let it clatter on to the wooden floor. 'He'll lose his chance of joining the community. He has to stay here with us!'

The sound of her voice seemed to rouse Aaron from his stupor. He raised his head and tried to speak. 'Wrong . . .' he mumbled. 'Holly, come . . .'

'We all have to leave,' Orlando insisted as we dragged Aaron to the porch step. He stopped only to pick up the knife. 'If the dam bursts this whole place will go under.'

The devil rises from the lake. Water breaks over his powerful shoulders. His green eyes glare and he spreads his terrible wings. The dam bursts and a huge column spouts thirty metres into the air. A wall of water thunders down the valley, taking everything in its path.

And before Orlando, Aaron and I could step down

from the cabin towards the frozen pond, shadows cast by the cliff behind us started to shift, the trees surrounding us twisted and came alive. Ziegler and Antony Amos stood there before us.

Time stopped. The two men appeared by the pond. Orlando and I supported Aaron. Holly froze in fear.

Branches bent and cracked, shadows deepened. Suddenly day became night.

I was face to face, unarmed against Amos, my dark angel. In my heart I always knew that it would reach this point.

'Oh, Tania.' Ziegler sighed. He was the first to move, advancing towards us and bringing the darkness with him. 'Why not keep on running?'

Terror pinned me to the spot. Ziegler's face was wolf-narrow, his eyes were the eyes of a hunter closing in on his prey. Behind him, Amos too started to approach.

'You won't win,' I told them, my voice hardly audible against the creaking, cracking pine trees. A wind tore through them, snapping branches and sending them crashing to the ground. 'You had me fooled for a while but now I know who you are.'

Antony Amos was my angel of death. Ziegler was his lieutenant. Now that we had come this far, I would speak their names and they would be ripped apart, destroyed, sent whirling back into the shadows. I would be saved.

'Oh, Tania,' Ziegler sighed again in mock pity. 'Our power to deceive is greater than you realize. I told you – you should have kept on running. But no, you played the hero, came back for your friends and now look what has happened.'

Cruel and tall, growing taller, towering over me, Ziegler's eyes glinted in the darkness.

The wind howled, the shadows moved, a hundred wolf eyes gleamed.

Amos stepped up beside Ziegler. My heart lurched. This was the dreaded time, the return for vengeance that my first dark angel had warned me of. The roar of floodwater filled my ears.

'Richard, what is this?' As Amos put his hand on Ziegler's arm, his voice was weak and quavering, almost lost in the wind. Behind him, a tree swayed, groaned and crashed to the ground.

'Old man, it is time for you to step aside,' Ziegler snarled as he thrust his boss back towards the pond.

Amos gave a startled cry, staggered and fell to his knees.

I let out a gasp, expecting Amos to rise again.

But what I saw was not my arch enemy after all. Amos knelt in the shadow of Ziegler the hunter. He saw Aaron and crumbled into confusion. 'How can this be?' he whimpered. 'Richard, you told me the boy was dead.'

Behind Ziegler, a pack of wolves appeared at the edge of the pond. Hackles raised, tongues lolling, they waited.

I looked from Amos to Ziegler, saw a being that was half man, half wolf, with jaws that would crush, teeth that would tear into soft flesh.

'Your time is over,' wolf-man Ziegler snarled at Amos. 'We have no more use for you.'

Antony Amos was on his knees, slumped forward. Yesterday, an hour, a minute ago he was the great philanthropist, the admired movie director, the idealistic founder of the community. Now he was broken, hardly able to raise his head.

'For a while we let you continue to believe in your new beginnings, your guiding principles,' Ziegler told him scornfully. 'You sent us into the wilderness to turn our hearts, to bond and learn how to trust, yet all the time we used you.'

Amos let out a groan. Using all his strength, he got to his feet, made one last appeal. 'Richard, I don't understand. What are you talking about? Who are you really?'

Smiling, Ziegler replied. 'We are your worst nightmare.'

'But who, who?'

'Nothing you can invent comes near to us. No movie

creation, no figment of your warped imagination – we belong to the dark side, we have power over you all.'

'I trusted you.' Amos felt the pain of betrayal. 'I believed in your redemption.'

The wolves at the edge of the pond stirred. One raised his head and howled.

'You believed what you wanted to believe,' Ziegler mocked. 'That's what everyone does. But let me tell you loud and clear, there is no ancient spirit, no creator in these mountains strong enough to protect you, no greatness, no harmony, no hearts at peace.'

'It was all a lie.' A sudden anger rose in the old man and he grew defiant. 'You betrayed me, Richard, just like you betrayed all these kids in the community. But you're not all-powerful. Whoever you are, you won't escape.'

As Amos moved feebly on to the attack, clenching his fists ready to strike, Ziegler called his pack. The wolves padded forward, slow and deliberate. Meanwhile, their wolf-man leader put up an arm to intercept Amos's weak punch. He thrust him back down on to the frozen ground.

This was too much for Orlando, who jumped from the porch and ran to Amos's side. He tried to help him back on to his feet.

The wolves advanced around the edge of the pond.

They padded softly, gathered behind Ziegler then waited again.

And I was reeling, locked into my own confused thoughts as I watched the scene unfold. Why did I get this wrong? I asked myself.

'Because we're good at what we do.' Ziegler read my mind and gave me my answer in a voice that snapped and snarled. 'We were in control every step of the way – it was simple to make you see it the way we wanted you to see it.'

Closing my eyes to calm myself and think, I picked up on the word 'we'. 'You and who else?' I demanded, watching warily as Orlando supported Amos and the wolves moved in.

'Hah!' Ziegler's laugh was more like a bark. He put up a hand to halt the wolves. 'Tell your boyfriend to stand clear,' he warned.

I didn't have time to speak, and anyway I knew Orlando wouldn't desert the weak old man. As I watched him draw the antique knife from his belt, my heart raced with fear.

Ziegler laughed again. With a quick gesture, he ordered five wolves to close in on Orlando and separate him from Amos. Orlando flashed the blade in their faces, slashing the lead wolf across the muzzle. The wolf whined and recoiled. Then Orlando took Aaron by the wrist and together they darted through the gap and disappeared into the shadows.

'Let them go,' Ziegler ordered angrily. He turned back to Amos. 'You had your uses but your time is over,' he reminded him.

This time Amos recognized the power of his enemy and didn't struggle to his feet. As the wolf pack closed in, he made no move to save himself. He waited until the last second, until the snapping jaws were so close he must feel their hot breath on his face, which was drained of emotion. He looked up at the dark sky and raised his arms wide in that gesture he used to summon the Great Creator, only now it was the gesture of a martyr accepting his fate.

Then, instead of waiting for cruel wolves to pounce and tear him apart, Antony Amos flung himself backwards into the black water.

18

The leader of New Dawn sank out of sight while the far-off siren wailed anew. Disappointed, the wolves stared down at their own distorted reflections.

Wolf man Ziegler laughed and barked.

A second emergency siren sounded, a renewed warning.

There was a loud explosion, a sudden boom and then the distant roar of water. Daylight filtered through the tall trees, the wolves lowered their heads and whined.

The corpses of West Point graveyard float free of their coffins, they rise to the surface. This is the time, the place of death, darkness, suffering. I float with the skulls, am flung by sinuous brown water against uprooted trees, driftwood, capsized boats. A current drags me down. I am drowned. The flesh is stripped from my body. I am bone.

As the Turner dam gave way and water poured through, I turned and ran.

I fled to high ground, fearing the wolf's breath, the swirl of icy water, the black monster rising. Ziegler appeared ahead of me, beside me, behind me, wearing his wolf pelt, fleet of foot, grinning at the chase.

There were five, six, seven of his ghostly images on the hillside, lurking under trees, leaping from rock to rock. Once he came close enough for me to smell his foul breath and see his face – more wolf than man now. He thrust his blunt muzzle into my face and I stared into what should have been his amber eyes. There was nothing – black holes, emptiness. He was a shadow, an illusion. Angrily, I dismissed him from my mind and changed direction. I carried on alone, climbing until I cleared the tree line.

Amos was not my enemy and Richard Ziegler was now my focus – a guy with a colourful history – daredevil stuntman and body double, petty criminal, convert. He was the team leader who'd been in charge of the rescue effort when Conner had drowned, who had driven Holly back to New Dawn after her accident, whose amazing good looks should have rung alarm bells in my head from the start. That's one of the things with the love thieves that makes them so powerful and deceptive – their unnatural, mesmeric beauty.

And Ziegler had said 'we'. The word had fallen naturally from his lips. There were other dark angels, of course – a whole army of them according to Zenaida, enough to outnumber the forces of light. And my job was still to work my way through their ranks until eventually I discovered their leader and named him.

For a few seconds the sun cleared the clouds, there was a breath of warmth on my face.

The fleeting suggestion of my dove's presence gave me confirmation that I was right to follow this plan, plus it gave me the physical strength to climb on into the snowy wasteland until I had a clear view of the valley below.

At first I didn't recognize the scene. The dam – the cement wall that had held back all those millions of litres for more than five decades was gone. A dark-brown deluge had engulfed the snow-lined valley. Power lines were down, the poles swept away like matchsticks, and the tiny, toy-sized yellow diggers and tractors sent to shore up the breach with sandbags were turned on their sides and swept away on a mocking tide of destruction.

And alongside the distant desolation, another factor began to play its part as I felt cold flecks on my cheeks, lifted my eyes to the grey sky and saw that a steady snow had begun to fall.

My stomach churned and tightened. How many

workers were already lost? Would residents at New Dawn make it to higher ground in time? Where were Orlando and Aaron?

Without answers to any of these questions, I pressed on up the mountain until I came to the place I recognized as Shaman Overlook – the flat ledge of rock with the overhang where Holly's Hawk band had camped overnight.

Relieved to see that the Explorer's old shelter was still intact, I hurriedly crawled inside. Protected from the wind and snow, I drew my legs up to my chest and tried to conserve my body heat. Snowflake flurries blew in through the opening so I retreated further under the tarp roof, only to find I was sharing the shelter with a sharp-featured, stinking, wild-eyed fox. More startled even than me, she snarled then bounded free of the enclosed space, out on to the mountain. I groaned, let my forehead drop onto my knees and waited for my heart to stop pounding.

'Be brave,' a voice murmurs. It's borne on the wind. It rattles the loose corners of the tarp roof. 'Hold fast to what you believe. Know your enemy, name your angel of death.'

I'm in my garden, the aspen leaves are still golden and my mourning dove perches on a branch. Zenaida macroura, also known as rain dove – I cling to the known facts.

She is not common-or-garden grey. Her feathers are flecked with brown and black, her breast and belly are pink. She rises with a whistle of wings and flies to a high branch where she can look out across the valley towards Shaman Overlook.

'I will guide you,' she promises. 'When the water bursts through the dam and carries all before it, do not be afraid. It will sweep away evil committed by the dark angels; the valley will be cleansed.'

I sit quietly in the sunlight.

'The dark angels will resist but the water is strong. Look for them in the wild places of the high mountains, remember they are subtle and vengeful, that they cannot escape the hell of their own making. They bring darkness with them.'

In my garden, in the evening sun of early autumn, I sigh at Zenaida's wise prophecy.

'Once they were like me, beautiful angels of light. The heavens were at peace. And then darkness entered their hearts – ambition and pride – and they fell through the immensity of space into eternal misery.'

I watch her and I understand with the finality of nails being knocked into my own coffin that there is nowhere to hide from my dark angel.

I gaze up at my dove, my guardian who sits on the branch amidst the golden leaves of fall, the mirror image of those fallen spirits. Where they plummet, she soars. Where there is a long, dark night, there will eventually be light.

Snow fell softly and the water rose. Hunched at the door of my shelter, I watched as if mesmerized the reddish-brown flood flecked with yellow foam. It rose and reached the door to the social centre at New Dawn and the porch of Jean-Luc's cabin. The irresistible current brought down the porch supports, sent the roof crashing in slow motion into the water. In the next inlet, the community's rescue boats were overturned and carried away. I was looking in dread for the black monster to rise and slough off filthy flood water, to spread his wings, not expecting the appearance of Jarrold further along the ledge.

I saw him and leaped out of the shelter, slipped and fell into a deep drift, struggled clear and started to run.

There was no chance – he was bound to overtake me.

He caught me by the shoulder and thrust me down, fell in the snow beside me and trapped me with one arm. 'It's cool!' he insisted. 'I'm not going to hurt you.'

'Let me go!' I fought back, slithered free. He trapped me again.

'Tania, Orlando's OK. Do you hear me? He and Aaron got out in Jean-Luc's car. They drove up the Jeep track to Spider Rock – they're safe.'

394

Suddenly my muscles went slack. I lay on my back, arms outspread, snow settling on my face. When Jarrold pulled me to my feet, I glanced down at my impression and saw that it was like the angel shape a kid makes in the snow.

'Everything's going to be OK,' Jarrold assured me. He lowered a backpack from his shoulder and handed me an extra jacket. When he saw that my fingers were too stiff to work the zipper, he helped me fasten it.

'Did you know – Amos is dead?' I whispered.

This was obviously new, but he tried to suppress his shock. 'How?'

'Ziegler.'

Jarrold stopped me before I could go on. 'Poor old guy, I knew it would be endgame for him sooner or later. Ziegler couldn't keep this dark angel stuff hidden for ever.'

'You know about that?' I gasped. I couldn't take my eyes off Jarrold's face. I saw his warm breath turn to mist, the white, crystallized frost forming on his pale golden lashes.

'Yeah, it's time we came clean,' he murmured, one arm around my shoulder as he led me back into the shelter. 'You know Conner – how he was sent here?'

'By the others – the angels of light.'

'So you know how the good angels work,' he nodded.

'I'm like him, I do the same job. They sent us both here to keep an eye on things and report back.'

'Why didn't you tell me?' I hissed. The dark, intimate space was filled by our urgent words as outside the snow kept on falling.

'I wasn't sure about you, Tania. You know how hard it is.'

'To know your enemy from your friend? Yes, I do.' We were in a warm cocoon of new friendship and trust. I can't tell you how great that started to feel.

'Ever since we met, I've been checking you out, wanting every day to trust you but never being sure. But since you came back for Holly and Aaron, I finally understand whose side you're on.'

'You've been checking *me* out?' I echoed. I wanted to believe him, found no solid reason not to, so in one split second I let my defences tumble. Boom! The water burst through the dam.

He read my mind. 'Finally, you get it,' he breathed. He smiled, leaned forward and kissed me.

This once, I forgave the kiss. The worst thing is to be alone. When the world falls apart and you need a hand in yours, you ease your boundaries.

'You're sure Orlando and Aaron are OK?' I checked as

we made our way along a ridge that Jarrold told me would lead us to a National Forest field centre. He described a hut high above New Dawn, where a team of meteorologists dropped by all year round to carry out weather measurements.

'I spoke to them myself. They definitely made it to that other shelter at Spider Rock.'

'How did you do that? We can't get a cell phone signal out here in the wilderness.'

'Two-way radio,' Jarrold explained. 'There was one in Jean-Luc's car.'

'And how about Holly?'

'I tried to contact Channing, but guess what – he wasn't answering his radio.'

'Can we use yours now?' I asked. 'It would be so cool to hear Orlando's voice.'

'Sorry, Ziegler took it away. I think he's starting not to trust me.'

'Likewise.' I grimaced, and I described my confrontation with Ziegler and the wolves outside his cabin. 'But he's not the main guy,' I insisted. 'Now that I know Amos wasn't in charge, it has to be someone else.'

'*Maybe* Ziegler.' Jarrold wasn't ready to let this one go. 'If not him, who?'

'I don't know yet.' Reaching out my hand as I stumbled

into yet another drift, I felt Jarrold steady me. 'Thanks,' I breathed. 'How far to the field centre?'

'Ten minutes. Maybe fifteen.'

We walked on hand in hand, two small figures trudging through the snowscape like two black crows on a vast sloping roof. At last, on a small flat ledge, I saw the hut we were looking for.

Noticing footprints leading to the door, I realized some of the Explorers must have made it to this shelter before us and felt excited by this. 'I wonder who we'll find.'

Jarrold glanced down at the flood water still sweeping down the valley, uprooting more trees and cabins. Weirdly, the highest part of the island in the middle of Turner Lake was still visible – the one point of safety for any animal unlucky enough to be caught out there. 'How scary is that,' he muttered, leading me up to the cabin door.

We stepped inside to find Ava, Kaylee, Marta and Blake huddled around a small wood stove.

'Hey, a witches' coven,' Jarold joked. 'Hubble, bubble . . . !'

Kaylee and Blake looked at us without surprise or amusement. Kaylee was feeding the stove with split logs that crackled and spat out sparks. Blake leaned idly against the far wall. Ava and Marta sat with their backs to us and didn't even turn to greet us.

I felt a jolt of unease.

'Good job, Jarrold,' a voice said from outside the door and I loosed his gloved hand and spun around to see Aurelie backed by Ziegler and Channing. They stepped in out of the cold.

I gasped and felt a dry click in my throat. When I looked at Jarrold he was still smiling.

'Endgame, huh?' he mocked.

'You swore to me that you and Conner were my allies, my angels of light.'

'And you bought it.' That smile of victory showed me his true heartlessness.

'You're worse than all the rest – even Ziegler or Channing. You betrayed me!'

'Finally you get it.' Jarrold carried on enjoying the moment, staring right into my eyes, seeing my heartbreak.

'You're shocked?' Aurelie's voice was pitying. Her black fur coat came high under her chin. She wore black leather gloves and boots.

Jarrold gave a laugh that sounded like a sharp bark. His face was darkening and changing shape. His body melted and morphed until it became half wolf.

'Oh, Tania, Tania!' Aurelie sighed. 'For all your

intelligence and psychic powers, still somehow you remain so gullible.'

Inside I wept, though I wouldn't let my agony show inside that small, crowded mountain hut. I held my head up in the face of my real dark angel, even as a wind blew through the open door and daylight faded. Channing and Ziegler stepped forward and bound my wrists behind my back.

I appealed to the only people there who I still believed in. 'Marta, Ava – don't let them do this. Help me!'

The two girls turned to face me. Marta's dark hair was loose, partly obscuring her pale-grey eyes. Ava stared straight ahead as if she didn't see me. Blake and Kaylee came to join them.

'Don't let them take me prisoner!' I made one last appeal as Aurelie stepped aside and let Channing and Ziegler drag me outside.

I resisted, looked over my shoulder and saw the four Explorer girls swallowed by dark, shifting shadows. When, seconds later, they followed us out into the snow, each was totally transformed into a sleek grey wolf.

Beautiful, shining eyes glared at me as they padded slowly forward and surrounded me. Thick, dense coats, tails tipped with white. Slender bodies with sloping backs, taut abdomens, strong necks. Jaws that would snap and grind my bones, teeth that would tear my flesh.

Marta, Ava, Kaylee, Blake – I had wild-walked with them and believed they were my friends, but each had hidden their secret dark souls. They too had betrayed me. I cried out in despair.

At my side, Ziegler and Channing had taken wolf-man form, foul pelts slung across their broad shoulders, heads hanging like hoods down their naked backs. Their faces and chests were striped with dark red war paint, their black eyes glittered.

And ahead of me, wolf-man Jarrold stood beside dark angel Aurelie. The lower half of his face was painted crimson, the upper half was white. His blond hair was matted, his eyes cold and cruel.

They mocked me with their smiles as they confronted me. 'Did you really believe I belonged to . . . the opposition?' Jarrold couldn't bring himself to say the words, 'angels of light'. He turned his head and spoke casually to Aurelie. 'You were right – fooling her was child's play.'

'I told you to play on her innocence.' Aurelie's tone carried spite and triumph in equal measures. They were evident in the twisted smile that played across her lips. 'Tania's heart is pure. She has no clear concept of how high we soared in the heavens, or how far we fell. But now she knows we will use any means – we will lie, cheat, flatter and deceive to regain power, even over one single soul such as Holly. And truly there is nowhere to hide.'

As Aurelie spoke, her glossy black coat began to dissolve and change shape until she stood in the snow with a wolf-cloak around her shoulders. Like Ziegler, Channing and Jarrold, her lean torso was bare to her waist, but unlike them, her beautiful face remained unpainted – flawless and eerily calm.

Jarrold grinned at me from beneath his yellowish wolfskin. 'Walk,' he ordered. And Channing and Ziegler dragged me forward.

We came at last to the Spider Rock, which stood on a ledge overlooking the lake – me and my two wolf-man jailers, together with Aurelie and Jarrold and the four she-wolves. The narrow finger of weathered pink sandstone pointed skywards, looming over us as we sought shelter from the wind and snow. Below us, the floodwater charged like a freight train through the valley. Despair blasted through me like the north wind.

There was a shelter by the rock, evidently built by the Wolf band after I left them.

'Channing, go inside the tipi,' Aurelie ordered. 'Tell Holly to bring Aaron and Orlando.'

Dark and silent as a shadow, he vanished into the shelter.

I recognized that here was another lie that had spilled from Jarrold's honeyed lips – that Orlando and Aaron had made it safely to Spider Rock. The fact was, they'd been tricked then captured, just like me. But the dread in my heart lifted a fraction, knowing that I wasn't so alone.

Channing came out again with Holly, but minus Orlando and Aaron. I felt a heavy thud of disappointment then a glimmer of hope.

'What happened to the guys?' Aurelie demanded sharply – wolf woman with a bark in her voice.

'Holly says one had a knife hidden in his belt. Orlando – he cut himself free then did the same for his buddy.'

'They won't get far in this blizzard,' Aurelie decided quickly. 'Ziegler, track them down. Kill them and throw their corpses into a crevasse, where the ice will form over them and they will never be found.'

Straight away Ziegler left with two of the wolves. Noses to the ground to pick up Orlando and Aaron's scent, they soon disappeared along the ridge.

'Sorry, Tania.' Jarrold gave a careless shrug. 'Looks like your boyfriend didn't care enough about you to hang around and help.'

I stared back at him, my heart in my mouth as we waited for Aurelie's next move.

'We go ahead with the celebration for Holly,' she decided calmly. 'Tania, we'd be so pleased if you would join us for your friend's initiation.'

I groaned and took a few steps towards Holly, who stood alone in the snowstorm, still in the lightweight tunic and skirt she'd worn for Amos's birthday party, and still deep in the wide-eyed trance I'd witnessed inside Ziegler's cabin. Channing had spun his web of flattery and lies and Holly was trapped, seeming to see nothing, hear nothing of what was taking place around her.

'Holly, don't do this!' I pleaded. But Jarrold held me back while Channing took his place at Holly's side.

'Spider Rock is as good a place as any,' Aurelie went on, her voice simultaneously soft and threatening. 'Papa always told me it's a sacred place where boys from the Navajo and Avesta tribes came on their quests. It is where the earth, air, fire and water join together to cleanse the spirits of young warriors.'

'A spiritual place, then.' Jarrold seemed to enjoy the irony. 'We're here on a different spiritual quest. No cleansing involved.'

'The opposite,' Aurelie agreed. Her arms and torso

were pale and her eyes glinting beneath the dark wolf mask that she pulled up over her head. 'This is the moment when Holly leaves behind her old life and steps over on to the dark side for ever.'

Jarrold's grip on my arm tightened. The roar of the water in the valley grew louder.

'Bring Holly to me,' Aurelie murmured, from beneath the black wolf's head. She stood at the very edge of the ledge overlooking the valley then raised both arms towards the sky.

Deep in her nightmare trance, Holly allowed Channing to steer her towards Aurelie. She teetered on the ledge, gazing down at the flood and swaying. At the same moment, more wolves crept out from behind the trees. I counted twelve, thirteen, fourteen as they formed a silent, crouching pack.

'Holly, listen to me!' Desperately I tried to prise myself free.

But again Jarrold held me fast. His hands had grown long, curved nails – the black claws of a wolf; his hot breath carried the stink of dead flesh.

And before my eyes Aurelie gathered herself then stepped from the ledge into thin air. She seemed to hover, her wolfskin cloak spread like wings behind her. Then she turned and spoke again.

'Holly, it is time,' she whispered eagerly. 'Join us, walk with us.'

With Spider Rock behind her, Holly stared at Aurelie, mesmerized.

'I am the dark power,' Aurelie chanted. Her voice chilled me, and her cold female presence.

In all of my nightmares I had envisioned a male figure like Zoran Brancusi – tall and lithe, with his shaven head and rock star swagger, or Antony Amos, whose quiet voice and charismatic beliefs drew you unquestioningly to him. Amos acted like a messiah. He was a movie maker and illusionist – a good candidate. But I never foresaw that my dark angel was a woman.

The shock of the unexpected blasted my mind – here was graceful, delicate Aurelie inviting Holly to step off the rock, over to the dark side.

She *was* my dark angel. I missed the clues but they were there.

A woman with short dark hair wearing sunglasses, capri pants and a pink shirt walks with Amos on to the lake shore.

A hellish vision slams into me, like a car crash. I see bodies beneath the lake.

I know my dark angel has shape-shifted and is lying low. She has forced my attention on to Amos and I don't recognize her, but she is rising again.

Another flashback – Aurelie stands with her feathered staff at the exit to the Explorers' parking lot at the start of our wild walk. 'Open your hearts,' she chants as we pass by. The feathers brush my cheek. I feel a bitter wind, I am blinded by snow and a sweating wolf man emerges from his lair of thorns with blood-stained claws.

These were the dreams, the sharp shards of evidence that had lodged in my brain but which I was too blind to see.

'I hold sway over everything you see,' Aurelie murmured. With a wide sweep of her arm she gestured towards the dark forest and mountain peaks, along the ridge to where the wolves lay in wait and down from the ledge towards the rushing torrent.

Facing the enemy, alone on the cold ledge, Holly swayed forward – shivering in her white dress, a sacrifice.

'Reach out your hands,' Aurelie commanded. 'Step across.'

Slowly, with great stealth, the wolves closed in.

Obediently Holly reached out to take Aurelie's hands. Her head was tilted back and there was a look of ecstasy on her face as the dark powers whispered and urged her to join her new mistress.

Step out. Feel the air beneath your feet. Do not be afraid.

Aurelie's wolf-eyes gleamed with victory. 'Hell is close to where you stand. Evil rises,' she gloated, holding out her hands, palms upwards. 'Our army is strong. We are everywhere!'

More wolves emerged from the forest, their coats darkened and matted with clumps of ice. They brought the night and a hot, sharp stench.

'You are innocent and loving, and now you are mine!' Aurelie whispered into Holly's ear. Holly shifted her weight, ready to move out into nothingness.

I'm not afraid! I thought. Suddenly, at the very last moment, I found my courage, broke free of my helpless dread and found new strength.

'The four winds are blowing,' a spirit voice reminds me. I've heard it before but I can't put a face to the voice – not Zenaida, not Conner or Maia. 'Call for the guiding spirit of the hawk or the swift crow. Call for the dove, who is your angel of light.'

The courage of the army of light flowed through me. 'You think you've won but you're wrong!' I told Jarrold, Channing and Aurelie – all of the dark spirits who could hear me.

High in the sky, a grey dove soared. And through the

trees behind us a figure appeared surrounded by light. He strode towards Spider Rock, thrusting aside the wolves who snarled and leaped at his throat to drag him down.

'Stand fast,' he tells me. Now I know the voice of this new angel of light. It is Regan.

Regan! With his bare hands he fought the dark spirits. The wolves howled, leaped again to tear at his face and neck. Jarrold released me. He and Channing ran to repel the intruder.

I heard more swift footsteps; a second then a third figure appeared from the forest – Orlando and Aaron! They stood beside Regan, Orlando carrying the knife with the long blade.

Orlando had stayed. He didn't flee the mountain. He loved me more than anything – my one fixed point in this dangerous world!

But now the wolves regrouped, ready to attack, and Regan gave orders to Orlando and Aaron. 'Stay back,' he warned. 'Let me deal with this.'

Already there was blood seeping into the snowy ground. Three wolves lay dead. Regan took Orlando's knife, thrust the blade into the chests of two more victims. The rest whined and retreated along the ridge, where they crouched and panted.

'You see!' I yelled at Aurelie, who still held out her hands to her dazed convert. 'You haven't won. We won't let you take Holly.'

My dark angel smiled and waited.

And now Jarrold and Channing launched their attack on Regan, Aaron and Orlando. With terrible howls of fury they flung themselves at my secret angel of light who had lived undetected at New Dawn.

'Stay back,' Regan said again to Orlando and Aaron. He kicked out at Channing, caught him in the stomach, toppling him and making him roll in agony. Then, as wolf-man Jarrold bared his teeth and pounced, Regan grabbed him by the throat and throttled him. Choking, Jarrold staggered back against a tree.

There was a pause.

'The wolves!' I pointed along the ridge to where two more hunters had gathered. Their hackles were up. They were back on the attack. But worse – a silent, shadowy figure crept up from behind. A third wolf man made his stealthy way out of the forest.

'Ziegler!' I cried.

19

Ziegler crept out of the forest.

We teetered on the ledge that separated dark from light, evil from good. Below us, the icy flood waited to sweep us all away.

Ignoring Regan's order to stay back and yelling their war cries like warriors of the plains, Aaron and Orlando sprang forward to drive back the snapping, snarling wolves. As the dark, feral hunters leaped for their throats, they wrestled them to the ground.

Meanwhile, Regan seized his chance to grab hold of Holly and draw her back from the ledge. He pushed her into my arms and told me to find shelter under Spider Rock.

'Stay strong,' he reminded me. 'Whatever happens, be brave.'

There was no time for more. As he finished speaking,

Ziegler came from behind and hooked an arm around Regan's neck. He bared his teeth and gave a snarl, using his savage strength to wrestle Regan to the blood-soaked ground. Dark versus light.

They wrestled and rolled towards the ice-covered ledge. Orlando yelled a warning before Jarrold closed in on him. Shoving the palm of his right hand under Orlando's chin, he jerked his head back, exposing his throat. Orlando staggered against a tree, where Jarrold trapped him and paused to mock him.

'How much does your girlfriend love you?' he mocked, sweat running down his painted face. 'A little – a lot?'

Orlando grunted and fought to free himself. He tore at Jarrold's wolf cloak, ripped the head from the pelt and threw it to the ground.

'Not as much as you'd like to believe,' Jarrold laughed. 'Give me one extra day – twenty-four short hours – and she'd have forgotten all about you, lover boy. She'd have crossed to the dark side.'

Enraged, Orlando found fresh strength and forced him backwards across the killing ground towards the ledge where Aurelie stood, still unmoved. Face to face, Orlando and Jarrold struggled on the brink.

Among the slain wolves, Aaron fought Channing. He sent him stumbling over a grey corpse, watched him regain his balance but didn't give him time to relaunch his attack. Instead, Aaron went in kicking and punching so fast and hard that Channing was forced towards Jarrold and Orlando on the ledge.

Hearing Holly give a thin, childlike wail as she made a move to join Channing, I held her back.

'Bring me the courage to stand in the blizzard and not to run from the wolf,' I plead.

My grey dove flies in a serene ark across a cloudless sky.

Orlando and Jarrold, Aaron and Channing were locked in combat. They slipped on the ice, wrestled and rolled closer to the edge. Fear gripped me by the throat, made it impossible to breathe.

And then the mightiest rivals of all – Regan and Ziegler – clashed again.

Regan's glowing light that I'd noticed as he emerged from the forest grew brighter, more intense, as if he'd summoned strength from Zenaida and all the angels of light to overcome Ziegler, who was darkness and torment. Angered, Ziegler summoned the remaining wolves and sent them in on the attack. One after the other they threw themselves forward, sometimes losing their footing on the ice, sliding over the edge of the cliff and disappearing with anguished yelps and howls. Regan was unharmed.

So Ziegler saw that it was down to him alone. Gathering

black shadows around him like a cloak, he advanced. I stared at the narrow wolf-face and the blood-streaked torso, remarking the columbine eyes that had first grabbed my attention on the lake shore – the only reminder of the human shape Ziegler had once adopted. Now he was dark and savage, intent on destruction.

Regan stepped between the bodies of the slain wolves, aware of Ziegler's every move. His eyes flicked towards Orlando and Jarrold, Aaron and Channing, still wrestling close to the edge. Regan took in Aurelie standing to one side, expressionless. Then his gaze swung round to me and Holly. 'The water is rising. Take her higher up the mountain,' he urged.

But I couldn't leave Orlando.

So I was there when Ziegler launched his final attack, surrounded by shadows, grappling with Regan, losing his footing on the ice, sliding into Channing and sending him skidding towards the edge. Channing whined as he scrambled for a hold, howled as he lost his grip. His own weight and the power of gravity pulled him down and he disappeared from sight. I held Holly back from running to the empty spot.

Then Ziegler roared and viciously hurled himself at Regan. Regan gave him eye contact, waited for him to reach the cliff edge and at the last moment stepped sideways. It was too late for Ziegler to put on the brakes. He launched himself from the rock. For a few moments he hovered, calling upon his dark angel power to become weightless like Aurelie. But the action was too fast and unexpected for him and Ziegler too crashed out of sight.

There was a long, high howl then only the roar of water.

Jarrold broke free from Orlando. On all fours he crawled to the edge and peered over the cliff.

Holly, Orlando, Aaron and I stared in horror. Two bodies had hurtled from the ledge into the rising water below Spider Rock, the place where air, fire, water and earth meet. Howling, they had disappeared beneath the dark surface. The flood water claimed them, dragged them down, would never let them go.

Knowing this, Jarrold whined. His painted face was streaked with blood and sweat. He panted hard.

'Tania, take Holly away from here!' Regan said again.

Still I delayed until I saw Jarrold retreat from the ledge and slink between the trees. Who was the coward now? Who but a treacherous, corrupted spirit would see his allies sacrificed and still want to protect his own tainted skin? Jarrold crawled away, head hanging in defeat – wolf man creeping back to his empty lair to lick his wounds, deserting his leader without a backward glance.

Aurelie had waited. She'd watched her lieutenants fail and now it was time to act. With one sweeping gesture, she raised her dead wolf spirits and they sprang back to life. With gaping wounds and jaws trickling with blood, they crept stealthily, menacingly towards Holly and me, herding us and pushing us towards the ledge.

'We are too many.' Aurelie's smile was cruel and unbending. 'We rise from the dead.'

And as Regan fought the wolves and Orlando and Aaron huddled by the ledge with Holly and me, only centimetres from the drop into the flood water of Turner Lake, Aurelie darted towards me, snatched me up and carried me far away.

She flew me through the whirling blizzard, above the brown torrent, with wind tearing at me and my brain in turmoil, until we landed on the snow-bound island in the middle of the lake. Here she set me down.

'Now who will help you?' she demanded pitilessly.

I gasped for air. I had no answer.

'Look around, Tania.'

I did as she said. We were alone on a snow-covered scrap of rock without trees or any kind of shelter. Heavy clouds clung to the mountains on either side and closed in on us, drifting as ice-cold mist against our faces. At our feet, the flood water raced by.

'You see. There is nothing to be done.'

'So do what you have to do,' I challenged. If this was the end, at least it would be cold and quick.

Aurelie's blank expression changed. Her dark eyes sparked and she let her anger show. 'Come, Tania – you're not usually so stupid. Remember that when we come face to face at last, we go at my pace because I am the one who holds all the power.'

I stared back, willing myself not to give in. 'Face to face,' I echoed with a faint smile of satisfaction. 'All this time I've fought to know who will punish me and take revenge – and now I do.'

Aurelie laughed. 'Poor Tania, we really made life difficult. We tricked you and twisted your visions, we got inside your head so that you suspected my stepfather. You wasted so much time.'

'But now I know,' I repeated. No more disguise or deceit – now I was alone with my dark angel.

A smile lingered – it contained mockery and suggested one last secret that she wouldn't share. 'You must be asking yourself – exactly what next? Look around again, tell me what you see.'

'Mist,' I said. It clung to my skin, was cold in my lungs.

'And what do you hear?'

'Water.'

'Rising. How will it feel to drown, Tania? To be dragged beneath the surface into the dark depths, to meet Death. How many times have you imagined what it will be like?'

'The same way it felt for Conner.' I might be close to the end, but I wouldn't let her forget what she'd done.

'And you know what lies beneath the water? Of course you do.'

A town, a church, a graveyard, a thousand serpents. And a giant beast with the head of a snake and cold green eyes, carrying a corpse. He rises and sloughs off mud and weeds. He bears a victim that before long will become me.

'Yes.' Aurelie smiled. She enjoyed the moment. 'The water rages. Are you ready?'

To say goodbye to Orlando, who stood with me and fought so hard. To my mom, who always believed, and my dad, whose world would forever feel empty without me. 'No,' I said, holding them in my mind and seeking a key that would unlock Aurelie's dark angel power and disarm her.

Know your enemy – search for her until you find her. Name her.

The key forged itself out of the love I felt for Orlando, stronger than the terror of this moment. It gleamed and gave me the psychic strength I needed.

'You don't win! Your name is not Aurelie Laurent. She's already dead. She drowned with her mother, off the coast of India.'

'Ah!' My dark angel didn't deny it. In fact, she was amused, as if I'd risen in her estimation and had at last grown into a decent opponent. In other words, this was a game which had suddenly become worth playing.

'You circle the planet,' I went on. 'You wait until someone dies then steal the body. This is how it worked with Zoran, and it's the same with you!'

'That poor girl,' Aurelie sighed. 'She was on deck when the boat began to sink and she could easily have taken to one of the lifeboats, but she was a loving, loyal daughter and so she went back to find her mother. She took the stranger child – the one Juliet was trying to save. But it was useless. Juliet, Aurelie, the child – all drowned.'

'You stole her body, climbed into one of the lifeboats then appeared to Antony Amos as if you had survived.'

'Almost,' she agreed through the icy mist and thundering water. 'But not quite.' She waited for me to fit the final piece into place. 'No?' she queried.

'Yes!' I cried. All around us, water crashed against

rock. I couldn't see land. I knew I needed to understand more.

For the first time a small doubt crept across Aurelie's expression – was I clever enough to find that still-missing piece?

'That wasn't all.' I queried everything, asked myself who at New Dawn could have deceived me the most – more than Jarrold and the other Explorers, more than Ziegler or even Aurelie. The answer came to me at last in words he himself had spoken. 'She's my twin. We've always been close.'

I whispered the crucial words: 'Jean-Luc is part of this.'

And as I said his name I looked up into the mist and saw a shape gradually materialize – another wolf man with a pelt around his shoulders, lowering himself on to the rock.

Jean-Luc stood beside his twin sister, swathed in mist but stripped of all fakery and lies. He wore the wolf-skin cloak, the lean grin and hungry eyes.

'You died in the shipwreck along with Aurelie,' I told him.

'Correct,' he replied. He didn't care that I knew. In fact, he seemed proud and disdainful.

'It was your mission to throw me off track,' I challenged.

'And I did an excellent job, you must admit. I charmed you with my talk of Paris and I took pleasure in deceiving you.'

'You made me blame Antony.'

'Yes – to gain time, to give Channing more opportunity to seduce Holly. It worked better than even I expected.' Turning to Aurelie, Jean-Luc invited her to share in his victory.

'Don't say any more,' Aurelie said quickly. She was on edge now as the water roared at our feet and I moved closer to discovering the whole truth.

Breathe. Breathe again. Aurelie and Jean-Luc – twins, inseparable in life and in death. Dark deceivers. I was almost there, at the heart of their lies.

But Aurelie and Jean-Luc hadn't finished their games of deceit – they held back one more shape-shifting shock.

'Shall we show her?' Jean-Luc wondered, switching between playful and sinister. 'Does she deserve to know?'

'I think she does,' his sister decided.

My skin crawled at the idea that they were about to reveal a final secret and I watched in terror as the evil twins turned and took each other's hands. Devil-eyes locked, they shrouded themselves in shadow, and I had a misty, stomach-churning image of two bodies fusing into one; of a female face and a male face merging and of a new, non-human body forming – a melding, a collapsing, an ultimate shape-shift. And when the shadows dispersed, cruel Aurelie and proud Jean-Luc were gone and in their place stood a devil wolf.

They were one and the same creature, neither male nor female – pure evil. My shape-shifted dark angel crouched low, its gleaming eyes fixed me with an evil stare. Its stillness terrified me.

I had time to take in the cruel features surrounded by thick grey fur – the small ears, the large, gleaming eyes, the sawing, tearing, grinding teeth. Saliva trickled from its mouth, its ribs heaved in and out.

It didn't move. At my feet, the torrent roared.

Nowhere to run or hide, only moments to go before the wolf leaped for my throat.

Be brave. Have the courage not to run from the wolf in the blizzard. Know your enemy.

It crouched, it raised its hackles.

Know your enemy.

The flood water pounded at the rock and sucked at my feet, sending spray high in the air. Then there was a roar in my ears, the water parted and the beast rose, black and covered in gleaming scales, its jaws wide open. Flickering its snake's tongue, it emerged from the sucking, foaming flood.

My devil wolf rose from its low crouch. It padded forward to deliver me to its overlord. The beast climbed out of the water. It spread its wings, reached out its empty arms.

Standing in the black shadow, I faced my wolf spirit.

Know your enemy. Name him.

The wolf – cruellest of all animals, dealing in death and madness, pitiless. And the tribes had a name for this most brutal of spirits. I sought in the darkest corners of my mind and tried to remember.

'Ahriman!' I cried into the mist, above the roar of the rising lake.

Ahriman, witch in wolf's clothing, child killer, creature of nightmares who brings death to the plains and mountains. The spirits of the lost tribes gather in the snow and wind. They are there to see me defeat my enemy. I am the cunning coyote, saviour of the world. I say the name and I jump down Ahriman's throat to saw up his wicked heart. I show no mercy.

Ahriman – the name halted the lumbering overlord of the dark lake.

'*He is revealed!*' Zenaida murmurs her approval.

Ahriman – it pierced the wolf like a knife to the heart. It stole its strength, robbed it of the power to exact revenge against me – the retribution that it had planned for so long. Anger and self-loathing blazed in its amber eyes – after all it was Jean-Luc, my twinned dark angel himself, who had told me this story, handed me the flint which would rip him apart.

Now its wolf-body was spent, its wolf-spirit defeated. In agony it threw back its head. It howled into the mist.

I heard the howl and saw blood ooze from its mouth. It bubbled through its killer teeth and dripped on to the snow. It howled again then sank low on the ground. I had torn away its last disguise.

And as my dark angel sank in defeat, the beast from the lake turned away, empty-handed. He lowered his giant bulk beneath the foaming torrent and the waters closed over him.

I stood trembling on the last scrap of land watching the demon wolf bleed. It whimpered and tried to crawl away but there was nowhere it could go.

It crawled and slithered, rolled in agony, reached the water's edge. The current licked at it, swirled around the spent body, lifted it and carried it away.

I watched it go.

Light wins. Darkness loses.

I am raised from the scrap of land. Angels of light carry me

*above the flood. It feels like I am surrounded by a thousand
fluttering, whistling wings.*

*We are above the snow, above the clouds. The sun shines
brighter than you could believe.*

'The water took him,' I tell my mourning dove. 'He vanished.'

'Forget him,' she says. 'He is nothing now.'

*I fly to safety. The clouds below are golden. I soar with
my angels.*

20

The disaster at Turner Lake destroyed the entire New Dawn Community. Not a single structure remained, and a total of fifty-three lives were lost. It made the international news.

What the journalists didn't say and the video footage didn't show was an army of dark angels being driven back, a valley being cleansed.

No – they reported that engineers were to be brought in to construct a new, high-tech dam, and already a permanent memorial to Antony Amos and his doomed enterprise was planned.

'He won't be forgotten,' Mom vowed. She was home from the hospital, able to wiggle the fingers of her left hand, religiously performing the programme of exercises her physical therapist had given her. 'Amos was a great man with a good heart. We have to make sure his work goes on.'

Dad smiled and told her to take things easy.

Orlando and I laughed at him for being so naive. Mom never relaxes, not even after brain surgery.

Orlando and me. He'd escaped from the wolves at Spider Rock. He and Aaron had got Holly off the mountain. Aaron had used Orlando's truck to drive her home.

'I never left you,' he'd told me. 'I swear on my life I was coming to find you.'

I knew it. There was no need for him to explain. 'Zenaida took care of me,' I whispered. And Maia, Conner and Regan.

Orlando and me. We were in my garden on Becker Hill, warmly dressed, sitting on a bench holding hands.

Grace and Jude had visited earlier and together we'd gone next door to see Holly. Aaron was on guard duty, letting in only one visitor at a time.

'It's cool; she doing good,' he'd assured us. 'Apart from the fact that she's exhausted and she says it feels like she got run over by a truck.'

'I remember that feeling,' Grace sighed.

I was the first to go up to her room and knock.

'Yeah, who is it?' Holly called.

I found her propped on pillows, hair loose, i-Tunes playing. She looked thinner, paler, with dark shadows under her eyes.

'Don't say it – I look like crap,' she said.

'You look better than I thought you would.'

'The wolves nearly got me, huh?'

'It wasn't the wolves I was worried about.' More Channing and the rest – Spider Rock, the ceremony, the edge of darkness.

'Don't let's go there,' Holly sighed. She'd flicked the switch, come out of the New Dawn trance and definitely didn't want to revisit. Except there was one thing she wanted me to clear up for her. 'So anyway, Tania, was I right?'

Now I knew that she was back with us, working on her surge power. I smiled as I sat on the edge of her bed. 'About what?'

'About Conner, of course.'

'What about Conner?'

'They killed him, didn't they? Come on, admit it – I was right!'

'I wish it was summer,' Orlando told me as we sat on the bench in the snow. The sky was blue, the temperature was minus four. Tomorrow Ryan and Natalie would drive him home to Dallas.

'Why is that?' We held hands, fingers intertwined, my

head on his shoulder, gazing out towards Carlsbad.

'Summer is our best time – long, lazy days, no pressure, midnight swimming.'

'Yeah, give me a piece of that.' It was the same for him as it was for me – that first precious memory of diving into the cold, clear water in the moonlight.

'College is over, I'm back here in Bitterroot; we're together.'

'It'll happen,' I promised.

Tomorrow I would stand in the drive and watch him leave. Today, right here, right now, my head rested against him, my hand was in his.

'I wonder what happened to Jarrold,' he murmured.

'The water rose; he got swept away with the others.'

'We don't know that for sure.' Gently Orlando kissed the top of my head. 'You don't mind me talking about this?'

'Jarrold's gone,' I insisted. Until the next time, the next place when someone like Jarrold, but not Jarrold, would rise again. Right now I didn't want even to think about it. I wanted to feel the wintry sun on my face, to breathe in and out in time with the guy I loved.

'What he said – about you weakening and going over to him, leaving me . . .'

'It wasn't true,' I said quickly, and I squeezed his hand. 'Forget him. He's nothing now.'

* * *

All night I lay in Orlando's arms, my dreamcatcher swaying above our heads. I slept soundly and woke early as the sun filtered through the blind.

He was still asleep. In and out, in and out, his chest rose and fell. Soon I would wake him but not yet.

'I know you have to leave,' I whispered as he slept. 'Drive away but leave the precious part of you behind – your love, your steadfast, beautiful self. Go and stay.'

Tania's story concludes in

BROKEN DREAM

coming soon . . .

Starry, starry night. I'm with Orlando in New York.

Repeat slowly – I'm with Orlando. We're together again after two months apart.

The picture we're staring at shows a whirling, swirling, magical night sky. The midnight blue is like nothing you've ever seen, the stars are crazy, the painter is Vincent Van Gogh.

New York in December. Two days ago Orlando flew into Bitterroot from Dallas and from there we took a plane to JFK. We gave ourselves five beautiful days to explore the city – time for me to attend a three-day film workshop and for us both to Christmas shop until we drop, watch movies and walk, walk, walk these bright, buzzing city streets.

Fourteen days before Christmas and outside the gallery it's snowing.

Earlier today the flakes froze on my eyelashes.

'How did Vinnie V do that?' Orlando murmured. The colour, the texture, the light.

Especially the light. I agreed that this painting was awesome beyond words.

We weren't alone in MoMA, obviously. Everyone who visits what must be the world's biggest collection of modern art wants to stand in line to see Starry Night, buy the postcard and go home to tell their friends. But the painting lifts you out of reality – the shuffling crowds, the air con and the uniformed security guards. You're in a dream, it really feels like it's just you and Vincent's stars.

'Let's go.' In the end Orlando had to take me by the arm and steer me away.

'Aww!' I sighed.

'I know, but it's time for lunch. We need to eat.' He led me through the museum. I floated past magenta, cobalt blue and chrome yellow paint dribbled, splashed and thrown on to white surfaces, plus multi-million dollar contemporary canvases that were pierced, slashed, scrunched up and scrawled on. I didn't care about any of them, only Vincent.

'Wow!' Orlando kept hold of my hand until we reached the exit.

'I know.'

Starry skies, midnight swimming in Turner Lake – that was how he and I first came together, in the mountains near our home. It was when he first told me he loved me and wanted to be with me always – under the stars in the cold, clear water. And now here we were in the heart of Manhattan, in a totally loved-up dream.

Questions and Answers
Eden Maguire

Where do the ideas for your books come from?
My ideas come from a mysterious region of the brain – the 'What if' part which must have a neurological label, but which works something like this: 'What if the world really is split between supernatural good and bad forces? What if we can all be tempted on to the side of shape-shifting, terrifying dark angels to fight against the angels of light?' With this basic idea, I can create a setting, a heroine and a whole cast of characters, plus a plot so full of twists and turns that even I don't know how it will end until I get there.

Who would your dream cast be if *Dark Angel* was made into a film?
Actors in a film of *Dark Angel*? Most of the ones I can think of are a few years too old (sorry!), but how about Natalie Portman for Tania (she's the right physical style and can play sensitive, tormented souls) and Robert Pattinson for Orlando (dream on!).

What have you enjoyed writing the most – *Dark Angel* or the *Beautiful Dead*?
The answer to which of my books I enjoy the most is always, 'The one I'm writing now.' So it has to be *Twisted Heart* (more on that later).

Who do you relate to more – Darina from the *Beautiful Dead* or Tania in *Dark Angel*?
I think Darina has more of the rebel in her – something I can relate to from my own teen years. I don't have Tania's psychic powers, but do share some of her thin-skinned sensitivity.

If you could invite five people to dinner who would they be?
Top of my list for ideal dinner guests are: Marilyn Monroe, Shakespeare, Catherine Earnshaw from *Wuthering Heights*, John Lennon and Atticus Finch from *To Kill A Mocking Bird*.

Where is your favourite place to write?
I can only write in one place and no other – it's my first storey office overlooking a river and a wooded hillside. No other room will do.

Who is your favourite author and why?
Favourite author is so hard – this time I'll choose one who is alive – it's Annie Proulx who wrote the short story *Brokeback Mountain* which they turned into a great film. Everything she writes is strong and disturbing.

What advice would you give to aspiring young writers?
People who really want to write don't need my advice. They're driven by some inner compulsion. It turns out right if they stick to the truth of their imaginations.

What book do you wish you had written?
A book I totally admire is *The Kite Runner* by Khaled Hosseini. I wish I could write something so moving and powerful and true.

How does it feel when you see your books in a bookshop?
When I see my own book on a bookshop shelf I have a mixed reaction. There's a big temptation to position it so that customers can see it more easily, but there's also an unexpected panic and a need to run and hide!

Tell us one thing your readers won't already know about you.
I once fell off a horse high on a mountain with no other riders around. My horse didn't run off – he stayed and waited for me to get back on my feet, thank heavens. Not many people know that!